FAINT SONGS

FAINT SONGS

Jeanette Uff

Book Guild Publishing
Sussex, England

First published in Great Britain in 2006 by
The Book Guild Ltd,
25 High Street,
Lewes, East Sussex
BN7 2LU

Typesetting in Baskerville by
IML Typographers, Birkenhead, Merseyside

Printed in Great Britain by
Athenaeum Press Ltd, Gateshead

A catalogue record for this book is available from
The British Library.

ISBN 1 84624 030 1

When men rise up at the sound of the birds but all their songs grow faint.

Ecclesiastes Chapter 12 verse 4
(New International Version)

PART ONE

Prologue

It began as a whisper, a trembling in the trees, but gained momentum as it swept around the churchyard, rushing between the gravestones scavenging for dry leaves to swirl and toss in its path. But the leaves were sodden and refused to be used for sport.

Soon another headstone would impede its chaotic pursuit. Frances Hall Cahill. 1882–1947.

As the interment began, the granite sky ruptured and, in fulfilment of its prophecy, unleashed its fury in a torrent of stinging steel, reddening the pallid faces of the mourners and causing them to gasp at its unexpected ferocity. Umbrellas unfurled and rose like a dozen black carapaces, concealing the identity of their owners and changing the balance of the scene so that it resembled a monochrome sketch with scarce any unmarked canvas escaping the severity of the charcoal. A study in shades of black.

'For as much as it hath pleased Almighty God of His great mercy…' the vicar intoned above the hollow thud of clay rapping against the pine. Absentmindedly, he flicked a small fleck of mud from the sleeve of his surplice. He had recited this so often, there should have been no need to read the words from the book he held in his left hand. '… to take unto himself the soul of our dear sister here departed…' His eyes skimmed from left to right and back, until his index finger located the next line '… we therefore commit his … hm, hm … *her* body to the ground…' Ah, he knew this bit by heart so he raised his head heavenward, allowing great beads of rain to course down his forehead and gather into one glorious crystal drop which hung, tremulous, suspended on the end of his not inconsiderable nose. His voice grew louder now as confidence amplified the drone. 'Earth to earth, ashes to ashes, dust to dust in the sure and certain hope…'

Francie studied him, tears distorting his silhouette. She blinked them away, scarcely conscious of their passage down her cheeks and neck, as she focused on him again.

He was so young, yet already his familiarity with the mechanics of death had given him a detachment that trivialised her grief. His dispassionate delivery of the words seemed somehow to diminish the validity of the relentless, aching loss she felt.

'He's too callow to have experienced this intense sorrowing pain,' she thought. 'He's never lived through the suffering and regret of old age, never felt such debilitating loss.' Her breath escaped in a deep, low moan. 'He had never known Ma.'

'...beseeching thee that it may please thee, of thy gracious goodness...'

'God wasn't hall that good to Fanny,' an elderly mourner wheezed to a stranger beside her, 'or 'e wouldn't 'ave done that to 'er face.'

The other looked down at her and allowed this thought to penetrate before she replied, 'Yes, that was unfortunate, but he gave her a beautiful spirit.'

The elderly woman considered this and slowly and painfully turning her head sideways and upwards, gave only the slightest nod of agreement. 'That's true. She was ha lovely lady.'

Bertha glanced at the two women. She recognised Ellen's daughter, Pearl, but the one who muddled her aitches, she had never seen before.

The woman was remarkable only on account of the fact that she alone was not enveloped in black. Instead, she wore a coat of some expensive material, the colour of newly ploughed earth, with an ostentatious, navy blue hat adorned with now, sodden and drooping pale blue flowers, more suited to the celebration of marriage than death. That it remained unwaveringly on her head was a miracle of millinery engineering since her body was bent at the waist in an almost perfect right angle, so that she would have faced the ground had she not rigorously schooled her neck to stretch upwards so that the parchment-like skin over her gullet was taut.

The eulogy ended and, as though on cue, the deluge ceased.

Bertha turned and took a few steps along the gravel path that separated the endless rows of gravestones, indistinguishable one from another, except for the long-forgotten names and platitudes chiselled for disinterested posterity into their eroded surfaces. She could smell the wetness of the stone.

She lit a Gauloise and her eyes followed the column of smoke upwards; a veil of pale grey gauze draped across a watery sun.

The air was still and quiet, apart from the relentless drip, drip, drip as the sky wrung out the last vestiges of moisture from the

4

clouds and drops of rain slithered down the branches until they joined with fellow stragglers and, confidence increasing with their union, gathered impetus and fell with a satisfying plop onto the saturated silk below.

As she sniffed back the tears, the snuffle drew in the soft, nostalgic scent of Coty perfume and she felt Francie's gloved hand lain gently on her shoulder. Without turning, she covered it with her own.

'I hate this place,' she hissed vehemently, so that the words darted out like a serpent's tongue.

'I know,' her sister soothed. 'So do I. It brings back such cruel memories.'

Bertha turned into Francie's arms and they stood, united in their misery.

'She deserved better, you know, Fran.' The words were strangled by wrenching sobs.

Fran nodded in agreement and held her more tightly.

With a strange sense of detachment, Olivia watched her mother and aunt and wondered how such disparate women could be equal in beauty. And how could poor Aunt Winnie have come from the same gene pool? Her gaze wandered across and focused on her youngest aunt. Her carrot-coloured hair, which usually floated like a cloud of summer gnats around her pinched, little face, was bedraggled and tamed by the deluge, like the physical manifestation of the subduing of her ebullient spirit by the weight of her grief. Yet Winnie and her grotesque little husband had led an idyllic life with such small demands. So much happiness! So much love!

As the group around the graveside dispersed, a raw shiver swept through Olivia's body and she allowed the tears, that she had struggled to suppress, to flow unchecked, so that they were absorbed into the wetness of her coat collar. She felt the incomparable comfort of Charles's arms drawing her closer, then easing her gently towards the waiting cars.

Ellen's daughter walked in front of them, the unknown ancient hobbling to draw level with her.

'I honly found hout by haccident that Fanny 'ad passed haway.'

'Did you know her well, then?'

'I knew 'er has a young girl,' replied Ruby. She glanced around, twisting her neck awkwardly. 'Yes, you could say I'd known 'er longer than hanyone 'ere.'

Chapter One

They thought … no, indeed, they felt quite certain that they could give another child everything. But the reality was very different.

There was no lack of any earthly comfort, since Thomas Hall was a man of substance, the owner of a thriving brickworks in Seaforth, a suburb of Liverpool. He had a strikingly beautiful wife, and two strong, handsome and intelligent sons who had both, of their own volition and without any coercion from him, chosen to follow him into the family business. It filled him with contentment to know that he was building a future for his descendents, and each morning he awoke in a mood of quiet ease, which stayed with him throughout the day.

How often in this life do we find perfect fulfilment? Yet it was manifest in Thomas. The one thing that might have caused him some regret, had he dwelt on it for long, was the want of a daughter.

Irene, too, shared her husband's calm satisfaction with life. They lived in a bubble of contentment, as gladdened by each other as when they had first met. She still felt an instinctive joy when he touched her, and thrilled when, by a word or gesture, he indicated agreement with some trivial observation that she had made. It was the stuff of adolescent besottedness.

Her one reservation was the yearning for a daughter but it was deeper and more invasive in her than it was in Thomas. In him it was a slight acknowledgment that it would have been nice but in Irene it was a profound and progressive canker. She dwelt on this more and more frequently as she approached forty. And so she had nagged him. Oh, ever so gently, but nagged him nonetheless.

'You have to consider our ages, my love.' He hesitated to say 'your' age for reasons of chivalry.

But, like the constant dripping of water on a stone, she had eventually had her way.

The beginning of April of 1882 was nothing if not unseasonable.

With dinner finished, the fires banked up and the servants departed to their own quarters, Thomas and Irene sat alone in the drawing room. Rising, Thomas drew back the heavy velvet drapes and stood for a moment, watching the amber cognac catch the reflection from the gaslights as it swirled around his glass. He raised it to his lips and stared out of the window at the late snow, weighing down the branches of the elm trees and covering the lawns and shrubbery in a thick, white fleece. He sensed that Irene had moved to stand behind him and then felt the gentle pressure of her arms around his waist. She laid her head against his back and they stood unmoving, sharing the poignant tenderness of the moment.

'Wouldn't life be perfect if we had had a little girl?' She swallowed hard but couldn't stifle a deep sigh. 'Do you remember when the boys were younger; so many times you promised me we would have a daughter? You actually said that as soon as I had got over the miscarriage we would try again.'

Irritation and alarm fighting for supremacy, he took her firmly by the shoulders and turned her to face him.

'That was a long time ago, Irene. Forty is too late to be carrying a baby and I am much too old to be a father again.' His brow creased. 'Aren't you happy?'

'Goodness, of course I am!' She hated being reminded that she was getting old, that the time had passed for it to be naturally apposite or socially acceptable to be a new mother. How could she expect a man to understand that the longing in her was, at times, a real physical sickness that dragged her down. Thomas was a dear husband, but he was still a man.

'So, my beloved Thomas, is it only for my sake you hesitate, or is it because you cannot face the prospect of being a father again?'

'Oh, Irene, how could you ask that? You know I would never refuse you anything. I am concerned only about you.'

Her grasp around him tightened but she didn't pursue the matter further and Thomas thought that it was the end of it.

That night, their lovemaking was an intense sweetness, more satisfying than anything they could remember. They rose to a peak of quivering ecstasy in perfect harmony, and rolling waves of utter joy rippled through their bodies and escaped in great gasps of pleasure. Thomas fell back, drained and bewildered at this resurgence of sexual fervour, his passion spent, replaced by lingering tenderness. And as they lay together watching the firelight

7

flickering on the bedroom ceiling, Irene couldn't contain her elation. A frisson of rapture rose up to her throat, because she knew.

Nine months later, a raw fear gripped Thomas as he strode backwards and forwards across his study. A fear that was not diminished by the fact that her confinement was almost at an end, because he knew the worst was yet to come. Her own mother had died giving her life. He let the breath that he'd been holding escape through pursed lips. He was paying for his indulgence of her now, and the cost was high.

Terror rose in him again, restricting his chest and making it hard to breathe. He moved to the door and, crossing the hall, sprinted noiselessly up the staircase and along the gallery to the door of Irene's room where he turned the handle gently, fearful of disturbing her shallow rest. Grace rose from her seat beside the bed and, with an almost imperceptible dip, moved across the room past Thomas and through the open door, carefully closing it behind her.

He filled up with tenderness as he watched his wife where she lay still and white against the pillows, glistening beads of perspiration catching the flickering gaslight and shimmering on her brow and upper lip. He was overwhelmed by her delicate loveliness. She was so precious to him that he had to fight back unmanly tears.

With the instinct often witnessed in deeply loving relationships, she sensed his presence and stirred, and her eyes opened. The flecks of gold that freckled her deep irises were echoed on the tips of her lashes. Her dark hair, now damp with effort, tumbled about her shoulders and this, too, was streaked with strands of gold that owed nothing to artifice. This harmony of colour gave her a unique appearance and, from what Thomas had learned from her father, was a dominant gene. Her mother had possessed the same distinctive colouring. Her lips parted in a wan smile when she saw him, and his anxiety began to lift.

As he left the room, Grace rose from the seat outside the door and glided silently to continue her vigil beside her beloved mistress. She sat, her hands clasped, rolling her thumbs one over the other, concern apparent in her face.

She had been in the service of the family since shortly before Irene's mother had given birth to her, and her devotion to her charge had been the pivot of her whole life. Thomas had to acknowledge that her concern was no less than his own. This was probably the reason that he had resented her in the beginning. She had been like a shadow all through their courtship. Whenever he had contrived to spend a few moments alone with Irene, Grace had appeared as from nowhere, never permitting them the shortest time of privacy, never interfering but always making Thomas aware that she was watching. He resented the inference that he would do anything to harm Irene. He objected to her proprietorial attitude towards her young mistress and he had taken consolation in presuming that after Irene and he were married, Grace's services would be needed no longer. However she had remained after Alexander was born and she had nurtured him with the same tender care and devotion that she had shown Irene, without ever relinquishing her charge over 'her girl'. Her rule over the nursery had continued after Richard had been added to the family and long after both boys had gone off to school, she remained in Irene's service.

Her anxiety in the present circumstances was palpable. The rolling of her thumbs continued, interrupted only to pinch her nostrils between her finger and thumb, her eyes closing for long minutes as billows of distress overcame her habitual calm.

Thomas returned to his study seeking some distraction but couldn't settle to any work. It was fortunate that the boys, though still young, were now able to run the brickworks between them and Thomas had no concern regarding the health of the business in his absence. He leaned back in his large leather chair, long legs stretched out before him, steepling the tips of his fingers, and allowed himself to relax and his mind to wander back to the early years of their mutual attraction and marriage.

He had requested a meeting with Mr Morse, one of the most prominent bankers in Liverpool, to review finance for some new kilns, and was invited to discuss the proposals at Morse's home in Crosby. Thomas had set out on the morning of the appointed day unaware that this was to act as a catalyst for his entire future.

The brougham turned into the long drive, but before it had reached the door of the imposing house, he saw through its window at some distance, a girl riding a chestnut mare. She was dressed in blue, was slender and graceful and had an excellent seat, carrying herself erect, back slightly arched, reins loose in her hands, in total control. She did not turn her head at the sound of his

9

approach, but reined in her horse and galloped towards the rear of the house.

The carriage trundled along until it came to a halt, and Thomas alighted. He was met at the door by the butler, and Mr Morse himself came close behind and ushered him into the library.

George Morse was a pleasant man and his face was set in an expression that suggested something amusing was occupying his mind constantly. He had a thick mane of sable hair which curled up on the nape of his neck, his features were aquiline and he was altogether distinguished.

The two men matched one another for height and they shared a degree of self-possession, which is the prerogative of the quietly confident.

They developed an immediate rapport and quickly discovered mutual interests and acquaintances. It was some time before the pleasantries were over and the business in hand had been concluded, and Morse invited Thomas to lunch with him. The older man excused himself and left the room. Thomas could hear him speaking to somebody outside, and after only a moment he returned. As they continued their conversation, there came a light tap on the door and it opened.

'Ah, my dear,' Morse said, rising again and moving towards the door.

Thomas turned his head and his mouth fell open as, with a quick intake of breath, he rose to his feet. He heard Morse speaking as the girl glided forward like a vision, but he didn't register what was being said and seconds passed before he recovered his composure. She was exquisite; absolute perfection. Her pale skin had a satin sheen. Her eyes were large and luminous, dark as coal but strangely flecked with gold. She had changed from her riding habit into a silver-blue day dress, which skimmed her slender body. Thomas froze, unable to move; hardly able to breathe.

'Mr Hall will be joining us for lunch, Irene,' Morse said, eyes twinkling at Thomas's discomforture. He felt the usual rush of proud pleasure which always accompanied the introduction of his only daughter to new acquaintances. The girl's face opened into a gentle smile and she proffered a slender hand.

As Thomas recalled that moment of contact, he trembled uncontrollably. Over twenty years later, he still marvelled that she had agreed to marry him. That she loved him!

*　*　*

He was brought back to the moment with a shock as Grace hurtled through the door even as she knocked, her air of dignified authority deserting her.

'Mr Thomas,' she gasped. 'It's time to send for the doctor. Miss Irene's contractions are coming quickly. The baby will be here this afternoon.'

Thomas sprung into action.

'Get Jenners right away! He's to take the dogcart and bring Doctor Bennett immediately. I'll go to your mistress. Get back as quickly as you can. Make sure Ellie's prepared everything for the doctor. Hurry now, and tell Jenners not to waste any time!'

He fired the orders, staccato, and was galvanised into action. Taking the stairs two at a time he tore along the gallery, heart racing, and into the room where Irene lay racked with pain. As he entered, a scream escaped her lips and her shoulders rose from the pillow. He took her hand in his and felt her grasp tighten. The pain reached a crescendo and her body collapsed as she moaned softly. He felt sick and helpless, a raw emptiness griping at his stomach, as twenty-five minutes passed with Ellie bustling in and out of the room, before Jenners came back with the doctor. The worst twenty-five minutes of Thomas's life. The doctor bundled him out of the bedroom and he lowered himself onto Grace's seat, his head resting on his knees, as another scream pierced his ears.

The door in the hall opened, and raising his head he looked down and through the balustrades of the gallery saw Richard, a light smattering of snow over the shoulders of his coat. Becket held the coat as Richard slipped his arms out and, simultaneously, moved forward to the foot of the staircase. He looked up and saw his father sitting on the low nursing chair, a ludicrous sight with his long legs reaching back up to his chin. It would have been comical were the distress on his face not so pitiful.

As he mounted the stairs Richard asked, 'What's happening, Father? Is the baby coming? Is Mother all right?'

He helped Thomas to his feet and slowly they descended together. Richard felt his father stiffen as another scream tore through the house, and he guided him into the sitting room and sat him in his chair before the blazing fire, to continue the wait. He had never seen his father so lacking in composure. Thomas was

11

usually a strong man, seldom showing emotion, never showing weakness.

'I've been such a fool, Richard. I should never have allowed myself to be persuaded.'

Looking at his son now, he saw an attractive young man, over six feet tall and strongly built. His appearance so favoured his maternal grandfather that Thomas could not look upon him without seeing George Morse two decades earlier when they had first met. Richard had the same stance, ramrod straight, head held erect. He had the same dark eyes, so deep in fact that it was not possible to discern the line that separated the iris from the pupil. A thick lock of curling hair fell over his forehead and, in an identical manner to his grandfather, he would run his fingers through it as he pushed it back into place. Even his voice had the same rich timbre, and the delivery of his speech mimicked his grandfather's exactly.

Thomas's musing was shattered by yet another cry, followed immediately by a wail of a different pitch. He looked up, startled. The doctor had warned him that Irene's age would cause problems, and he had expected a long and difficult labour.

He was on his feet immediately, his strength and sagging energy renewed, and leaving Richard in the hall, he climbed the staircase, knocked on the door and without waiting, pushed it open and entered. He felt a surge of relief as he took in the scene before him. Grace was leaning over the crib where the baby lay, already swaddled in a white shawl, while the doctor, resting against the wall beside the wash stand, his sleeves still rolled up, dried his hands. Ellie stood snivelling in the corner, repeating over and over again, 'Oh, Mr Thomas.'

'Stupid girl,' thought Thomas as he crossed the room to where Irene lay, her hair streaming out in wet tangles.

He took her hands between his and lifted them to his lips and she turned her head towards him.

'It's a little girl, Thomas. We have a baby daughter.' She heaved a deep sigh and succumbed, at last, to the exhaustion that overwhelmed her in surging waves.

Thomas smoothed back her hair from her face and kissed her forehead. 'Oh, Irene, Irene, that's wonderful. You have made me very happy.'

He choked back tears of relief as he turned to the small bundle in the crib. Grace came forward and lifted the baby. She looked

12

directly into his eyes, holding his gaze for several seconds. She hesitated imperceptibly before placing his daughter in his arms.

She was so tiny, so fragile. He looked down into two large eyes peeping over the shawl. She was beautiful. Thomas placed his fingers on the edge of the shawl and drew it down.

He almost dropped the child in horror.

Chapter Two

After the age of seven, Fanny seldom revealed the gaping cleft that disfigured her upper lip but became adept at covering it. She had a way of wrapping a long, raven lock of hair around her finger, putting the tip of her thumb into her mouth and lowering her head to look up through gold-tipped lashes. This further emphasised her startling dark eyes and gave her an air of charming vulnerability that enchanted those who saw her. She'd also developed a mannerism with her right hand, by which she would close her fist and crook her index finger over the cleft, laying her thumb beside it so that the gap was covered.

This deformity apart, she had inherited all of Irene's beauty, and her inevitable shyness gave her an otherworldliness. She would never venture beyond the garden of the house unless concealed behind the windows of the blue brougham.

She became a most accomplished pianist and would spend many hours at the piano in her music room next to her bedroom. It had long windows, which overlooked the garden at the rear of the house and was appropriately furnished to allow her to give short recitals for the entertainment of the rest of the family and their close friends.

Her brothers doted on her, the difference in their ages making them even more protective than is usual for brothers towards younger sisters. One of them would always be available to accompany her wherever she needed to go.

She was seventeen when everything began to change, and she was sadly bewildered to find herself increasingly isolated as nature took her course. Alexander's time was taken up with his wife and children and the running of the brickworks, and Richard, whom they had begun to think would never marry, fell in love with Ruth.

Fanny's birthday that year was particularly sombre. In October, severe influenza had confined her grandfather to his bed for six weeks and this illness was to mark the beginning of a decline in his previously strong constitution.

It seemed to George Morse that he was scarcely ever without pain, and each morning his waking was accompanied by an unaccustomed lethargy which despite his greatest efforts he was unable to shake off. He was never to recover completely.

Reluctant to cause the family concern, he would make light of it.

'If I wake up in the night and I can't feel the pain,' he would tell them, 'I think I'm dead.'

'Don't try to laugh it off, Father,' Irene would respond. 'I'm very worried about you.'

'I'm getting old, my dear, and wearing out. I'm not going to last forever.'

But as things worked out, it was Grace who was to wear out first.

At the end of November, when she had reached the advanced age of ninety-eight, she contracted pneumonia. Irene had her moved from her cottage on the estate into the big house and, refusing to allow Grace's nurse and companion to tend to her needs any further, she took on her nursing care herself, never leaving her bedside except for short periods of fitful sleep, insisted upon by Thomas. When, as was inevitable, Grace succumbed, Irene was inconsolable. Great empty sobs wracked her body incessantly and she could neither eat nor sleep.

Since she had lost her mother when she was only hours old, she had no memory of her death, and the passing of Grace was her first experience of the wretched sorrow that bereavement can bring. She mourned, not only for her beloved nurse, but at the loss of her own ignorance and innocence. The sudden realisation that took her peace of mind away, that something which had been there from the beginning of time could cease to be.

Desperate to calm and comfort her, Thomas wanted to take her to the Mediterranean, hoping that the more clement climate might relieve her melancholy, and help her to recover her composure. But she wouldn't go.

The funeral seemed appropriate to the mood of the time and it appeared to Fanny that the whole country shared her state of abject depression.

Rumour was reaching the ears of her subjects that their beloved Queen was in failing health, and people went about their business with downcast spirits. The appalling weather did nothing to

15

brighten the lugubrious aspect. In early December torrential rain poured down relentlessly, so that rivers burst their banks and before the effects of this had subsided it became so bitterly cold that it turned to snow, which covered the roads and the fields until they blended together into one vast shroud. There were drifts several feet high against the garden walls, the elms were eerily visible, white upon white, at the end of the garden, and the brickworks yard was blanketed under an unforgiving deluge of whiteness.

Even after the yard was cleared and the snow piled up into huge, glacial mountains at the edges of the field, the ice filled in the crevices between the wooden sets so that the men's clogs and the horses' hooves skidded over the surface like skates on a frozen pond. Work was all but impossible. Fires were kept banked up in the works, dormitory and quarters, and heavy rugs hung inside the doors. Thomas ordered extra blankets for the bunks and increased the men's rations but still many of them became ill from exposure and production fell to an all-time low.

This was at a time when the output was already well down. Indeed, industry across the country was suffering.

Manufacturers began to demand that tariff reforms be introduced in an effort to stop industry sliding into recession, but many who were in Parliament had vested interests in avoiding a protection policy. They advocated free trade, and since they were the ruling caste, they were prevailing. Consequently, men were being laid off, especially in the iron and steel and associated industries, and Christmas was upon them.

The building trade didn't escape the fallout and the demand for bricks fell.

'It's going to be a struggle to keep all the men on, Father.' Alexander opined.

'It has to be a top priority,' Thomas replied. 'I'm not going to see any of our people on the dole at Christmas. We'll have to tighten our belts but we'll get through it.'

But he didn't feel the optimism he affected.

The new century brought no comfort and the sombre mood continued to hang over the nation like a cloud of doom. The Queen, at eighty-two, suffered a stroke and succumbed to her final illness. She had been on the throne for sixty-three years and since she was the oldest, longest-reigning and best-loved monarch, it was no surprise that the whole kingdom – the whole empire – was distraught. In London, over a million mourners lined the route of her funeral procession. Elsewhere in England, buildings and people were swathed in black crepe. The Welsh Valleys were mute in mourning. In Scotland, people wept in the streets for the loss of their beloved 'Mrs Brown'.

Even Ireland, so eager to escape the confines and perceived oppression of her sovereignty, wore its flags at half mast, and, arriving at Dublin docks, a young Irishman named Charlie remembered how he had hitched a ride from Cork only months earlier, to join the throng that cheered her through the streets of Dublin.

Now he was on his way to England.

The Dublin Steam Packet Company vessel departed from the quay at eight sharp each evening. By seven o'clock traffic began to stream into the docks, disgorging baggage-laden passengers who, arriving on the connecting trains, had made their way from the station to the landing stage. For a brief moment in time, the resultant confusion threw together cloth-capped Irish labourers and top-hatted gentry, before they were irrevocably separated into the first class and steerage, to which they had been consigned by accident of birth.

This time, Charlie wasn't coming back!

'By five o'clock in the morning, I'll be standing on the Liverpool landing stage,' he thought with mounting excitement.

For the past six years he had made this journey every June, to work on the farms in the North West of England, and every July he had returned with his pocket a bit heavier than when he went. But this time was different. This time, he was not coming back!

He pushed his cap back on his head and began to fight his way through the mêlée of bodies towards the ticket office queue, his fingers curled around his two precious half-crowns. When he reached the window, he slapped them down on the sill with some satisfaction. This time there would be no inflated fare to return home. He would not be among the crowd who, being made richer by their labours than when they left, would be compelled to pay a higher price for the return journey. This time he was not going back!

With a pang of anxiety, he remembered the note he had left for Ma to find after he'd left that morning. She would have had thirteen hours to recover from the shock of finding that her eldest son had left with no intention of returning, at least in the short term. He knew her well. They were close, Charlie and Ma, and he could imagine her emotions as though he lived in her mind. First she would feel the shock. 'Charlie not coming back!' Then, after a while, the anger and questioning would follow. 'How does he dare to decide this without consulting me?' Self-pity would flood in next. 'How could he do this to his poor old ma?' And, finally, after it had sunk in, sorrow!

Of all her nine children, Charlie had remained her favourite. Her first-born and the darling of her youthful heart, before she began to weary of the world in general and of her lout of a husband in particular. When Charlie was born, Mick had been young and strong and full of hope and they had shared such joy together as they awaited his coming into the world. But disappointment and despair had turned him into a weak but, paradoxically, bullying wretch of a man.

Still, the die was cast and Charlie was determined that he was not going back to the hunger, the poverty, the squabbling and Pa's drunken temper. Ma would feel forsaken, it's true, but the year would speak against the day and when he had made enough money and had somewhere decent to live, he would send for her. Then she would know that he had been right to leave. That he had done it for her.

He was being carried along now by the impetus of the crowd. He could smell the sweat of the heaving mass of bodies and last night's beer on their exhalations, but it was a comforting atmosphere, the feeling of comradeship and empathy; men together, driven by necessity to a mass exodus to become sojourners in a foreign land. It sounded noble and courageous in his head and gave him a feeling of belonging, of being a part of something powerful and determined. He hardly dared admit, even to himself, that he had always loved the time of year that took him across the Irish Sea to England.

The ship's side was looming, vast over him now. Sure, it was a fine, handsome thing. With every conceivable modern convenience including the new electric lighting, the Steam Packet's powerful vessels were fast and offered a comfortable, uninterrupted night's rest for those who could afford to pay the higher tariff.

Last year, Charlie, unable to sleep, had prowled around the deck leaping the barrier that separated the steerage passengers from the

18

first class, and had peered through a cabin porthole where the light was shining between the partly drawn curtains. There was a double bed, embellished on each side by the new electric lights which cast a rosy glow over the room, with its sombre-coloured quilt turned down, revealing crisp, starched, snowy sheets and pillowcases. In the corner nearest to the porthole, there stood a burgundy leather easy chair with a throw draped carelessly over its arm. On a rosewood washstand stood a bowl and pitcher, decorated with cabbage roses. Soft white cotton towels hung over a wooden rack next to it. A deep maroon and cream rug covered the floor beside the bed. There was no one in the cabin and no evidence that it was occupied. Empty! Waste! The opulence had staggered him.

As he recalled the moment, he vowed, 'When I send for Ma, I shall post a first class ticket for the journey and she shall experience the luxury that these privileged travellers take for granted.'

He was brought back from the warm pleasure of his reverie by a sudden surge forward as the mass of bodies reached the top of the gangway. Soon he had boarded the boat, and was being propelled by the throng to the stern. He managed to extricate himself from the crowd and escape to the rails. The mails were still being taken aboard as the first bell sounded and late passengers were hurriedly weaving their way through farewell parties, their porters following closely, laden with luggage. He watched the tearful leave-takings and last-minute embraces, until the second bell was rung and the cry came from the sailor at the top of the pier steps.

'All ashore! All ashore!'

Visitors began to emerge from cabins and hurry down the gangway, suddenly fearful that they should be carried irrevocably out to sea. The third bell sounded as the gangway was pulled in and the ropes were thrown aboard, and the steamer began to glide away from the dockside. He moved to the middle of the stern and leant on the rail as the boat swung out into the open bay. It was gathering speed now and soon cleared the harbour, its red funnels belching out two swirling shafts of black smoke. Charlie could taste the brine on his lips and feel the cool, sweet wind ruffling his fair hair and caressing his skin. His euphoria was overwhelming; as though his stomach had risen into his chest so that he could hardly breathe. He was on his way and this time, he wasn't coming back!

The seagulls screeched as they wheeled overhead, turning back towards where the verdant green of the land sank slowly into the

19

sparkling, silver sea. As it disappeared, Charlie experienced the familiar climax of excitement that always came upon him at the prospect of the adventure that lay ahead, but for the briefest moment, it was eclipsed by a frisson of panic. He was not going back!

He gave an involuntary shudder, suddenly realising that the sea breeze had made him cold, and drawing his threadbare jacket around him, he entered through the double doors and down the steps to find a space to spend the night.

'Please God,' he said, closing his eyes tightly, 'let there be a decent place for me to lay my head.'

Opening his eyes, he saw that there was a vacant corner, surrounded by bodies, some talking, some playing cards, some dozing and some already asleep. A red-haired man sat propped up against the wall to the left of it and on the right, a big brute of a man had fallen into a deep, noisy sleep. Charlie stood leaning against the door jamb, looking around uneasily, but when after several minutes nobody had come to lay claim to the site, he stepped over the reclining bodies and, bending down, asked the red-haired man if it were spoken for. Without answering, the man shuffled further along, making more room for him, and hardly believing his luck, Charlie put his small, shabby case against the wall and lowered himself, thankfully, to the floor.

Sleep eluded him, for his head was swirling around with the wonderful, grandiose possibilities that England opened up to him but finally, he drifted off with the ship's rise and fall to the rhythm of the waves.

He seemed scarcely to have closed his eyes before the awakening bustle around him proclaimed the breaking of the day. The engines were beating time to the deep surge of the sea. At first he felt no desire to leave the comfort of his dream, but the thrill that he always felt as he reached the Mersey Estuary began to rise in him, and drawing his legs in beneath him, he came to his feet. Picking up the battered suitcase that had made the journey many more times than he, and which had done service as a pillow during the crossing, he stepped gingerly over the still reclining bodies of his fellow travellers.

When he went up on deck, the sun's rays were casting a scarlet veneer over the massive grain elevators, which were just visible in the distance. The air was sharp and cool and he drank in the wonder of it greedily, feeling no little pleasure as it hit the bottom of his lungs.

As the ship moved up the river past Canada Dock, the gas lamps were still lit along the waking docks from Seaforth to The Dingle. The quayside was stirring with the arrival of the stevedores and porters, calling out to each other in good humour. The occasional bowler hat of the early clerical staff could be seen among the cloth caps, and a tallyman was already in position at Salisbury Dock, checking off the day's boxes.

As far as Salthouse, there were signs of awakening on the ships. Barques, topsail schooners, four-masted sailing ships and brigs crowded the Salthouse Dock, so that the early morning movements were like a rustling through a ghostly forest of denuded trees. As shafts of sunlight struck the domed roof of the Custom House, the world of shipping was coming alive.

The skyline brought to Charlie's mind something that his da had told him when they first made the crossing together.

'There was a fellow called Daniel Defoe. He used to be a writer ... he's dead a long time now. He came to Liverpool in 1720 and when he caught sight of it for the first time, he said that there was no town in all of England that could equal it for the fineness of its streets, so he did.' Mick had stroked his chin, a wistful look in his eyes, and gone on, 'I envy you, lad. It is a great moment when you see this splendid city for the first time.'

And he was right! Yes, without a doubt, Liverpool was a city of fine, handsome buildings. Beyond the George Basin, St Nicholas's Church dominated the waterfront. From medieval times, and through many incarnations, it had chronicled the history of the port as it stood, a silent watchman, overseeing the spiritual life of the docklands. The clock face showed that it was half past four. Gulls tripped across the surface of the water, rippling it into combs of white foam before rising into the sky with a screech of sheer ecstasy that matched Charlie's joy.

Charlie loved Liverpool. The sudden resurgence of euphoria was tinged with a pang of guilt as he remembered that its eminence as a port depended largely on its trade with Ireland, and he attempted to assuage this feeling of disloyalty. Sure, Dublin was a great city too, and where in the world was there a vision like the sea around Cork, as the sun bounced off the waves?

But Liverpool! That was something different. There was an

incomparable majesty, an aura of power, a unique feeling of permanence. He had never watched it receding in the July evening sun without a pang of regret.

This time was different. This time, Charlie wasn't going back!

The ship began to regurgitate its cargo of drowsy humanity and Charlie was once again carried along by the flow of bodies as they were deposited onto the dockside. He walked up the floating pier and came out into the daylight, blinking in the brightness of the morning sun, and crossing the road he made his way to the Seamen's House, a magnificent example of nineteenth-century architecture in 'Sailortown' and took a room for one night.

He stood in the centre of the ground floor and looked up at tier upon tier of wrought iron balustrades. The landings ran around four sides of the building with green painted doors leading off, behind which were rooms not much larger than closets.

The interior was austere in the extreme and Charlie was struck by the comparison between the stark cast-iron interior and the splendid elegance of the outside of the building. It was only for a night. He climbed the stairs to the third floor and opened the door to his allocated room. It was almost bare. Between the iron bedsteads was a small table. Charlie emptied his pockets and shook out his last Woodbine, crumpling the empty packet and throwing it onto the table. He sank down on the bed, his hands behind his head, and inhaled with relish the first cigarette of the day.

His case lay unopened on the other bed. It could wait until he had finished his smoke. He felt a drowsy satisfaction with life and began to doze, moving only to drag on his cigarette and inhale deeply.

He started at a knock on the door, and a burly man with a head of dark, curly hair came in. He was about six feet tall with broad shoulders and carried a fiddle case in one hand and a bag slung over his shoulder. He looked at Charlie for several seconds, unsmiling.

'That's a dirty habit you've got there,' he said at length.

'And hallo to you, too.' Charlie replied, nevertheless removing the offending cigarette from his mouth and stubbing it out in the tin saucer on the table.

'It'll kill you, so it will,' went on the stranger. He swung his bag onto the spare bed but laid his fiddle down lovingly. He lifted Charlie's battered old case and held it in the air. 'Have you paid for both beds then?'

Charlie rose from his bed and took hold of the case.

'No. There's nothing in it worth the rent.'

The stranger smiled. 'Connor O'Donnell. Dublin,' he said.

Charlie took the hand held out in front of him and replied, 'Charlie Cahill. Cork.'

And that handshake marked the start of a friendship and respect that was to become deep and mutual.

Chapter Three

Charlie leaned heavily against the jamb of the dormitory door, staring unseeingly across the yard as the evening sun ricocheted off the brickworks, windows onto his face. His bones were tired, but there was a pleasure in the weariness and the sun had not completely lost its comforting heat.

The day had been long and hard but he was being amply rewarded for all the extra hours he had laboured. Indeed, all the men were treated fairly by the Gaffer. Hadn't that been one of the most important factors in his coming to Seaforth? Forty-three men had applied for jobs at the brickworks but only four had been taken on. Over the last ten months, Charlie had progressed from unloading the clay and through processing, until his keen eye and instinctive understanding of brick quality had gained him the opportunity of training to assess the bricks as they were drawn from the kiln.

He worked under Josh and they had an easygoing relationship.

Mr Hall had been impressed with his quick grasp of the manufacture. He could reckon the durability and frost resistance of a brick just by the feel of it and he was eager to learn from the more experienced men where the best locally available materials came from. He quickly became able to separate the well-fired from the less well-fired bricks to suit particular locations and applications, those appropriate for the outside wall face and those which were fit only for inner and partition walls. His ear had become attuned to the clear ringing sound of perfectly fired bricks as he gently tapped them, one against another, and he took great pride in his work.

Mr. Hall had called him 'a natural' and had confidence in the thoroughness of Charlie's inspecting, sampling and testing. He had given him two small pay rises in only ten months.

Charlie breathed a deep sigh and his lips curled upwards as he thought of the nest egg steadily swelling in his battered suitcase.

24

Precious little of this had come from his previous job, working on the harvest. Labouring on the farm had been back-breaking and the barn that had been set aside as the hands' sleeping quarters had been smelly and damp, despite the long hours of June sunshine. The men had worked hard last year, with not one malingerer amongst the whole gang. They were nearly all men he had worked with before, and though they enjoyed their jug of ale, none of them allowed it to interfere with their work. They had toiled in the hot sun from daybreak until they could scarcely stand up, driven by promises of a bonus for an early harvest ahead of the rains predicted by the local diviner. But when all the sheaves stood with military precision down the length and width of the fields, beautiful in their symmetry, the bonus had been miserly and the season had been foreshortened by their excessive industry.

The farmer had been arrogant and dismissive as, seated in the great barn framed on either side by his two ungainly sons, he called each man forward to receive his final pay. At one point, it seemed to Charlie that there might be an explosion of violence as the murmurings of dissent rose to a crescendo and the massive fist of hot-headed Mick Cavanagh smashed down on the makeshift table, causing the money to fly up into the air and come to rest in the mire between the cobbles.

'Pick 'em up!' shouted the farmer, heaving his massive bulk inches from his seat to lean forward and peer at the paltry number of coins. 'Pick 'em up. Get your things and bugger off!'

When Mick refused, he bellowed again, his face purpling with anger as he struggled to lift himself out of his chair. 'Bugger off!'

The famer swung a wild punch into the air. His aim was true but his reach was well short so that the momentum of the swing continued and carried his bloated body with it so that he almost landed on the floor.

Some of the men tittered nervously, while others moved forward, in a show of unity.

One of the farmer's sons caught his father as he fell and eased him, fuming, back into his seat while the other picked up a pitchfork and advanced towards the hapless Mick.

Connor stepped forward from his place in the queue and positioned himself between the two men, his hands held up in front of him, palms out towards the son, in a placatory gesture.

'Now there's no need for that, is there?'

25

His voice was soothing, yet it carried authority so that he was able to calm things down, bending to retrieve the money, moving from coin to coin where they had fallen.

Wiping them on his sleeve, he put his arm gently but firmly about Mick's shoulders and turned him out of the barn. Mick submitted to Connor's pressure but, at the door, he turned and gave the old farmer a murderous look before turning away, his face crinkled with pain and his stomach heaving at the humiliation and the injustice. There was no way of winning against the bosses. The police would be called and the labourers would pay the price.

Charlie had been fortunate to have found himself not only working at the same farm as Connor, but also to have been allocated a sleeping area next to him, yet again. The Dubliner was a strapping, healthy fellow of around fifty – older than most of the Irish labourers that made the journey for work each year – and he had been coming over to England for twenty-six years, so he knew more than all the other men put together. After work was finished and they had eaten their meagre supper, he would tell them stories from Ireland's history and serenade them with Gaelic ballads in a deep melodic voice.

He had first come over in the triumphant year of the initial secret ballot.

'Almost sixty Irish Home Rule MPs were elected to Parliament.' His voice would move up an octave as the memory took hold of him. He sucked in air through pursed lips as he recalled the rejoicing in the streets of Dublin. 'That was a day to remember, so it was,' his voice would fall again, 'but it didn't last long.'

'What happened, Connor?' The young men would lean towards him as though his enthusiasm would rub off on them.

'Ah, well, 'twas not long before we realised that Disraeli's new lot was not about to recognise the result. No, his one purpose was to obstruct the progress of the bill. Yous'd never believe the anger when the people found out that they'd been double-crossed. There was civil disobedience everywhere in the city. Aye, and beyond. That's when I first decided that I would come to England to stay.'

'Why did you go back then, Connor?'

'Well me ould da died and that changed everything. I slaved for five years as a tenant farmer over a small patch of land after he passed away; it wasn't even me own land,' his sigh shuddered in his chest, remembering. 'But the miserable scrap of stone and bog failed.'

He told them how five years later he was driven back to work in Lancashire by the poor harvest, which brought about near famine in Ireland. And then, when he had thought things couldn't get any worse, cheap grain poured in from America, lowering the price of the pitiful amount the land yielded.

After work, as they lay with only hay between their aching bones and the hard ground, Connor would relate to Charlie and the other young men what it had been like when the Irish National League, that was under Parnell, fought for reduced rents.

'They tried to persuade supporters in County Mayo to refuse to harvest the potato crop and they urged the other counties to do the same, too. It was hard, though; you didn't work, you didn't eat. Anyway, yous've heard about Gladstone's second Land Act?' Irish heads were nodded and English heads shaken, but all were strained forward in concentration. 'Well, Parnell, God bless his gentle soul, forced Gladstone's Second Land Act, in … that would be about 'eighty-one … but they threw him into jail, so they did, because he told them straight it was a paltry concession and he just went on whipping up opposition. And he was right.'

Connor explained wryly that although after the 1885 General Election Parnell's Irish Parliamentary Party had won only eighty-six seats, this still gave it the balance of power in the Commons. It was the turning point on a long, hard road to freedom.

Connor never showed resentment towards the English, but instead insisted that the quarrel was between the rich and the poor, the powerful and the weak. He had met as many ill-used and exploited Englishmen as Irishmen on the farms and roads of Lancashire. It was, he told his audience, a situation conceived and born of class, not of nationality, a philosophy that made every man and boy listening, whichever side of the Irish Sea they came from, Connor's friend. Nobody could help but respond to his quiet Gaelic charm and slow, thoughtful manner.

It was Connor who had told Charlie about the job at Hall's Brickworks, helping him to get there and putting a word in for him with Mr. Richard. Charlie owed a lot to Connor. He owed a lot to Mr Thomas too, who had given him total trust in his own sphere of responsibility, and now even allowed Charlie to drive the dogcart into the town on the groom's day off or when he was busy with his stable duties.

The rays of the late afternoon sun washed the dirty, grey surface of the cobbles in a golden swathe and the office building cast long shadows across the yard. It was time to collect the work sheets. Would he see his pretty lady this evening? At this time each Thursday, as he crossed the yard to the office, she would appear from around the corner, flustered and breathless, shyly holding her shawl across her face. This was his favourite time of the week.

He glanced up at the window of the big house where he had seen her standing on many occasions, just in time to see the curtain swing back into place.

Chapter Four

The house at Seaforth had been extended over the years and now boasted a two-storey wing on either side of the main three-storey building. It stood as a testimony to the quality and the beauty of Seaforth brick.

There had been Halls in Seaforth before records began and the old house, which lay in ruins two hundred yards from the surrounding wall of the garden, had stood since the mid-eighteenth century. It now housed a colony of swirling and swooping house martins. Thomas's father had begun construction of the present house at the turn of the century. A palisade surrounded the 'T'-shaped veranda and the steep overhanging roof was supported by six white pillars and cast a long shadow across the lawns, which slanted down to the lane. The two wings were set at right angles to the front elevation so that the house extended on three sides around a rear courtyard. The huge iron gates opened up onto a wide drive. To the right of the house there was a pergola with a rose garden planted in front of it, and laid out symmetrically on the opposite side in front of the stables and coach house was the tennis court. Facing the west wing was a massive double sliding door with a smaller door cut into one half of it, and this led across the yard to the staff and tradesmen's entrance. The sliding doors allowed access to the carriages whilst the smaller one alleviated the need for it to be opened when people went in and out on foot. From the long windows at the end of the annexe, the kilns could just be glimpsed through the tall elms that separated the house from the works.

It was May and the elm trees were in full leaf, screening the quarters from the rear of the house and the rear of the house from the quarters in mutual self-consciousness, but here and there were gaps where hawthorn trees were coming into blossom. The grass, luscious and verdant, conceded defeat to the assault made upon it by armies of daisies and clover that effortlessly dappled it in patches

29

like some luxurious quilt which had been laboured over with love, skill and dedication by nature's needlewomen. The rain had ceased and innumerable shiny droplets, made fluorescent in the reflection of the sun's rays, hung tremulously before relinquishing their hold and falling, shimmering, to the ground.

The air was balmy and full of the promise of summer, and Fanny's spirit sang with expectancy of some unknown, yet clearly anticipated, delight. Across the valley, the earth stretched out in satisfaction, displaying the promise of a bumper harvest.

The scent of rain on the leaves and grass rose in a gentle haze from the sun-warmed, damp earth, and Fanny's heart leapt at the wonder of all this, and at the sight of a tall figure glimpsed through a natural lych-gate of mayflowers.

She had had the piano moved closer to the window, ostensibly the better to read her music in what little light penetrated beneath the low eaves, and now she perched on the piano stool, the heavy drapes of the music room screening her from outside view. From this vantage point, she could survey the works yard between the trees without exposing her position. She could see the Irish boy leaning against the dormitory door, the pale blue of his eyes, indistinguishable in any event at this distance, hidden by his squinting into the sun. But Fanny knew the exact shade of their blueness. She could see it with her eyes shut. She saw it when she was asleep; she saw it when she opened her eyes in the morning and when she closed them at night. His eyes haunted her, waking and sleeping. She drowned in them; she delighted herself in them.

Now, he raised his hand to shield them from the sun and looked up at the house. Abruptly, she let the curtain fall and glanced at the clock impatiently. Soon it would be time for him to go to the office. She turned back to her piano and began to tinkle the notes with the fingers of her left hand but the close proximity of the Irish boy proved too distracting for even this simple exercise. She turned again to the world outside, drawing the curtain a little and becoming absorbed in what she saw ... and what she recalled.

Whenever Fanny caught a glimpse of him she almost choked with happiness. Whenever they came face to face, that smile would expand, as in slow motion, to encompass his entire face, and she would lower her eyes lest he should see the complete surrender in them and, heart racing, would wrap her shawl more tightly around her face and hurry away. When she had rounded the corner she

30

would stop, leaning heavily against the wall to steady herself and breathing the air in deep gulps until, at least on the surface, she had regained her composure. Nobody had ever looked at her the way the Irish boy did.

There had been young men, but for the most part they had known her since their childhood and though her good nature may have caused them to overlook her mysterious deformity had they seen it, so large did it loom in her mind that self-loathing would not allow her to conceive of being desired, and so she gave no opportunity for any but the most platonic and reserved relationship to develop.

She had heard Richard speak to her father about the Irish boy during dinner on the first evening of her return from her stay with Grandfather Morse at Crosby. Richard had been very free with his praise of him, and it was two days later when she had occasion to walk over to her father's office, that she had her first meeting with him. He had come out of the office and held the door open for her to pass. His eyes had given warning of that devastating smile that spread like the slow rising of the sun until it filled the whole heaven. It creased his face like ripples on a pond, and his pale blue eyes disappeared into folds of pleasure.

Now Fanny recalled the impact of that first meeting: a fear, a joy, an excitement that she had never experienced before, her body discovering meridians that had lain dormant waiting to be awakened. Two people discovering, instantly, that they shared an affinity, though they had never met before and had never spoken. Passion roared through her like the inaugural opening of a sluice gate and as the outer door swung shut and he was gone, Fanny fell against the wall, her head and chest bent forward to aid her breathing, her left hand clutching her stomach where there was something like a pain, and yet, different. She stayed there for several moments but it was several hours before she could claim that she felt something approaching normality. This was a feeling that she would experience again and again without any lessening of intensity, each time she came close to the Irish boy.

She came to realise with amazement over the succeeding months that he, too, regarded her in this special way, not because she was Thomas Hall's daughter, but because love, like some delighted and mischievous voyeur, was mixing a volatile cocktail in his veins that imposed upon him the same madness that engrossed her. In the ensuing months she fluctuated between flights of euphoria and utter despair. She was to feel surging joy as she remembered electric moments when their eyes met, only to come crashing down as self-loathing held up a glass to her deformity and cried out, 'How could he love that?'

There was, as a matter of policy, a dearth of looking glasses in the house, but now, from time to time, she would seek one out to examine in detail the contours of her mouth. At times she would try vainly to convince herself that love had come like a ministering angel in the night and corrected the deformity, but it stubbornly remained and accused her of deceit. Then she would hope that passion and the overpowering magnetism that drew them closer with every encounter would, of compassion, waft a cloud of dust into his eyes concealing the cleft and preventing him from ever discovering this massive barrier that rose between them like a colossus.

She was abruptly brought back to the present by the striking of the clock and she realised with alarm that he would be crossing the yard to the office even now. She picked up her shawl and flew along the gallery and down the staircase. Slipping her feet into her shoes, but not stopping long enough to fasten them, she opened the heavy back door of the kitchen and, leaving behind an astonished kitchen maid, hurried down the path through the emerging shoots of the vegetables and herbs through the lych-gate of may and into the yard.

Some excuse for her sudden appearance always occurred to her between the kitchen door and the office.

For his part, Thomas was greatly pleased that the girl seemed to be becoming more willing to leave the house. She was maturing, he thought, and beginning to realise that she could not allow a harelip to go on tyrannising her all her life.

As Fanny approached the yard she pulled her shawl more securely across her face and then, turning the corner, she caught her loose shoe in the sets and tripped. She felt a hand catch her elbow as she let loose her shawl, which fell away, and she was staring into the pale blue eyes of the Irish boy. Her hand fluttered like a wounded dove, full of pathos and despair, to hide her mouth. Long, slender, tapering fingers with perfectly shaped nails trembled as they searched blindly for her upper lip and came to rest over the offending cleft. She gave an audible moan.

The shock, which struck Charlie's heart, never reached his face. He held her for a moment and then, gently easing her fingers from her lips, he said, 'What beautiful hands you have.'

He took her other hand in his and, turning both palms upward, he lifted them to his lips and kissed them. For a brief moment Fanny was stunned, until, recovering her composure, she loosed her hand to cover her mouth once again. But this time there was no resistance when Charlie took it in one of his and, kissing the index finger of his other hand, traced the outline of her lips with great tenderness.

A frisson of excitement shook Fanny's body and her heart contracted.

Enclosing his hand in both of hers, she held it between her breasts and Charlie thought elatedly, 'She loves me.'

Chapter Five

Fanny took a sudden, unexplained fancy to reading that summer and she now began to take her book into the garden at the rear of the house. There, in a gap between the elms where the may trees had formed the lych-gate, a stone tablet, like a coffin rest, had been placed to one side and there she would sit with her book in her lap, just visible from the house, engrossed in her novel. She was reading Louisa M. Alcott's *Little Women*, and Miss Alcott herself would have found it profoundly strange that the first pages of this work, it would seem, should be longer than *War and Peace*.

Her time was now divided between the music room, which afforded an excellent view of the dormitory, and the lych gate. Invariably she would saunter out of the kitchen door half an hour before luncheon. Initially, Rose would look up from her preparations in mild curiosity but after a short while, she would come to barely notice her coming and going. After a little time had passed, Charlie would appear and lean against the bole of the may tree furthest away from the house, hidden from view by the cloud of its copious white blossoms, so that it appeared to any casual observer from the house that Fanny was alone. That they were unable to touch was a sweet torment; they were simply happy to be together. Fanny would watch him eat his bread and cheese, his cap pushed back and his legs stretched in front of him. At this time of day nobody used the lych gate, so that they were never discovered, but the clandestine nature of their daily tryst heightened the thrill of their newfound delight.

June passed in this way and July was upon them. The palette of azure was broken by full, white, cumulus clouds hanging low in the sky. The larks sang as they wheeled overhead and the heat seemed to linger under the elms as though it were it were solid matter.

There were none of the faint breezes, which had caused the tremulous elms to flutter in the earlier weeks, to provide respite from the constant glare of the midday sun.

Charlie would release the kerchief from around his neck and, bunching it up to form a sop, would wipe the perspiration from his neck and face, and Fanny would remove her hat and fan herself languidly. If anybody at the house wondered at Fanny going out in the heat of the midday sun, they did not see fit to question her, although Connor, aware of Charlie's absence from the common room, watched perplexed as Charlie rounded the corner day after day. Then, assuming him to be happiest in his own company, he dismissed him from his mind.

Sometimes Charlie would slip away moments early and would wait behind the may tree for Fanny to appear. He yearned to sweep her up in his arms and twirl her around as though she were no weightier than a rag doll, and he restrained himself only with the greatest effort of will.

It happened that on one of these occasions, when Fanny was exercising patience so that Charlie may be there waiting when she arrived, she was standing like a sentinel in the music room window looking out over the garden, when she realised with horror that the may tree had begun to shed its blossom and Charlie's waiting form could be glimpsed through the denuded branches. In the same moment, Thomas appeared beside him.

Oh, smiling Fortune that had prompted her to linger! She saw that Charlie, far from displaying discomfort or concern, was answering her father's question with an easy smile and, to her astonishment, they walked together along the path towards the house, talking amicably, until they came to a halt at the edge of the kitchen garden. She realised that she had been holding her breath involuntarily and now it escaped her in a half sigh, half gasp. Laughing together, Thomas laid his hand on Charlie's shoulder before continuing to walk towards the house.

Charlie stood alone, looking towards the upstairs window of the music room. Now that he was closer to the building, the perspective made him slightly taller than the receded may tree and, for a moment, Fanny fancied him to be a bridegroom standing beside his lover, decked out as a bride. There remained sufficient blossoms on the tree to give an impression of a white lace veil concealing the secret happiness of the exquisitely gowned bride and fallen petals lay like showers of confetti around their feet.

What would happen when all of the blossom had fallen and the bride was revealed in stark totality? The last petal would be the only whiteness, the tooth that was visible through the ugly cleft in her lip.

She let the curtain fall and composed herself with an effort. She was glad that it had been she, and not another, who had noticed the may tree's unwitting exposure of their trysting place, and now she applied her mind to seeking a solution to the problem this presented. Their narrow escape brought to her an awareness of the consequences of their liaison being discovered. Surely her father would forbid further meetings and would, most certainly, send Charlie away. And yet, he had treated him kindly when he discovered him in the garden. She could not understand what had happened. Drawing back the curtain once more, she surveyed the garden again. Through the shimmering heat she could discern Charlie behind the tree, still unaware that he was visible from the house.

The kitchen door was ajar in deference to the oppressive heat. Fanny, slipping through it, made her way down to the lych-gate.

'What happened?' she asked, breathlessly. 'Why did my father take your being here so calmly?'

'I told him I'd seen a rabbit going into the kitchen garden and I was going to frighten the little divil off. Would you believe, he commended my good sense and concern.' His face creased into his inimitable smile and Fanny's heart contracted, as ever.

'We're going to have to be more careful, though,' Charlie continued. 'I don't think I could bear not seeing you. It's precious little I have of you anyway.'

He put his arm around her shoulder and drew her close but Fanny, tremulous inside, pulled away from him.

'We can't be here together, I have to go. I could see you from the music room window because the trees are losing their blossoms. If anybody looks from the kitchen window, they will see us. We'll have to find another way to meet, my love, but I'll think of something. I'll leave a note for you tomorrow under here.' She indicated a small stone.

Charlie cursed silently and his spirits fell. He had known that this must come sometime, but he and Fanny had got themselves into a hopeless situation. There was no going back now. He didn't know how, but he had to find a way for them to be together. As she made to go, he held on to her hands. He bent to kiss her fingertips as they slipped out of his grasp, and then she was gone.

36

Fanny ran up the path, through the lavender bushes, which formed a low hedge on either side, until she reached the kitchen door. She paused with her hand on the doorknob as she heard voices inside.

Cook was asking Rose, 'Do you know where Miss Fanny is? I declare I don't know what's happening to that young lady. She wanders around the place in a dream, never here on time for luncheon. Go see if you can see her in the rose garden.'

'I'm sure I don't know where she is and it's not my job to go searchin' for 'er. I've got quite enough to do without chasin' after that little madam. Where's Ruby? Why can't she go and find 'er?'

Angered by what she had overheard but too alarmed by the realisation that the kitchen staff had noticed her daily routine to confront them, Fanny slipped around the corner and entered the house through the side door. This led into a stair well with stairs going down to the cellar under the kitchen. A door to the left led into the kitchen itself and straight ahead there was another, which went into the corridor between the kitchen and the dining room. Fanny intended to go through this door and enter the kitchen as though from the house but as she pushed it open, she felt a resistance behind it as if something had been stacked up against it. As she pushed harder, she heard a gasp followed by a sharp cry and the door gave way to reveal Rupert, the groom, catch Ruby as she stumbled and fell. Consternation ensued with Ruby realising that her indiscretion had been discovered, and Fanny, whilst having great sympathy for the girl, was none the less ready to take advantage of her dilemma.

'Please, Miss Fanny,' whimpered Ruby. 'Please don't tell the mistress. We won't do hit again. Please don't give hus away. I'll do hanything.' She began to snivel, holding her starched white apron over her face, and revealing a faded, blue and white striped dress beneath.

Rupert now joined in her pleading until Fanny dismissed him with a wave. Cap in hand he shot past her and through the door, his gallantry dispelled like ether as he realised that his fate rested in her hands.

'Ruby, come to me in the drawing room after lunch. Make sure that there is no one else in the room. If you are challenged, say that I have instructed you to come so that I can tell you how I want the music room rearranged.'

They went through the door straight ahead into the corridor, Ruby still whimpering and apologising. Fanny pushed her towards the dining room and, composing herself and smoothing down her hair and dress, she pushed open the door from the front house to the kitchen and walked through regally, mustering all the authority she could. Cook looked round from the huge black range, which dominated one wall, and wiped her hands upon her apron.

'There you are, Miss. We thought as you was outside. Madam has asked for the lunch to be ready a bit earlier 'cos she and the master are going out.'

'Sweet Providence,' thought Fanny, 'that gives me time to sort out Ruby's problem … and my own.'

After Thomas and Irene had left, there was a timid knock on the drawing room door and Ruby, now changed into her black house dress, entered with her head held low. She curtsied and crossed to where Fanny was sitting with her embroidery. Fanny stuck her needle into the material and set it down on the side table.

'Now, Ruby, if I am prepared to say nothing of what I have seen. If I am to overlook any future improprieties, within reason,' she added hastily, 'you will have to do something for me.'

'Hanything, Miss.' Her relief was palpable. 'Hanything, you only 'ave to hask.'

'And you must say nothing to anyone else about our little arrangement.'

'No Miss, not a word.' By now, Ruby was faint with gratitude. Not only would she not be sent home in disgrace, she and Rupert could continue to meet. Of course, they must be even more discreet than they had been. Suddenly, she began to wonder what Fanny could possibly want her to do in return.

Fanny took from her sewing basket, an envelope. Ruby smelt a gentle waft of perfume and her eyes widened. Fanny handed it to her.

'You are to take this to the men's dormitory at the brickworks and ask for Charlie. You could, perhaps, suggest that he is your beau. When you are alone with him, you must give him this letter and wait for a reply. Don't speak to anybody about this or we will no longer have an agreement and you will be dismissed. When you next meet with Rupert tell him that I shall require a favour of him also. If I send him word by you, he must feign illness and take to his bed for the day. Make sure that he knows what the consequences of his not agreeing will be. In return, I shall procure keys to the inside doors of the stairwell, so that he can lock them when you are together. If someone should try to open either door, he can let you out of the other one and leave himself by the garden door, after unlocking the door where entry is being sought. Do you understand? Is that fair?'

By this time, Ruby was so broken up with relief and thanksgiving that she could hardly stand. And so the bargain was sealed and Ruby, with a bob, left the room, letter safely concealed in her apron pocket.

After waiting until dinner was finished that evening and she had been dismissed for the night, she made her way through the kitchen and down the path, passing through the lych-gate to the dormitory. Connor opened the door and went to fetch Charlie, surprised that his young friend had given no indication of his interest in the little housemaid. Charlie stepped outside the dormitory and took the note from Ruby who lingered, waiting for a reply. He was perplexed that Fanny was taking such a risk, but having looked under the stone which she had designated and found nothing, he had gone about his work with a heavy heart so he was too relieved and happy to dwell on this for long. He edged around the corner of the building and opened the letter.

'My darling Charlie,
We can trust Ruby not to betray us. She has much to lose.
She will act as our go-between. I have devised a means by which we can spend some precious time together. You need to do nothing but wait and be ready on Thursday afternoon.
Until then, my love. Fanny'.

Rupert had every fourth Thursday off and Fanny, remembering this, contrived to arrange a visit to Grandfather Morse at Crosby on that day. If her father should order Rupert to take her on his day off, she would call in her favour from Ruby.

Chapter Six

Fanny had left the announcement of her intended visit until the preceding Sunday and, on her return from church, whilst she casually removed her gloves, she ventured, 'I thought I might like to go over to Crosby on Thursday after lunch.'

'What a good idea, darling,' said Irene, surprised at this sudden turn of events. 'I am sure your grandfather will be delighted to see you and I shall be relieved to have news of his health. He is still far from well.'

Thomas interrupted. 'It will have to be another day. Rupert's off this Thursday.'

'Is there no one else who can drive me? If not, I shall drive myself in the dogcart.'

Astonished, Irene said, 'You can't, Fanny. You never ride in an open cart, let alone drive yourself.'

This was true. She hated to be on show. For Fanny to appear in public was equally abhorrent veiled as exposed. Idle conjecture was as discomforting to her as the blatant curiosity of the brazen stare. Nevertheless, her insistence was determined and, alarmed, Irene appealed to her husband.

'Thomas, what about that nice Irish boy? I have seen him driving the dogcart and he seems sensible and trustworthy. If Fanny is agreeable to riding in the open cart, surely the boy could drive her?'

Fanny smiled inwardly. This was proving easier than she had dared to hope. Thomas, puzzled at the sudden unexplained boldness of Fanny's attitude, hesitated for some moments. Reluctantly – yet he knew not why – he acquiesced rather than agreed, but stipulated that they should take the tubcart. Fanny demurred. She did not want to sit opposite Charlie in the tubcart, she wanted to sit beside him, and so she dug in her heels.

So it was that on Thursday afternoon, the two found themselves sitting side by side on the dogcart behind the pony. Fanny had been

40

almost unable to contain herself during luncheon and had watched the hands of the clock, which on several occasions, she felt sure had stopped.

For Charlie's part, he was pleasantly bewildered at this turn of events, knowing not how it had come about that their fortunes had taken such a turn for the better, when his spirits had been at their lowest ebb and their hopes and desires had seemed so far from being realised. Nevertheless he had made himself ready and wearing his one good shirt, his face shining like a scrubbed schoolboy, he sat behind the pony, outside the kitchen door. Thomas had spoken to Charlie while Fanny ran upstairs to pull on her hat and shawl, and had given him firm instructions in the care of his young daughter.

As the cart passed the end of the brickworks, Connor looked up from his work and muttered to himself, 'Sure, there's trouble brewing there.'

Now Charlie and Fanny were trotting along the lane with such a heightened sense of sheer pleasure in each other that neither spoke for several minutes. The fields stretched out verdant green, trimmed with the last blossoms of lacy may, which divided them into neat squares like elaborate pocket-handkerchiefs. The heat rose in a haze from the road ahead and, from time to time, mirages shimmered before their eyes. The birdsong echoed the delight of the young couple and Charlie felt heady. He recalled having a similar sensation on Dublin docks when he had rather too much to drink so that he was faintly, pleasantly dizzy, and he hoped that the morning would not be the harbinger of the remorse and regret that had accompanied that particular adventure. He moved the reins into his right hand and permitted his left to rest lightly on Fanny's like a frightened mouse, tentatively testing before committing itself to the unutterable pleasure of the soft, fragrant nest. There it rested, absorbing the rapture of first love, content for the moment with this small, permissive delight. He felt her fingers respond to his with a thrill like a short electric shock at the contact, but she did not resist. She was fearful of moving lest the spell should be broken.

That ride was never to be forgotten, even in the throes of later, more intimate moments. Fanny wished that time would stop – that the world would end. She felt that nothing in life would ever approach the ecstasy of that moment. They came to an avenue of candled chestnut trees, where the sun dappled their path through the leaves. Charlie reined in the pony and they sat together, side by side, their blood racing through their young bodies, their hearts beating in unison and their close proximity paralysing them. The atmosphere was leaden with confined passion. Now and then a frisson of voluptuous delight would break the stillness.

The young pair sat like this for a half-hour, neither advancing the contact between them. Eventually, Charlie broke the enchantment of the moment. He said nothing but withdrew his hand from the resistance of Fanny's fingers, which slid reluctantly from his grasp. He urged the pony on, and still they remained silent as the minutes went by, words incapable of expressing emotion. At The Five Lamps, where St George's Road intersected with Crosby Road, they stopped once more to let the pony drink from the trough on the small island. Again they held hands, and this time it was Fanny who eventually drew away.

'We must be getting on. Grandfather will be wondering where I am.'

They passed the terminus at Victoria Road and turning, followed the lane until the house came into view and the cart rolled over the same stretch of drive where Thomas had first caught sight of Irene on horseback, four decades earlier.

George Morse's face was creased with concern. He became anxious easily since his illness and he had expected Fanny this last half-hour. He stood in the long window of the library and took out his hunter. Although he was enjoying his ninetieth summer – for enjoying life he still was, despite his failing health – yet he stood upright without using a cane and held his head high, seeing without the aid of eyeglasses. His hair was full and thick though it had given up the struggle of maintaining its strong curl and now lay in white waves above a handsome profile. He was a most distinguished-looking figure; one might almost have considered him aloof, had he not retained that spark of humour in his dark eyes which even time and widowhood had not been able to eradicate. When he spoke, it was in measured tones, choosing his words with care and delivering them with authority, in a pleasant, resonant voice.

Now seeing, with no little surprise, Fanny seated unselfconsciously beside the groom on the approaching cart, his worried countenance brightened, and hurrying out of the library he found Quinn already at the big front door of the house. As he opened it, Fanny hurled

42

herself inside, skirts flying and the shawl which perpetually adhered to her face, fallen back from her shoulders. She held her left hand before her mouth in a loose fist, her index finger crooked beneath her nose, her thumb lying beside it resting against her nostril. Her large brown eyes were bright with excitement and her taut, high cheekbones flushed. She wore on her head a deep, brimless cap pulled down to fashion a frame around her face. Her hair, like wayward streamers, enjoyed a considerable degree of success in escaping its confines. She looked, at one and the same time, vulnerable and insouciant.

'This,' thought George, 'is Fanny at her most happy. 'Why,' a blend of amazement and delight overcame him, 'the girl's in love!'

Turning her face into his shoulder, she reached up and threw her right arm around the old gentleman's neck, remaining there for several long moments. It was as though, having been unable to embrace Charlie, all her unspent passion was spilling over in her grandfather's embrace.

'Hey, hey,' George smiled indulgently. 'What's this then? Are you trying to squeeze the breath out of an old man?'

'Oh, Grandpa,' she cried, 'I am so happy. It was such a beautiful ride. The sun shone all the way and the fields and trees were so green and, oh Grandpa, I'm so happy.'

'Could you contain your delirium at seeing me long enough to come into the drawing room?'

George disentangled himself from her embrace and gently pushed her to arm's-length, searching her face for further confirmation of his pleasant suspicion, his hope. She faced away guiltily, unable to disguise her joy, and in order to give her time to compose herself he turned to ask Quinn to bring them tea in the drawing room. Then he ushered Fanny inside and sat her down. He remained standing before the empty fire-grate, waiting for Fanny to spill her bright shining secret before him, but instead she asked, 'How are you, Grandpa? Have you been keeping well? Mother and Father send their love and Richard and Alexander, of course.' She continued garrulously in this vein and George listened to her chatter with amused patience until the tea arrived, but still she did not stop. 'Shall I scald the tea?' she asked. Not waiting for a reply she released the pin at the rear of the steaming, silver teakettle and, tipping it forward, poured the boiling water into the waiting Georgian pot. She replaced the pin, and picking up the douter, she

43

snuffed out the flame of the methylated spirit lamp then began to pour milk into her cup.

'None for you, Grandpa. A slice of lemon?' She poured and handed the fluted china cup to her grandfather. The three tiers of the wooden cake-stand held plates of egg and parsley sandwiches, hot toasted crumpets and strawberry cream scones, prepared specially to her taste by Mrs Flower, but Fanny didn't avail herself of any of this, her favourite fare, but continued in a loquacious stream of idle chatter. George moved to the sofa and sat down beside her.

'Fanny,' he interrupted, 'suppose you say what you have really come to tell me?'

'Pardon?' Fanny rose, obviously flustered.

He took a shot in the dark. 'Suppose you tell me about this young man.' Fanny's heart skipped a beat. How could Grandpa know about Charlie and her? Nobody knew. She was sure nobody knew. Ruby would not have told anyone.

'Who is he?' her grandfather continued. 'How long have you known him? Do we know his family? Come, come Fanny my dear. Don't keep me in suspense. I can see that you're in love. Not all the darkness in the world could put out that little light. Come,' he repeated. 'Sit down again and tell me.'

Fanny sank back onto the sofa, confused and dismayed. If Grandpa knew, somebody else must know; somebody must have told him.

'He's not my young man,' she stammered. 'He's just someone who works in the yard. It's the groom's day off and Father said the Irish boy should drive me here in the dogcart.'

George's eyes narrowed and the furrow between them deepened.

'My dear Fanny, I'm not supposing that you're in love with the groom,' he assured her laughingly, 'but I felt sure that some young buck was responsible for your euphoria. Are you telling me that you haven't fallen in love?' Seeing her stricken face he went on, 'Oh well, perhaps I am mistaken. Perhaps it is seeing me that has wrought this wondrous change in you.'

He felt a deep sense of disappointment and remorse. His poor little Fanny with her split lip. Her tears did not escape the confines of her lower lids but settled in translucent pools on her lashes. He had thought, hoped, that some young fellow had seen beneath the surface to the depth of Fanny's true beauty. Now he saw that her eyes glistened with tears where, moments before, they had shone with happiness. What an imprudent old fool he was.

But Fanny's relief was almost palpable. It was the cause of the tears that sprang to her eyes.

George changed the subject hurriedly, concentrating his conversation on family matters and they talked for some time but the atmosphere was strained and George felt bewildered. She turned to look at the clock. It showed nine minutes to four. Charlie would be waiting for her. Now she longed to get away, to be alone with Charlie once again and to feel that thrill extending to every part of her being. Every moment seemed like an hour until she felt she could, with some degree of politeness, take her leave.

'See the time, Grandpa. I have to get back. I told Mother I would be home by five,' she lied.

George's eyes followed her gaze. She had not been there twenty-five minutes and now she was anxious to be gone. Yet stranger. Truly, some great change had come over his Fanny. She had risen to her feet and turned towards the door, but now she turned back as she drew her shawl over her cap, across her mouth and over her right shoulder. It was a hot day to be so attired!

'Grandpa, I don't want Mrs Flower to feel that I don't appreciate her having prepared my favourite tea. May I take a scone for the journey? I'll bring the napkin back next week.'

Not waiting for his reply, she bent forward, holding the shawl to her shoulder, and with her free hand she unfolded the cloth and placed in its centre two scones, wrapping the snowy white linen over them. George watched in mild amusement this very strange behaviour. Not only was Fanny going to sit atop the open cart where the world could see her, but she now proposed to eat two strawberry scones in public!

'This scenario gets more curious by the moment,' he thought.

Charlie, who had spent the intervening half hour in Mrs Flower's kitchen where he endeared himself without effort to all the staff, was already standing beside the dogcart, his face leant back to catch the sun, eyes squinting against it and cap tilted onto the back of his head. Charlie was in love, and he gave no thought to consequences but lived only for the moment, so that when Fanny emerged through the massive door, he was oblivious to her grandfather's presence in the shadows behind her.

He moved forward to take her elbow, but, Fanny, with unaccustomed arrogance, fearful that he was about to embrace her, shook off his hand and glared at him. Charlie stepped back in shocked surprise, falling against the side of the carriage. George, too, was surprised. He had never known Fanny to treat any of the household staff with anything but respect and her nature was normally sensitive and kind. Anxiety flooded through him, and as Quinn came up behind, he turned to impede the old butler's view and said softly, 'Never mind, Quinn, I am seeing Miss Fanny out.'

Charlie rode for a while, angry and confused at this new turn of events. Fanny was the first to speak.

'I'm sorry if I seemed rude, Charlie, but Grandfather was suspicious and it felt wrong to let you touch me while he was watching.'

'There was no need to treat me like that,' he retorted. 'I would have helped any lady into the cart. It signified nothing. But then you people use salvers so that your hands don't have to touch a butler's, so what can we common labourers expect?'

Tears sprang to Fanny's eyes as she realised that they were having their first quarrel.

'Don't let's row, Charlie,' she said. 'I'm sorry if I offended you. I'm just so afraid that someone will find out and tell Father, and we will be prevented from seeing each other.'

Charlie made no reply.

'Please Charlie,' she implored. 'Can we go down to the shore? Just for a few minutes.'

Charlie turned the horse towards the shore road. He was still burning with embarrassment but he could not remain angry with her for long, and by the time the dogcart reached a deserted spot on the coast road his anger had passed. He wrapped the reins around a branch and helped Fanny down.

'Is it all right if I take your hand, M'lady?' he mocked childishly.

He took the rug from the cart and they walked hand in hand along the beach until they came to a gnarled tree where he laid it down and lowered Fanny onto it. As he sat down beside her he felt something beneath him and, transferring his weight onto his left thigh, he put his hand beneath the rug and brought out a smooth, shiny, lemon-shaped shell about two and a half inches long. It was mahogany, spotted and strafed with cream.

'There now,' Charlie said, holding it out to Fanny, 'isn't that a beautiful thing?' And putting it in the palm of her hand, he closed her fingers over it and held them there. 'That's my first gift to you. Treasure it, for although I may give you a keg of gold when I've made my fortune, yet it will be as nothing compared to this. For sure, it's God's own handiwork.'

Fanny ran her fingers gently over the shell's surface. She curled her hand around it and let her fingers rest along its opening, their tips feeling the serrated edge.

'It's beautiful.' She smiled at him below her lashes. 'I will always treasure it.'

And the eyes that had enchanted Thomas forty years before now held Charlie in thrall. Fanny leaned her head against his shoulder as she continued to admire his gift to her. Together they ate strawberry scones and watched the waves, defying gravity, as they crept up the steep beach before receding to be swallowed up by the ocean.

Chapter Seven

Summer turned to autumn and the valley was mellow and lethargic after the bustle of cropping and harvest. The stately elms had already begun to drop their first leaves, the underlay, in preparation for the laying down of a deep carpet of burnt umber, amber, fiery oranges and reds. In the small orchard at the end of the kitchen garden, the apples were already falling from the heavily laden boughs, round and red and russet.

Charlie and Fanny continued to meet whenever the opportunity arose.

In September, Thomas at last persuaded Irene to spend two weeks on the shores of the Mediterranean and during their absence the young couple enjoyed a freedom previously unimaginable.

On Charlie's Saturday afternoon off, sneaking separately from the house and dormitory, they rode the train on the overhead railway to Liverpool. They climbed on board at Seaforth Sands and, being a Saturday afternoon, the train was heaving with humanity. From Monday through to midday on Saturday, the railway was used to carry dockworkers, seamen and shipping clerks between the docks in pursuance of their business but when Saturday afternoon came, it became a playground for sightseers. From their lofty position high on the viaduct over the suburbs, docks and city, travellers enjoyed a unique, moving pageant of colour, shape and sound.

Fanny's excitement mounted until it was explicit in her every tremulous gesture. Never had she reached such heights of quivering expectancy. She swivelled around on the wooden slatted seat in the second-class compartment of the foremost carriage, hungry to absorb every detail of her surroundings. She saw that the train was composed of two carriages coupled together, end to end. In the last rows of the front carriage and the first rows of the rear carriage, people travelled in some style. The seats were upholstered in leather with deep-buttoned backs, and they were wider spaced than in the rest of the train. They were occupied by gentlemen in frock coats, accompanied by fashionable ladies. The rows at either end of the train were filled with working men and women who were, nonetheless, attired in their best clothes. Recognising that in the first class compartment behind her there might well be friends or acquaintances of her father or brothers, she sank down into her seat for fear of being seen.

She linked her arm through Charlie's and asked, 'How do they turn the train around when it gets to the end?'

'See,' replied Charlie, indicating the driver's cabs at either end. 'The driver's boxes both have all the switches and levers needed to drive the train. When it gets to the terminus at The Dingle, the train goes into an underground tunnel. The driver carries the key – that's that lever thing in front of him, it operates the train – he carries that from the front cab to the back, which then becomes the front, if you see what I mean.'

'I am becoming more confused than ever.'

He released his arm and put it around her, pulling her towards him.

'That's because you're a little goose.'

The train lurched forward and began to gather speed. The driver gave it full throttle and soon it was thundering along as suburbia flew past. It was indeed a unique experience. From her elevated position, Fanny took in every detail of the six miles of moving theatre. They passed through Bootle, past the Alexander Dock, past the Canada Dock, past Waterloo Dock, past the great grain elevators that Charlie knew so well and the massive ocean-going liners, giants of the high seas, being loaded by the ships' chandlers and provision merchants. Fanny pointed excitedly as a lifting bridge rose high into the sky to allow a load to pass into the docks. A barge negotiated the dock entrance and horse-drawn wagons plodded across the bridge. The world was awash with cranes, hoists, shunting locomotives and people, people, people! Fanny had not realised there were so many people in the world. She felt so excited that she was almost sick. Charlie was opening up a new world to her, the busiest locality in Europe!

Finally, they alighted at the exit for Lime Street Passenger Station. Liverpool!

For Charlie, it was a delight to share with Fanny some of his love for this great city and her excitement and pleasure was pure joy to him.

They gazed in wonder at the tall buildings on Dale Street then turned right into St John's Street with the Solicitors' Chambers on either side. They wandered around the large shops and found their way to St John's Market. Fanny thrilled at the vibrant colours, the pungent, mellow, fruity smells, the echoing sounds of laughter and shouting and the bustling busyness of the market. They bought some fruit, and Fanny thought her mother would have apoplexy if she could see her daughter eating in a public place and, as though in defiance, she threw aside her customary embarrassment and revealed her deformity to the world, as she munched on an apple. It tasted glorious.

They marvelled at the magnificence of St George's Hall, walking around to look at the Progress of Justice reliefs, which had caused so much controversy when Rathbone commissioned them from Thomas Stirling Lees. Fanny wondered how the council could have taken offence at such a beautiful, realistic sculpture until her attention was caught by the figure of a young nude girl and, embarrassed to have discovered this in Charlie's presence, she dropped her eyes. Charlie moved on, and slowly she lifted her eyes to examine the figure again and she suddenly felt an overwhelming envy of the girl. Confined as she was in the restrictive costume of a lady, she imagined what it would be like to slough off not just the shawl, which concealed her deformity, but all her outer garments, her shift, her bloomers, her stays and stockings, and dance up and down the steps of the Hall dressed in diaphanous clouds of gossamer like the notorious Isadora Duncan.

Charlie came up behind her and, folding his arms around her, he gazed over her shoulder at the sculpture.

'Isn't that just beautiful?' he whispered in her ear, and they stood for several minutes admiring the magnificent work of art. And it was all right to admire it.

Then, his arms tightened around her and she felt his lips brush her neck and she turned around to face him. He took her by both hands and, laughing, led her to the edge of the plinth then, letting her right hand fall they crossed the street together, dodging a pagoda-roofed electric tramcar. They stood in the vastness of Lime Street Station, watching the trains from London come steaming into the building. They read the posters outside the Empire Theatre

50

and watched the rich people going into and out of the Adelphi Hotel, past the portly commissionaire with his shiny brass buttons and his waxed moustaches. They had tea in a small café down a side street.

Ma would have to just wait a little longer. Charlie had taken a considerable lump of his savings for this afternoon and it was almost gone, so that he was beginning to worry that he would not have enough to see them through the rest of the day. As much to remove the need for spending money that he did not have, as to any artistic inclination, Charlie steered Fanny towards the Walker Art Gallery and, climbing to the top of the steps, they turned around and surveyed the city lying below them.

'Oh Charlie, I didn't know I could be so happy. I never want today to end. When I am very old, and you are no longer with me, I shall think about this and remember how happy I was.'

She threaded her arm through Charlie's and leant against his shoulder, and he lowered his head to kiss the top of hers. He felt a sudden sadness at the realisation that their time together must come to an end. The thought of life without Fanny was worse than no life at all. But he must not allow anything to impair the brilliance of that afternoon. 'After all, some people live long lives and never know a moment like this,' he thought.

They entered the magnificent building. It was like a wonderland to Fanny. Nothing she had ever experienced had prepared her for what she saw. It was as though Heaven's gates had opened and displayed all its treasures to her.

Here was Leighton's *At a Reading Desk*, all palest rose and gold, and Moore's *The Shulamite*, crimson, yellow, ochre and gold. Delight! Every new canvass sent her into raptures. They mounted the stairs together, and as they entered the first room, she gasped in sheer pleasure. There in the position of distinction on the facing wall, dominating the entire room, was a picture of the interior of a house of quality. Five Roundheads sat imposingly around a table, interrogating a young boy dressed in pale blue. In the background were his mother and sister, the small girl weeping and the woman quivering with apprehension. There was a second woman, her relationship unclear. The legend read, *And When Did You Last See Your Father?*

She reached out blindly for Charlie's hand.

'Oh, I love it! That dear little boy ... so innocent. He is sure to tell the truth and then, oh what? And see his tiny sister crying in the background. Oh Charlie, it's so sad.'

'One day I'll buy it for you.'

Charlie gave rein to the desires of his imagination. He couldn't even buy her a picture postcard, let alone this Yeames masterpiece.

Time passed quickly and Charlie became anxious in case they should be back late but he could not persuade Fanny away from this Aladdin's cave.

The staff at the big house became more anxious with every passing hour, until Cook sent Ruby down to the yard to get Connor. He put on his coat and hurried up to the house behind the girl. When they arrived at the kitchen door, Cook told him of her concern, 'Take a couple of the men and look for Miss Fanny would you, Connor? She's going to be the death of me. I'm that worried about her. Whatever the Mistress and Master would say if they knew I don't dare to think, and I'll be right glad when they're home.'

Connor had a good idea, if not where she was, then with whom, but he said nothing. He collected two of the boys from the dormitory and, purposely sending them away from the direction of the road, he himself walked towards the town. Before he had gone far he recognised, through the gathering gloom, the figures of Charlie and Fanny. As they approached, he first addressed Fanny.

'Cook is very anxious about you, Miss Fanny, perhaps you should run on ahead and set her mind at rest.'

To Charlie he said, 'Have you gone barmy? Where have you been? If the Gaffer finds out about this, you'll not only get the boot, you'll be lucky to escape with your fat head on your shoulders.'

Unhearing, Charlie watched Fanny's back with mounting anxiety as she hurried up the kitchen garden, then, as she reached the door, he turned to Connor.

'Connor, for pity's sake, don't tell anyone. I really love her, Connor, I really do. Please keep this to yourself.'

'I've seen this coming,' said Connor. 'I blame myself. Get inside before anybody realises that Miss Fanny was not the only one who didn't get back for supper.'

Fanny flounced through the kitchen without a word to Cook or Ruby, and she made no answer when Cook shouted after her, 'Do you want your supper now, Miss Fanny? I've been keeping it warm.'

Bristling at receiving no reply, she wiped her hands on her apron and muttered under her breath, 'You just wait until your parents get home, young lady.'

The deep furrows in her brow became more pronounced as she reflected that Fanny's shoulders were draped in a man's threadbare jacket.

Chapter Eight

There was an atmosphere of celebration when Thomas and Irene returned home and, in the pleasure and excitement of the moment, Cook either forgot or thought better of her threat, for she said nothing. Fanny's feelings were ambiguous. It was wonderful to have Mother and Father home, but she knew that it would curtail her freedom and that she would see less of Charlie.

In the early evening, she would stroll down the garden before dinner and then race across the meadow to where the old house stood, dark and intimidating in the gloom. Charlie would be waiting; his day's work finished, and they would spend an hour together wrapped in each other's embrace. He would tell her stories of his childhood and youth in Ireland. As is the wont of Irishmen abroad, he made it sound like an enchanted place, and she made him promise to take her there one day. On such a night as this, she sat beside him with her head upon his shoulder, his arms enclosing her from behind.

'When we are married ...' she began. She felt him stiffen and he eased her away and turned her face towards him.

'Fanny,' it was a hoarse whisper, 'you know we can never be married. Your father would never permit it. All this must come to an end. We know it Fanny; we have always known it. I can't bear to think about it but you will be married off to some dashing young fellow and I shall have to watch you day after day with someone else. I can't bear to think about it,' he repeated.

Her head moved back to his shoulder. 'I shall never marry anyone else.' Her large eyes were round and moist. 'Nobody ever made me feel beautiful except you. I shall kill myself if you don't marry me.'

He drew her close again and rocked her gently to and fro. 'Then you will have to elope with me and I'll carry you off to Killarney where we'll live in a little cottage and keep chickens and a pig and a cow for milk.'

'Don't joke, Charlie, this is serious. I don't want you to go away, Charlie. I want to be with you always. I couldn't face life without you. I couldn't go back to being alone.'

'What is to be done, Little Goose?' he asked.

'You'll have to talk to Father'.

'And tell him what? That I am a penniless Irish navvy with nothing to my name but three shirts, two pairs of trousers and my Sunday suit, and I want to marry his only daughter who just happens to be an heiress. Fanny, he would boot me out quicker than you could sneeze!'

'Then I'll go with you. I won't be separated from you.'

'The quickest and surest way to be separated from me would be to tell your da.' Charlie was becoming exasperated and it was evident in his tone of voice. 'Let's just leave it awhile and carry on as we are. Don't spoil it all, Fanny.'

Tearfully, Fanny asked, 'Is it my lip, Charlie, are you ashamed of me?'

'Ashamed of you? You silly Little Goose, how should I be ashamed of you? You are so beautiful. Fanny, we are all made up of different parts, some good and some bad. Everything about you is exquisite except one tiny imperfection. Most of us are many flaws with, maybe, one small virtue. You are all virtue with one small flaw. Beside, if it were not for that slight defect, you would never be entertaining the thought of marriage to the likes of me. It's only because you perceive your lip as a barrier to any other man falling in love with you that we are here together now. There is another thing. I would never have dared to speak to you if I had known who you were. You wear a shawl. I never saw a lady wearing a shawl before. I first fell in love with you when I thought that you worked at the house. When I found out who you were, it was too late. I bless that little fissure that made you mine.'

His arms tightened around her.

It was quite dark by now and, one by one, the stars began to come out. The clouds were scudding across the moon, making the house like a moving lantern show; now brilliantly lit, now in shadow, now dark and the two young lovers, so close, so alone, melted into one beneath Fanny's heavy cloak. Charlie crooned softly to her, an old Irish lullaby.

Connor, as he passed by the ruins on his way home from the public house, cocked his head and froze as he realised the source of the faint, gentle voice that mingled with the sound of birdsong in the gathering dusk, and once again he thought, 'Sure there's trouble brewing, there.'

Chapter Nine

In December, it was decided that because of the miserable Christmas of the previous year, the celebrations would be really special. The house was bright and cheerful. The trees were delivered a few days before Christmas Eve. One stood in the corner of the drawing room, while the other majestically dominated the old barn which, being used as a store throughout the year, had been emptied and thoroughly cleaned out for the occasion. The walls were decorated with branches of spruce and with holly and mistletoe. Fanny had helped the kitchen staff fashion massive bows from red crepe, and festoon the windows and doors with them. The pot-bellied stoves were lit on the morning of Christmas Eve, so that by the time the trestle tables were being erected, the vast venue was cosy and warm. The men brought the dry logs from the store and, working to a roster, they kept the stoves going all through the day. In the kitchen of the big house, Cook and Cissy had been preparing food for several days and now plates of raised water pies, baked potatoes, fat brown sausages, capons, hams, hard-boiled eggs, cakes and tarts were laid out in readiness for the feast. Wonderful smells found their way out of the kitchen through the smallest apertures, heightening the expectations and causing the remaining men to chafe to stop work.

Today, along with the midsummer picnic, was one of the highlights of the calendar for the staff and workers, and spirits and expectancy were running high. At four o'clock, the men from the clay room finished their work and made a noisy beeline for the bathhouse where steaming water boiled in large black kettles that were emptied and refilled continuously. Their loud laughter and boisterous joviality could be heard all through the works, increasing the impatience of the remaining men to be finished.

The first shift emerged through the bathhouse door like scrubbed shiny-faced schoolboys. Before the last of them had left the building, the kilnsmen were rapidly replacing them, sluicing the warm, comforting water over their sweat-stained bodies. Finally, it was the turn of the supervisors and the last of the great black kettles were emptied into the tub, the heat of their bubbling contents dissipating on contact with the cold water so that it increased the temperature by only a few degrees. Charlie, the last to finish, now gleaming with cleanliness and naked but for the towel around his waist, his bare feet numbed by the stone floor, stood before the glass looking at his reflection. He raised his arms and pushed back his flaxen hair, now darkened by the water. He knew that he was good to look at. The hair went back from a broad, strong brow and the eyebrows were disciplined and well shaped, low where they sprang from above his nose and rising until they tapered out on either side. The nose itself was aquiline, masculine, the mouth strong and determined and the jaw, though square, finished in a point. He knew, too, that the eyes were his best feature. It seemed as though they had a smile of their own, independent of his mouth, that began as a trickle and ended in cascading pleasure. Looking at himself now, he saw the slight glide of his eye, which confirmed that he was his father's son. It appeared whenever he concentrated for long but then, as he looked away, his vision returned to normal. There was strength in his arms; his shoulders were broad and his chest firm without being overly muscled. He was satisfied with what he saw, not in an arrogant, self-absorbed way, but in contentment and gratitude for his normality and his youthful vigour. He was suddenly aware of how cold he felt, standing there alone and still in the empty bathhouse, and he began to rub himself down vigorously. Moving to the door, he located his boots and slipped his freezing feet into them. He ran the 20 yards through the biting cold to the dormitory and entering, slammed the door shut behind him. He dressed with care in his only suit and spit upon his shoes to polish them. Tonight he would be at the centre of the universe with his Fanny, and though no one else might know it, yet he and she, untouching, unspeaking, would be together for the first time in the presence of those people who made up their world.

The single men crossed over the yard to the festive barn. They were in good cheer, drunk with the pleasure of it all, without having yet imbibed any of the ale provided for them. The younger ones had set their hearts on their fancies before the celebration began, but they outnumbered the girls five to one, so there would be plenty of disappointed swains before the evening was out.

Charlie hung back, silent and hidden on a stool in the corner, waiting for the moment when the Halls would appear with his Fanny in their midst. He felt at once brave yet fearful, calm yet excited, hopeful yet apprehensive. Would she dismiss him in the perfunctory and humiliating way that she had at Crosby or would her beautiful eyes shine at the sight of him, the way they had in Liverpool?

After the workers had eaten their fill and the children were popping chestnuts on the stoves, tossing them from hand to hand and blowing on each palm in turn, the musicians struck up the music for dancing. The bravest and most confident of the men claimed their prizes, whilst the more timid and self-conscious drank too much, too soon, too quickly – their consolation.

The barn was warm now, the heat from the pot-bellied stoves and the human bodies combining to raise the temperature inside. The atmosphere was buzzing with euphoria, and then suddenly she was there, standing behind her father and her eldest brother, her grandfather beside her, with Richard and Ruth following closely. Mrs Hall, with Alexander's wife Gabrielle and the children, brought up the rear. The music stopped and everyone turned to face the makeshift platform, constructed for the purpose. They waited expectantly for their benefactor to speak, and Thomas began to address them.

'Friends,' he began.

But Fanny wasn't listening. Her eyes were sweeping the room trying to locate Charlie.

Thomas finished by thanking them all for their efforts throughout the past year. 'Now, everyone, charge your glasses and drink with me to a Merry Christmas and a Happy and Prosperous New Year!'

Glasses and mugs were raised and emptied, and Thomas's grand-children moved among the company giving a small gift to each of the other children.

All through the speech, Charlie had watched Fanny's eyes darting from one group to another, searching for him, but he kept himself concealed, savouring and saving the moment like a child who keeps the best of the treat till last.

Thomas took Irene's hand and together they led the dancing. Alexander and Gabrielle joined them and soon they were twisting and twirling in the centre of the barn floor. Now Charlie, unable to contain himself any longer, rose and Fanny caught sight of him before he had reached his full height. Her hand placed strategically in front of her mouth, she crossed the barn until she stood before him and, without a word, his arm was about her waist and they were gliding across the barn floor, oblivious to the shocked, questioning glances and the whispers behind hands. Fanny let her hand drop. She cared not at all, who saw her lip so long as Charlie thought her beautiful.

George Morse recognised, with shock, the youth that had brought her to visit him and Connor stared at the floor and shook his head.

Breakfast was strained. Thomas sat at the head of the table while Irene faced him down its length, flanked on either side by her grandchildren. The children sensed the tension and sat meekly in their places. The dining room was festive and a log fire burned in the grate but it was not the happy occasion that they had planned and anticipated.

Fanny had not made an appearance. After waiting for several minutes Irene said, 'I really think we should begin breakfast without Fanny. There is so much for the servants to do before church if luncheon is to be on time. They really will be wanting to get on.'

No second invitation was needed to break the embarrassing silence and everybody began to talk at once, as they helped themselves from the servery. Conversation was artificially animated so that no one noticed that both Thomas and Irene continued to be silent and withdrawn.

When Fanny came into the room the talking stopped. She looked elated and radiant and quite unaware of the anxiety she was causing, and she did not cover her face. She smiled widely, with the result that her lip was not as pronounced as when in repose, since all her teeth were visible and the fullness of her lips was narrowed. It was as though she had completely forgotten the bane that had ruined her young life up to this time. The adults in the room struggled to appear not to have noticed this unprecedented action, but standing up and firmly pointing a finger in Fanny's direction, Alexander's eldest child cried out, 'Look I can see Aunt Fanny's mouth. She's forgotten her veil!'

'Quiet, Andrew.' Gabrielle chided him, and looking straight at Fanny remarked, 'Fanny you look charming.'

The tension, at once, was eased and everybody readily agreed that

Fanny did indeed, look enchanting. It was as though she had been liberated.

Rising, Richard drew out a chair for her and she sank gratefully into her place as the conversation and attention turned to other subjects but she was aware that Thomas's eyes were still upon her, remonstrating with her silently. Now, self-consciously, she concealed her mouth with her napkin, her fragile confidence receding once again under the onslaught of his gaze.

Looking around the table, she bridled with the unfairness of it all. Father had Mother, Alexander had Gabrielle, and Richard's fiancée, Ruth, was seated beside him, but Charlie was back in the dormitory and she was alone in the midst of all this company. She caught her grandfather's eye. Grandfather, who was also alone; alone for all these years since the grandmother she never knew had died. He winked at her and gave her a conspiratorial smile, and she loved him almost as much as she loved Charlie.

Breakfast came to an end and their mother took the children upstairs to make ready for church.

As they settled into their pew, Fanny, seated between Gabrielle and the children, looked around the old church and her heart leapt as, in a shaft of sunlight fragmented by myriad colours from the stained glass window, she saw Charlie's head illuminated. His eyes were closed and he looked like an angel.

She was surprised to see him sitting amongst the other young men from the yard because she knew that he followed the Roman Catholic faith, and yet he had come to this Anglican church just so that they might catch a glimpse of each other for a brief moment on Christmas morning, and say a prayer together in the silence of their hearts. The moisture gathering in the corners of her eyes threatened to betray her as she thought that they would not ever be permitted to sit side by side in church. They asked only to be allowed to be together, to touch hands.

Her grandfather, following her gaze, saw that her eyes rested on the Irish boy who had driven her to visit him at Crosby. He saw the boy's eyes open and meet hers immediately, as though he had focused on her through closed lids, and a devastating smile spread slowly across the solemn face. There could be no doubt that these two were in love.

'What a travesty!'

*   *   *

61

They came in from the cold, stamping feet and clapping frozen hands. Gloves and muffs, mufflers and coats were cast aside in a flurry of laughter and good cheer. Only Thomas and Irene remained downcast and withdrawn. Even Fanny's melancholy had lifted now that she had seen Charlie. The ladies carefully removed their bonnets and the children changed out of their outdoor shoes, loudly hazarding guesses as to what delights awaited them under the tree in the drawing room.

The room was warm and welcoming, the log fire having been stoked up and the mantles and candles lit so that all was ablaze with light. Parcels in multicoloured paper were stacked high under the tree, and a sparkling burgundy punch stood in a chafing dish on the sideboard. With much chattering and banter the gaily-wrapped presents were distributed, and shouts of pleasure rose above the general hubbub as each one was opened.

Amid all this gaiety, Fanny's heart and thoughts were with a sad-eyed, flaxen-haired boy who, half sitting and half lying on his bunk in the dormitory, shunned the jollity and companionship of his fellows and thought only of Fanny.

George, Thomas and Irene, each independently, watched Fanny's vacant stare as she sat mournfully with a new pale cashmere wrap draped across her face.

Lunch was a happy occasion for most of the gathering, but Fanny, her parents and her grandfather were all preoccupied, and both Fanny and Irene left their food virtually untouched.

When the meal was over and the men were finishing their cigars in the smoking room, Richard, anxious, in the manner of young men, to be back with Ruth, excused himself and Thomas said to Alexander, 'I wonder if you would mind, Alex? I would like to speak to your grandfather alone.'

Alexander simply nodded and rose, and stubbing out his cigar, he left the room without speaking.

George waited expectantly, knowing that the conversation was to concern his granddaughter, and as though reading his thoughts, Thomas began, 'It's about Fanny.'

George said nothing but just nodded his head.

'She appears to have taken a fancy ... I don't quite know how to say this ...' he trailed off.

'Let me help you,' said George. 'She appears to have taken a fancy to the Irish boy and, if I am not mistaken, he to her.'

'It's so ridiculous.' Thomas was relieved that his father-in-law had broken the ice. 'The situation is impossible.'

'Why is it impossible?' asked George. 'You have said yourself on many occasions, if my memory serves me aright, that he is a good young man with a bright future …'

Thomas interrupted with a snort. 'He is a nobody. An Irish immigrant, without a penny to his name and a papist for sure. For goodness' sake, George, they have been out fighting with the Boers against their own country. By a bright future, I meant that he could have eventually become manager of the yard, not that he should become emotionally attached to my daughter!'

'Are the two mutually exclusive?' asked George. 'Isn't it possible that he could become manager and be in love with Fanny?'

Thomas made to interrupt, but George raised his hand.

'No, Tom, you have done me the honour of asking for my opinion, now do me the courtesy of allowing me to air it. When we began this conversation a moment ago, I confess that my feelings were the same as yours. In fact, I had been uneasy for several months.'

'You knew?' spluttered Thomas.

George's hand went up again. 'I shared your concern but now, I ask myself, why. Why should he not be considered using the same criteria as you would use for any other young man? True, his social position and penury are disadvantages, but they must be weighed against any virtues he might possess. Fanny is happier – yes, and unhappier – than I have ever known her. This young man has brought her alive. He has given her self-confidence and trust and affection in a way that we, who have loved her for all the years of her young life, have never been able to. When he looks at Fanny he doesn't see her imperfection, he sees all of her radiant beauty. Tom, you and Irene have given her everything money can buy, but he has given her something that cannot be bought. This is Fanny's first love. It is very unlikely, by its very nature, that it will be her last. Let her enjoy it while she can. The young people will move on, but Fanny will have more confidence, more self-worth. See the difference he has made already. I tell you, Tom, we aught to be eternally grateful to this young man.'

There was a moment during which neither of them spoke, then Thomas said thoughtfully, 'What will people say? I don't want them whispering behind their hands.'

'What about Fanny? She has endured years of whispering. It's time she had some real happiness. What do you care what people think as long as she is happy? Providing she is chaperoned, it can do nothing but good.'

'I need some time to think this over, George. There is indeed much sense in what you say but there are many ramifications. I just cannot come to terms with the idea of the boy working in the yard and living in the dormitory with the other men while being – er – attached to Fanny. It's not what Irene and I had hoped for her, but I'm sure you are right and that she will come to her senses. He is a good boy, no doubt about that, and he is quite obviously responsible for Fanny's new openness, so I confess that he must be good for her, too. You know well, George, that Irene and I want only what is best for her. I'll talk to Irene and see if we can't arrange limited access to Fanny … with a chaperone. Well, that's settled.'

Thomas rose and took his father-in-law's elbow.

'Perhaps we'd better join the others. They'll be wondering what we're hatching up. I confess that I feel much better about it now. Thank you, George. May I ask something else? How are you feeling? Irene is in a perpetual state of concern for you since that last bad illness. I worry she is going to make herself ill. Have you seen the doctor recently and has Irene really got anything to worry about?'

'I'm old, Thomas. We all wear out in time, and to tell you the truth, I am tired; time is running out for me. I'm sorry Irene is worried about me because I have had a good and a long life, and I have been alone for much of it. I never really got over Florence's death. We only had two years of marriage and most of that time I wasted in overwork. My only regret is that I gave her no support during those years; that I was impatient with her deep concern and compassion for others. To be honest, Thomas, it is all I think about at the moment. I wish there were some way in which I could make it up to her. Don't you make that mistake with Fanny, don't trivialise her passion and desire.'

On New Year's Eve, the family gathered to bring in 1903, and at midnight flaxen-haired Charlie, coal and a bright shining coin in his pocket, knocked on the door of the big house, dark and swarthy Connor with him, to fulfil the rest of the tradition.

/

Chapter Ten

In the New Year, invitations were extended to Charlie to take tea at the big house. Although he accepted, it was with no small degree of reluctance, since it entailed his self-consciously leaving the yard early, passing the men still working, to go to the bathhouse. After dressing in his suit in the dormitory, he would make his way through the lych-gate, up the vegetable garden, past the staff in the kitchen, where he was met by Fanny, and into the drawing room.

'Why am I doing this to myself?' he muttered, but he knew the reason. It was those thirty seconds, after the kitchen door closed and before the drawing room door opened, when he could bury his face in the heady sweetness of Fanny's hair, taste the faint saltiness of her lips and touch the softness of her skin. If this is what it took, half an hour of purgatory in exchange for half a minute of ecstasy, he had no doubt it was a good exchange.

The young couple found their permitted time together very unsatisfactory compared to the close and loving hours they had enjoyed previously. Sitting on the edge of his chair, his cap in his hands between his knees, Charlie would liken these times of testing to Jacob, labouring twice seven years for Laban, in return for Rachel's hand in marriage and he fully expected that Thomas too would find some way of keeping them apart after the bride price was paid.

Irene, though she appeared outwardly calm and tranquil, enjoyed these afternoons no more than Charlie. She was ill at ease with the young man. Nothing in her experience had prepared her for this situation and she would offer the opinion when alone with Thomas, that he should have stayed at home in Ireland! She wished with all her heart that he had never come to Seaforth. As she poured the tea, she enquired about his mother and father and his home in Cork and, pointedly, when he would be returning there. There were times, as she became aware of Fanny's increasing confidence and happiness that she had to admit to herself that the Irish boy had been a blessing to her daughter.

On the occasions when Thomas was present, he would sit quietly conscious of the polite, strained conversation and wonder how it would end. From time to time he would question Charlie about his work and Charlie would relax and come to life, leaning forward a little in his enthusiasm and blending into the company and conversation almost without being aware of it. He loved clay, he loved bricks, he loved their exactness, their disciplined stacks, the feel of them, the smell of them. It was as though he was born to work with bricks. But when anybody else joined in this conversation, it was as though a spell was broken and, like a discarded puppet, he'd slump forward, resuming his awkward, motionless perch on the edge of the seat.

After these afternoons, he would return to the good-natured taunts of the other men. At first, none of them appeared to resent Charlie receiving these privileges and they seemed happy for him, but gradually they left off joking and became quiet at his approach, so that he began to feel that he belonged nowhere. Josh began to treat him with reticence and the men had become cautious about what they said in his presence. He no longer seemed a part of the workforce, and he certainly did not feel at home with the people at the big house. He had become an outcast, a misfit. Only Connor's attitude towards him did not change.

Things continued in this vein until spring began to break through and Charlie and Fanny were reminded of the wonder of being free to enjoy their secret trysts at the edge of the garden and in the old house, and then their frustrations grew greater with every passing tea time. Eventually Fanny could stand the situation no longer and, taking the small window of opportunity between the kitchen and the drawing room, she slipped a note into Charlie's hand.

Charlie took his place on the edge of the chair, cap in hand, the note burning a hole in his pocket. He yearned to read it and studied consciously not to reach into his pocket to feel it. The time passed slowly until he was out of the house and he could open it. She had written,

My dearest love, these futile, sterile meetings are torture to me. We sit face to face, with a whole room between us, uttering inanities when all I want is to hold you, to reach out and touch you and to be with you twenty-four hours a day.

Charlie, my darling, please, speak to my father – today. Every day that passes, I am dying a little more.

A shiver ran through his body, though he could not determine whether it was pleasure or fear. It seemed to him that Fanny was living in a hopeless dream, yet it seemed, too, that the feelings of deep despair engendered by these strained moments under the watchful gaze of her family were almost as great an agony as not seeing her at all. She had told him that she was prepared to go away with him if her parents opposed their liaison, but she could not know what she was suggesting. She had always had everything she desired, and with Charlie penniless and out of work, her love for him would soon be strangled.

As he lay on his bunk that night, he once again considered the possibility of South Africa. He would surely have enlisted by now had it not been that he would have had to leave Fanny. The fighting would keep his mind off his misery. He could take it out on the Boers. The frustration rising in him, he felt an unaccustomed emotion, as tears welled up in his eyes, spilling over and running down his face. He put out his tongue and tasted their saltiness on his cheek, then sitting up with his elbows resting on his knees, his head between his hands, he wept. He had never been so low, so empty, so hopeless. He must approach Mr Thomas … or go to the war.

He stood in the drawing room, Fanny close by his side, and felt her fingers briefly entwine themselves around his. He was conscious of the gentle squeeze of her hand, and he began to speak. A croak escaped his lips. He cleared his throat and tried again.

'Sir.' He coughed. 'Mr Thomas, Sir.' He felt Fanny's sharp kick on his ankle. 'I want to marry Fanny,' he blurted out, his face reddening. 'I know I have little to offer her and I am sure that I am not the husband you had hoped for her, but I love her dearly.'

Silence.

'I could wish myself wealthy or I could wish Fanny poor but I could never wish for a deeper, more satisfying love.' Now he was in full flow, nothing and no one could stop him. 'I would devote my life to looking after her. I don't care how hard I work. If I can't be with Fanny there will be no point to my life. I would never hurt her, nor let anyone else hurt her. I love her.' He looked down at his cap, twirling it around between his hands 'I love her…' he trailed off. His whole body shuddered and he turned his lowered head away, to hide the desperation showing in his face.

Thomas was speechless. He had had weeks to prepare for this moment yet he had no response ready. In his own defence, he thought he had never really believed it would happen. He was sure that Fanny would have come to her senses. He turned away and, moving to the long window, stood looking out over the lawn, his hands clasped behind his back. Charlie and Fanny remained silent, unbreathing, hearts thumping in the hush, and still Thomas did not reply. There was nothing to be said. This was not happening. His only daughter, like some dissolute kitchen maid, wanting to marry a labourer, a labourer from his own works, pitifully poor, Irish and a Catholic. There was nothing to be said.

Minutes passed in silence until Fanny, impassioned, cried out, 'I love Charlie, Father, and he loves me. We don't care about money. We want your blessing, but we will marry with or without it. If you stop me marrying Charlie, I am going to go to Macedonia as a volunteer. I have already enquired, just in case you sent Charlie away. The people there are starving and dying and they need volunteers to distribute food and clothing and medicines and it's so dirty and cold that I shall probably die of infection or disease, but to die like that will be better than living without Charlie.'

Thomas turned to look at her. Tears were pouring down her cheeks and her face was contorted with anguish.

'Don't be so melodramatic, Fanny,' he snapped. 'The young man has made a proposal of marriage. Please permit me time to consider it and to speak to your mother.' Turning to Charlie, he continued, 'I have listened to what you have to say, young man. We will discuss it further, in private, without the benefit of female hysteria.'

So the ice was broken, but the water beneath appeared cold and murky to Charlie. Still, it had been done. The ball was rolling and there was no going back.

Chapter Eleven

'Have you written to your parents yet?' Fanny looked up from her writing desk as Charlie shook his head. She rose and crossed the room to where he stood.

'Oh, Charlie, you should have let them know at once. They are the most important guests and they need time to prepare.'

'They won't come,' muttered Charlie. 'They won't have the money and Ma won't come without Da. Besides, they don't even know where I am.'

'Haven't you written to tell them about me? Don't they even know you're getting married?'

'No, I've not been in touch with them since I left Cork.'

'Charlie.' Her voice was shocked and accusing. 'You haven't written to your poor mother? She doesn't know where you are – whether you're dead or alive? Oh, Charlie, how cruel, how could you?'

'It's best this way,' said Charlie, gruffly.

He explained that he had intended, when he left, to save his money and send a ticket for the Steam Packet, but that his money had never amounted to enough. He hadn't written to his ma because he hadn't wanted her to know that he had failed to fulfil his hopes, hadn't rented that little cottage for her that he had dreamt of, hadn't wanted to give his father the opportunity to mock him and make scathing remarks to her about her son being a failure. No, he had put his family behind him. They belonged to the past. He had moved on. But his heart ached as he remembered Ma and guilt welled up inside him.

'So, you'd rather your poor mother thought you callous and uncaring than that you had not become a millionaire?' she taunted him. 'Oh, my dear, you must write to her at once.'

Charlie shook his head. 'Believe me, it's best this way.'

But Fanny was persistent, and when Charlie refused to budge

from his firm opinion that they would not come to the wedding, Fanny pointed out that it would do no harm, in that case, if she sent them an invitation.

'If it will make you happy,' Charlie reluctantly allowed, knowing that there was no way by which his parents could ever find the money for the journey.

Fanny sent an invitation and enclosed a crisp, new, white £5 note and a letter which read:

Dear Mr. and Mrs. Cahill,

As you will see from the enclosed wedding invitation, Charlie and I are to be joined in marriage and he has asked me to write to you and invite you to be our honoured guests. Charlie misses you greatly and so looks forward to seeing you and sharing our special day with you. I, myself, anticipate our meeting with delight and my parents wish me to convey their kind regards and suggest that you may wish to come some days prior to the wedding, so that we might all get to know one another before the happy event.

My sincerest good wishes, your dutiful future daughter-in-law, Fanny Hall.

She waited anxiously for the reply, which arrived without delay:

Miss Hall,

You can tell your fiancé that his mother passed away last Christmas. Do not mourn for her. She was spared the agony of knowing that her son was to join her proud Irish bloodline with an English heretic's.

Mick Cahill.

Devastated and shaking in her distress, Fanny opened the envelope to return the letter to it, and as she did so, a piece of paper fluttered to the ground. It was the £5 note.

She waited all day in deep despondency for Charlie to come home. She met him at the door and, taking his hand, led him into the drawing room.

'My love, I'm afraid I have some dreadful news for you. I don't know how to tell you.'

Her large, brown eyes flooded with tears which, escaping her

70

lower lids, slid down her face onto the bodice of her dress where they remained as darkened spots on the silk.

'It's Ma, isn't it?'

His eyes were already shining with unshed tears as he took the envelope from Fanny's hand. He read his father's letter, looked up at Fanny, and read it again. Then he stared bemused at the £5 note, finally realising that Fanny must have sent it and Da, his drunken father who would never let the chance of money for a drink pass, had returned it. Then he knew the depths of his father's hatred for him. Charlie's head dropped onto Fanny's breast and he wept with abandon, his tears combining with Fanny's to form an expanding patch of darkened blue. She cradled him like a child as his shoulders rose and fell. When his crying subsided, he felt empty, as though he were skin, stretched over a frame of bones, containing nothing.

The wedding was postponed for eight months, so that it fell in January when, once again, winter was bringing the world to a stop. The day before the wedding it snowed; snow that was like shards of ice, sharp and painful as it flew into the faces of the people. Overnight the temperature rose, only slightly, but enough to bring the rain and wash away first the snow and then the resulting slush. The sun shone brightly so that early in the morning, steam began to rise from the ground. It was as though nature was making clean the whole earth in time for the wedding. The staff arose long before the sun was up and everyone moved at a rapid pace to put the final touches to the reception preparations so that they could all be witnesses to the wedding. Mrs Flower arrived with her kitchen staff to take over from Cook, Rose and Ruby who readied themselves for the ceremony with unrestrained enthusiasm.

Fanny was driven the short distance to the church in Grandfather Morse's handsome green victoria with his unicorn crest emblazoned in gold on the doors. The driver and footman were sat atop the box, dressed in the same livery of dark green serge with gold buttons. It had been agreed that they should borrow the carriage, the driver and the footman, in order to free Rupert to attend the wedding with the rest of the staff.

Her grandfather, in increasingly failing health, insisted on rising from his sickbed to be present at the church though he was to return to his room immediately the service ended.

Fanny was, at her mother's insistence, and as a concession which she counted to her credit against the debt of her parents' reluctant approval, wearing a white wool georgette dress with a matching cloak trimmed with fur. She carried a small bouquet of Christmas roses and wore her veil forward, obscuring the radiant and rapturously happy face beneath, as she sat beside her father in the carriage. It was a blessing to be able to abandon her constant vigilance in the concealing of her mouth as the veil gave her an unaccustomed freedom.

As Fanny approached the altar where Charlie and Connor were waiting as bridegroom and best man, she felt completely happy. Insofar as she was unaware of the turmoil in the minds of those who were dearest to her, the only flaw in an otherwise perfect day was that Alexander and Gabrielle were unable to attend the ceremony.

'Most inconsiderate of Gabrielle to arrange to visit her parents at such an inconvenient time,' Irene opined. 'Surely she could have chosen a more appropriate date, but then I suppose she is French and one must make allowances.'

It was not in Irene's nature to be snide, but it was tacitly understood that Alexander had deliberately arranged to be out of the country when the marriage took place, and it was easier to put the blame on her daughter-in-law than to admit to her eldest son's hauteur.

During the service, her weeping was perceived to be the tears of poignant melancholy, a mother weeping as her only daughter is about to leave the family home, but they were, in fact, tears of disillusionment and despondency at what she perceived to be her own failure as a parent.

Chapter Twelve

'We insisted on consultation prior to design commencing, when we discussed choice of materials, jointing and bonding. They were told verbally and we confirmed later in writing, that they must use hydraulic lime mortar with pozzolan additives. We couldn't have made it plainer, Father. We advised against non-hydraulic at the architectural stage. Look, here, it's all in writing, "hydraulic blue lias lime". We gave them authoritative guidance on all matters of specification.'

'Alexander, giving guidance is not the same as giving instructions. It should have been written into the contract that, if they did not follow our definitive instructions, we should not be held responsible. They are claiming that the advice that we gave them was purely arbitrary and they followed the architect's specification.'

'Then it's the architect they should be suing, not us!' retorted Alexander. 'They wouldn't go to a dentist to have their appendix removed so why accept the architect's advice on a matter of brickwork?'

Richard, who had been silent until now, spoke up. 'We've been doing business like this for years, Father. We don't take a dictatorial attitude with our customers. We have always advised them and worked together with them, without tying up the minutiae in the contract. This is how you taught us that gentlemen conduct business, confer and shake hands. After all, both parties have a common aim, the success of the project. Why, then, should we anticipate that they would deliberately ignore our advice?'

'Because, Richard, times are changing. People will go to litigation at the slightest provocation. But laying that complaint aside, they also contend that the bricks are showing signs of efflorescence.'

'It isn't true, Mr. Thomas,' Charlie joined in the discussion, 'I have been to inspect the bricks at the site and there is no evidence of crystallisation. What they are referring to are sulphates, leached up into the lower bricks from the soil. There is no problem there. We know our clay, Mr Thomas and it has a very low soluble salt content. It's just a mere sprinkling of salt particles, an acceptable level.'

'If there are problems with brick quality, that's Charlie's fault not ours. You'd better take it up with him. Richard and I have got other things to do.' Alexander shot Charlie an icy glare.

'Before you go, Alexander, what I have said about not letting your mother know anything about this still holds good. You too, Charlie, don't tell Fanny. We've had the worst three years that I have known in this business and if this thing goes ahead, I think all of us here realise that it could be the end of us. The two of them have enough to worry about with your grandfather being so ill. Between them they are nursing him night and day and I don't want your mother put under more strain.'

Of all the members of the family, Alexander was finding it hardest to cope with the social disparity between them and his brother-in-law, and relations between him and Charlie had deteriorated since the marriage.

Thomas and Irene had grown to accept that they must adapt to the circumstances and, in any event, they were not very social people and enjoyed their own company very well.

Richard and Ruth were too involved with each other and their own growing relationship to worry too much about what others thought of Fanny and Charlie, but for Alexander it was different.

At that time, and in that place, every aspect of life was defined by distinctions in financial and social class and Fanny's peccadillo, as Alexander crudely thought of it, caused him untold embarrassment and shame. He was altogether unable to accept the fact that Charlie was now a member of the family and had been promoted within the firm. His discomfort when meeting business colleagues and friends was acute. He could not forgive Fanny for having, as he regarded it, brought shame upon the family, and he could never accept Charlie as a brother-in-law! If the rest of the family had been able to overlook the difference in their stations, Alexander could not. He could not see any method by which the misfortune could be reversed, and so he wanted Fanny and Charlie as far away as possible. Indeed he felt that even if they were to go away now, it would be too late, since the news was travelling around Liverpool like a forest fire in a cyclone.

74

It occurred to him that it might prove necessary for he, himself, to take Gabrielle and the children, move away and start again where nobody knew them. Gabrielle had fretted to return to Paris. This might be expedient under the circumstances.

He had loved Fanny as dearly as anyone, but she had betrayed him. She had refused to listen to his reasoned arguments and had stubbornly insisted on proceeding with the wedding, not even agreeing to a short delay. It had been postponed once and she would wait no longer. Well, she had made her bed and she ought to be made to lie on it.

Alexander had had discussions with Thomas and tempers had flared. He had proposed that a settlement be made on Fanny so that she and Charlie could go and live somewhere where their circumstances were not known. A trust could be set up for any children of their union, and there was no reason why Thomas and Irene should not visit them as often as they wished, providing they went to live far enough away to avoid further scandal.

He burned with embarrassment as he remembered his visit to the club some days after Charlie and Fanny had returned from their short honeymoon. Anxious for news of the tariff reforms, he had stopped the carriage and mounted the steps. The porter came forward to open the door and, handing him his hat and gloves, Alexander made his way to the smoking room where several of his friends and acquaintances were sat in the deep leather armchairs behind their newspapers. Harrison and Fawcett sat opposite each other on either side of a low table. Harrison lowered his copy of the *Mercury* momentarily, acknowledged Alexander with a curt nod, and returned to his reading. The silence was eerie and Alexander felt uncomfortable as he moved across to the ticker tape. His head was bent over the machine when a peal of laughter broke the stillness. Straightening up he had seen, reflected in the window, the two men looking at him. Whatever Harrison had said, had caused Fawcett to guffaw with mirth but as he turned around, each suddenly became engrossed in his paper again. Tears of anger burned behind his eyelids. In his mind, he weighed up his options. He could either follow his instincts and hurry out, thereby acknowledging his shame or he could face them. He chose the latter course. Crossing to the table, he sank uninvited into the seat between the two.

'What are you finding so funny?' He asked stiffly.

'Just discussing marriage, old man.' They both smiled widely at him.

'What particular aspect of marriage do you find so amusing?' Alexander retorted.

'Sh!' Several hushed voices chorused.

'Don't take on, old fellow,' smirked Fawcet, 'we're only teasing you. You've got to admit it's a strange kettle of fish. We were just wondering if you were going to be an uncle soon.'

Alexander pushed back his chair in fury. It was not enough that Fanny was marrying an Irish labourer, it was being gossiped about that she had need to.

He leant across the table and struck Fawcett full on the face.

'You malicious bastard,' he cried, and, ignoring the mêlée that ensued as Fawcett's chair toppled backwards and emptied him onto the floor, he strode out of the smoking room. Hurrying down the stairs, collecting his hat and gloves as he went, he passed out into the open air and breathed deeply. His face was purple with rage.

As expected, he had received a letter by hand, requesting him in the strongest terms to appear before the committee on the following Monday. He never returned there.

This confrontation with his peers was to prove the catalyst for what later became a devastating argument that split the family. Thomas and Irene refused to be drawn in, and both Charlie and Alexander felt betrayed by their unwillingness to take sides. Fanny flared up at her eldest brother who silenced her with a withering stare.

Charlie, angered beyond control by the visciousness of Alexander's tirade, stormed out of the room and when Fanny, in tears, had followed him to their bedroom, she found him packing. He had turned and given her an ultimatum.

'Choose. Your family or me.'

'I can't make a choice like that, Charlie. It's not fair of you to ask me. Please, Charlie,' she implored. 'It will blow over. Just be patient with Alexander.'

'It's not just Alexander. I've worked hard to be accepted by this family and I've made every effort to overcome your brother's prejudice and yet none of them made a stand for me. They stood by while he poured out his malice. I feel humiliated. No, Fanny, I can't stay here where I am so despised.'

Fanny put her arms around him.

'I'm sorry, my love. I really am so very sorry. Perhaps you are right. We need a place of our own but we don't need to do this in a hurry. Just bear it for awhile longer, for my sake.'

After much persuasion and using every feminine wile, she managed to placate him, but the last and greatest row was still to come.

Chapter Thirteen

George leant back in his chair, his hands clasped behind his head. He had few regrets or unsatisfied longings, or if he had either, they both concerned his insatiable appetite for the books that lined every inch of the walls around him, the digestion of which he now knew for certain, he would never complete. Even as he had added to them, as a miser hoards up his treasure greedily, he had known that he was increasing this frustration.

The pain surged again like a breaker and he rode its crest until it eased.

No, his only real regret was that he had been less than tolerant of his young wife's eternal ache for the plight of abused women and children; her deep longing for, and pursuit of, social reform. The monies that he had committed to her charity were mere hypocrisy, born of guilt. The crumbs that one throws to a beggar to induce him to remove himself from one's sight, and thus assuage one's feelings of guilt. He had indulged in all the pleasures of the senses, and that indulgence had been an anathema to her. The very gentleness and caring that had attracted him to her became to him a stumbling block.

He recalled their first quarrel. She had been sitting in the drawing room after dinner some three months after their wedding when she had lain aside her needlework and said, 'George, my darling, may I talk to you about something very dear to me?'

'Hm.' He continued to read his book.

'No, George, you must listen to me. You must put down your book and listen!'

George lowered the book onto his knee.

'No, George, put it down!'

She spoke in an unfamiliar manner. No longer his gentle wife but demanding. One might almost say strident.

'What is so important that you feel the need to harangue me?' he asked impatiently.

'I am sorry to upset you. It will avail me nothing if you feel you are being coerced into listening. I need your voluntary goodwill.'

'Go on.'

'I want to make a difference to somebody's life.'

George did not answer but his brows furrowed.

'I lead such a privileged life, my darling. I have had a wonderful home and two most excellent and loving parents. My sisters have been my dearest friends and we have each received an unparalleled education. I have fallen in love with, and married, a remarkable and truly adorable man and I live in the finest house in Crosby. I have been so favoured and my position is so enviable, I want for nothing, nothing. But … Oh George … how can I say this? How can I make you understand? I need to make a difference to somebody's life.'

'Well, Florence, you have made a remarkable difference to my life. Yes indeed, my life is completely changed since we met.'

'Thank you, George, but that is not what I mean. There are so many other women out there, yes, and children too, who are destitute and homeless. How can I spend my days writing out menus, arranging flowers and doing my needlework when there is so much human misery beyond my door?'

Alarmed to observe tears rolling down her cheeks, George crossed to where she was sitting and, kneeling beside her chair, put his arms around her and eased her head onto his shoulder.

'There,' he said, stroking her hair, 'there is no need to get so upset. Of course you must do what your conscience tells you is right. It's good and proper that we should care for those less fortunate than ourselves. Tell me, what is it that you want from me? How can I help? If it is money you need, you know you only have to ask. I'll do anything to make you happy.'

She turned in his arms and lifted her face to him, her smile shining through the tears. 'Darling I knew you'd understand. Thank you so much. Thank you so very, very much.'

Quite suddenly, she became business like, speaking rapidly in her enthusiasm.

'We can turn the whole of the top floor into little, one-room apartments. There will be enough rooms for six women and their children, eight if we divide the two largest rooms. We can put extra washing and toilet facilities where the box rooms are and we can all have our meals together.' She turned to see the confusion on his face and assuming this to be his reaction to her last remark, she went on, 'Of course, if you would rather eat separately, that can be arranged.'

'Stop! What on earth are you prattling about? You can't possibly be thinking of bringing your pathetic creatures here? I have had you to myself for only three months and now you want to fill our house with your wretched women. Come, Florence, I have been very accommodating as far as your little charities have been concerned. Have I ever tried to stop you attending meetings? Haven't I been generous towards your collections? Have I ever criticised your do-gooding? Have I ever refused ...?'

'My little charities? My do-gooding?'

Bewilderment and anger mingled in her mind as she flounced out of the room. George heard her footsteps tearing up the stairs.

She had locked the door and thrown herself across the bed, weeping. George had knocked on the door in vain and she had finally sobbed herself to sleep.

Now, George gave a profound sigh at the irony of it. '*I* want to make a difference to somebody's life, as she did, before this thing takes me,' he thought.

He rose and moved to the long window that opened onto the garden. The slight breeze caused a gentle undulation of the water, hardly worthy to be called a ripple, but it created shards of late sunlight which fractured the surface. Only the quivering of the aspens broke the stillness of the verdure, and barely perceptive birdsong added to the serenity. The elusive scent of wallflowers floated in the warm evening air, a will-o'-the-wisp, yet when he tried consciously to recapture its essence, it escaped him.

As he stood, he was suffused with a feeling of calm certainty. This is what she would have wanted. His mind's eye superimposed upon this untroubled tranquillity, an over-vision of women resting under the trees beside the lake. Small children calling to each other as they swayed back and forth on swings suspended from the branches. Chubby babies crawled across the grass, gurgling with pleasure. This opulent, gracious edifice, which had housed one selfish old man for over seventy years, would become home to generations of under-privileged women and their children.

His greatest sin had been to love too little, he thought. If he had loved more, he would have understood her total emersion in the distress of others. Her compassion was so great that she could not be happy where others were suffering. She felt a part of a humanity where one person's pain hurt all – is shared by all.

This plan, he felt, would be a panacea for the deep disappointment of the thwarted promise of ageing together that had faded even before it was born.

How long he stood there, listening to his breathing rising and falling almost imperceptively, he did not count but dusk was gathering about him when he stepped outside. A fine drizzle, like the flutter of a butterfly's wings, beat against his skin and released in its vapour the sweetness of the wallflowers and night-scented stock.

He sought behind closed lids to recapture a distant memory, which eluded and taunted him. He felt he could have reached out and touched it, but it was as though it had turned a corner. This intense and delightful felicity permeated his whole being, as though he had received her forgiveness, a benediction, a gentle purging of his fallibility and weakness. A whisper of breath escaped his pursed lips, carrying on its wings, the last vestige of doubt and leaving in its place a deep, abiding contentment.

That night, the pain that had been his constant companion for eighteen months relented, and his sleeplessness produced a slow-moving panorama of waking dreams.

George waited impatiently for the arrival of his daughter and her child, his head filled with memories of the past and plans for the future. Thinking, he observed, was almost wholly taken up with the past and the future, and only the smallest proportion of it related to the here and now. Behind him lay lost opportunities, lost love. Before him on his desk lay the future, seven sheets of copperplate writing, the harvest of his sleepless nights. The topmost two concerned the proposition from the banking conglomerate, an immense sum of money, far more than the market value of his shareholdings. The longer he had held out against the amalgamation, the higher had been the proffered rewards, until now, when he would have been pleased to acquiesce to any proposal which could ensure him a benign and dignified end, they had increased their original offer to an unrealistic high.

The third and fourth sheets were a survey and a very satisfying valuation of the house. The fifth and sixth were the preliminary architect's drawings for the necessary alterations. Beneath these lay the reply to the letter he had sent to Josephine Baker. Ageing now, and unable to help directly, she had nevertheless recommended to him several eminent social reformers who would make worthy trustees, and of these, three of the four he had approached had signified their willingness. He had known Josephine for many years now and had a deep respect and admiration for her. She reminded him, in some subtle way, of Florence.

There was a knock on the door and Quinn announced the arrival of Irene and Fanny. As he greeted them, George looked at these two beautiful women and he filled up with pleasure. He indicated that they should sit down, and returned to his seat behind the desk.

'Well, Father, you are looking a little better today. Don't you think so, Fanny?' She busied herself with her gloves.

Fanny agreed that, indeed, her grandfather looked more animated than he had since Christmas, and she asked, 'What is so important that you have summoned us with such urgency, Grandpa? Have you got some good news for us? Are you feeling so much better?'

'I am fine, child, but I have something which I very much want to discuss with your mother and, as I feel it concerns you too, I have asked her to bring you along. What I am about to tell you will affect your future and I want you to consider it very carefully before you tell me what you think.'

Now he addressed Irene. 'You know that before you were born, your mother had a great interest in underprivileged women, especially those who were unmarried and with child. She abhorred the system that allowed men to force themselves upon women, abandoning them when they became pregnant and leaving them to face the shame and ignominy whilst they themselves walked off unscathed. She grieved too for the children of such unions, whose lives were blighted from the moment of conception.' His eyes took on a glazed expression and he shook his head slowly. 'I wasn't always as understanding of her as I should have been. I don't know, perhaps some people are born with greater empathy than the rest of us, but I know that she felt real and deep pain no less than if these villainies were happening to her.'

'Some years ago, another great lady with similar compassion needed some financial advice on borrowing and since I was a banker, a mutual associate introduced us. It concerned the Brownlow Hill Workhouse, and during our meeting, she suggested that I should visit the place and see for myself, first hand, her reason for wanting the money. That is how I first came to see the Oakum Cellars where these poor wretches lived and worked.'

He described to them the atrocious conditions and the humiliations that these women were subjected to. Throughout this account, the two women remained silent.

George continued, 'Over past years, I have supported her charity. I suppose it is my memorial to Florence, to your mother and grandmother. Anyway, I have always felt that it was she and not I, who made the donations.' There was a long pause, during which nobody spoke or moved. George stretched himself, painfully, to his full height.

'And now I am about to die.'

Both women rose from their seats.

'Grandpa. No, don't say such a thing!' Fanny cried out in distress, but Irene moved around the desk and placed her head against her father's breast. She knew the truth of it.

After several moments, she looked up at him. The past months had scored deep lines into that beloved face. She felt heavy with sorrow.

'Sh, Fanny, darling. Go on, Father, what is it that you want us to do?'

'Do? Nothing. No, I don't want you to do anything, Irene. It's what I want to do. I and your dear mother.' He choked. 'I want to tell you how proud I am of you both. Well, of all of you really. You, Irene, have always been well cared and provided for by Thomas. I know how much he loves you, how much you love each other, and I know that you will not want for anything. And you, Fanny … Charlie is a good man and now that he has been made manager of the works, you too will be well provided for. Tell me, Irene, is the business doing well? Does Thomas have any problems or money worries?'

'No, Father. I'm sure that everything is satisfactory. I know that there have been some concerns, something about free trade and tariffs … you know I don't understand these things, Father, but I am sure that everything is all right now. Neither Thomas nor the boys have mooted any problems. In fact they seem to have ridden the storm. They never discuss the brickworks at home now. Things seem to be more peaceful than they have for a long time.'

'Good. Here is what I want to do. I intend, that is I would like, to turn this house over to a charitable trust. To make things as simple for you to understand as possible, most of the private banks in Liverpool have been acquired by, or amalgamated with, the big London banks, and I have had a very substantial offer. I am proposing to accept it and put the proceeds into the trust. The interest will enable the house to be run as a home for unmarried mothers and their children for the foreseeable future, until such time as the authorities recognise their obligation and adopt it. The sacrifice will, of course, be yours and not mine and I would never allow you to make it if I thought that there was any chance that you might be in need of the money in the future. You must think very carefully about this before you tell me what you feel.'

'Oh, Father, there is no need for time to think. It is a wonderful idea! Of course, I hope that it will be a long time before it happens, but we are proud of you, too. It is such an admirable thing to do. How can we help?'

They spread the drawing across the desk as George listed the modifications that would have to be made and explained the steps that he had already taken. He felt exhilarated, as though he had cheated death. He now had something to live for, something to work towards, and he felt that he was to some small degree compensating for his lack of understanding; his insufficient love.

Before they left the house, he assured Irene that her mother's jewellery would be hers; his hunter watch and other personal effects would go to Thomas. Irene excused herself and, using the opportunity, George drew open the drawer in front of him, took out a small box and beckoned for Fanny to come around the desk. He opened the box, and taking her hand from her mouth he placed on her finger an exquisite ring. A magnificent ruby surrounded by diamonds.

'This was your Grandmother's engagement ring. Treasure it.'

On the first day of spring, when the earth around him was burgeoning into life, George died.

Chapter Fourteen

Their happiness was overwhelming as they stood before the house, the key in Charlie's hand.

'Our first home,' whispered Fanny.

Her hand trembled beneath his fingers and he squeezed it tightly. Charlie turned to look at her and saw that tears of joy were overflowing and spilling down her face. She made to take the key from his free hand, but he pulled it away.

'No, wait. This is our first real home, yours and mine. Do you realise, Fanny, that this is our very own house? We'll be together with nobody else to consider.'

He put the key in the door and unlocked it, and then, sweeping her off her feet, pushed it open with his thigh and carried her across the threshold. As he put her down, her arms remained around his neck and she kissed him interminably, not wanting to stop.

'All good things come to an end,' he laughed as he gently pushed her away. 'Come on, Little Goose, let's look at all the rooms again.'

There were three floors to the house. On the ground floor, the small vestibule led onto a long, intensely dark, windowless passage. The staircase ran up the left wall and the first door on the right opened out into the front parlour. Their furniture had been sited in position, but Fanny noted the adjustments that needed to be made. Her piano stood on the left wall, the furthest away from the window. Her back would be to the light. They would move it around tomorrow. Behind the next door was a room of very small dimensions, dim and cosy. Ahead lay the roomy kitchen with a scullery going off it to the back of the house and the yard. It was bare of furniture. Some of their precious savings would have to be used up on a table and chairs. Fanny voiced her concern.

'Don't worry your pretty little head about that,' Charlie said. 'I'll have a job in no time and we'll be able to have it just as we'd like. It'll be our own choice and all brand new.'

He followed Fanny up the first flight of stairs. Three doors opened onto the landing. The bedrooms seemed small to Fanny, used to more space, and they needed decorating badly. Brightening, she thought of the pleasure that they would have planning and painting them together. One room was very much larger than the others were and this, they decided, was to be their bedroom.

'Can we paint this lilac?' she asked, going to the centre of the room and twirling around, her head thrown back to face the ceiling. 'I have always wanted a lilac room. The ceiling and woodwork can be white and we can paint the bed frame white, too.'

Fanny's elegant single bed stood against the left wall of the smaller bedroom. It looked forlorn standing alone but they would buy some more furniture and it would become the guestroom. The smallest room of the three would make a perfect nursery. They stood together in the doorway, their imaginations furnishing the empty space with a bassinet, happiness welling up inside them. At the top of the next flight of stairs there were two tiny rooms, boxrooms really, only big enough for a bed and a dressing table. They could wait to be furnished and wouldn't need much, anyway.

They set about unpacking the boxes in the kitchen, stacking pans, crockery and precious china on the shelves. Then they found the sheets and made up the bed. They had forgotten pillows. At last, all the packing cases were empty but the house still looked bare, and they made a list of all the things they would need to buy immediately. It looked ominous. How could they have thought that they had everything? Checking off the list, Charlie made a rough calculation of how much money they would need, but said nothing to Fanny. But Fanny was doing the same exercise in her head.

'Perhaps I should go back to Seaforth and ask Mother if I can take some of the more essential things. They have so much more than they need,' she ventured.

But she paled at the expression that came over Charlie's face, and no more was said about going 'cap in hand', as Charlie chose to think of it, to Thomas and Irene.

The first few days in the house on Walton Road were spent in a haze of delight. Fanny cleaned the whole house from top to bottom, enjoying the novelty of her labours, and the cases were stored away in the one of the attic rooms. They happily shopped together for those things that they couldn't do without. On one of these forays into the town they were walking down Castle Street when, suddenly, Fanny cried out, 'Oh, look, Charlie, my picture!'

Grabbing his hand, she pulled him across the pavement. There in the window, much reduced in size, was a print of Yeames's painting. Fanny's face was transformed with delight.

'Oh, Charlie, we must buy it. How wonderful! Don't you see? It's an omen. We're going to be so happy in our new home. Please, Charlie, say you want it, too.'

So, they returned home with a picture of a boy in blue, that they could ill afford, and hung it in pride of place on the parlour wall, behind the piano.

The time went quickly, until on the fifth day, Charlie began to look for work. He bought a copy of the *Liverpool Echo and Evening Express* and scoured the columns for news that might result in a suitable management position. He was unprepared for the continuous, almost scornful, rejection that he met day after day. He lowered his sights and applied for a foreman's job, but he was no more fortunate. A week turned into a month without so much as an interview, and he was now reduced to looking for labouring work, and still there was nothing. Their money began to dwindle away, although they were being careful, not to say parsimonious. Fanny was finding it very hard to keep up Charlie's spirits as he came home each day, utterly dejected.

He began to leave before sunrise to walk to the docks and stand amongst the stevedores, waiting to see if there would be any work offered. But he soon found that there were skills needed to work on the quays, skills that he did not have, and there were plenty of men with the necessary experience, whose abilities were known by those in whose gift employment lay, who went home disappointed.

How could this be happening to him? He had proved himself at the brickyard before he had come to know Fanny, and he had risen to a position of authority and responsibility on his own merit. He had had experience of handling men when he had been made manager, and he had received a thorough training before and after their marriage. He began to regret that he had not asked Thomas for a reference, but they had left in haste and anger, and his pride would not allow him to approach his father-in-law now.

As he persisted in turning up at the docks among the first half-dozen, daily, he was sometimes selected for work, but soon realised from experience that the other men were far more able than he and the days that he was chosen were so rare as to be worth celebrating.

After one such occasion when he had had a complete day's work, he was passing the butcher's shop as he neared home. Fanny had been feeling ill in the morning before he left, and he was concerned that she was not getting sufficient nourishment from the paltry meals they were sharing, since it was not the first time she had been sick of late. He looked in the window of the shop and decided that he would use some of the precious money to buy her some beef. It lifted his spirits as he continued on his way home, to feel the miniscule piece of meat in his hand and anticipate Fanny's pleasure. She had never complained, nor once thrown it back at him that he had insisted on leaving her parents' house and would not accept anything from them. He loved his Little Goose and he would make it up to her one day.

When he arrived home, Fanny was feeling quite well again. She was touched that Charlie had brought the meat for her, but insisted that they share it. How could she eat meat while Charlie had none! However grateful she was for his sacrifice, part of her felt agitated that he had spent his hard-earned money on this food, because she was going to have to ask him for more. She waited until after they had finished their meal and she was washing up their plates. Charlie came behind her at the sink and put his arms around her waist.

'Charlie,' she began tentatively, 'I have something to ask you. Please don't be angry with me. I wouldn't ask if I didn't need it. Could you let me have sixpence?'

Charlie drew in his breath. 'Sixpence?' he echoed. 'What do you need sixpence for, Fanny? Of course, you shall have it, but what on earth do you need it for?'

His happiness dissipated as he turned her around to face him. He felt a deep misery as he realised to what depths of poverty they had sunk. He had failed her. She had asked him for a meagre sixpence and he could not afford to give it. He had failed both of the people he had really loved in his life through his arrogance, first Ma, and now Fanny. He turned away in shame. Fanny, mistaking his dejection for annoyance, as he slumped against the sink, his hands on its edge and his head hanging low, began to weep.

'I'm so sorry Charlie. I hate to have to ask you. I didn't want to tell you yet but I need it for the doctor.'

Charlie whirled around. 'Why, Fanny, my love, what is the matter with you? I thought you were feeling better. What have I done to you? Why did I bring you to this?'

His arms went around her again and he pressed her, painfully, against his chest.

'I think I'm going to have a baby.'

Relief flooded through him as he picked her up. 'Oh, all the saints in heaven,' he exclaimed, 'that's wonderful! Oh Fanny, that's marvellous. I thought you were ill. I thought you were going to die. I thought I was going to lose you … and you're pregnant. Wonderful!' he cried, yet again.

'You're not angry,' Fanny said. 'You're pleased. You don't know how I have dreaded telling you. How will we manage, Charlie? We can't keep ourselves and we're going to have another mouth to feed.'

'We're going to have a baby, Little Goose. Nothing can take away this joy. We'll manage. Our luck will have to change. I'll try harder, Fanny. Just trust me. Don't spoil this moment.' His thoughts came out staccato, mixed with his laughter. 'There is nothing in the world I want more than another little Fanny.'

Fanny laughed, too. His pleasure was like a contagion.

'It might be another little Charlie,' she said.

'I don't care if it's one of each.'

Fanny's pregnancy went smoothly, but as the weeks went by she fretted desperately that she could not tell her mother. At times, she toyed with the idea of writing to let her know that she was going to be a grandmother again. She comforted herself with the certainty that Charlie would mellow after the baby was born. Surely when the baby was here he would want to show it to the whole world. There would be time enough later to show Irene and effect a reconciliation. Little did she know that it was already too late!

Chapter Fifteen

Gradually the supervisors at the docks came to recognise Charlie, and they knew that they got a fair day's work from him, so the times that he turned away dejected became fewer. He enjoyed the physical labour, and also got great pleasure from the companionship. Every Saturday he managed to put a little away so that their nest egg grew slowly. They agreed that they should not spend any of it until the baby was born.

Fanny, too, had come to know some of their neighbours. She would meet Ellen, who lived next door in the alley that ran behind the house, when she was hanging out the washing. Ellen was in her thirties and she and Jimmy had nine children, ranging from Terry, a boy of thirteen and the baby who was only eighteen months old. Her washing line traversed the alley several times and every day without fail, including, to Fanny's horror, Sunday. At first Ellen found Fanny's refined manner of speech disconcerting, but as her condition became more apparent, Ellen, realising it and noticing too, that the girl appeared to have no relatives or friends, took her under her wing. She might talk a bit posh but she had a nice, friendly personality and was not in the slightest bit swanky, she was to tell her husband Jimmy, when he came home on the first day that they had spoken.

That first meeting was not a success. Fanny noticed Ellen looking at her as they hung out their washing at the same time. When Fanny turned to look at Ellen, the other woman's stare did not flinch, and it was apparent that she was examining Fanny's lip without embarrassment. Her first glimpse of Fanny had been from the side as she pegged out the sheets, and her profile had been so stunningly beautiful that Ellen had been unable to tear her eyes away, so that when Fanny turned to face her, the shock had been profound.

'Oh, God in 'eaven!' she exclaimed. 'Whatever 'ave you done to your lip?'

Fanny was taken aback. She had almost completely forgotten the cleft since she had left Seaforth, since she saw nobody but Charlie and he saw nothing except her beauty. The corner of the sheet fell to the ground as her hand flew to cover her mouth in that well-remembered, instinctive gesture.

'I haven't done anything to it,' she snapped through her fingers. 'I was born like this. Haven't you seen a harelip before?'

She hated the term but it suited her to use it to register her self-loathing, as she remembered it with shame.

'What a pity,' Ellen went on, as though she did not notice Fanny's annoyance, 'an' you so beautiful an' all. You want to see a doctor about that. They might be able to cure it.'

'Nothing can be done about it.' Fanny strove to control her anger and indignation. 'It's just the way I am.'

'Then, why don't you 'ave that tooth taken out?' Ellen went on, peering closely at the offending lip. 'It'd look an 'ole lot better if that tooth wasn't there.'

Fanny had the old familiar feeling of scalding tears behind her eyes and she felt her face crimsoning. Putting the last peg in the sheet, she gathered up her skirt and ran into the house, leaving the washing basket behind. She hurried to the pier-glass and studied her face. She had almost forgotten that she was disfigured. Running her tongue across her lip, she stopped at the protruding tooth, then covering it with the tip of one finger, she was surprised to find that it improved her appearance considerably. She pulled at the tooth, trying to move it backwards and forwards to loosen it, but it held firm and fast. She was to worry that tooth constantly in the months that followed.

Answering a knock on the back door later that day, she found Ellen standing on the step, Fanny's washing basket at her feet and a bucket in her hand. She put the bucket on the floor and rubbed her ruby encrusted fingers down the sides of her apron till they reached her knees, and up once more to rest regally upon her ample stomach.

'I've just been doin' the steps,' she said, 'an' I wondered if yer'd like me to do yours, too, you bein' in the family way?'

Without waiting for Fanny to answer, she bent over and unpacked her scrubbing brush and cloth and a donkey stone. She continued speaking as she worked, asking when the baby was due and whether they wanted a boy or a girl. When she had finished she stood up and, hand on hip, arching her back, she said, 'There y'are, duck, that looks better now, doesn't it? I'll do the front step next and if there is anythink else yer want doin', just you give me a knock. Yer've got to be takin' a bit o'care o' yerself.'

Fanny was overcome at the other woman's kindness and said, 'Thank you very much. It's very kind of you. I was just about to put on the kettle. Would you like a cup of tea?'

It was strange, Ellen thought, for these two, obviously poor as church mice, to have such fine china and linen when they had hardly a stick of furniture, and even stranger that Fanny should set up the table so grandly, to have a cup of tea with a neighbour. But she held her peace. She did not want to upset Fanny further than she had done already with her thoughtless remarks about her lip.

Several days after the two became friends, Charlie and Ellen's husband Jimmy arrived home together and, over the evening meal, Charlie told Fanny that Jimmy was a supervisor at the dock and had recognised Charlie as he waited in the crowd for an offer of work. He had taken Charlie on for the day and told him to come to the same yard in the morning. It was the first piece of good luck they had had since they had realised that Fanny was with child.

From that time on, Charlie brought home a complete week's wage every Saturday, and by the time Sam was born they had a Moses basket which had held nine babies, the gift of Ellen and Jimmy, and their littlest one's cast-off clothing.

They had determined that they would not spend any of their savings until after the birth, but Charlie, with only weeks to go, relented. Fanny was huge and ponderous with the child and had nothing in which to wrap herself other than her shawl, which barely met across the mass of her stomach. It was her birthday, and Charlie broke into their precious hoard to buy her a dressing gown. She opened the box excitedly and folded back the tissue paper. Charlie leaned over her, drew out the robe and draped it about her shoulders. It was large and roomy, and although Fanny hoped that it would be much too big for her before long, she was too thrilled to point this out to her husband. There were tiny flowers in pink and blue and green on a cream background.

'It's beautiful. Oh, it is beautiful.' Her delight was palpable, and Charlie knew that he had done right to break their agreement.

'Happy birthday, dearest Fanny.' Standing behind her, he

wrapped his arms around her shoulders and buried his face in her hair.

They had enough money to decorate the nursery and buy fabric for curtains, which Ellen ran up on her treasured Singer, and sufficient remained for a rainy day.

Sam was a lovely baby. He had Charlie's flaxen hair and had inherited his gentle nature. He was a contented child, too. When he was not sleeping or feeding he would lie happily in his cot, gurgling and spluttering. After the first four months of his life, he slept right through the night, until Charlie awoke to get ready for work.

Fanny wondered if it was time to broach the question of whether, or when, they could present the baby to her mother. Uncertain of whether her father would welcome a visit from them, she tried to devise a way to test the temperature of the water, before committing her thoughts to Charlie. It would be devastating if, having persuaded Charlie to mend the breach, her father were to refuse to allow her mother to see them and yet, the quarrel had been with Alexander, not with her parents. If they had known where to find Fanny and Charlie, they would surely have contacted them by now, but nobody at Seaforth knew where they had gone. She could find out how the land lay from Ruby. Ruby still owed her.

The day came when, leaving the baby with Ellen, Fanny donned her best clothes. Though they were a little close-fitting after the baby, they still looked as good as the day they were new, since she had had little opportunity to wear them in Liverpool. The horsebus service had been withdrawn four years previously and, although she did not at all like the new-fangled electric trams, out of necessity she boarded one of the pagoda-roofed vehicles and took her seat.

She watched out of the window as the buildings went by. Several people were pedalling the new-style bicycles with pneumatic tyres, and they looked so fast and smooth compared with her old penny-farthing. She fantasised about buying one for Charlie, but she knew that they cost about £4 and that was now a fortune to them. She saw several steam-driven horseless carriages, and she leant her head against the cold glass and thought how quickly the world was changing and how different her life had become since she married Charlie.

She alighted at Seaforth and began the long walk to the house. As she turned into the lane where a lifetime ago, or so it seemed, she had hurried home through the gloom with Charlie after their adventure in Liverpool, the rear of the house loomed into view. It rose imposingly on the brow of the slight hill, visible through the naked elm trees. She could just make out the lych-gate, which had been their trysting place. She was happy with Charlie in Walton Road and yet she felt nostalgia for this place, her home for over twenty years. Her pace quickened. She was not sure how she would manage to speak to Ruby without anybody seeing her, but she would have to improvise.

As she drew closer she could sense a great busyness around the house. Packing cases were strewn on the yard at the side, in front of the stables and there were people moving backwards and forwards. She recognised no one. It was as though the whole outdoor staff had been replaced. Changing direction, she passed by the lych-gate and turned the corner of the garden wall. She went through the small cut-out in the stable yard door and stood for a moment, watching the activity. A groom approached her. It was not Rupert.

'Can I help you, Miss?' he asked courteously.

'I'm looking for Rupert.'

'There's no Rupert 'ere, Miss. There's nobody much 'ere at the moment. The master and mistress will be moving in on Tuesday.'

'Moving in? The master and mistress?' Fanny echoed his words. 'Where are Mr and Mrs Hall?'

'Mr 'all has moved away. 'is wife died six months ago and 'e sold the 'ouse and the works is gone. Mr and Mrs Forrester is movin' in, as I say, Tuesday. You've just missed 'em. They was 'ere this mornin', till about lunchtime. Can I give them a message?'

Fanny slid to the floor, her face deathly pale. She felt a wave of nausea as the house and stables began to whirl around her. In her daze she remembered Charlie's face, crumpled with pain and tear-stained, as he heard of his mother's death. And now, history was repeating itself. How could this be happening again? Why had they not learned from their past experience? Everything went black!

By the time Jimmy and Charlie came home from work, Ellen was in a state of anxiety. She was waiting at the door in the cold darkness, Sam wrapped securely in a grey shawl in her arms, and she told Charlie that Fanny had not returned home.

'Where did she go?' Panic rose as he spoke.

'She said she was goin' 'ome. I don't know where that is but she was to be back by three o'clock an' Sam's been crying. 'E 'ardly ever cries but 'e's 'ungry and I 'aven't got a bottle for 'im.'

Charlie pulled himself together with a great effort of will.

'Can you look after him for a bit longer while I go and see what's happened? I'll get a bottle if you could warm some milk and just give him enough to take the edge off his hunger. I'll be back as soon as I can, so I will.'

In moments, he had organised things and was on his way to Seaforth. Arriving there, he went to the back of the house but it was deserted and in pitch darkness. There were no lights in the windows but, still, he hammered on the kitchen door, feeling his own impotence. He shouted out Ruby's name, and Rose's, but there was only the stillness of the empty house. Seeing a light in the window of the butler's cottage, he ran across the yard and knocked on the door, shouting for Becket as he did so. A stranger came to the door, and Charlie, unable to speak, stood gasping against the jamb, despair overwhelming him. Recovery took several seconds.

'Have you seen my wife?' he managed between great gulps of breath.

'Come in.' The stranger opened the door wider and took Charlie by the elbow. He wore the uniform of a butler though without his tailcoat or stiff collar.

'I think she's in shock. The groom brought her here after she passed out. She hasn't moved for hours. She has really given us a turn. She was looking for the groom who was here before but we couldn't contact anybody because we didn't know where he had gone.'

While he had been talking, Charlie had crossed the room to the couch where Fanny lay, looking pale and dazed, her face streaked with tears. She could not speak, but her arms closed around Charlie as she continued to weep as though her heart would break.

'Fanny, my love, what is it; what's happened? Where is everybody? Where are your mother and father?'

The butler and his wife exchanged glances. Here was an odd couple! It looked as though the girl was the daughter of the previous owners and this man, strange as it may seem, was her husband. The wife went to the hob to pour a cup of tea for Charlie but her husband said, 'Perhaps the young man would like something a bit stronger, Martha.'

'Tea'll do just fine,' said Charlie, holding Fanny still tighter.

His mind was whirling around. Why had Fanny come here? He had asked himself the same question a hundred times on the journey to Seaforth. Where had his father-in-law gone? Where was the staff? What on earth had been happening while he was at work? Why, oh why, had Fanny returned home against his expressed wishes? Fanny, still unable to talk, continued to sob in his arms as he rocked her to and fro, making a hushing sound in her ear. He had never seen her like this before, even in their worst moments. She was helpless in his arms.

How he got her back to Walton Road that evening, he would never quite understand, but he remembered it later as a waking nightmare.

Fanny was slow to recover from the shock. She moved around the house aimlessly and hardly noticed when, having forgotten to feed him, Sam became fractious. She would fall into a deep reverie, unaware of the tears that she was shedding, and she could not be consoled. Each morning Charlie left for work, fearful of what he would find when he returned, but he could not afford to remain at home with her. She had stopped going to church and on Sundays, when Charlie was home, she would remain in bed until midday when she would roam around the house with hair and clothes dishevelled. When Charlie sought to distract her with love, she lay like an acquiescent lamb waiting to be slaughtered, feeling nothing, giving nothing.

From such a union was Francie conceived.

Chapter Sixteen

Slowly, Fanny began to return to normality. She still wore her sorrow like a shroud, but began to fulfil her household duties and take some pleasure in Sam once again. Her appetite returned and the thinness which had been the physical manifestation of her misery began to disappear as her arms plumped out and the haggardness of her face faded.

They were more comfortable financially now, though they still had to exercise discretion over the allotment of Charlie's earnings. At least he was on a weekly wage, which gave them some security compared to the capriciousness of the daily work. Charlie had alternate Saturday afternoons off, and the week following the discovery that Fanny was again pregnant, he felt it was time to lay her ghosts, so he suggested when he arrived home that they should take the overhead railway to Seaforth. For old time's sake, he had said, and to let the little one see where his mother had come from.

Fanny shrank from the suggestion initially, but gradually she came around to the idea, remembering with so much longing and joy the carefree day that she had taken the same journey in reverse. After she had made Sam ready, she once again took down her best clothes, not worn since the fateful night of her previous visit to Seaforth, and she dressed with care. They walked down to the docks, past where Charlie spent his days, and along to the Pier Head. It was early spring and the wind from the river was cold although the sun was shining brightly. The walk was invigorating. They passed the tall sailing ships and stopped to stare at the great liners. Fanny rediscovered the euphoria she had felt on their first visit to Liverpool, of being in the midst of crowds of people, which she thought she had long since exhausted. Sam lay in Charlie's arms, oblivious to it all.

They passed St George's Basin and the landing stage lay ahead of them. They stood for a while, watching the incoming *Royal Daffodil,* and the *Royal Iris* as it left to make its journey across the Mersey. One day soon, they thought they would come down here and cross on the ferryboat, but today they were going to Seaforth. The train was already in the station when they went through the turnstiles, and the old excitement returned to thrill them, as they settled themselves into their seats.

The journey was full of nostalgia as they pointed out old landmarks to one another. Once Fanny caught sight of a blue landau, and was so sure that it was her father's that she wanted to get off the train, until it turned parallel with the railway and Charlie pointed out that the crest on the side was not the Hall's.

They alighted at Seaforth Sands and walked around for a while, recalling exquisite moments of delight from the past and forgetting that their joy had been coloured by what they thought of as the insuperable social chasm that lay between them. As they had longed for this day then, they longed for that day now. In the way that memory airbrushes the visions of the past to remove the harsh edges that would spoil the picture, they perceived even their heart-wrenching pain as sweetest pleasure.

The time passed quickly and, mindful of their last, sad visit, neither suggested returning to see the house. They boarded the train for the homeward journey and Fanny sat next to the window, looking out at the passing scene, but before the train began its return she jumped out of her seat and, thrusting the baby into Charlie's arms, pushed her way past his knees shouting, 'Quickly, Charlie, there's Ruby. I must speak to her. Hurry!'

She moved so fast that Charlie could not restrain her and he had no option but to follow her, though he was certain that it was only her wishfulness suggesting Ruby's presence to her, as had been the case with the blue landau. But as Fanny, running, caught up with the girl in the beige shawl and turned her around, Charlie saw that it was, indeed, Ruby!

The three sat around a table in the small teashop, the baby on Charlie's knee. Ruby, amazed to see Fanny and Charlie again and delighted by their tiny child, answered the questions that Fanny fired at her.

Mr Alexander had gone shortly after Fanny and Charlie, and taken his wife and the two children with him. She had heard a rumour that his wife had wanted to go to live near her family in France and they had just 'upped and gone'. So before poor Mrs Hall had got over her father's death, she had lost both Fanny and Alexander, and her grandchildren. She had only lived for five months after she had taken ill, and Mr Hall just faded. There was no other word for it. He just faded. He sold up the place, though it seemed that the business had gone down the nick. He didn't go near the brickworks while Mrs Hall was ill, and never went back again. There was a rumour that he had gone to live with Mr Alexander in France.

'What happened to Mr Richard?' asked Charlie.

'I don't know,' she replied. 'We was given hour wages han' ha week's extra pay han' we was hout of there hin ha few days, hall of us.' She was obviously well satisfied with the outcome of the tragedy and went on, proudly, expressing much air with her ghostly aitches and tilting her head upwards a little. 'Rupert han' me, well, we took hour money what Mr 'all give us han' put it with hour savin's han' we rent a little shop in the 'igh street. The Candy Box, we call it. That's ha Hamerican word – candy,' she added with pride. 'Hit's doin' well. We're goin' to look for hanother soon. Maybe it'll be ha little grocer's.'

She looked at Fanny for approval, but was disappointed to discover that the recitation of their success had gone unheard by Fanny … but not by Charlie. Here were a kitchen maid and a groom, the lowliest people in her parents' household, and they were in a much superior position to his poor Fanny. He signalled for the bill, paid it, and hitching Sam up onto his shoulder, he put his other hand below Fanny's elbow.

'Come on Fanny, we'll miss the next train.' To Ruby he said, 'Well it was really nice to meet you again, Ruby. Perhaps we'll come to see you in your shop next time we come to Seaforth.'

'Oh, that would be lovely. Rupert would really love to see you, too. You take care of yourself now, Miss Fanny,' she said, bending her head down and looking at Fanny's face from below, noticing again the disfiguring upper lip that she had first seen on a Christmas Eve many years before when Fanny had displayed it to the world as she danced with Charlie.

Fanny arose at the pressure from Charlie's hand, all her energy drained from her, and as though unaware of her surroundings, she allowed him to steer her towards the door and out onto the street.

Chapter Seventeen

Francie's birth was as uncomplicated as Sam's. It seemed that Fanny was made for childbearing. It was something that she did with ease and calm and, not only that, but the babies she bore were beautiful. Francie was dark haired, like Fanny, and had all the beauty of the Morses.

As the doctor drew the baby away from the mother, Fanny could see without asking that it was a little girl.

'Let me see her mouth.' Fanny thrust aside her tiredness and lifted herself on one elbow. 'Is her lip alright, Ellen?'

By way of answering, the doctor bent down and held the child in front of Fanny's face.

'She is perfect,' he said, 'quite the most beautiful baby I've ever delivered.'

He cut and tied the cord as the child began to cry, and handed her to Ellen who, after wiping the baby's eyes and mouth, wrapped her in a white sheet, laid out in readiness. She laid the baby, still bawling, in Fanny's arms.

'She's got a good pair of lungs on 'er,' she said. 'Just listen to 'er takin' on. You're goin' to have a right 'andful 'ere, Fanny, you mark my words.'

Charlie came into the room. Although he had changed from his working clothes, he still managed to look dishevelled. His white shirt, without the collar, was open at the neck, his sleeves were rolled up and his vest unbuttoned. His flaxen hair stood on end, evidence of his having run his fingers through it, as was his habit in times of stress. He stood beside the bed, looking down on his wife and child, his fingers recommencing the teasing of his hair upward from the scalp. He was quite unable to overcome his excitement sufficiently to speak or move.

'It's a girl, Charlie. Are you pleased?' asked Fanny unnecessarily. It was quite obvious from his demeanour that he was bursting with delight.

'We've got a boy and a girl. How lucky we are.' He bent over and kissed Fanny, his forefinger opening the sheet, the better for him to see his beautiful child. Turning to the doctor, he asked, 'Why is she crying so much? What's wrong with her? She sounds as though she is in pain.'

'There is no pleasing some parents.' The doctor's sigh was humorous. 'If the baby doesn't cry, they panic, and if it does, they complain. There's nothing wrong with her, she is perfect, she's just had a very difficult and tiring journey and she wants to be left alone. Come on, Ellen, we'll leave the proud parents with their new acquisition. My goodness!' he exclaimed, 'She sounds just like a train running through a tunnel.'

Left alone, they watched their child as she began to suck and, red-faced and worn-out, finally fell asleep.

'We'll call her Frances.' Charlie spoke into the ringing silence. 'She looks like you.'

'We can't call her Frances,' said Fanny, 'It would be too confusing having two Fanny's in the same house. Besides, I had hoped to call her Irene.'

'You have never said anything in all these months. I had really set my heart on calling her Frances. We could call her Francie for short. What about Frances Irene?'

And so the sleeping child was to become Francie and to grow into a charming toddler, her curly, dark hair with the Morse signature gold tips and her velvet eyes flecked with gold.

Wherever they took her, people stopped to look closer and remark on her loveliness. It became so commonplace to be stopped by strangers that Fanny became used to her shopping trips taking twice as long as they should. People would engage her in conversation about Francie's unusual beauty several times during each trip, so that when she was short of time, she would take the girl to Ellen to be looked after while she went out with Sam. Charlie adored the child and spent his evenings and weekends with her sat upon his knee. It would have been to the exclusion of Sam had his son not been equally besotted with the infant, but as it was, he would stand beside Charlie's knee and play with his small sister as she lay in her father's arms. It just seemed to Fanny and Charlie that they could not be happier or more fortunate.

Ellen had told Fanny that she could not become pregnant while she was breastfeeding, so it had come as a considerable shock to find that she was with child again when Francie was barely three months old. It was not that they did not want more children but they could have wished that a longer period had elapsed, both because of the difficulty of caring for three tiny infants at the same time, and for the extra strain on their already stretched income.

The pregnancies were taking their toll on Fanny's body, too, so that she felt continuously tired during the ensuing nine months. Apart from that, her health was good, and two days after Francie's first birthday, she bore another beautiful baby girl, golden and cream and crimson, like the Leighton painting she had seen in the Walker Art Gallery, even outstripping Francie with her beauty. When it came to deciding on a name, Fanny, realising that she did not know what Charlie's mother had been called, asked him, and on learning that her name had been Bertha, it was decided without further conferring that their second daughter should be named for her.

Bertha would lie in the wicker cot, quietly gurgling, just like Sam had lain before her and Fanny felt that she were being given such beautiful children as a consolation for the years of torment she had endured from her harelip, and took great pride in each of them.

People who had drooled over Francie now turned all their attention to Bertha. It was as though the sun had come out and eclipsed the moon, and though Francie was too young to suffer from suddenly being usurped by her baby sister, Fanny felt an unease at the rebuff. It seemed that Francie had suddenly been demoted, devalued, denigrated.

'People are fickle,' she thought, 'and made unkind by it.'

As the girls grew older, the occasions when this was apparent increased.

Their financial position was still stretched by the three small children. It seemed as though they were never able to put anything aside. Each week some new thing was needed, so that even when Charlie was working long hours regularly, they never lost the anxiety which was the offspring of poverty.

A joint party was arranged to mark Francie's third birthday and Bertha's second, and Ellen was to bring her three youngest children. When Ellen arrived with the children, she told Fanny with some excitement that a shop was opening on Walton Road which specialised in the new photographic technology. The proprietor had placed a notice in the empty window prior to opening, announcing a competition to find the prettiest child. The prize was twofold. The winner would have his or her photograph taken and placed in the window for the opening of the shop, and – this was the part that interested Fanny most – a five-sovereign prize was offered to the most beautiful child, with two one-sovereign prizes for the two runners-up. Fanny pulled her shawl around her and, leaving the children with Ellen, flew along Walton Road to where she had been told she would find the shop. She stopped before the window and read the notice. The rules stated that the child had to be between three and seven years old and the judging would take place a week next Friday. Parents were asked to bring their children along to the shop at eleven o'clock in the morning. Francie was three today! Fanny had no doubt that her child would win. She was euphoric at the prospect of the five-sovereign prize, or at the very least, one sovereign.

She discussed it with Charlie when he returned from work, and he agreed that she should take Francie along on the appointed day. Ellen offered to look after Sam and suggested that they might make a new dress for Francie for the occasion since, as Ellen pointed out, all the other contestants would be splendidly dressed in their prettiest clothes. The economics of this had not occurred to Fanny, and thinking it over, she had a better idea. On the Thursday afternoon, she dressed once again in her finest clothes from earlier, more prosperous days, took the precious ruby ring from her box and slipped it upon her finger. Her hands were workworn but it could not be helped. She alighted at Castle Street and made her way to the Bon Marche.

When she entered the store, she adopted the haughtiest attitude of which she was capable and glided through the glass doors, her lace handkerchief over her mouth and her head held high so that she looked down her nose. She wandered through the children's department until an assistant approached her and asked subserviently if she could be of help to Madame. Fanny nodded graciously and began to examine dresses, discarding them as 'unsuitable'. She had already seen what she wanted, a beautiful ivory-coloured, oyster-silk dress, but she continued to rummage through the racks as though nothing quite came up to her extremely high standards. Gauging the size, she held out the chosen dress.

'Perhaps this would do, but my daughter is not with me, so I am not sure it will fit. Perhaps I will take it on approbation,' she

103

continued, as though she anticipated no objection to this suggestion.

'Of course, Madame,' said the sales assistant ingratiatingly. 'I'll get the manager, I'm sure there will be no problem but he will have to authorise it.'

Fanny waited, feigning impatience, until the manager hurried towards her. He dismissed the assistant with an imperious wave.

'I understand that you would like to take the dress to try on your daughter at home?' he gushed. 'Beautiful, isn't it? It is our new season's stock. I'll just have it wrapped while I take your details, Madame.'

Her details were duly taken. She reverted to being Fanny Hall of Seaforth and assured the manager that, should the dress fail to suit or fit the child, she would return it, or send one of the servants with it, the next day. So Fanny, holding in her hand the box containing the loveliest, and probably the most expensive, child's dress in the store, went onto the street, out of the same door through which she knew she would re-enter on the next afternoon, to return the beautiful garment, in as immaculate and pristine condition as she now took it.

The house was abuzz with excitement on the Thursday evening. The kettles were boiled and Francie was immersed in the hot tub before the kitchen fire and Fanny plunged her energies into the preparation of the child for the challenge that lay ahead. The atmosphere carried a warm vitality and the steam held in its swirl the faint, elusive scent of Attar of Roses, soap specially purchased from their dwindling resources for the occasion. Her hair was washed and encouraged into its tight curl. Her nails were scrubbed and special attention was devoted to the cleaning of her ears. Not to waste the good hot water, Bertha was tubbed after Francie had been taken out and dried. Ignoring the economy that their poverty gave rise to, a pair of white stockings had been bought for the occasion. New boots or shoes were out of the question, but Fanny had resolved to carry Fanny into the judging in her stockinged feet.

The following morning, Fanny arose early and dressed herself in the clothes she had worn to town on the previous day. Having made Bertha ready, she left the dressing of Francie to the last. She was meticulous in her preparation, and Francie took self-important pleasure in once again being the focus of admiration. Taking her wooden box from the sideboard drawer, Fanny took out her shell and, curling her fingers around it, held it against her cheek before slipping it into her bag. At a quarter to eleven, Ellen knocked on the door to collect Sam. She smelt strongly of raw onions, and Fanny, with uncharacteristic insensitivity, drew Francie to her as though fearing contamination, but this instinctive protection of the child's aura went unnoticed by Ellen.

'Doesn't she look adorable!' she enthused. 'Why, Fanny, she is more beautiful than ever. She can't fail to win. You be off now. I'll shut up 'ere and mind you come right back and tell me all about it.'

Leaving the cloistered calm of the house, Fanny's senses were assaulted by the clamour. Clattering of hooves and clanging of tramcars jangled in her ears to the rhythm of the turmoil in her mind. There were still moments when she longed for the rolling countryside of her youth. The cold air bit through her thin coat and her heart raced as she struggled along Walton Road, Bertha clinging hard around her neck, dragging Francie by the hand, conscious that necessity revealed her deformity to a world of strangers, who shouldered their way past her along the pavement, brutally indifferent to her anxiety.

She was trembling by the time she arrived at the shop. A queue of women clutched children of differing degrees of attractiveness. Some of the mothers were as poor as she, but some of them were quite obviously better off and there more for an endorsement of their child's unique qualities and the kudos of having his or her photograph taken, than for the need of the prize money. Many of them seemed to know one another and they talked animatedly and in loud voices. Fanny began to wonder if she had been wise to set her store on winning the precious five sovereigns. She looked around confirming that her child was surely the most attractive and yet, wasn't that what every doting mother there was thinking? Here were certainly some very pretty children. She was tempted to go home, but remembering the trouble to which she had gone to get this far, she decided to persevere and began to exhort herself not to get upset if Francie didn't win. With a great effort, she willed herself into a state of calm, dropped Bertha to the ground and smoothed out her own coat, examining her reflection in the plate glass window of the shop. She slipped her hand inside her bag and her fingers closed around her precious shell, reminding her of who she was, where she had come from and, more importantly, that she was loved. The three mirrored in the glass were loved. She breathed deeply and smiled. It always worked. Letting go of the shell, she calmly formed a loose fist with her hand and laid it in front of her lip. Now she was all serene and peaceful, her shoulders relaxed, and she stood a little taller.

The door to the shop was opened by a young man, who instructed the women to enter in an orderly fashion and sit on the seats arranged around the room. Fanny was close to the end of the queue, and found when she went inside that she had to stand for a while, but she felt a relief that the room was warm and she was able to slip off the shabby coats that the girls were wearing. She was acutely aware that the comparison between the quality of her coat and the children's hand-me-downs marked her as a selfish mother. But Fanny's dress beneath was exquisite.

Composing herself, she surveyed her surroundings. The pale cream walls were covered with likenesses of elegant women in various poses. There were images of imposing buildings and idyllic country scenes of mountains and rivers. That they were so lifelike was astonishing to Fanny. Her eyes feasted on each subject, dissecting it hungrily before she passed on to the next. She was reminded of the Walker Art Gallery, so long ago, and recognised the same satisfaction that she had felt in her spirit at being introduced to the wonderful works of art that had adorned the walls in that magnificent building.

Tearing her eyes away and giving her attention to the room once more, she saw that the seats were covered in light brown, buttoned leather and the wooden floor had a strip of gold, russet and burnt umber carpet along its length. It reminded Fanny of her old home in Seaforth, the lych-gate in autumn.

It seemed to take an interminable time to get through the hopeful parents, each child being given about five minutes, but gradually the numbers in the waiting room declined, the low hum of conversation ceased, and soon the mother and child ahead of Fanny were called in. Ten minutes elapsed and Fanny, committed by her temperament to anticipate rejection, began to worry that this child had received a longer consideration than the others, so that when the mother burst forth from the inner room, exuding a self-important pleasure, she felt a debilitating despair.

With difficulty she rose and asked one of the remaining women, if she would keep her eye on Bertha. The woman agreed, but Bertha began to whimper as Fanny made to leave. Fanny, ignoring her with difficulty, picked up Francie, slipped off her boots and, placing the lace handkerchief that she kept for such occasions over her mouth, moved to stand outside the door.

When the boy came out and called pompously, 'Next please', Fanny went before him through the door, with Francie in her arms. If she had had doubts as to whether Francie could stand up to the competition, they were dispersed immediately. There was a sudden hush, followed by a hum, around the table where the three judges sat as she sank down upon the chair in front them, settling Francie on her knee. They looked at each other, exchanging barely perceptible nods. They subjected the child to intense observation before asking Fanny some questions and busying themselves with their pens. Eventually the most eminent-looking judge, who had a clipped beard and eyeglasses, stood up and moved to Fanny's chair.

'Would you stand Francie on the floor for us, Mrs Cahill?' And to Francie he said, 'Hello little girl and what is your name?'

Francie turned her head into her mother's lap and encircled Fanny's legs with her arms. Peeping out from the folds of her coat, she said, 'Francie.'

'You are a very beautiful little girl, Francie, did you know that?' The child nodded shyly as he began to study her from all sides.

'And how old are you Francie?'

Francie looked at her mother for encouragement and Fanny gave her a smile and gently turned her around to face the man.

'I was three. I just had a party. I have got a big brother. His name is Sam. I've got a sister too; she's called Bertha. She's only little.' Suddenly her head cocked on one side and she said, 'She's crying. Can you hear her crying?' and turning to Fanny she said, 'Ma, Bertha's crying.'

'Mrs Cahill,' the man said, 'Francie is an amazingly beautiful child.' He turned back to his colleagues, 'I think we have found our winner, gentlemen,' he said, and the other two nodded agreement with him. 'We do, of course, have to wait until we have seen the other contestants, but if you can spare a little longer, we will recall you after we've seen them.'

A rhapsodic smile transformed Fanny's solemn face, but when she returned to the waiting room, she tried to hide her pleasure and relief, so that the repose on her face was at odds with the turmoil churning in her chest. She waited, elated, while the other children were being judged. Bertha was still whimpering and Fanny tried to placate her with shushings and bouncing her upon her knee, while Francie, aware that for some reason everybody was pleased with her, laid her head upon her mother's other knee and swung a stockinged leg backward and forward in delight. While the mother of the last contestant was gathering up her things, the man came into the room and said, 'Perhaps you'd like to come back in now, Mrs Cahill,' and noticing that Bertha was still whimpering, her face pressed against her mother's shoulder, he said, 'You'd better bring in young, erm, Bertha, wasn't it?'

At the sound of her name, Bertha turned to look at its source, and seeing the old man, her face wreathed into a disarming smile, wrinkles gathering around her intense blue eyes, her head tilted to the side so that her golden curls cascaded down one shoulder. The old man stopped in his tracks. His body still turned away, toward the door of the interview room, his head remained looking over his shoulder, his stare transfixed on this devastating nymph. Turning, he took Bertha from Fanny's arms.

'Here, let me carry her for you.' He addressed no one in particular as he walked, without taking his eyes off the delighted Bertha, into the room where the other judges waited.

'Look what I've got here,' he said, showing Bertha to the others. 'Isn't she the most adorable child you've ever seen?'

The other two men arose and hurried around the table to coo over Bertha, one playing with her foot in the scruffy boot, the other twisting her curls around his finger; they were like besotted adolescents. Fanny, perplexed at this new turn of events, and Francie, sadly discarded and ignored, stood looking on.

With a great effort of will, Fanny controlled her bewilderment sufficiently to say, 'Bertha is only two. She is too young to enter the competition.' She urged Francie forward. 'That's why I only brought Francie.'

But Francie, sensing with the special intuition of children that she had in some way failed this most important test for which she had been prepared for several days, became truculent. Turning, and holding her mother around the legs, she began to cry loudly, emitting the singularly unattractive sound of a train running through a tunnel. Bertha, on the other hand, became ever more coquettish, bestowing upon them, as though it were a palpable gift, an incomparable, beaming smile.

With all the embarrassment of a love-struck young boy and a smile that went beyond his control, the judge boomed, 'I think that we can expand our remit on this occasion, gentlemen. The three-year stipulation was only introduced because it was inconceivable that a child below that age could ever be relied upon to follow instructions, but I'm sure that we can agree that little Bertha, here, has poise and maturity beyond her years. She is remarkable in every aspect, a natural model. I can really do some wonderful work with this child!'

The two remaining judges were muttering words of agreement, which were being drowned out by Francie's continuing impression of a locomotive. Conflicting emotions ran through Fanny's mind, creating confusion in her head. She was offended on behalf of her eldest daughter by the callous insensitivity of these three men, and her instinct was to sweep up her two precious children and run from this place. But five sovereigns!

'What about Francie?' she interjected weakly.

Suddenly aware that both the mother and the child were upset by this turn of events, the man said in a placating manner, 'Oh, yes, of course, Francie, too, must have a prize. I think, gentlemen that both of these little girls are outstandingly beautiful. I have no doubt that, when we have finished our deliberations, we will find that we are in agreement that Francie shall be first runner-up.'

Francie continued to wail and Fanny remained hostile.

'Perhaps we should agree to increase the second prize to two sovereigns.'

The two seated beside him looked a little disconcerted and Francie's bellowing became a sniffle, as though she knew the value of two sovereigns.

Two sovereigns! Five sovereigns and two sovereigns, seven sovereigns! Fanny was transported. Her feet almost left the ground. Seven sovereigns, it was a fortune. A fortune! She felt numb with disbelief. It was more money than she had dreamt of. She was suddenly aware that a second man was speaking now.

'Are you able to stay for an hour or so longer, Mrs … erm …,' he glanced down at the form which lay in front of him on the table, 'yes, Mrs Cahill? Mr Peterson would like to take some photographs of Bertha and, erm, Francie.' He struggled to find the name in the recesses of his memory. 'Before we raise any hopes too high, we must make sure that the little girls are photogenic.'

'Photogenic?' Fanny queried the unfamiliar word as, fruitlessly, she looked around the room for a clock. She had to have the dress back before the shop closed, and time was passing. She was already over an hour later than she had told Ellen she should be. Weighing up what now seemed to be the comparatively paltry cost of the dress against the seven half-promised sovereigns, she decided that she must stay.

Holding Francie, she was ushered through another door. Mr Peterson, still carrying Bertha in his arms, had preceded her. He sat Bertha down on a layer of dark velvet material which had been spread over the mound made by a cushion on the floor. He moved around her, placing electric lights and other unfamiliar equipment in different positions until, finally satisfied with the ambience he had created, he moved across to the black-draped box which stood upon a tripod at the back of the room.

Bertha sat contentedly on top of the cushion, displaying an astonishing precocity, like a seasoned professional. Mr Peterson enthused, 'Wonderful! That's beautiful, my little dove.'

The two-year old Bertha clapped her hands in glee, soliciting yet more compliments and epithets from her admirer. Mr Peterson straightened up and moved to rearrange the lighting.

It was as though they were alone. These two were in a world which excluded the other four people in the room. Mr Peterson vanished beneath the dark curtain time and again, squeezing a rubber bulb, and the resultant flash caused Bertha to laugh delightedly. He stopped between shots, moving a light or crumpling up the velvet, but never needing to orchestrate Bertha's imput. They were a natural team.

The second man said eventually, 'Do you think we should have a look at Francie, now, Patrick?'

The older man stopped. The puzzled frown on his face suddenly lifted as he realised that Francie was still there, waiting to be tested.

'Yes, yes, yes.' He came over to where Francie waited with her mother, and took the child by the hand. 'Come now, Francie,' he coaxed, 'sit beside your sister.'

For the first time, he positioned the children, Francie with her arm around Bertha, who automatically brought her head forward and sideways onto Francie's shoulder in an enchanting pose. Peterson chuckled with pleasure, shaking his head and pinching her cheek. After he had completed two studies, he lifted Bertha up from the floor and crossing, placed her on her mother's knee. As he did so, he paused and looked Fanny straight in the face.

'It is easy to see where the children get their beauty. Why do you persist in covering your mouth? You are a very beautiful woman. I'd like to take a photograph of you with the children.'

As he said this, he placed his finger beneath her chin and lifted her head, turning it at the same time, to examine her in profile. In doing so, he moved Fanny's mouth from behind the handkerchief revealing her lip and she flinched. She no longer shrank away in terror as she had in the past, since she was now used to showing her face without embarrassment. This she owed to Charlie, whose acceptance had made the imperfection inconsequential and irrelevant, and to her children after whose arrival, the luxury of concealment had been lost to her, as she busied about the general duties of a wife and mother. Peterson examined the defect, like a surgeon assessing the extent of the reconstruction necessary to correct the deformity.

'Hm,' he said softly. 'I see why you hide yourself. What a pity! I am sure that you could have something done about that. That tooth should come out, to begin with.'

Without hesitating he turned around and proceeded to pose Francie, who constantly looked to her mother for encouragement and reassurance. Achieving the effect he desired, he took just one picture of Francie and then they were finished.

Nothing could be finalised that day, Fanny must understand, but Peterson, winking at her, advised her not to worry, they would be in touch with her in several days. If the little girls were confirmed as winner and runner-up, dresses would be provided for the official photographic session as part of their prizes.

The ivory silk dress was returned by a truly guilt-ridden Fanny to a now frosty assistant in the children's department of the store, with moments to spare before closing time.

Chapter Eighteen

Fanny suffered in her heart for what she perceived as her betrayal of
Francie, but as Francie herself soon forgot the incident, the feeling
passed, leaving her with only a positive, sustaining pleasure in her
children's beauty.

Day after day, she waited anxiously for confirmation of the result,
and when a week passed without hearing anything from the
organisers of the competition, Fanny wondered if she had misread
the situation. Charlie tried to calm her down, telling her that it
really did not matter. They were no worse off, since they had never
had the money, but Fanny had spent it several times over in her
head. For herself, she had coveted a visit to the dentist to have the
protruding tooth taken out. She did not mention this to Charlie
since he had disapproved of the suggestion that a pefectly healthy
tooth should be removed, when Fanny had first mooted it and had
persisted in trying to loosen it for herself. Having treasured this
dream since she heard the words 'five sovereigns' and 'two
sovereigns', she now felt dejected once again.

On a day when the sun shone so brightly that even in the dark
kitchen, the motes could be seen dancing in beams of light, the
letter came. It was delivered by hand, and at first Fanny could not
open the envelope for shaking. She was blackleading the grate and
her hands were dirty with Zebo but she gingerly took out the letter
and held it against her breast, her eyes closed and a fervent prayer
on her heart, before spreading it out on the kitchen table and
reading it. In wild euphoria, she picked it up, flew next door to
Ellen's house and hammered on the door.

'Ellen, Ellen,' she shouted. Ellen opened the door. 'They've won!
First and second prizes! Seven sovereigns, Ellen! Seven sovereigns!
Oh, I can't believe it.' Tears were streaming down her cheeks
and she lifted her apron to wipe them away. 'Seven sovereigns,
Ellen!'

Ellen's delight was no less than her own. Leaving her eldest child to look after the younger ones, she went with Fanny into her house and, telling her to sit down and calm down, she put the kettle on the hearth. They sat at the table and reread the letter, smudged as it was with Fanny's fingerprints.

'Goodness me, girl!' Ellen exclaimed. 'Just look at the colour of the thing. The little dears'll be disqualified if the judges see this. I do 'ope yer don't 'ave to take it with yer when yer go to claim yer prizes. Bless me, just Fancy! Two proper little beauties they are an' no doubting.' She continued, unstoppable, like an almighty torrent, drowning Fanny in a deluge of words, and they laughed together and clung to one another as they stood, bathed in a shaft of joyous sunlight, in the centre of the kitchen.

Then there was the wait for Charlie to come home from work. Controlling her excitement, Fanny put on a soulful face and waited until he was seated at the table before she gave him the letter to read himself. She watched his expression progress through sombre, to calm, into the familiar grin that creased his face like crepe, and he rose quickly, wrapping her in his arms and lifting her off her feet. It was the same smile that had won her heart half a lifetime ago, and the template of the smile that had conquered Mr Peterson's just over a week ago. Over their evening meal, they discussed what they would do with the money.

'I'd like to give some to Ellen, Charlie. She's been so good to me and she looked after the children while I went. If it hadn't been for Ellen, I would never have heard about the competition.'

Charlie agreed unhestitatingly. He also had much for which to thank his neighbours. It was Jimmy who had first helped him to get regular work at the docks. After discussion, they decided to offer them one of the precious sovereigns. While Fanny cleared the table and washed up, Charlie went up the stairs to see the two delightful children through whom this good fortune had come, and when he returned to the kitchen, Fanny was sitting at the table, deep in thought.

'You know, I should have taken Sam as well. We would have had another sovereign. I'm really stupid, Charlie.' She brightened as she added more cheerfully, 'Don't we have the most beautiful children?'

'You're becoming greedy, Little Goose,' he smiled. 'We have so much to be thankful for. There was a time when we thought we could never be together. I am so grateful to you for giving up

113

everything for me.' He went around the table and, once again, placed his arms around her. 'I know that you must have wished, so many times today, that your mother and father and your grandfather could have seen how beautiful the children have grown. I know how proud Ma would have been if I could have shared you and the children with her. She would have loved you so much, my Little Goose.'

He fought back the unmanly tears that glistened in his eyes, as he squeezed her tightly to his chest.

That night, as they lay together, relieved at the prospect of not having to worry constantly about money, they unknowingly took upon themselves two further burdens. Their names were to be William and Winifred.

But, for the moment, their shared life seemed complete and idyllic.

It was almost Christmas and the snow had come early that year. Fanny was heavy with child as she waddled around her kitchen, preparing for the festive holiday. Life had become much easier since their windfall from the photographs, and there had been several other small opportunities resulting from that success. Bertha's photograph had been used to promote a brand of baby carriage, and though no money had changed hands they were allowed to keep the perambulator, which would prove most useful with another child imminent. A company that manufactured powdered baby milk offered a substantial reward for Bertha to promote its product, but this would have entailed travelling down to London and Fanny was advanced in this very disabling pregnancy.

During her previous pregnancies, Fanny's figure had remained relatively unchanged except for the actual enlargement of her stomach, but this time her whole body seemed bloated, like a pregnant cow. She moved around clumsily, walking heavily on her heels, and suffered from excruciating backache. Charlie would massage her in the evenings when he returned from work, but she could not get relief. She spent most of her time in the house, scarcely going out except for the most essential reasons. Charlie felt that she needed some fresh air and tried many times to coax her to visit Seaforth again, but she just wanted the pregnancy over. The child was constantly kicking within her and she longed for a temporary respite from the assault. Charlie moved from their shared bed to the couch in the small sitting room between the parlour and the kitchen, but he hated the lonely nights and the waking alone.

Unbeknown to her, he asked Ellen if she could manage the three children for a couple of hours on a Saturday afternoon, so that he could take Fanny out to see the new building at the Pier Head. Ellen had been so grateful to them for the sovereign, and so unable to believe the extent of their benevolence, that she would jump at any opportunity to repay their kindness.

So, when he returned from work at midday on the second Saturday before Christmas, he took Sam, Francie and Bertha next door and, after washing away the grime and changing his work clothes, announced to Fanny that he was going to take her to see the majestic building he had watched rising, in domination of the Pier Head and which he had been telling her about for months. The weather was bright but bitterly cold. Reluctantly, Fanny readied herself, trying hard to disguise her fatigue and the aching, which she felt in every part. They caught a tram, Charlie helping Fanny to heave the great mass that was her body, first up the two steps onto the platform and then up the third into the body of the tramcar. She shivered violently as she perched on the edge of the hard, narrow, wooden seat nearest the door and pain shot through her as the tram trundled along jolting over every joint in the lines. But when they reached the end of the line, what she saw justified every discomfort she had suffered.

The Liver Building stood imposingly at the Pier Head, dominating the waterfront, the crimson sun striking off the foremost bird, so that it looked like a phoenix, rising out of the ashes in a blaze of glory, while the four clock faces, like Ezekiel's wheels, showed that it was three-thirty and, as though further proof were necessary, the faces on the clocks of St Nicholas's Church to its left, confirmed the hour. They stood at the side of the George Dock Basin and gazed up at the wonder of British architecture that rose above them. As Fanny stood, her head tilted back, she was shot through with a searing pain, so acute that she shouted out in agony, and drawing her head forward and down, leaned against Charlie. She would have been doubled over had not her massive stomach denied her the relief afforded by that position. The wave of physical anguish receded, but she was left shaking at its intensity.

'Take me home, Charlie,' she gasped. 'I'm so sorry. Forgive me Charlie, I'm glad you brought me but I must get home.' She clung to him as he steadied her and steered her bulk towards the tram stop.

The seat nearest the platform faced inwards, allowing more space, and the people seated there moved hurriedly to make way for her. As she settled on it, the next wave of pain roared in. She felt as though her stomach would burst open as she slid from the seat and dropped onto the floor of the tramcar. There she remained on all fours until she felt the pain reach its limit and recede. Charlie was beside her on the floor, holding her, soothing her, and comforting her with words of confidence that he did not feel. The short journey down Scotland Road to the house on Walton Road seemed endless, and Fanny experienced several more spasms of pain of increasing severity before Charlie had her on the sofa in the parlour. The room offered no respite from the cold, but there was nowhere for her to lie in the kitchen and he could not risk moving her upstairs at this stage of her labour.

'Will you be all right for just a moment?' he asked. 'I'm going to slip next door to get Ellen.'

Ellen came bustling in. Charlie lit the fire. Jimmy remained with the children of both families. He had volunteered to get the doctor, but Ellen had insisted that it was too late. She bustled about boiling water and collecting towels and sheets while Charlie stayed beside Fanny, holding her hand and attempting to comfort her, blaming himself for having arranged their outing. The baby wasn't due for two weeks yet. He could not have foreseen its arrival today.

But now, Fanny was bearing down and Ellen exhorting her to push. Then there was a lull while Fanny moaned before the next crescendo of pain and push and pant. The child was born quite quickly, a girl, her lusty crying confirming that she was well and robust, relishing her release from the confines of the womb. But Fanny felt no relief from the birth. The afterbirth seemed huge and slow to slough. Fanny felt no different after the child was born, she still felt heavy and bloated. Ellen took the baby and wrapped her in a towel. She was active and strong, happy to be alive, her little red hands punching at the cloth that restricted them. She was very dark and very loud.

The pains persisted. None of her pregnancies had been like this. Ellen reassured her that once the afterbirth had come, she would feel very much better, but Fanny knew that something was not normal. She still had an incredibly strong need to bear down, and she realised, of a sudden and to her amazement, that she was giving birth to another baby.

'Charlie, there is another baby!'

At first Charlie did not comprehend what she was saying.

'We have twins. There is another baby about to …'

But before she could finish her sentence, her face went purple with the effort of expelling the tiny little boy into the world. It seemed that an eternity passed before William, to the relief of his waiting audience, gave a small whimper; a portent of the fragile existence to come.

The days that followed were fraught with unspoken fears for their frail son. Winnie thrived with an insatiable voracity for life. She was demanding when she was hungry, but at other times she seemed to exist almost independent of any outside help. Feed her and clean her and she wanted nothing else. When the older children came to look at her in the lone cot, her hand would reach out to push them in the face, as though intentionally, as she continued to live in the world she had created around herself; the world that belonged to her alone.

William, on the other hand, lay unmoving in the large drawer that served temporarily as his bed. Though he fretted constantly, it was difficult to tell from where the sound emanated. He was, it seemed, too weak to suck, and indeed, it seemed that Winnie drank enough milk for both of them. As the days went by and there was no improvement in William's condition, Fanny became more anxious until, on the evening of the tenth day, she lifted him to give him his evening feed. Her shout of alarm reverberated along the hall and Charlie, hearing it, dropped what he was doing and came running. Fanny held the tiny mite in her arms, and Charlie could see that he was motionless and his face was blue. Fanny swaddled his prone body in a blanket and then in Francie's shawl, and grabbed her own shawl, wrapping it around herself and the child, while Charlie ran next door to summon Ellen. Together they hurried along the icy road, stumbling in their anxiety, Fanny holding her precious child close to her while Charlie's arms encircled them both. The street was awash with Christmas trees and holly, with mistletoe and decorations. They circumvented a circle of carol singers, their steamy breath rising in the air to the strains of Good King Wenceslas. As they passed by the shops, smells of nutmeg and cinnamon, warm pastry and apples, coffee and tea assailed their nostrils, preparations for the festive season. The atmosphere of jollity and celebration seemed to taunt them in their anguish and despair.

Arriving at the elegant terrace where the doctor's house was, they hammered on the door. It was answered by a sour-looking woman, gaunt and thin and unsmiling, offended by this rude interruption of her evening repast. The doctor was having his meal. They would have to come back later. Before she could slam the door shut, Charlie jammed it open with his foot.

'He'll be no use to us later. Our baby is desperately ill and we're not about to leave until the doctor has seen him.'

The doctor loomed behind the woman, come to see what the altercation was about. Wiping his mouth with the corner of a large white napkin that was tucked around his neck, he peered at the child through thick lenses, which shrank his eyes to two small dots. He was short, though alarmingly stout, and so had to lean around the imperious woman to see them. As he took in the urgency of the situation he pushed her aside unceremoniously, removing the napkin with one hand while, at the same time, taking Fanny by the elbow and hurrying her into the house.

'Lay him on the trolley here,' he said, plunging his arms into a white coat before scrubbing his hands at the washstand in one corner. He deftly unwrapped the blanket and lifted the baby's gown, placing a stethoscope on the exposed chest, the urgency of his movements revealing more than words could have done to Fanny and Charlie. His head turned away from the anxious parents so that they could not gauge from his face what the prognosis might be. After several seconds, he straightened up. His demeanour became gentle and sorrowful and, in the manner of those who have bad news to impart, he shook his head slowly.

'It would be wrong to fight for his life.' He spoke softly. 'The child's lungs are not properly developed. If, by some miracle, he should pull through, what life he might have would be short and cruel. Take him home and love him for what time he has left.'

Pulling down the gown, he wrapped the blanket around the small, still body, lifted him with a clumsy tenderness and placed him in Fanny's arms. All her confined fear exploded in a great shudder which shook her whole body as she hugged the child to her breast and turned her head into Charlie's shoulder. The doctor left the room and the three of them stood together like some tragic statue, their grief merging to make them as one.

Together they returned, empty and lost, to the house on Walton Road. As they lay, unsleeping, that night in the big brass bed, depleted and sore of soul, Fanny whispered, 'However long I live, I shall never feel such misery as this again.'

Eight days later, at the start of a new year, as an icy blast swept across the country, they wept over a tiny coffin in a small grave in Anfield Cemetery.

Chapter Nineteen

The birth of William had sapped the physical strength from Fanny and his death, the spiritual. She railed against God and refused to attend services at the nearby church. The agony of her loss impounded on her so profoundly that, in the long term, she was never able fully to recover the contentment that had marked her life at Walton Road, whilst in the short term, she eschewed all efforts at comfort from her husband and her children. It could not be said that she denied them her dutiful concern, but it was as the tender caring of a paid attendant, rather than the willing devotion of a loving wife and mother.

Charlie, banished once again to the solitary occupation of the sitting room, experienced the sensation of rejection that had followed the discovery of Irene's death, so that he became reluctant to return to the house when his work was done. He took to slipping into the embracing comfort of the public house on his way home, delaying the moment that he must confront the zombie that had been his darling Fanny, his Little Goose.

Inevitably, he sought comfort in the company of his workmates in his leisure time and, inevitably, he found it. He met during one of these gatherings, a young and pretty redhead called Kathleen. Initially, they met by chance and it was no more than a lonely man sharing a drink with an attractive companion, but as the weeks turned to months, they began to meet by design ... and alone. In the space of three months the friendship blossomed into affection, cultivated by Kathleen's genuine attraction to the charming Irishman.

He began to smile again, and the months of pain were assuaged in the short hours he spent in her admiring company. It was not doing any harm, he thought, but he feared Fanny would discover his indiscretion, and rehearsed answers and explanations for his tardiness and increasing periods away from home. But Fanny never asked, nor did she seem to notice his absence. When he was late, she would place his evening meal in front of him, dried up and lukewarm, no hostility, no complaint that it had been spoilt by his late arrival and no apology for its unappetising state.

She cared for the children and managed her household duties efficiently, but she inhabited a silent, morose world of her own. There were times in the still silence of the bedroom where they had reached such moments of tenderness, such joys of intimacy, such heights of ecstasy, that she longed for the comfort of his arms. She lay sleeplessly, willing him to come to her, but he remained, unaware of her need, in the sitting room below. Her isolation was unbearable and yet she was unable to admit anyone into the deep distress of her grief. Even Ellen could not penetrate the wall of self-pity that she had built around herself. The tyranny of her mourning precluded comfort.

And so her desolation made a perfect breeding ground for infidelity. Charlie, in his utter misery, felt that he had lost a child and a wife. He just wanted to recapture something of the joy of living that they had shared for a decade, but he felt impotent to arouse any ardour in Fanny. It was Fanny he loved, he had no doubt about that. Kathleen was a good companion, but she could never take Fanny's place. It was not just that she frequented public houses; she had nothing of the gentleness and sweetness of his Fanny. He resolved to put her aside, and arriving home one evening after a particularly stressful day, empty of all feeling, he tried to take Fanny in his arms. Bowing her head, she turned from him, pushing him away with her hands.

'Fanny, we've got to talk about this.'

'Not now, Charlie.' She did not elaborate. It was a bald rejection.

Incensed beyond words, he grabbed her roughly by the elbows and swung her around.

'Yes, now.'

One of the children in the room upstairs began to cry and Fanny turned to go, but he pulled her back savagely.

She had never seen him enraged before and she was frightened by his unaccustomed fury and viciousness. Striking out, she hit him hard across the cheek so that he staggered back against the wall and she fled up the two flights of stairs into the girls' room. Charlie, following behind, flung back the door to find her with her arms around Francie and Bertha, the three of them cowering in the furthest corner, as though sheltering from some monster. The baby in Fanny's room below began to cry, and Charlie, seething with indignation, stormed down the stairs and out of the front door.

The icy blast bit against his burning face and penetrated his thin jacket as he pounded along the road towards the docks, his anger anaesthetising him against the harshness of the cold. The Cock and Feathers was about half a mile from the house, a distance that Charlie needed to recover his composure. He stood staring at its door, unaware of how he came to be there. It was not his intention when he had raged out of the house to assuage his pain with drink, but now he pushed open the door and allowed the warm, beery ambience to embrace him. The smell of hops was inviting. The first drink acted as an opiate for his pain and he rummaged in his pocket for the price of a second pint. He was calming down now, and leaning on the bar he turned and surveyed the room. There were several men whom he knew, but he acknowledged them without joining their company. Tonight he wanted to be alone, just to observe, and enjoy the solace of the ale. His money depleted, he put his third pint on the slate and was lifting it to his lips when the door swung open and Kathleen entered with two men. Their eyes met, but Charlie turned away in embarrassment. He had met with her often in these surroundings, but tonight he thought, 'No lady would ever intrude on this masculine domain and yet Kathleen is as at home in here as any man!' He felt a tap on his shoulder and he looked round.

'Not speaking to me tonight, then, Charlie?' Her long, red hair, usually neatly rolled and pinned at the nape of her neck, fell loosely about her face, wayward and wild. Tonight, in his intoxicated state, her easygoing and affectionate manner seemed more like abandonment, and Charlie responded to it.

He ordered another pint and a gin to be put on the slate, and they drifted over to a table in the corner of the bar, her erstwhile companions peeved by her desertion. They sat together in silence for a while, until Kathleen said, 'What's the matter, Charlie? Something's troubling you, and you know that if you want a shoulder to cry on, I am here for you.'

She touched the bruise that was colouring his cheek, and laid her other hand upon his arm. He looked at it in glazed wonderment, unsure of how it came to be there but, instinctively, he covered it with his own. Hesitatingly at first, he began to confide in her some

122

of the incidents that had taken place between him and Fanny, omitting, out of shame, the slap, but feeling his face sting again as he remembered. He felt as though he might cry, and the possibility appalled him. He rose quickly and went outside to the closet in the yard where he leaned his back against the door. What was he doing? How did he come to be telling Kathleen about his problems? But when he returned to the bar she was already on her feet and she took his arm and led him out of the public house and into the cold of the night and the warmth of her tenement.

It was after midnight when he returned home, and Fanny heard his key turn in the front door as she lay dry-eyed and desolate. She listened as he opened the door to the yard, and she could even hear his retching outside, so acute was the tension within her. She let out a shuddering sob and the baby stirred and whimpered.

Charlie was late for work on the following morning, and moved about his labours in a desultory manner, full of bitterness at Fanny and remorse with himself. He tingled with mortification at the memory of what he had done, and repented bitterly.

When he arrived home in the evening he let himself into the house and went straight to the sitting room where he now slept. There was a gentle tap on the door, and Fanny came in. She stood looking down on him where he sat and they both remained still and silent, regarding one another with moist eyes. As she moved towards him and knelt beside him, he gathered her into his arms and wept into the sweetness of her hair. They stayed like this for a long while.

'What has happened to us, Charlie?'

'I don't know, Little Goose. I don't know. Sometimes I feel that we are two different people. I feel so far away from you. I can't get through to you any more.'

He stroked her hair and, taking out the pins, let it fall around her shoulders and for that moment, she was his Fanny again. He laid her gently on the couch that served him as a bed and, that night, she did not go back to her own room. But this was just an isolated loving moment, not to last, as Fanny, reluctant to be happy for fear that tragedy would strike again, reverted to her morose detachment and Charlie, failing to understand her self-imposed seclusion and hating his enforced isolation, sought comfort where it was willingly given.

Chapter Twenty

The following March, Francie came home from Sunday school in a state of heightened pleasure.

'Miss Warner says I might be the May Queen this year. The Sunday school teachers are having a meeting this week and they are going to announce it next Sunday during the morning service. Miss Warner says that she is going to put me forward to be Queen.'

Fanny was cheered by this news. For the first time in the months since William's death, she showed interest in something. Her spirits could always be lifted by approval and confirmation of her children's beauty. Only Charlie noticed Bertha's sullen discontent. During the week that followed, Fanny consulted with Ellen about the making of a dress and veil for the occasion, and asked Charlie for money to buy white shoes.

'Don't you think you ought to wait before building up Francie's hopes? She's going to be very disappointed if she isn't made May Queen. Let's leave it until we're sure.'

'Miss Warner has practically told her that she will be selected, and we can't leave everything until the last minute.'

'It's six weeks off, Fanny. There's plenty of time to get shoes if she is chosen.'

'Your daughter is being picked out of the whole Sunday school for this honour and you begrudge the price of a pair of shoes.'

Charlie said nothing but rose from the table and made for the door.

'That's right!' Fanny shouted. 'Turn your back on us! Whenever there is something you don't want to discuss you simply walk away. Alexander was right about you ...' the words were out before she could stop them and she reddened with shame, but pride would not allow her to apologise. Charlie turned and stared at her sorrowfully, then he left the kitchen and went into his sitting room.

She knew that what she had said was unforgivable, but she was

124

pregnant again and her hormones were causing her nerves to jangle unmercifully. She had not told Charlie she was expecting another baby. A wave of self-pity overwhelmed Fanny. Charlie was so mean. He knew how much Francie becoming May Queen meant to her. Well, she wouldn't let him spoil it for them.

The next day, she and Ellen gathered up all the children and trooped down to the market. They bought some white voile, sewing thread and small pearl buttons. Fanny counted the remaining money. Something would have to be sacrificed if she were to get the net for the veil. She bought the net anyway, and they returned in high spirits to Ellen's house. Fanny was measured, the material was pinned and cut, and the dress began to take shape. The following day it was finished, save for pinning up of the hem, and Francie was regaled in a diaphanous cloud. She looked exquisite, her dark, gold-streaked hair contrasting with the whiteness of the dress and veil, and Fanny thrilled at her child's loveliness.

On the following Sunday they awoke in a flurry of excitement to ready themselves for church. Special attention was paid to Francie's appearance and she was full of happy anticipation. As they took their seats in the pew, Fanny lowered her head to pray, and as she lifted it and opened her eyes, she saw Charlie's bowed head in a shaft of refracted light from the stained glass window, and for a moment in time, she was back in the little church at Seaforth on Christmas Day. The poignancy of the moment struck her, and her heart flooding with a happiness that she had thought she could never feel again, she gave thanks.

They waited impatiently for the hymns and prayers to be over and the vicar to begin to make the announcements. There was to be a wedding in a month's time and the banns were being read. Bible study would take place on Wednesday and there was to be a christening next Sunday. Then, at last, the Leaders' Meeting to discuss the selection of the May Queen had taken place on Friday and it had been decided, unanimously ... here he looked directly at Fanny who tried hard to disguise her pleasure ... it had been decided, unanimously, to elect little Bertha Cahill.

Fanny froze and her shawl fell from her face, Francie looked around in astonishment before bursting into tears, Charlie simply sighed, but Bertha stood up and clapped her hands in delight.

Francie was inconsolable, and Bertha, quite impervious to her sister's distress, crowed and preened herself in a most provocative manner. Fanny was furious. She didn't mind which of her daughters was chosen, but to have given Francie the impression that the honour was to be hers and then to have robbed her of it, without even giving them time to prepare her for this violation, was an outrage. Neither of her children would take any part in the celebration and none of them would attend the church further!

'Nobody told you that Francie would be chosen,' Charlie tried to console her once they reached home. 'It was just the wishful thinking of a small child. We should have waited.'

'What sort of a father are you? Your daughter is embarrassed in front of the whole church and all you can say is "I told you so". All that money and work, and they change their minds.'

'Fanny, they haven't changed their minds. Their minds were never made up and anyway, the dress can be altered to fit Bertha.'

'Altered to fit Bertha! Do you really imagine that I am going to let Bertha be May Queen after this? I shall go and see the vicar tomorrow.' She took off her hat and stabbed the pin into it, vehemently. 'If you are too weak to do anything about it, I shall have to.'

True to her word, Fanny left the children with Ellen and sallied forth to do battle with the vicar, with the result that Francie, as consolation, was to be maid of honour and Fanny, though feeling herself to be betraying her eldest daughter, acquiesced to this arrangement.

The dress could not be made to fit Bertha. Francie had grown much faster than her younger sister over the last two and a half years and had always been taller for her age than Bertha, so try as she might, Ellen could not recover the garment. Fanny brought down the dress which Francie had been given as part of the prize for the photographic competition, and they tried it on Bertha. It was small for her and needed to be let out and the hem taken down and edged with lace, but it 'needs must suffice', Fanny observed.

So May began, with Bertha installed as Queen and Francie consenting to be her maid of honour, wearing the dress it had been hoped she was to have worn as Queen, and soon forgetting her disappointment in the pleasure of the occasion. On the evening of the crowning, Fanny was happy, her fretfulness forgotten in her pleasure of the day. She returned from church in the early evening, her sweet nature restored, and as she reached up to remove her hatpin, her coat parted and a button flew across the corridor.

Charlie looked down at her gaping coat and placed his hand on her swollen stomach,

'Fanny, are you putting on weight?'

She laughed and danced away from him, following the children, still in high spirits from the activities of the day, into the kitchen where she began to bustle about preparing Sunday tea. The evening was spent in an atmosphere of happiness such as they had not enjoyed since the death of William, and when the children had been put to bed, Fanny went to her room and undressed. When she returned to the kitchen, she was wearing the dressing gown which Charlie had bought her for her birthday when she was pregnant with Sam.

The rest of that month was an anticlimax, and Fanny, attempting to extend her buoyant mood beyond its natural limits, would saunter into the parlour and gaze upon the portraits of Francie and Bertha at three and two years old. How very different they were, and yet both such beautiful children. She would sit at her piano and her spirits would be lifted for a while, and during these moments she would be fused with energy. On such a day as this, she crossed to the bay window and gazed out on the street outside. The sun shone brightly and brought out the people in their summer clothing. Fanny thought about Seaforth in late May and June, remembering how she would sit on the coffin rest, her head lowered unseeingly over a book, waiting for Charlie. She closed her eyes, shutting out the view of Walton Road and projecting onto the pinkness of her eyelids scenes of trees, heavy with may, and quivering elms dappling the grass. In her heightened imagination she rose and strolled through the vegetable garden, and the kitchen door opened in front of her and Rose and Ruby came out carrying a carpet, which they hung out to be beaten.

All the servants would be busy at this time of year since the spring-cleaning was always left until May. Her eyes opened wide as the thought struck her. She would spring-clean! She would clean and paint the rooms and wash the curtains. She would start today.

This ill-advised effort in the fifth month of her pregnancy resulted in Joe being born prematurely three months later, but he showed no signs of being disadvantaged by his untimely arrival. He was similar in disposition to Winnie. Enquiring into everything, constantly investigating the world around him ever interested, ever absorbed. They had to keep their eyes upon him at all times. An open door was an invitation to venture beyond it without fear or caution, and he kept everyone on their mettle. He was well loved by his parents and siblings, the baby of the family and a delightful and charismatic child.

Two days before his second birthday, Great Britain declared war on Germany.

Chapter Twenty-One

On a stifling hot day in June, Pandora's Box, the lid of which had been creaking for several decades, burst open thousands of miles away in Sarajevo when a confused, unknown boy, for no better reason than to engrave the name Gravilo Princip in the history books, crooked his index finger and instigated the slaughter of over ten million of the flower of eight European nations' youth.

The flexing of a finger of the Black Hand was all that was required to spark off the tinderbox of Serbo–Russian suspicion and hostilities and their competing alliance systems. The assassination of the Austrian Archduke, Franz Ferdinand, was the catalyst that caused events to go spiralling out of control six weeks later, when Great Britain declared war on Germany and Charlie joined the throngs of men eagerly enlisting to join Kitchener's Army. It was rumoured that a Liverpool Regiment was being formed and trained to replace the First Line on the Home Front, and no amount of remonstrating or pleading from Fanny had deflected Charlie from his determination to be among the first in the queue to become part of it.

The work of organisation began immediately and he joined the motley crew of volunteers marching to drill at Sefton Park or for field days to Arrow Hall or Allerton.

November found him marching to Exchange Street Station on his way to Blackpool. The cheers and encouragement of the crowds who had defied the cold to line the street, clapping, waving hats, whistling and wishing the marchers 'God Speed', lent the town an atmosphere of celebration in stark contrast to that which awaited them on the Fylde Coast. He had not been billeted for twenty-four hours when the realisation of what he had let himself in for began to dawn on him. Icy winds swept across the bay as the battalion began early morning parades, and by the time they had finished the incessant drilling on the sands of North Shore, he could no longer feel his fingers and toes. In the evenings, when all he wanted to do was to return to his billet and collapse onto his bed exhausted, there were lectures to be attended and no quarter given to any man who failed to remain alert.

Returning with his roommate on a particularly raw night to the miserable boarding house that was their billet, Charlie said, 'Is this what I left home and family for, to die of frostbite and fatigue? I'll tell you what, Reg, it doesn't have the same ring as dying for King and Country, does it?'

'I don't want to die for anything,' muttered Reg. He struck a match and lit up.

'Do you think we'll ever see the war, or will we still be playing soldiers when it's all over?'

'Well, you see, the problem is, when they said the war would be over by Christmas, they thought you and me'd be out there but they've stuck us in this God forsaken 'ole and forgot about us. Could go on forever if they don't send for us soon.'

The following morning, as though in response to this opinion, a request was received for men to leave for the front to undertake the digging of trenches, and Charlie's enthusiasm was rekindled with a vengeance. It was not quite the same as shooting Huns, but at least it was action.

The Allies, having lost so much territory by now, clung fiercely onto every scrap of land they occupied, and so needed men not only to replace the natural wastage of war, but also to maintain and repair trenches.

Much to his elation, Charlie was among those selected from an overwhelming number of volunteers and wrote, in a state of high excitement, to tell Fanny, fully expecting her to share his fervour and pride.

Fanny was distraught on receipt of his letter, and in her desperation, she sought the distraction of activity, which had always served to divert her frantic mind. She resolved to clean the house from top to bottom. She worked through each room, beginning in the parlour and working upwards. On the third day she reached the top of the house. Carrying Joe, she settled him in a corner of the girls' room and gave him a wooden cart to play with. Her mind was still in turmoil as she knelt on the double bed, which Bertha and Francie shared and which stood against the wall, and pulled up the sash window. The cold rushed in like a whirlwind usurping every vestige of warmth. Scooping up the bedclothes, she carried them out of the room, careful to close the door behind her so that Joe should not fall down the stairs. Burdened with the bedding, she descended them and struggled along the corridor and through the kitchen and scullery into the alley. One by one she hung the blankets over the line, securing them with pegs. As she began to lift the heavy eiderdown she heard a scream and Ellen came hurtling out of her back door.

'Fanny, Fanny, I've been calling you. Oh, God in Heaven, Fanny! It's Joe.'

Dropping the coverlet, Fanny shrieked. 'What, Ellen? What?' By now she was shaking Ellen.

'What's happened? Joe's upstairs. Oh, God! Oh, dear God!'

Without waiting to hear Ellen's answer, she ran into the house and raced up the two flights of stairs, screaming as she went. 'Joe! Joe!'

She flung herself through the door where she had left him, but he was nowhere to be seen. Running into the boys' room on the other side of the staircase, still screaming his name, frantic with terror, she collided with Ellen.

'I tried to tell you, Fanny.'

'Where is he? Ellen, where is he?'

Ellen, one hand covering her mouth, pointed the other to the open window of the girls' room and Fanny's eyes followed the direction of her finger. Her feet fastened to the floor as, rigid with horror, the realisation dawned upon her. She had shut Joe in. With great effort she crossed the room and leant out of the window. There on the pavement below, surrounded by a gathering crowd, lay the limp, motionless, tiny body of Joe.

This, indeed, was déjà vu. The same bleak cemetery, the same grave, the same minister, the same desolate little group of mourners and the same deep misery that reached into the bowels of her soul. Although it was August, the day was unseasonably cold as though nature were empathising with them in their distress. Fanny stared ahead unseeingly. A single tear escaped her left eye, slid down her cheek, and came to rest in the cleft in her upper lip. The tip of her tongue appeared and gently, slowly, drew the droplet back into her mouth, loathe to permit the loss of what seemed to her, the last vestige of moisture that her body possessed. She was unaware of

Charlie's fingers closing around her hand; she was alone in the utter desolation of her anguish. What was it all about? What was the point of carrying on? 'Vanity, vanity, all is vanity. A chasing after the wind.' How many more of her precious babies would she lay beneath the inhospitable earth of this desolate, Godforsaken burial ground? What persecution would He afflict on her next?

'What more will He wrest from me before his wrath is slaked?'

Charlie inclined his ear towards her to catch her murmuring, but she turned her head away and walked from the graveside. Bewildered, he followed her and placed his arm around her shoulder, but she shrugged him off and he was left, torn between his wife and his children, remaining at the grave. He ran back to where Ellen stood, eyes closed and head bent down.

'Ellen, would you take care of the little ones? I have to go to Fanny.' He bent down beside Sam and the three girls. 'Stay with Ellen and Jim.' He hugged them together in a bundle, feeling the coldness of their cheeks against his own, and turned to follow Fanny, but she was nowhere to be seen. He turned in every direction, moving between the tombstones to catch sight of her but though he ran to the gates and back, he could not find her.

The interment was over and still there was no sign of Fanny. By this time Charlie was frantic. He leant heavily on a tombstone and wept. And wept. The funeral cortege had departed by the time his grief was exhausted. His pity for Fanny turned to anger. Joe was his child as well. He had his own agony of loss to contend with, but it seemed as though she thought that the pain of bereavement was exclusive to her. He strode to the gates of the cemetery and turned right towards home. He walked briskly for half an hour, his eyes darting in all directions, searching. The sun gave no heat, and around him, people were hurrying, heads down and shoulders hunched against the cold. A group of boys in ragged jerseys were playing marbles with blue hands, in the gutter. Three small girls took turns to twirl a hoop around their waists, shouting out with pleasure as they sustained the circling motion with their bodies. Some children were teasing a mongrel, throwing a ball into the air and watching him jump to retrieve it in his mouth. They skipped and clapped and laughed with pleasure, and Charlie wanted to shout out to them to stop. To stop laughing! To stop playing! To stop living! Joe was dead! The pain wrenched at his gut again. A tram had stopped in front of him and and he jumped on it as it moved away,

132

remaining standing on the platform, holding on to the chrome upright. His eyes were still fixed on the road outside, searching the faces as they flew past. He alighted in Scotland Road and raced along it until he reached Walton Road. He let himself in with his key. The house was cold and quiet and empty. He sat on the bottom stair, his fair head clutched in his hands.

His compassionate leave would be over tonight. Tomorrow he must rejoin his regiment and prepare for France or Belgium or wherever he was to be sent.

'Oh, Fanny,' he cried aloud in anguish, 'Where are you? Don't let me leave like this. Please, Fanny!'

But the house remained eerily silent.

Pulling himself together, he went through to the kitchen and put his head under the cold tap and gasped as the icy stream touched his skin. He pushed back his sodden hair with both hands and as he did so he caught sight of himself in the mirror that overhung the fireplace. For a moment in time, he recalled Christmas Eve, a long time ago. He stood, once again, in the washhouse at Seaforth, happily anticipating an evening close to his beloved Fanny, and he filled up with nostalgic melancholy. They had been through so much together.

Still heavy with worry at Fanny's absence, he collected the children from next door, fed them and oversaw their washing and dressing, mechanically. The three older children wrapped their arms around his legs and pressed their heads against his thighs. Sam was sad-eyed and silent, whilst Francie and Bertha sobbed quietly into the rough fabric of his trousers, but Winnie sat contentedly on her bed, engrossed in the undressing of her rag doll.

Charlie had been glad to occupy his mind with the children, but now that they were all in their beds, the fear of what might have happened to Fanny returned to fill him with terror. As he descended the stairs, the door opened and she stood framed in it, the setting sun behind her surrounding her with a shimmering aura of gold, and casting a long shadow down the hall.

'Fanny,' his cry pierced the stillness. 'Where have you been?' He stumbled down the remaining stairs and gathered her numbed body into his arms. 'I have been distraught, my beautiful Little Goose!'

He looked at her. The skin of her face had a pale green cast, her lips were colourless so that the hair lip was barely visible, and the only shade of colour in her face was the redness of her once beautiful eyes. Charlie's heart was filled with pity and he drew her into a close embrace. They wept together. At last, they were one again, in their shared tribulation.

They fell into bed and clung to each other, reluctant to relinquish the comfort of their physical contact. Eventually Charlie released himself from Fanny's grasp and rose. Gently, lovingly he removed her clothing where she lay and helped her into her nightdress. She began to shiver and he draped his greatcoat over the eiderdown. Taking the jug from the washstand, he went downstairs to the kitchen and heated some water. He filled it and returning to their bedroom poured the water into the bowl. He soaked a flannel and wrung it out and then crossing to the bed he wiped Fanny's tear-stained face. Taking her hands, one at a time, he stroked them with the cloth. This done, he undressed, rinsed his face and hands in the same water and climbed into bed beside her.

'I have to go away tomorrow, Little Goose.' His voice was a whisper. 'How can I leave you like this?'

By way of reply, she turned fully towards him and drew his head onto her breast. Charlie felt a sudden quickening and felt, too, Fanny's response. It was the furthest thing from their minds, and yet, the passion of their misery and anguish, transmuted into the carnal passion of their senses.

The following morning, Fanny's fragile heart finally broke, as Ellen and Jimmy restrained her and Charlie reluctantly escaped the ferocity of her embrace.

134

PART TWO

Chapter Twenty-Two

The family gathered together around the table were actually poles apart in their thoughts. Eleanor felt no inclination to eat. Indeed, she felt as though she might throw up if she tasted so much as a mouthful of the meal so elegantly spread upon the sideboard. The table was laid with her finest napery and Cook had outdone herself. Robert would surely remember his last breakfast with the family as a sumptuous affair.

Robert was also finding it hard to eat, but the reason for his lack of appetite was the intensity of the excitement in the pit of his stomach. At last, he was on the way with his chosen regiment. He couldn't believe his good fortune in getting his first choice, one of the most distinguished infantry regiments of the line and the timing could not have been more perfect. No more playing at war, this was the real thing. This was what the last six months of sweating on the parade ground had been all about and now he was going to the front. It was all very jolly. He and his friends would show the Hun what was what. Little did he realise that his privileged existence had done nothing to prepare him for the horror of the carnage that lay ahead.

Sophie had very mixed feelings. Without a doubt, she felt great pride and pleasure at the sight of her brother in his smart officer's uniform, but her pleasure was tinged with anxiety. It was one thing to walk in the village with him standing straight and tall by one's side, acutely aware of the glances of approbation from their neighbours and friends, but when he went her dear little brother might well be wounded – or even killed. Heaven forbid! An involuntary shudder ran through her and she dropped her fork on her plate with a reverberating clatter that caused all eyes to focus on her and flushed her crimson with embarrassment.

The Colonel felt nothing but bursting pride and satisfaction. His boy was going to chase the Hun back where he came from and give him a sharp kick up the derrière while he was at it.

He wiped his moustaches with his napkin and said, self-importantly, 'We can't abandon our obligation. We have to back up our treaty with Belgium. Let the Kaiser get away with that and how long do you think it will be before he attacks Blighty? Eh? Eh? No, no, we've got nothing to worry about from the Germans.'

'How can you say that, Cuthbert?' remonstrated Eleanor, 'The German infantry has a tremendous reputation in Europe and it is evident that they have been preparing for this war for some time, whereas we have had it thrust upon us. For what reason should we interfere in a squabble between Germany and Belgium? I really don't see why Robert should risk his life for some Belgians whom he has never met.'

Eleanor became tearful and dabbed her eyes with her handkerchief. It was too bad of Cuthbert to take such a gung ho attitude when she had struggled so hard to remain calm in the face of Robert's departure.

'Father's right, Mother,' her son said. 'It's not only a matter of us honouring our treaty to maintain Belgium's independence, the Kaiser has designs on the whole of Europe. Anyway the German Cavalry and Artillery are inferior to ours. I'll wager it'll take less than another month to get them on the run. We could still be home for Christmas.'

'I read that Lord Kitchener expects it to run for three or four years and millions of men will be killed and he should know, he is Secretary of War,' Sophie declared.

'Don't be foolish, Sophie. You know nothing about it. Kitchener's been out of the country for forty years. What does he know?' said the Colonel.

'But, Father ...'

'Now don't argue with your father, Sophie. If he says Kitchener is a buffoon then a buffoon he must be.' Eleanor did not like the direction this conversation was taking and, seeking to placate her husband, she deftly changed the subject. 'Have you seen his picture on the posters? They're everywhere. They say, "Join Your Country's Army" and "Women of Britain say – Go!" I must tell you, I don't say "Go!" I really don't want Robert to go at all.'

'Don't be silly, woman. Kitchener's mad. We don't need untrained men flocking to the Continent. What would we do with them when they got there? Where would we get enough uniforms and guns and ammunition to fit out thousands of inexperienced men and how would they know how to use them, if they had them?'

'Oh, well dear, I'm sure you know best.'

'Of course I do,' he replied tetchily.

'Oh, come on, chaps, I expect it will be immense fun. I'm really looking forward to it now,' interrupted Robert.

The bell began to clang and Robert rose. Making a ball of his napkin, he threw it on the table and hurried to the door.

'That'll be Cecilia. Do excuse me.'

As he opened the door, Cecilia and her mother were following Tomlinson across the hall towards the drawing room.

Robert intercepted them. He opened the door to allow Mrs Simonstone to enter. She was a small, slight lady with a birdlike quality. She seldom spoke unless she was spoken to, and her eyes were perpetually cast down towards the ground. By contrast, her eldest daughter was tall and erect and could be quite acerbic when she so chose. So much so, that there were occasions when Robert wondered whether he was doing the right thing, but it was what everybody expected and there was no one whom he preferred. As her mother passed into the drawing room, Robert held Cecilia back and, putting his arm around her waist, kissed her full on the mouth as though to assure himself that she was, indeed, the right girl for him. They drew apart quickly as the dining room door opened and the Colonel came through followed by his wife and daughter.

Cuthbert gave a loud 'Harrumph' and smiled broadly. Robert was making a good marriage. She was a very suitable match, Cecilia. It is a pity that she was not more like her dear mother, Rosemary. Now, there was a real lady. Modest, knew her place, never passed opinions on matters about which she had no knowledge, and kept a nice house and a wonderful table.

The Colonel moved across the room towards Rosemary, right hand outstretched and left arm ready to encircle her shoulder. His wife came behind him and embraced her friend warmly.

'Rosemary, how very nice of you and Cecilia to come to wish Robert bon voyage. I'm sure he appreciates the kindness of your gesture, don't you Robert?' She turned to look at her son, tall and clean-cut in his uniform, with Cecilia on his arm. 'And Cecilia, so lovely to see you, darling. Do come in and sit down. I wish it were a happier occasion.' She dabbed her eyes.

'Come now, Eleanor. Don't start that again. The public is almost unanimous in agreeing that we must honour our treaty with Belgium. You should be proud that your son is going to defend his country's honour.'

'I'm sure I am, Cuthbert, but I am worried for his safety, too.' She laid her arm upon her son's, her eyes glistening with unshed tears, and with her other hand seeking the arm of the girl standing beside him, she went on, 'I'm certain you must feel the same, Cecilia. I'm sure you understand how I feel.'

Robert shifted, embarrassed at being the subject of this unseemly display of emotion.

'Will you excuse Cecilia and myself if we take a walk in the garden?'

'All right, my dear.' With an effort she pulled herself together, 'But don't be long, your train leaves in forty-five minutes.'

The young couple left the room and went out onto the manicured lawn. They strolled down the length of the garden until they had entered the shrubbery beside the summerhouse, where Robert took Cecilia into his arms and kissed her with an almost desperate passion.

'Robert, you're hurting me, and see how you are making a mess of my hair, my hat is half off my head.'

'Sorry, Cissy darling. I just can't help myself. I'm so distraught at having to leave you.'

'I can understand that, Robert, I feel just as desolate as you, but we have to go back into the house and the parents will see my disarray. Please try to be a little more careful.' She adjusted her hat and smoothed down her dress. Softening, she went on, 'I do wish you didn't have to go to this stupid war. I'm going to be so lonely without you.'

'Will you wait for me, Cissy? Will you promise to wait for me? It would be such a comfort when I am out there in the trenches, to know that you were waiting for me here back home.'

'Of course I will and I'll write to you every day. Oh, Robert, I do love you.'

Robert led her to the seat inside the summerhouse and fumbling in his pocket, he brought out a small red box. 'When I get my first leave from the front, will you marry me?'

Eyes widening, she held out her left hand. 'Oh, yes, yes,' she choked.

He slipped the ring on her slender finger and she held it out in delight.

140

'It's beautiful.' She waved her fingers high in the air, watching the diamonds shimmer, pleasure rippling through her body and bursting over her face. 'Can we go in and show mother?' She rose to her feet and was moving across the lawn before Robert knew what was happening.

'Hey,' he laughed, running after her. 'Don't I even get a kiss?'

'Of course.' She slowed, turned without stopping, and raised her cheek to his lips then, quickening her pace, she arrived at the French windows before him, waving her hand towards the four people inside. 'Look. Robert has asked me to marry him. Just look at the beautiful ring he's bought for me.'

They all moved towards her like metal shavings to a magnet, and Robert, standing in bewilderment in the middle of the lawn, wondered where he fitted into the picture.

'Robert!' Eleanor called to him. 'You'll have to hurry. Dorcas is putting your bags into the motorcar. We mustn't miss your train … Lovely ring, darling … you are a dark horse.' She laughed as she stabbed the long pin into her hat

Sophie, fighting back the tears, stood apart watching. Her beloved younger brother was going to the front and to make matters worse, he had proposed to the abominable Cecilia. She had come between them, and now Robert was passing out of her life without even noticing her. Much to Sophie's distress, Robert and Cecilia rode in Rosemary's car and the Colonel drove the family car himself, with she and Eleanor in the back.

When they arrived at the station, the train had already pulled in and the platform was buzzing with an unaccustomed excitement. Bags were unloaded and put aboard the train. Tearful goodbyes were said, and the guard was shouting, 'Stand back, now! All stand back!' Doors were slammed shut and he was waving his flag. With a final blast of whistle and steam, the iron monster lurched forward and began to gather speed.

'I'll wait for you.' Cecilia dabbed her eyes with her handkerchief. 'I'll write every day.' Then she mouthed the words 'I love you' and he was gone, a tiny speck of khaki framed in the window of the train. The vision was imprinted upon Sophie's memory like a snapshot in a photograph album.

Robert settled into a corner seat of the carriage and glanced around. Opposite sat a rather common-looking woman with her

141

legs stuck out straight in front of her. They were so fat that she could not put her calves together, so that her feet splayed. Her skirts were hitched up and he could see, even through the thickness of her stockings, that her legs were mottled with red as though scorched from sitting before a fire. She kept taking huge sniffs of air and exhaling with a loud noise. He shifted uncomfortably and toyed with the idea of moving to another carriage, but his considerable luggage was stashed above his head and he was not prepared to be parted from it; not when such strange people seemed to travel first class these days. One could no longer be assured of a comfortable journey with people of one's own sort.

From time to time the woman would snort again, and Robert would shake his newspaper in annoyance and glower at her over its top. The woman returned his scowl and they continued thus, in an undeclared and unspeaking war.

Finally, she hauled her not inconsiderable bulk out of her seat and reached, with great difficulty, above her head to recover her valise. Relieved that they were to part company, Robert stood up smartly.

'Here, let me help you with that.'

She smiled coldly, recognising the condescension in his voice, and taking the bag from him, she left the carriage and he returned to his seat, feeling a complacent pleasure at his own graciousness.

Now, he stretched out his legs and considered the crease in his trousers and the shine on his shoes with satisfaction. He relived the happenings of the last few hours. He was glad that he had asked Cissy to marry him. He so much needed to know that someone was waiting for him when he returned home. Now that he thought about it, he wished he had acted sooner so that they could have been married before he left. It would have been spiffing to have left a baby ripening inside her in his absence. To have come home to a ready-made family. But it was too late now.

He considered Cissy. He wished that she were a little bit … softer. That she had given him some small token of her caring for him. A little more than the chaste, hard-lipped kisses she had bestowed upon him. Some touch a little more yielding than her corseted waist. Of course, he respected the fact that she was not a girl who would give herself lightly. No man wanted a woman who was wanton. If she had been careless of her virtue with him, she would surely be the same with some other fellow. At least he could be certain that she would not submit to another man in his absence. His brows furrowed. It was a challenging dichotomy. A virtuous woman came at a very high price.

He stood, and taking down his attaché case, took out the copious notes that had been compiled at the front for those who were preparing to embark and began to study them. As he did so, the excitement rose in him once again and he felt a great urgency to be there in the trenches, taking pots at the enemy.

His first disillusionment came two weeks later, as he boarded the troopship that was to take him across the channel to Le Havre on the way to Honfleur. He had not realised that, even as an officer, his first fight would be to keep warm as the ship was tossed and thrown by an angry sea. He had, at the very least, expected a berth, if not a cabin. How was it that with all that he had read and heard nothing had prepared him for this beginning of the spiralling descent into Hell?

Chapter Twenty-Three

Fanny was in the kitchen when the bell on the wall began to clang. Wiping her hands upon her apron, she moved down the long hall and opened the front door. She peered into the blackness and, as her eyes adjusted to the dark, she gasped with surprise as she saw standing there, with a grey blanket containing something heavy slung over his shoulder, a ghost from the past.

'Connor,' she managed, 'Charlie isn't here. He has enlisted and he left for somewhere on the Continent yesterday.' She swallowed hard to contain her emotions.

It was the first time that Connor had seen her lip since that brief glimpse on Christmas Eve so long ago, but he was more shocked by her general appearance than by the deformity. Her red-rimmed eyes were sunken and her hair was dishevelled. She wore a navy-blue and white striped kitchen apron over a shabby pink blouse, and dark skirt of some rough material. He would have passed her in the road and not recognised her. Was this the beautiful, immaculate Miss Fanny Hall?

'I know. It's not Charlie I've come to see, Miss Fanny. Can I come in?' He heaved the burden higher upon his shoulder.

'Of course,' she replied, stepping back into the hall and opening the door wider. 'Come in, come in.' She was flustered by the appearance of this unexpected visitor and wondered how he had known where to find them. He followed her down the hall. 'Is it all right if we talk in the kitchen? It's warmer in here. Oh, Connor it's so long since I saw you. So much has happened. Charlie will be so disappointed to have missed you.'

'I was with him last night, just before he sailed. I met him on the docks.'

'You saw Charlie? Sit down ... Sit down. I'll put the kettle on.'

As she was turning to lift the big black kettle, Connor swung the bundle from his shoulder to the floor, and the blanket fell open, scattering coins across its length and breadth. Fanny stared in amazement.

'Connor, what on earth is all this?'

'Charlie asked me to bring it to you. I work at the docks now and I came upon him quite unexpectedly on the quayside. A group of soldiers were playing poker with the last of their English money and Charlie was there among them. He was on a roll and the money just kept piling up in front of him. He had no idea what he was going to do with it and then he saw me. Just before he boarded the ship, he asked me to bring it to you. The blanket was the only thing we could find to wrap it in.'

'It must be a fortune,' said Fanny, kneeling down and letting the coins trickle through her fingers. 'How was he? I would have gone to see him one more time if I had known he was there. Oh, how was he, Connor?'

'It's hard to tell what Charlie's feeling, Miss Fanny. You know what he is like. He says very little, but he did tell me that he was heartbroken to leave you and the children. He asked me to tell you that he loves you.' He lowered his eyes as he spoke the last words, embarrassed as though he had inadvertently stumbled upon some intimate moment of passion.

Fanny retreated into herself as she lifted the kettle once more and began to fill it. Several moments passed before she turned again to face the big Irishman and, with an effort, smiled at him and said, 'How much is there? It looks like an awful lot.'

'It's only small coins; farthings, ha'pennies and pennies. Joeys and tanners are about the largest denominations and there are only a few of them.'

'Still, there must be hundreds and hundreds of pennies.' They began to stack the money into piles on the kitchen table until half the surface was covered with miniature copper towers. Fanny was delighted. The money meant so much more now that Charlie had gone away and it was in such short supply. The kettle began to boil and Fanny took down two of the remaining cups and saucers. The delicate china looked incongruous on the rough, scrubbed table. She scalded the brown pot and spooned the tea into it. While it brewed, she turned back to Connor.

'What has been happening to you? You never went back to Ireland? Were you still at Seaforth when my mother died? Do you know where my father is? And Alexander and Richard? Oh, Connor, please tell me all you know. Please tell me what happened after we left.'

'I can't help much, at all.' He took the teacup from her hand. 'Mr Thomas just went to pieces. We were all given our notice. Mr Alexander had already left. The rumour was that he went to France. He came back for the funeral but returned immediately after. I reckon he will be regretting it now that war is raging over there. I never heard anything more and I never went back. I came here to Liverpool and got work on the docks. I didn't feel that I wanted to return to Ireland. I would have enlisted if I had not been too old.'

Fanny looked at him more closely, now. He had altered very little. His hair was greying at the temples and his face, always rugged, had a few more wrinkles, but he was still a good-looking man and obviously fit and healthy. So much time had passed since the night that he found them returning from their wonderful day in Liverpool, that it seemed like another life. She was comforted that he had come because he had shared in that distant time that now seemed so desirable, so perfect. She felt less alone.

'Are you living nearby?'

'I have a place in Lovett Street off Scotland Road. It's handy for work.'

'Will you come and see us again? It's so good to be with someone who remembers the old times and with whom we can share those memories. I'd like us to be friends, Connor. I need someone to talk to about Charlie and you must meet the children. They're asleep now, but could you come and have tea with us on Sunday?'

She told him about the children as they drank their tea and they arranged that he should visit them on Sunday afternoon. As he turned to leave the cosy warmth of the kitchen, Fanny flung her arms around his neck and buried her head in his wide chest.

'You can have no idea how much good your visit has done me. I was so desolate with Charlie gone.'

She sobbed into his shoulder and he held her gingerly, acutely aware of the social chasm that had existed between them, until her tears abated and she had calmed down. She smoothed back her hair and straightened her apron and led him to the front door, watching his bulk grow smaller as he disappeared into the night

Back in the kitchen, she looked at the stacks of coins.

'Oh, Charlie,' she whispered to the emptiness, 'you are wonderful!'

Chapter Twenty-Four

During their four days of wearying tedium in the front line they were never dry. Earlier in the war the Allies had flooded the country to impede the Germans, but the waters were not partisan and they remained to create total, abject misery for the perpetrators. To add to this, torrential rainstorms had raged for the past three days, so that the trenches were filled up to mid-calf. Each day stretched out in long, grey, drenched boredom until, when evening came and the rain-soaked clouds completely eclipsed the watery sun and the ranks struggled to remain conscious, a terrorising barrage of artillery would begin. If it were designed to demoralise, it was completely successful.

Men who had left the comfort of their homes to join in the glorious fight for their country found themselves building up the subsiding parapets or baling out with whatever they could lay their hands on. There were insufficient hand pumps to go around because no one had anticipated such an indescribable morass.

Struggling through the bog on his evening inspection, the young subaltern thought about morning. Tomorrow he would be going back to the farmhouse for three wonderful days. Robert closed his eyes. He could almost feel the warmth of the water about his limbs and smell the steam rising from the hot meal he would savour.

He leant against the side of the trench and his mind wandered to England and home, and he meandered from room to room enjoying the familiarity of each small object. It was strange how sound, smell, taste and touch came into their own with remembrance. The smell of baking wafted from the kitchen and his tongue slipped over his hard palate and across his lips as he dimly recaptured the taste of warm, sweet pastry. It was still lingering on his lips as he moved to the Colonel's study and went inside, and the intense smell of tobacco and leather assailed his nostrils. As he drew it deep into his lungs, the pleasure momentarily vanquished the stink of mud and urine and death. He lingered in the drawing room with its strong aroma of beeswax furniture polish, mingled with the scent of cut flowers from the garden. In his trance-like memory, he walked outside and breathed in the smell of hay in the loft, manure in the stables and dubbin in the tack room, felt the warmth of the sun on his face and heard, in the far distance, the sound of a cuckoo. 'Cuckoo!'

But a faint sound penetrated his dream, grew louder and harsher and shriller as a hail of bullets screamed past his head, shattering the serenity of his vision, its suddenness filling him with terror. When it had ceased, he inhaled the rancid air and, calmer now, tapped his pocket to feel the slight bulge of his pipe. He would smoke the last of his tobacco when he returned to the bunker. He had written to Sophie asking her to send some more, and he hoped that it would come soon … perhaps tomorrow? He hoped, too, that there would be some word from Cissy. He had not received any post from her in twelve days, but Sophie's letters were only taking two or three days to arrive and he heard from her at least twice a week.

Another burst of machine gun fire, and a shower of mud rained over him as a sandbag slipped from the side of the trench into the murky water. The adrenalin rushed through his cold and aching body, energising him for a few moments before the tiredness set in again.

Was it like this when his father faced the Boers? Why, then, had he painted such an exciting and romantic picture of battle? Perhaps he had forgotten what it was really like. He dismissed this thought from his mind. He would never, never forget a moment of this stinking purgatory. Wiping the mud from his watch face, he saw that it was time for the evening relief, and stretching himself to ease the stiffness in his drenched and frozen joints, he began to wade through the mud towards the bunker. He had taken two steps when his foot struck the fallen sandbag and he cursed softly. Bending down to lift and replace the sodden heap he grasped what he realised was flesh. To his frozen fingers, the face still felt soft and slightly warm, and with indescribable horror he let it drop, to sink back into the mire. In no more than three seconds he was on his knees, churning up the muddy water as he grappled to get a grip on the dead man's shoulders. He lifted the head out of the sludge and cradled it against his chest, rocking backwards and forwards and sobbing loudly, all the pent-up dread and agony of the last weeks escaping in a fierce explosion of protracted misery.

148

How long he remained, mud covering him up to his chest, his sobs renting the fetid air, he didn't know but later, he remembered the moment when strong hands had wrenched his apart and lifted the body out of his arms.

The dead man was heavy with the weight of the water and the mud, like cold treacle, clung to its prey, so that Charlie found it no easy task to lift him onto the fire step. When he had ensured that the corpse was securely composed, he returned to where Robert sat, waist high in sludge, and gathered him into his arms, silently comforting him. When Robert had emptied himself of pain, Charlie held him at arm's-length. Without speaking, he caught the cuff of his battledress jacket over the heel of his hand and ran it across the white rivulets that ran down Robert's face, until they merged together with the dirt and all visible signs of his distress were wiped away. From behind, he guided him along the trench to the nearest traverse. He could feel the young officer's body shaking beneath his sodden greatcoat and it sapped Charlie's strength to prop him up as they crossed the seventy or eighty yards to the support trench where he braced the shattered subaltern beside the entrance, and with the lightest pat upon his shoulder he was gone.

Robert stumbled inside. On the plank-lined floor of the thinly roofed shelter, reclining figures could be discerned snatching a couple of hours' sleep. Robert sank to the ground and leant trembling against the wall. He couldn't go on. He couldn't.

Charlie found the sterilised petrol tin and, pouring some of the water from it into a billy-can, heated it on the dying embers of the coke brazier. Minutes later, he was wrapping Robert's frozen fingers around a steaming hot mug of sweet cocoa.

'Thought you might feel like a drink, Sir,' he said for the benefit of any officers who might be merely dozing, 'as you're coming off duty.'

He was Irish, Robert marvelled. His angel from the bog was Irish, and if his ear did not deceive him, from the south. He had never trusted the Irish. He had heard stories of them running guns from Germany to assist in their uprising and yet here was an Irishman showing him kindness and real compassion.

Next morning, the rear and advanced battalions changed places. As the first brigade fell in for the long march to the transport rendezvous, Robert caught sight of Charlie, but the Irishman showed no sign of recognition. Despite their weariness, both had lain awake for hours, unable to sleep, and it seemed that no sooner had sleep overtaken them than it was four-thirty and they were standing to arms and line inspection. Robert had performed his duties with routine lacklustre, collecting the reports on the enemy's activities during the night and making cursory notes of damage to parapets and the condition of the wire. He'd longed for his daily rum ration.

There was a parcel from Sophie, but still no word from Cecilia. When he was back in the farmhouse, he tore open the brown paper. Inside, in addition to his Navy Cut, she had sent three pairs of thick khaki socks, a cardigan, some marmalade, a tin of biscuits, writing paper and envelopes. He blessed her aloud as he laid out these treasures on his bed and shook out the cardigan, pitching a silver flask onto the floor. His spirits rose as he unscrewed the stopper. Brandy! Tears of gratitude came to his eyes as he sniffed the amber liquid and then touched it to his tongue.

Having bathed and towelled himself, he exalted in his clean, dry skin and hair as he pulled on the socks and held the cardigan against his cheek, relishing its newness. Falling back on the bed, he closed his eyes. He never wanted to go back to the front. He squeezed his eyes tighter.

'God grant that this foul war will end soon or that I might stop a bullet and be sent home. Or that I might just … stop a bullet.'

He remembered last night. He didn't want to remember it, but it forced itself into his thoughts. He had broken down but, worse, he had been discovered by an other rank! Part of him was angry with Charlie for having been there at the wrong time and yet, would he have pulled through without the man's quiet calm?

Charlie held Fanny's letter against his chest. He would open it when he had washed. He longed for a bath. Tomorrow the company would march to the divisional baths for delousing and a blessed immersion, like a water baptism washing away every sin and vile thing.

Their clothes would be cleaned and fumigated and they would be like new men. Fanny had sent him some soap in her last parcel. He had cupped his hands around it and held it to his nose, breathing in its fragrance. He had used it only to wash in a bowl, but tomorrow its luxuriant lather would engulf him. He wondered how much it had cost her.

He began to strip and wash in the bowl, starting at the top and proceeding to clean and scrub every part of him. He poured some fresh water to rinse his head and as he rose and pushed back his wet, flaxen hair, he caught sight of his reflection in the glass. The sudden memory of that Christmas Eve in another time, another life, struck him with such a force of nostalgia that it forced tears to his eyes. The hair was shorter now and beginning to grey prematurely, the face was older, older than his thirty-five years, the body ached and the soul was weary. He leant heavily on the washstand his head hanging on his chest.

'Oh, Fanny.'

Back on his blanket on the floor of the factory, where the other ranks were billeted, he took out her letter and held it to his nose, inhaling its scent. He turned it over in his hands. It was thick. For a moment longer he lingered over it, extending the moment of pleasurable anticipation, and then he carefully tore back the envelope and took out the bundle. There were photographs of the children. The joy of the moment overtook him as he fingered through each image. Sam, smiling radiantly, his hands fastened together in front of him, self-consciously. Francie, serious, unsmiling, her dark, shiny curls successfully escaping the confines of the ribbon that strove to hold them back. She was a beauty. Charlie's eyes were riveted to the face that was a perfect replica of his darling Fanny, but flawless. Bertha, pale, curly hair tumbling down around her shoulders (he remembered the gold of it). Head tilted to one side, she beamed with an impish, teasing smile that gave her such warmth. Bertha exuded charm. The last likeness was of Winnie. What manner of child was she? A stick-like creature, all arms and legs and frizzy hair. Not quite four and yet with an independence of spirit and the total self-absorption of some eccentric academic. He lifted the photograph to his lips and kissed the thin little face. He opened the envelope wide, and turning it upside down, he shook it. No photograph of his darling Fanny. She would be heavy with his child now, and he realised that she would hate to have her photograph taken, obsessed as she was with her lip. Still, it would have meant so much to him to have a recent likeness to carry in his pocket. He thumbed through the photographs again. He should get some home leave soon. His eyes closed over the vision of his precious children. Unfolding the letter, he began to read.

151

Charlie, my love,

I was so happy to receive your last letter today, though some of it was difficult to decipher. The conditions out there must be quite horrible and to think of you scribbling your love for me on the fire step (whatever that may be) of a trench. It is little wonder that it was so hard to read. I will put a sharp pencil in your next parcel.

The part where you said you loved me and missed me was quite clearly written and I read it over and over and over again. How I wish this war would end, Charlie. I am only half a person without you and life is no life at all when you are so far away.

I must stop being maudlin and give you all our news. Sam is doing very well at school and his teacher says that his handwriting is remarkable for one so young. He has written a letter for you, which I have enclosed. The girls are all well. Francie and Bertha quarrel incessantly but join forces against the world if anyone tries to intercede. Bertha is a terrible flirt. I quite worry about her growing up as she makes eyes at everyone and everything, including the milkman's horse. Winnie keeps very much to herself. I sometimes wonder if she feels outside of things because Francie and Bertha are so close. She might have been more sociable if William had lived, or even Joe.

I hope the photographs will be a comfort to you. Jim has purchased a Box Brownie camera. It is the cleverest little thing that I have ever seen and he paid five whole shillings for it. He took the photographs of the children as a gift for you.

Connor continues to visit us at the weekends and it is such a comfort to be able to speak about you with him. The children love him; they call him 'Uncle Paddy' but he doesn't seem to mind.

It is so interesting to read about your young subaltern. How fortunate he is made by this strange coincidence.

I grow weary with the new baby and I shall be glad when it is born, especially as you will be home by then and we will be a little family again. We will never, never quarrel any more. Our being apart must surely have taught us how foolish we have been to have allowed dissension to arise between us.

Everybody asks about you, even the tradesmen, and the vicar includes you in the prayers each Sunday for those who are serving their country. There are a considerable number of men from this parish who are serving in Low Flanders.

I wait to hear from you, my love but even more, I wait to hold you and touch you and kiss you again.

With all my love, Fanny.

P.S. I will send a parcel next week. Try to let me know if there is anything you would particularly like and I shall endeavour to include it. You never ask for anything.

Charlie lay back on his blanket, the letter on his chest. He was crestfallen as he thought of how often he felt like crying in recent weeks. He lay there for several minutes as he went over and over the letter in his head, then he sat up and read it through again. Sam's letter was folded up very small and he opened it and smoothed it out on his upper thigh. The writing was, indeed, very mature, each letter beautifully formed, uniform in size and evenly spaced. He wrote of school and told of being chosen for the football team. He said that he was missing Charlie but that he would look after his mother and sisters until he came home because Ellen had said that he was the head of the family while Charlie was away. The girls sent their love.

Charlie pulled out his duffle bag from under the workbench beside his sleeping area and took out a biscuit tin. He put the letters and photographs into the tin and stowed it away again. That night, he slept well.

When on the front line, the officers and men considered themselves fortunate if they were able to catch six hours' sleep in twenty-four and so the battalion had been excused daily drill on their first morning and filled the time with answering letters from home and studying the latest newspapers, hoping to find out what was happening on other parts of the front. After breakfast, Charlie joined the line that marched to the baths.

When night came they would begin work repairing roads or carrying stores to the trenches. The work was not only back-breaking but dangerous, as the German searchlights would beam across the open ground and the enemy would strafe any area of movement with gun fire.

On return from one such nerve-wracking duty, Robert, having laid out his trousers, tunic and belt, collapsed into a deep sleep and was awoken with a start by the sound of horses' hooves clattering on the cobbles of the farmyard. He flung his legs over the side of his bunk and sat there listening intently. Presently an order came from the adjutant and he rose and dressed quickly.

Test all equipment. At last! They were advancing. The relief at anticipation of actually fighting instead of waiting around for the enemy to take pot shots overcame his fear. Dressed and briefed, he arrived to find the town astir with the activity of preparations for attack.

Chapter Twenty-Five

Robert could feel the pain as though it belonged to someone else. It was a contest between his utter fatigue and the throbbing in his shoulder, as to whether he should collapse into sleep or unconsciousness. While the battle had been raging the adrenalin had kept him alert and acted as an analgesic, but the Prussians had pulled back and an eerie silence had settled over the deserted meadow and he struggled to stay upright. He stood in a dip, which formed a natural breastwork, and leant forward against the bank. His eyes closed and his head began to whirl as tiredness swallowed him up. He was brought to attention with a shock by the sound of Captain Rutherford, like the voice of the Almighty, calling his name. He jumped to attention, a conditioned reaction, for he had no inkling of where he was.

Sleeping on duty, an offence punishable by death!

'What kind of an officer are you, man, when those under your command remain vigilant and you sleep. What in God's name were you thinking about? You realise that this is an offence of cataclysmic proportions. I have no alternative but to report you.' The captain's tirade was interrupted by another voice with a soft Irish brogue.

'Amen and thank you, Sir. I'm feeling much better. The power of prayer is a wonderful thing.' Turning to Captain Rutherford Charlie said, 'I beg your pardon, Sir, I didn't see you there. My eyes were closed for a moment while the Lieutenant was praying for me. I have been hit, Sir.' He displayed his blood-soaked side. 'I thought for a minute there I was going to die and we all know the Lieutenant is a godly man, so I asked him to pray and, Glory to God, I'm feeling quite better.'

'You gave me no opportunity to explain, Sir.' Robert, fully cognisant of the situation, now brought a note of umbrage into his voice. 'I was not asleep! I was beseeching the Lord for mercy on this man. Indeed, Sir, I will do anything for my King and Country but I do not interrupt my prayers for anyone. God comes first with me and if that is treason, then you must court martial me.' By now he had so convinced himself of his righteousness that he was filled with indignation and he felt an overwhelming sense of injustice.

The scarlet-faced Captain, confronted with this outpouring of resentment, muttered an apology and stammered that it was an easy mistake to make. Shamed in the presence of the Irish soldier, he dismissed him with instructions to go to the field station and have his wound attended to.

As Charlie moved away, Rutherford continued, 'Private.' Charlie turned back. 'God bless you.'

The incident passed off with no further mention. The Captain, shame-faced at his own insensitivity, wanted to forget the matter completely and Robert, after he had reflected on his narrow escape, was happy to let it go. He felt truly fortunate as, in retrospect, it seemed like a scene from a farce; he could hardly believe that the Captain had accepted such an unlikely excuse. He looked out for the Irishman, to thank him, but on the two occasions when he was close to him the other showed no sign of recognition and gave no opportunity for conferring.

Chapter Twenty-Six

Connor had become a regular visitor since that first night in August, and was now considered almost one of the family. He would bring little treats for the children, things that were never seen in the corner shop, and Fanny did not allow herself to worry too much from where they came. The children looked forward to Sundays and would stand in the parlour window watching for him. They squealed with delight when they caught sight of him looming up to the front door, and he never got time to clang the bell after that first Sunday afternoon.

'Uncle Paddy,' they would sing in unison as they raided the deep pockets of his jacket.

For his part, he adored them. He remembered the first time he'd seen them hanging onto Fanny's skirts and peeping out from behind her. They were so beautiful that he stood shaking his head slowly without speaking, his eyes travelling from one to the other in fascinated disbelief. Francie was dark with golden overtones like her mother, but Bertha! Bertha had the face of an angel and hair like pale, spun gold. Sam was the image of his father and he thought that Fanny must remember Charlie with total clarity of vision when she looked at his son. Winnie! She was like a mischievous little monkey.

Winter was upon them once again and Christmas came and went. It was the time of year which Fanny hated most, not only the short, dark days and unrelenting icy weather, but the remorseless memories of that grim night of William's death, that came back to haunt her as she sat alone in the flickering gaslight. She took no pleasure in Christmas and hated the celebration of both Sam's birthday and her own. This Christmas was profoundly worse than previous ones because Charlie was not with them, and she was glad when January arrived and the paper garlands and the tinsel, which had mocked at her grieving for two weeks, were put away for another year.

The baby was not due for four months but already she was

walking heavily upon her heels and she tired easily. She began to rely upon Ellen for the heavy work and, as always, her neighbour proved herself to be an invaluable friend.

The eight-year-old Francie was well able, and very willing, to help with small jobs around the house and could be relied upon to run messages to the corner shop. Both she and Bertha were growing up fast. They would sit in front of the dressing table in their bedroom and dust their faces with flour and colour their lips with cochineal from the kitchen. When Winnie asked to be included in these charades, they would join forces against her, push her out of the room and put a chair under the handle, denying her access.

'Go away, Winnie. You're too young,' Francie would shout.

'Yes and ugly, too,' Bertha added. 'Skinny Winnie! Skinny Winnie!'

Winnie, far from being offended, would pre-empt her expulsion and add to her plainness with grotesque contortions of her face and a fulsome display of her tongue, then, lifting the back of her skirt to show her bottom, would flounce away laughing.

There were times of deep melancholy, when one of the children would be reminded of Charlie. A depression would descend over the whole household and the girls would become tearful, but it was Sam who missed him most of all. He felt a dull ache in the pit of his stomach whenever he thought about his father.

When spring came, Fanny felt a flutter of excitement because Charlie was due leave, and she dared to hope she would have given birth before he came. She wondered whether spring-cleaning the house might accelerate it, but she was too weary to do more than contemplate it briefly. She would lie in bed in the early morning and listen to the first birdsong of the season and plan for Charlie's return. Her hand would move in a leisurely fashion over the sheet beside her and she would imagine waking to find him lying there. In her musing, he would hold out his arms and draw her close and he would kiss her hair, her throat, her breasts and they would make love until they touched the edge of heaven. Her body shuddered with remembered ecstasy.

'I must have this baby before he comes,' she would whisper to herself. 'Please, God, don't let me be fat and cumbersome when Charlie returns.' And she would run her hands over her distended belly, as though feeling the shape of the baby that lay within but it refused to leave the drowsy comfort of her womb.

Chapter Twenty-Seven

Just at daybreak the regiment began to move forward across the meadow. Now in the cold light of morning, it lay quiet and still under a heavy mist. The atmosphere was eerie and a sense of foreboding hung like vapour over the scene.

Robert had drunk some tea but he had been unable to eat even the sparse breakfast of bread and butter. He had had an almost sleepless night, spent preparing for battle. Trenches were to be dug under cover of darkness and exits cut into the wire and filled temporarily with coiled barbed wire. After he had lain down, the nagging pain from his lower back sent spasms through him, and his body and mind had ached with an unsatisfied desire for oblivion, but the tension and the thunder of gunfire had prevented all but the slightest drift of sleep.

Shaving and dressing had been a torture, and he had wondered, 'were these the same bones and sinews that had yearned for this confrontation with youthful urgency and longing?'

But now they were advancing, and Robert could just make out the holes where a patrol had audaciously crept up on their bellies through the darkness, and cut the wires in front of the enemy parapet. When he considered the agony of crawling over such a distance in the darkness, clutching heavy wire cutters, and the fear as they lay yards from the Germans, severing the wire, then inching their way back, a paralysing terror came over him.

'How did I ever think that I had had the makings of a soldier?' he asked himself. It seemed that the lowliest rank in the army had more mettle than he.

He watched the first wave of men rise and break into a charge. As they reached the bottom of the shallow rise, they were mown down by enfilade but by this time, the second wave was charging forward to take their place. With only the slightest pause they, too, fell under a salvo of bullets. Nevertheless, they were followed by a third wave and by the time they were up and running, those remaining from the advanced sorties, were through the German defences, bayonets fixed and charging the enemy's front line. The German gunners joined in the hand-to-hand fighting, which gave time for the following lines to charge.

Now it was Robert's turn and he was urging his men forward, over their dead comrades until they, too, were falling into the carpet of bodies. The Germans were firing again now and bullets whistled past Robert's head as he moved forward in a trance. As he saw his men falling around him, his fear turned to rage and he plunged into the Prussian trenches, bayonet stabbing again and again and again. Fury seethed within him, obscuring all other emotions. The Germans were no longer human beings; they had no more humanity in them than the hanging sacks upon which he had been trained in another life, in another country. He didn't count how many he slaughtered after the first three, but he couldn't stop. He raged until there was no one left upon whom to empty his fury.

He could hear orders being shouted in German, too rapid for him to decipher, and the enemy began to drift away. He climbed up onto the parapet of the trench and watched them retreat. He lifted his hands high in the air and threw back his head in hysterical laughter.

A bullet whizzed past his head yet he did not realise that it had grazed his skull because all other feeling was blunted by the wrenching pain that shot through his shoulder as he was pushed to the ground from behind. Clutching the wound with one hand he heaved the weight that had fallen upon his body off him, and turned to gaze into the face of the Irishman. He looked unharmed. His eyes were open, but glazed over and when he tried to speak, the effort was too great. Robert put his ear to the other's mouth.

'Tell Fanny I love her. Find ... her ... tell her ... I'm sorry.'

'Find her where? Where, man, tell me?'

'Liverpool. Find ... tell her ... my Little Goose'. The words ended abruptly and his head fell to one side.

Robert put his arm around the man and lifted him, then feeling the oozing discharge between the shoulder blades, withdrew his blood-soaked hand, staring at the viscous crimson in frozen horror. He clung on to Charlie as he had clung on to the dead soldier in the trench on the night they first met, but that had been merely a

160

rehearsal for the scene that was being played out now. This was the epitome of all his agonies. This was to drain the last of his tears; to end all weeping. He would never cry again.

Chapter Twenty-Eight

Searing pain broke through the constant throbbing of his shoulder with every jolt of the stretcher as he was carried to the casualty clearing station. Throughout the night Robert had drifted in and out of consciousness, unable to distinguish between what were his nightmares and the reality of his situation.

A doctor made a hurried examination, after which, Robert was conscious of firm, strong hands that wound the dressing around his head and beneath his chin. The same hands gently lifted him and cut away his jacket, as he slipped into oblivion again.

Struggling up through swirling, blue-black waters until he broke the surface, he emerged into the half-light of the grey evening. He was able to look now at the appalling number of casualties that surrounded him, and could hear the moans of the other anguished victims of the terrible battle. The stench of blood and, inexplicably, the smell of iron, overwhelmed him. He could taste it in his mouth and it caught in the back of his throat, adding considerably to his discomfort. He lay there for some time, watching the fast-moving, fat grey clouds scudding across the sky, desolation wrapping itself around him like a black shroud. Eventually he was lifted back onto the stretcher, and it began again, the rhythmic, searing pain with every step, as he was carried to the hospital train.

On the journey to the port where the Royal Mail Steam Packet ship was docked, waiting to carry a thousand wounded and dying adversaries, men of both factions, back to England, Robert relived the last fateful hours of the battle before he had surrendered to the onslaught of the pain.

Had the Irishman been a real flesh and blood person, or was he some angelic spirit, a guardian angel? He had heard, though with much cynicism, of the angelic host that appeared over the battlefield at Mons. He had never spoken to anybody else who had seen the Irishman, and yet he had appeared to Robert at every

162

moment of crisis. If he lived through this, he would seek out the other men in the regiment and enquire if they knew of this man who had lost his life, so that Robert might keep his.

A huge lump in the back of his throat was preventing him from breathing properly. He swallowed hard.

Remembering how Charlie had come between himself and a hail of bullets, so that only one had grazed his head, and one entered his shoulder, he squeezed his eyes tightly to halt the tears that oozed from beneath his lashes. Clickety clack, clickety clack, clickety clack. Mercifully, he once again swooned.

As dawn broke, the liner was steaming up Southampton Water. Never had England looked so beautiful to those patients who lined the deck rails, even in their waking dreams at the front. The view of the ship was beautiful, too, to the blue and grey-clad figures along the waterfront, who watched her sail majestically past the Military Hospital at Netley.

The magnificent red-brick building, nestling in the woodland that edged the shore, stretched for a quarter of a mile along the water-front. The early morning sun, glinting off its windows, gave it an ethereal aura of radiance. It could have been the inspiration for Xanadu with its walls and towers and gracious dome, surmounted by a cupola.

The final leg of the wounded men's journey covered the few short miles to what was to become their home, prison or mortuary depending upon their nationality and the extent of their wounds.

His stretcher came to rest on the floor in a long corridor that extended across the full width of the hospital, hard and unyielding beneath Robert's back, as he waited for a bed in one of the officers' wards. As he lay there, eyes closed, feeling the sun cutting a swathe of warmth through the raw air, he felt a movement by his head and turned to look.

There beside him was a pair of stout legs, strafed with crimson scorch-marks that showed through the stockings. He had seen those legs before. His eyes followed them up over ample hips covered by a navy-blue dress, and continued to the starched white Matron's cap set above an all too familiar face, which looked upon the reclining subaltern with a maliciously obvious recognition. If lips can purse and smile at the same time, then that is what Robert saw! He heard a familiar snort, and walking past him followed by a small entourage,

163

she moved to the next patient and gave the orderlies instructions for this man's relocation and comfort.

But Robert remained uncomforted, resentful and regretful.

Eventually, he was moved to a ward and to the consolation of a real bed, though Netley was overcrowded to the point where men were being accommodated in marquees in the hospital grounds.

Robert's recovery was slow and left him too much time to think. He went over the incidents with Charlie again and again, in his head. It was as though there were some subconscious link between the two of them. Almost as though Charlie were with him, living in him, through him. He felt such a warmth of love of, and closeness to, the Irishman whom he had barely known. As though he would never be alone again. Charlie would always be with him. A heart-wrenching melancholy welled up in him whenever he remembered the older man's selflessness.

The wound to his head had almost healed but his shoulder was proving more resistant to treatment.

He was cheered by a letter he received from Sophie, telling him they had been informed that he was in Netley and she and Eleanor were coming down to visit him on Wednesday. But he was saddened by neither letter from, nor news of, Cecilia. Wednesday morning dawned crisp and bright and, by six o'clock, he was washed and anxiously waiting for his mother's and sister's visit, but the day dragged on. Breakfast came and went without their arrival. He got through the morning trying, without much success, to concentrate on the *Tatler*, and by lunchtime was feeling quite dejected. At two o'clock precisely, Sophie hurtled down the ward ahead of her mother, running in her eagerness to be with her brother. She flung her arms around him and burst into floods of tears.

'Darling Robert, how I've missed you. We really thought that you were going to die. You have no idea how difficult it has been for us, not knowing how you were. I'm just so relieved and happy that you are all right.' Robert winced as her arm made contact with his shoulder. 'Oh, you poor darling. Your poor shoulder.'

Gently, he eased her away with his right arm.

'Have you any news of Cissy? Do you know if she is coming to see me? I haven't had a letter from her in weeks. Is she all right?'

He shot the questions out like the rattle of a machine gun, and Sophie fell back, crestfallen. Here she was, having travelled all this way. She had ached with unsatisfied longing to be with him, and he thought only of that dreadful, selfish girl. She hated her! The whole world was half in love with Cecilia, and she received that affection as her due, without gratitude or requital. Sophie had watched her at the Hunt Ball dancing and flirting shamelessly with the young officers who were fortunate enough to be on leave, or remaining in England, while Robert suffered all kinds of horrors at the front.

Her face crimsoned with fury.

'Hallo, my darling.' Eleanor had come alongside the bed now and was leaning over to kiss Robert on the cheek. 'How are you my brave boy? It is so good to see you sitting up and looking so well.'

'I'm very much better, now. My head's almost healed and the doctor says my shoulder will recover fully in time. Mother, I can't tell you how wonderful it is to see you. Wonderful!' he reiterated, the intensity of his feelings, causing his voice to break.

'Your father would have come down with us but he had a very important meeting in London. He sends his love, of course.'

'Have you seen Cissy lately? Is she all right?'

'She and Rosemary came over to The Hamptons for tea yesterday. Yes, she was looking very well and so pretty. She can't wait to see you; she is missing you so much. I asked her if she would like to accompany us today, but unfortunately she had an appointment at her dressmaker's. She was saying that she must look her best when you arrive home.'

How shallow the waiting world seemed, after the intensity of the struggle for survival a few hundred miles away. This was another life, concerned only with the pomp of London meetings or occupied with such trifles as organza and chiffon. He no longer had anything in common with these people, except perhaps with Sophie, who at least displayed some empathy with his ordeal. These were his closest relatives, and yet he felt a greater bond of brotherhood with a dead Irishman, the dead Irishman whose shadow haunted his waking and sleeping. Suddenly he wished them gone, but the afternoon dragged on with no less celerity than the morning of yearning for them.

Cecilia arrived on Monday, looking elegant and lovely in maroon velvet trimmed with dark fur. She brought no offering, no token of affection that might have evidenced some previous kind thoughts of him. As she leant over to brush her cheek against his she whispered, conspiratorially, 'How I hate hospitals.'

'My dearest Cissy, thank you so much for coming. You can have no idea how much I have longed to see you. I've missed you more than

165

I can say. I thought about you all the time, pined for you. Oh, Cissy.'
He buried his face in the fur of her collar and wrestled with the
emotions that engulfed him.

Cecilia's eyes above his bent head widened and swept wildly across
the ward. She was totally unaccustomed to exuberant shows of
affection in public, and did not care to be the subject of what
seemed to her to be a reprehensible over-reaction to her presence.
She revelled in a relationship which made her its whole existence,
but was incapable of returning such exclusive devotion. Her eyes
sought a passing nurse and silently implored her to intervene, but
she was oblivious to Cecilia's discomfort and Robert clung on still
more tenaciously.

At last, when his passion had subsided, he implored her, 'Can we
be married before I return to the front?'

'Oh Robert, darling, surely you won't be going back. It will be an
age before you are fit again and the war will be over by then.' She
saw his face, disconsolate and dejected, and continued, 'But of
course we can marry anyway, as soon as you would like. I shall start
arranging it immediately.'

He relinquished his hold on her, and once again she settled into
the more familiar setting of graceful manners and good breeding.
Cecilia had no reluctance to being a bride. Indeed, she thrilled
at her idealised vision of herself, attired in voluminous silk and
lace, poignantly pronouncing her vows to love, honour and obey
an heroic and romantic young subaltern, before a saintly vicar in
the picturesque village church. She did not look beyond the
fantasy

And so, a marriage was arranged.

Much to Eleanor's dismay, the weeks that followed were turbulent
in the extreme, with frantic arrangements for a wedding by special
licence. To her mind, it was unseemly to marry in such haste and
would, without a doubt, cause much speculative gossip. She had
long envisaged, for both of her children, the glamorous festivities
that would surpass any wedding celebration of their generation. She
was beginning to abandon her hopes for Sophie, who would, she
felt sure, never find any man who would compare with any degree of
favour to her younger brother, but for Robert ... It would be so
much more sensible to wait just a little while, until the war was over
and things became more plentiful. A wartime wedding would, of
necessity, be a compromise.

166

Rosemary, too, would have liked more time to organise the reception and other requirements, but she said nothing and, as always, accommodated everybody else's wishes. Despite these forebodings, the wedding was a great success and Robert was able to walk to the altar unaided. The bride, resplendent in white, was radiantly happy, delighted to be the sole object of admiration and well satisfied with her handsome, gallant groom.

They spent their honeymoon in London visiting the theatres and concert halls and shopping in the West End, and it was during these early gay and carefree days of marriage that their first child was conceived.

Robert, his body restored to full health, returned to France before Cecilia's confinement.

Chapter Twenty-Nine

It was a truly happy house as Fanny and the children prepared for Charlie's homecoming. Sam, Francie and Bertha, with their newly washed bodies and damp, curling hair glowing in the dancing firelight, sat around the table in their nightclothes, making streamers from coloured paper. From time to time, little good-natured squabbles would break out and be reconciled in showers of childish laughter, and Fanny would smile with warm contentment. It was a long time since she had felt such happiness.

The bell began to clang as it swung on its spring, and the three children jumped down from the table and raced to reach the front door first.

The tin bath stood in front of the fire and Fanny was bathing Winnie in the water that had previously sluiced away the dirt from Sam, Francie and Bertha. A large towel of some indeterminate colour lay across what would have been her lap, were it not for the swell of her stomach. One edge of it dropped into the water as a victorious Francie tumbled through the doorway holding aloft the orange envelope with obvious pleasure. Fanny slowly wiped her hand on the corner of the towel, and without turning her head to look at it, took the telegram from her eldest daughter and pushed it into the pocket of her striped money-apron. Tears rolled down her cheeks from unblinking eyes. The children fell silent, bewilderment showing in their faces. They knew from the sequence of events that the cause was that inoffensive-looking envelope; but how could it cause Ma so much pain when she hadn't yet opened it?

Fanny lifted Winnie out of the tub and rose slowly, unseeingly and silently left the room.

That night Bernard was born.

Fanny had hardly felt the pain of his birth, because the pain of her loss overwhelmed all other feelings. She wanted to die; anguish swallowed her up so that she existed in a blackness that was not of

168

this world. She could not cry, and she felt nothing except this deep, griping agony of abject misery. She was unaware of the child which she had just birthed; she was unaware of her other children, huddled inside the door of her room, mystified and full of fear. She knew only the unrelenting pain of her misery. Charlie was gone!

Ellen was roused from her nap by the sound of Sam banging on the door and screaming her name.

'Good gracious, Jim, what on earth can be wrong?' She hurried to open the door to reveal the child, dressed only in his underwear, tears streaming down his face. 'What's the matter Sam? Is it the baby? Is it comin'?'

Sam, ignoring the question, grabbed her hand and begged, 'Please, Ellen. Ellen, please. Please come.'

Filled with apprehension, she threw her shawl around her shoulders and shouted to Jim. 'I'm just goin' next door. I think it's the baby but there's somethin' terrible wrong.'

Winnie stood frozen, naked and wet in the doorway. Bertha was at the head of the staircase crying plaintively and shouting, 'Aunty Ellen, Aunty Ellen, up here.'

When she reached the top of the staircase, breathless and in great anxiety, she found Fanny lying lifeless on the bed, the skirt of her dress caught up, and a small, red infant lay crying between her thighs. Francie was trying to lift the child but it was still fastened to its mother by the cord. For a moment Ellen thought that Fanny was dead, until a moan escaped her lips and she moved her head from side to side. The pathos of the scene caused Ellen to fall back against the bedpost, but with great effort, she composed herself and went into action.

Ushering the children out of the room, she said to Sam, 'Take Winnie downstairs an' dress 'er, then take 'er an' Bertha to our 'ouse an' tell Uncle Jim I said you were to stay there. Francie, you get some towels an' a pair of scissors. Where does your ma keep her sewin' things?'

Sam guided the two girls out of the bedroom, but Francie stood in the corner of the room sobbing, the top button of her nightdress in her mouth, shaking her head. It was evident to Ellen that the girl was traumatised.

'Sam,' she called after the retreating boy, 'ask Uncle Jim for some white tape out of my sewin' basket. 'Urry now.' And to Francie, 'You go with them. Go now!'

169

Francie shot out of the room like a frightened mouse and stumbled down the stairs. When she reached the foot, she huddled into the corner of the hall beneath the staircase, threw her nightdress over her head and continued to sob.

Ellen turned her attention to her friend, lying like a corpse on top of the counterpane. She dragged the cover from beneath her, laid it over the end of the bed and covered her with a sheet, carefully lifting the baby and arranging it around him. Taking Fanny's hand in hers, she slapped it.

'Fanny, Fanny, can you 'ear me.' But the only response was that deep, mournful moan. 'Do you 'ave any brandy in the 'ouse?' Still there was no reply. 'Dear God, I could do with some 'elp 'ere,' she muttered.

The sound of the bell clanging reverberated through the house.

'The children 'ave left the latch on,' she muttered to herself, but before she could reach the door of the room she heard Francie opening the door and shouting, 'Uncle Paddy, Ma's dead!'

Francie threw herself at Connor and he lifted her in his arms and held her tightly. Looking up, he saw Ellen at the top of the stairs, crouching down to see who it was.

'Connor,' she shouted, 'Thank God you're 'ere.'

Still clinging on to Francie, he took the stairs two at a time.

'Miss Fanny's dead?'

'No, no, but she's in a proper state. I've only just got 'ere meself. She's 'ad 'er baby but God knows what's been 'appenin'.'

She stood aside for Connor to enter, and placing Francie on the floor outside, he went into the room and crossed to where Fanny lay like a cadaver in a morgue. Sam returned with the scissors and tape and Ellen deftly cut and tied the cord. She had slipped up to the girl's room as Connor passed and now wrapped the child in the sheet she had brought from their bed. Whilst she was doing this, Connor faced away for the sake of Fanny's modesty, and as he did so, he caught sight of the white paper lying beside the distinctive, orange envelope on the washstand.

'Oh, no!' he gasped. 'Oh, dear mother of God, no!' He picked up the telegram, read it and reread it, turned towards the supine figure and moved across to the bedside. 'Oh, my poor Miss Fanny.' He placed his arm behind her head and, lifting it to rest against his chest, he stretched out his other arm behind him towards Ellen and, wordlessly, handed her the telegram.

170

'Give her the baby,' he instructed Ellen.

Whilst Ellen, now openly weeping, brought the infant, Connor, with great effort, for she was a dead weight, lifted Fanny in the bed until she was half sitting and Ellen laid the baby in her lifeless arms.

'It's no good,' she said, as Fanny made no move to support the child, 'she's unconscious.'

But Connor held her arms around the tiny bundle. He could not secure the child in her grasp because her fist was closed like a steel trap, and as he prised it open, a mahogany-coloured shell, spotted and strafed with cream, fell to the floor.

'Can you undo her buttons so that she can suckle him?'

As Ellen did as she was told, the baby began to suck voraciously. Fanny's eyelids fluttered open for a second and life came back into her arms as she lay with her new born infant nestling in them.

She had wanted to call the baby Charles, but his name was a knife in her heart and so, remembering that Charlie had spoken of his younger brother Bernard, she named him for the Cahills.

Chapter Thirty

Thirteen months later, over two hundred miles away, another child was about to be born.

Cecilia turned sideways to look at herself in the cheval glass. She turned away in horror. How could Robert have done this to her? For the sake of a few moments of excitement, he had made her pregnant and then swanned off to play at being soldiers again, and had left her alone, growing more gross with every passing week. She eased herself down onto the bed, belly up, and covered her face with her hands. The baby moved inside of her and she lowered her arms so that her hands could feel the contours of the child.

'Monster,' she spat out the word viciously. 'Just you stop doing that, or I won't be responsible for my actions.' She gave her stomach a sharp slap, hoping that the thing that had grown inside of her would feel the pain. She hated it almost as much as she hated the man who had caused it.

A shaft of spring sunlight penetrated the shadows in the room and where it fell upon the eiderdown, it transformed the material from a moth-grey colour to a rich, vibrant pink. Turning her head to the side, she traced a flower with her finger. She should be out on this beautiful day, at a regatta or a garden party, in her new organza frock, which she had had no opportunity to wear since her so-called honeymoon. She closed her eyes and visualised herself walking with a spring in her step, all her admirers falling over each other to get closer to her, as she flirted with each in turn. There was no harm in it, of course. It was just an innocent bit of fun, and yet she longed to meet someone new and exciting, to feel her pulse racing again at the prospect of charming some young devotee.

'Some hope!' she thought and she opened her eyes and looked down at herself. Who would look at her like that again? She was like a beached whale. She would never, never be the same. She hated Robert more than she thought possible.

And now he was coming home. Well, at least she would not have to endure his sexual advances. In her condition, no one could expect her to share her bed with him.

'Never, never, never.' She thumped the pillow aggressively and then buried her head in its downy softness.

Robert, totally unaware of his young wife's emotional turmoil, sat comfortably in the corner of the carriage, anticipating the rapture of their reunion. He was on his way home and his child was about to be born. A warm contentment flooded through him. He hoped it would be a son. It would be nice to have a little girl but she would come later. Yes, they should have a boy this time. Someone to look after his sister and see that she came to no harm. It was always useful for a girl to have an older brother to introduce her to the right kind of chap as she grew up and to make sure that no unsuitable fellow made advances to her. Good heavens! She was not even conceived yet and he was marrying her off already. Still one had to plan ahead, make sure that she didn't mix with the wrong class of people.

His mind went, once again, to the Irishman. He would have been considered the wrong class of man, but Robert would have been proud for any daughter of his to marry a man like Charles Cahill.

It had taken some time to identify the private who had sacrificed his life for him, but he had eventually tracked down his records and, now that he had, he'd determined to honour the dead man's request to visit his Fanny in Liverpool. He wondered what he would find there, some poor, uneducated woman, worn out before her time, no doubt. But that was for another day.

Right now he was almost home, and this time it was for good. It was worth the constant pain of his wound to be out of that hell and back in England.

The train was approaching his station so he stood up, lifted down his valise and moved eagerly towards the door. He pulled on the sash that lowered the window and as he stuck out his head, he caught sight of the small group of people standing apart from those waiting to board the train. He felt an awkwardness, a slight panic, as though he were about to sit an examination. As the train drew into the platform, he recognised his parents and Sophie, but of Cecilia there was no sign.

'She's probably waiting in the car,' he thought. She was, of course, very close to her time and so he should never have expected her to venture out of the vehicle.

Opening the door and stepping onto the platform, he embraced his mother, at the same time shaking hands with his father who stood behind her.

'Darling boy, it's so wonderful to see you and you look so well. Let me have a good look at you. It has been so long.'

Robert disentangled himself from his mother's grasp and turned to hug Sophie, and looking over her shoulder asked, 'Where's Cissy? Is she in the car?'

'Rosemary thought it better for her to wait for you at home. The baby is due at any time now and the poor dear has been so sickly. Come, let's get you into the motor car. I'm sure you're absolutely exhausted after your long journey and longing to be home. You can tell us all about your great adventure over tea.'

They came out of the station to where the car stood waiting and, still, Robert could not resist looking around to see if Cecilia had come in another car.

They were quiet on the drive home, each feeling inhibited, like strangers meeting for the first time. Robert sat morosely looking out of the window but the drive was quite short and soon they were drawing up to The Hamptons. Tomlinson opened the door and stepped forward to take Robert's valise.

'Welcome home, Sir,' he said and stepped aside to let Robert pass. 'Tea is in the drawing room, Sir.'

'Thank you, Tomlinson, is Miss Cecilia in there?' He handed the servant his cap and swagger stick and strode quickly to open the drawing room door.

From behind him, Tomlinson answered, 'No, Sir. Miss Cecilia is not here.'

Robert's eyes swept around the room and then turned to look at his mother.

'She didn't come, darling. I suppose she is waiting for you at The Cedars. You can get over there as soon as you've had your tea.'

He looked at her in amazement. How could he think of tea at a time like this? He had waited for months to see Cissy and when, at last, he had thought to hold her in his arms, to feel their precious child moving in her womb, she was not here. Then it occurred to him that the family must have been keeping something from him. Something disastrous had happened, something was terribly wrong.

'What's happened? What's wrong with her? Is the baby all right? What is it you're not telling me?'

'Shush, now,' Eleanor tried to calm him, 'she's fine. They're both fine. She's just a little tired. Come and have a cup of tea and then Dorcas will drive you over.'

'No, I must go now. I'm sorry, Mother, would you mind if I forget the tea and go straight away? I'd expected that she would be here with you. I don't understand. After all, she is my wife.'

He turned and called out, 'Dorcas,' and as the man appeared in the entrance hall, 'can you drive me over to The Cedars straight away?' He picked up his cap and swagger stick from the hall table and went out into the drive.

'It's too bad,' Eleanor muttered in bewilderment. 'All this time I have waited to see my son and he can't even stay long enough for a cup of tea.'

'It's that dreadful woman's fault.' The bitterness sounded in Sophie's voice. 'One would have thought that she would have been here for her husband's homecoming. Poor Robert, he's distraught. He's beginning to see to what sort of a creature he has got himself married. Oh, I hate her, Mother!' she added, vehemently.

'Now, Sophie, don't talk like that. Just wait until you are nine months pregnant and see how you feel then!' But, secretly, Eleanor was very much inclined to agree with her.

'Can we have some tea now? I'm starving.' The Colonel, who had been quiet throughout the contretemps, now spoke up, bringing his womenfolk back to a semblance of normality, but tea was awkward and conversation was forced as everyone strained to contain their opinions.

It took Dorcas twelve minutes from door to door, and as they drove the last few hundred yards through the long arch of cedar trees, Robert's fingers were already around the door handle. Before the car had come to a complete stop, he had flung himself out of the vehicle and up the steps of the house, and was hammering the huge knocker.

The door was opened by the housekeeper, with Rosemary following closely behind.

'Robert, my dear, come in.' Demurely, she turned her cheek to be kissed. 'Cecilia is just having a lie down.' Turning, she continued, 'Mrs Simpson, would you run upstairs and tell Miss Cecilia that

Captain Robert is here?' She made to put her arm through Robert's and lead him into the drawing room, but he slipped out of her grasp.

'Mrs Simonstone, mayn't I go up and tell her myself?' Before she could answer, he was taking the stairs two at a time. Reaching the top, he turned and looked over the balustrade. 'Which is our room?' he called down.

'You will find her in the room straight ahead at the end of the gallery. She may be asleep. I wouldn't ...' but before she could finish he was gone from her sight.

At the end of the gallery, he drew in his breath and, gently laying his hand on the ornate handle, he slowly and soundlessly eased it down until he felt it click and the door glide open.

The room was darkened, but a shaft of sunlight fell across the bed and, as his eyes adjusted, he was aware of a fussily feminine room with a heavy scent of musk that caught at his throat and made him feel faintly sick. Across the bed, swathed in a frilly lace peignoir that fell open to reveal the swell of her belly, Cecilia lay, unmoving. At first he thought her to be sleeping, but as he walked lightly across the room to where she lay, she became aware of his presence and gave a start. She tried to rise but the immensity of her stomach held her down as rigidly as any straitjacket and, unable to right herself, she began to panic.

'Who is it? What do you want? Knock before you come into my room!' Her voice was strident.

Robert had reached the bed by now and, leaning over, he placed a hand on either side of her and, smiling, lowered his mouth towards hers. She turned her face to avoid the contact of his lips.

'Robert. Robert! How could you sneak up on me like that? You gave me such a fright. Didn't anybody teach you to knock before you enter somebody's bedroom?'

Robert drew away from her. He placed his right arm under her shoulders, his right knee on the bed beside her, and lifted her into a sitting position.

'I wanted to surprise you, Cissy.'

'Oh, you did that all right,' she growled. 'Go downstairs and wait for me. I'll be down in a moment.'

'You don't seem very glad to see me.' It was a bald statement, delivered in a plaintive whine, which made her despise him the more.

'Of course I'm glad to see you. I just don't want you to see me like this. Please, Robert,' she placed her hand in the middle of his chest and pushed him away, 'go and talk to Mummy while I make myself presentable. Well, as presentable as possible under the circumstances.'

'You look beautiful. Can't I stay here and help you. Oh, Cissy, I've missed you so much. I can't tell you how I've longed for this moment. Please, don't shut me out. Let's stay up here for a while longer; we've got so much to talk about. I don't want to be with anybody else just now. I want it to be just the three of us.' He took a step forward and, with pain and pleasure mingling in him, tenderly placed his hand on the swell of her stomach,

She knocked it away impatiently. 'Don't be tiresome, Robert. I'm not in the mood.'

Robert's bewilderment turned to alarm. 'What is the matter, Cissy? Why are you so cold? I really had expected you to meet me at the station, or at least to be at The Hamptons when I got home but I have to come over here and then you treat me like an intruder. For God's sake, woman, you're my wife.'

'There's no need for blasphemy and there is no need to remind me that I'm your wife. If you're not going to be civil to me, you may just as well go now. In case you haven't noticed, I am about to give birth to this ... this ... child. You've abandoned me all through this wretched pregnancy and now you think you can swan back into my life and start taking over, talking to me like some little housemaid. Well you can't.' By this time her voice was echoing through the house. 'Now I feel quite ill.'

They were both startled by a timid knock. Rosemary placed her ear against the door, her heart beating fast against the wall of her chest. Always verging on acerbity, her daughter had become impossible during her confinement, and poor Robert had walked straight into it unawares. She knocked again, more boldly now.

'Would you like to come down and have tea?'

Robert strode out of the room, competing emotions struggling for control. His eyes stung with anger or unhappiness, he himself could not have told which. Running down the stairs and stopping only to pick up his cap and swagger stick, he made to leave, but Rosemary, almost tripping over her own diminutive feet as she hastened after him, called, 'Robert, my dear, please don't go just yet. Come into the drawing room so that I may talk to you.' She had

177

caught up with him and was holding onto his sleeve with tiny, bony fingers. He acquiesced and permitted her to lead him into the room, where tea was laid out on a trolley.

'Please be patient with her. She has had a difficult time. Cecilia has been so used to having all her own way. Her father spoiled her dreadfully when he was alive and the result has been that she is quite fractious at times but you are the best thing that has ever happened to her. She became less ... wilful when she first met you. You seemed to have had a beneficial effect on her and I was so happy when you married. She will be different after the baby is born if you can just be patient with her, dear Robert ... please?'

There was a pleading in her voice and Robert warmed, once again, to this diffident little woman. Perhaps Cissy was entitled to be a bit brusque and bristly in this phase of her pregnancy. He moved to Rosemary's side and placed an arm around her slight shoulders. She barely reached his armpit and he felt her fragility and vulnerability.

They drank their tea in silence and he was rising to leave when the door opened and Cecilia walked in, now dressed in an elegant cranberry-coloured velvet gown, which was far more becoming than the lace. She came straight over to where he stood and took the cup and saucer from his hand, placing it on the table. Her arms wrapped themselves around his neck and in a cajoling voice she purred, 'Robert, my darling, I'm so sorry. It was just that you took me by surprise and I so wanted to look nice for you when you came home but just look what a mess I am. I know that you must be horrified at the very sight of me but I'll be rid of this lump soon and quite back to normal. Kiss me and tell me you forgive me.' Her eyes closed and she lifted her face to be kissed.

Robert hesitated for only a moment, glancing at Rosemary who slowly shook her head, then leaning forward to circumvent her massive stomach he kissed his wife on the lips.

Chapter Thirty-One

Cecilia lay red-faced and livid, the child lying quietly beside her in its crib.

Robert ventured, 'I am so glad he is a boy. I wanted a son first.'

'First, first? Never again!' she hissed venomously. 'No more children, ever, ever, ever! I don't know how you can even think of it after what I have endured. I have gone through purgatory for your sake.'

She turned over, her back towards Robert, her martyrdom exhibited as profoundly as any tormented saint. 'Have you no compassion? I almost died. I think I could still die and already you are talking of putting me through this again. Go away! I hate you!'

'You don't mean that, darling. You are just exhausted after your ordeal. You'll be all right in a few days, and we don't have to have any more children if you don't want them.'

He concealed his distress admirably, but he had a dull ache in his gut. Somehow, he felt, Cissy always managed to impair the pleasure of every joyful event. She expected to be pampered in all situations, as a child might, and he was wearying of her constant grousing and carping.

She did not want to be 'churched' as 'she had nothing to thank God for', she simply refused to breastfeed the child as 'no lady would entertain the thought of doing anything so odious', and she left the care of her son to the nanny as 'that's what she is paid for'. She remained in bed for two weeks, though the doctor told her that she needed to exercise if she wanted to regain her slender figure. She responded that she just wanted to be left alone to die. Robert spent hours by her bedside encouraging her to take an interest in the child, and pleading with her at least to take a walk in the garden. At the end of the second week he approached the subject of the child's christening.

'The vicar can fit us in next Sunday at three o'clock. Everything is

179

ready. Your mother wants him to wear your christening robe and we really need to discuss a name for the little mite and whom we will ask to be his godparents.'

'Whatever you want.'

'Cecilia, you really must start taking an interest.' He recognised the beginning of impatience in his voice and breathed in deeply before modulating it. 'I thought we might ask Sophie to be godmother.'

'Tut! If that's what you think.'

'Cissy, I'd like him to be called Charles.' No response. 'What do you think about that?' No response. 'Cissy, we need to discuss these things, darling.' Then, trying an approach more close to her heart, he went on, 'What are you going to wear? Would you like me to take you into London to choose an outfit for the occasion?'

She stirred at this, and turned over to face him. 'When would we go?' She sat up in the bed. 'Sophie can be godmother if it's what you want, but I hope she makes a bit of an effort. She always looks so dowdy. Perhaps we could ask that nice Daniel Carter-Simms to be godfather. He was so good to me when you first went back, and I'm sure he's a good Christian and would be a fine guardian of, what's his name, Charles? We have no Charles in the family, as far as I know, but it's a good, strong name. Yes, I like that; Charles.'

Robert thrilled inside at this token of success. And Cecilia, encouraged by the thought of being the centre of attention in a new ensemble, managed to rise from her bed.

'Well,' she thought, 'the little monster will, no doubt, think it's his day but I'll show him. I'll wrap him up so tightly in the stupid christening robe that no one will see him.'

Robert, mistaking her smile for pleasure and delighted that her melancholy had receded so suddenly, took the chance to approach another contentious matter while she was still in good humour.

'You know that Sophie has been seeing Frank Ferguson and I think it is rather serious. I know that he is very much older than her but she is very mature. He's an elder at St Stephen's and, since a baby boy should have two godfathers, I wondered how you would feel about asking Frank to be the other one.' Before she could answer he continued, 'It would really please Sophie and I should like it, too. It seems very fitting that Charles should have a pillar of the church to oversee his spiritual development.'

Cecilia, still considering whether she should wear ecru, which suited her complexion so well and made her look demure and interesting, or should buy pink to brighten her pallid skin, replied absently, 'Of course, dear, whatever you think.'

Sunday dawned, a bright and glorious midsummer day, and Cecilia, splendidly attired in an exquisite dress bought at extortionate expense, held the tiny Charles in her arms, looking, for the first time since his arrival, like an adoring mother. She had on her head a cloche hat of pale feathers, and wore cream elbow-length gloves. It could not be denied that she looked devastating, despite the extra weight she had gained during pregnancy, and appeared utterly charming, so that many guests were heard to remark what a fortunate young man was Robert.

Sophie was deliriously happy on the arm of Frank. Of course, he was not like Robert, not so handsome, not so intelligent and not so adorable, but given that she was unlikely ever to find her brother's equal, he was a very acceptable second best. Now that the detestable Cecilia had not only married her brother but also borne his child, she had to find someone else on whom to lavish all that devotion.

After the christening was over and everybody had returned to The Cedars for lunch, Frank, upon whom the two attractive young people, obviously deeply in love and dedicating their baby to the Lord, had made an indelible impression, was moved to ask Sophie to marry him. In the euphoria of the day, Sophie, sure she had met her life's love, enthusiastically accepted his proposal and they set a date in June of the following year.

Things did not improve between Robert and Cecilia. She made a life for herself outside the house. She played tennis twice a week in summer at the local club and became obsessed with bridge when the days grew shorter and the autumn air began to bite. These things apart, she sat on several committees and gave and attended endless coffee and tea parties. She had little time for her child, who was cared for by a live-in nanny.

Robert travelled daily to Camberley and threw himself into his work, staying late at the barracks until he was too tired to feel the pain of Cecilia's rejection. On occasions when he sought to stir some reaction in his wife, she would turn her back and close her eyes and remind herself of the horror of childbirth and the restrictions a child put upon its mother's life.

One evening, after they had been out to a particularly pleasant party, they drove home in a relaxed mood. For once Cecilia was in good humour. When they had entered the house, Robert poured them each another drink and took the glasses upstairs, where Cecilia was preparing for bed.

'Wasn't that a jolly evening?' Cecilia looked at Robert's reflection in her mirror as he approached. 'I can't remember when I've enjoyed myself so much. We must have the Robinson's back very soon. In fact, darling, we should have a party. It's ages since we entertained, well, except for dinner parties and that's not the same thing, is it? I know,' she swung around to face him, almost knocking the whisky from his outstretched hand, 'sorry, darling, let's have an engagement party for Sophie and Frank.'

'But you don't like Frank, and anyway, they've been engaged for three months.'

'Oh, that doesn't matter. It's just an excuse to have a party.'

Robert put his hand on her neck and eased her face around until he could kiss her on her ear. 'All right, if it will make you happy. I'm sure Sophie will be thrilled, but I don't know about Frank, he is a very retiring sort of chap.'

'Wonderful.' She sipped her whisky 'I'll start arranging it tomorrow. When shall it be? Two weeks' time; no, three! That'll give people time to be sure they don't make any other arrangements for that evening.'

'Cissy, don't you think you ought to ask Sophie and Frank first?'

'Nonsense. I won't give them an opportunity to refuse. I shall make all the arrangements and then they will have to agree. Oh, darling, I'm so excited. I can't wait to get started.' She rose and moved into Robert's embrace, and they kissed.

As they lay in bed, Cecilia still fired with enthusiasm for her new venture, Robert turned her in his arms and his hand moved under the strap of her nightdress and he slid it off her shoulder. She immediately froze, and pulling away, she replaced the offending strap and hissed, 'Stop it! What are you doing?'

'Cissy, it's been over a year. I do so much want to make love to you. Please, darling, I'll be careful. Really I will. You won't have to worry about getting pregnant again. Please, Cissy,' he implored.

She loathed this wimpishness in her husband. She would far rather have married a man who took what he wanted than one who whined and cajoled. It was sickening!

Reluctantly, she lay prone on her back, turning her head away. 'Hurry up then.'

Robert hesitated. He knew that her condescension was not what he wanted, and yet he feared that if he rejected this pitiful submission now, he could never persuade her that this was something to delight in, something to be cherished. Their union was cold and unsatisfying, and as he moved to his own side of the bed, Robert felt the old familiar stinging behind his eyes. God, he was spineless!

'Thank you, darling,' he whispered.

'Just make that last another twelve months!'

Chapter Thirty-Two

It rained incessantly on the day Frank and Sophie were married; indeed, it scarcely seemed to get light all day. Rain soaked the feathers on the ladies' hats and the gentlemen's top hats dripped large globules of translucent liquid from their rims. The bride and groom were damply happy and not discomforted at all by the inclement weather.

Their wedding had been brought forward by a month because Frank was being transferred to the London office and the company required him to be there on the first day of May. Immediately after the reception, the newly-weds were driven to the station amongst tearful farewells and left The Hamptons and the family for all time. Sophie was never to return again, not even on a visit.

They found a little house in a leafy street in St John's Wood and Sophie set about making it into a home. She had never been so happy, nor had she dreamt that such happiness were possible. To her great surprise, she missed the family not at all. Robert came to visit from time to time when he was in London and that, too, was idyllic because she had him all to herself since Cecilia never accompanied him.

The three of them would go together to the Music Hall or a theatre and eat out afterwards in one of the a little cafés near Leicester Square. Sophie would be in heaven as she walked home, her arms linked in those of the two people dearest to her in the entire world. When his visit took place in the afternoon, she and Robert would visit an art gallery or stroll on Hampstead Heath or through St James's Park.

During the day, while Frank was at work, she would put on her coat and hat and, carrying her basket over her arm and her purse in her bag, she would make her way to a small mews, which was being converted into shops. Already there had opened a delicious little emporium with every kind of cheese imaginable, a baker's which smelled of warm fresh bread straight from his ovens, and a greengrocer's with a striped awning where, in the summer, were laid out colourful fruits and vegetables in its shade. To walk down this delightful cul-de-sac, one could scarcely believe that there was a war on. There seemed to be no shortage of any good thing. The greengrocer told her, during one of her morning forages, that a butcher and fishmonger were to take up the remaining establishments, which were nearing completion, so that everything that she required for Frank's delectation could be obtained from this charming, tiny alley. She registered with each retailer as they opened their premises. This preparation for her husband's comfort was all her joy.

The fact that there were no children of the marriage was a deep disappointment to them both. Despite taking advice from both old physicians and old maids, despite prayer and not inconsiderable effort, they remained childless. It was the only blight on an otherwise enchanted existence.

Evenings were the most wonderful time of the day for Sophie. She would make ready for Frank's homecoming, tidying and polishing the small house and cooking him some delicious meal. His slippers would be placed before the fire to warm, and the cushions on his easy chair would receive a good plumping-up before, finally, his distinctive knock fell on the door. Then she would hurry into the hall and open the door and they would fall into each other's arms, for all the world as though they had been separated for many years. He never used his key, because he enjoyed this little ritual that they played out each working day

On one particular evening, she opened the door to find him with a self-satisfied smile on his round moon-face and his large, plump hands clutching a wriggling bulge in the breast of his topcoat.

'What have you got there, my love?' She squealed with delight as her fingers encountered a bundle of white fur. 'What a darling little dog. Oh, Frank ... for me? Thank you so much. Oh, he is so beautiful. I adore him.' She lifted the puppy out and preceded her husband into the sitting room.

Frank had removed his coat after taking from his pocket a bag of jelly sweets.

'I bought these for you, too.' He handed them to her. 'They're your favourites.'

'Thank you, my love.' She reached out and took the bag and

peering into it she said, 'Jujubes.' She turned her attention back to the dog. 'I shall call you Jujube.'

Sophie wrote weekly to her brother, long excitable letters about her wonderful husband and their happy life in North London. Robert wondered at the capriciousness of fate that swept away the anticipated bliss of his marriage to someone as beautiful and desirable as Cecilia, who was all he had ever wanted, and yet bestowed upon the unremarkable Sophie and Frank this heightened state of ecstasy.

The visits to his sister and her husband were his most happy times, though they tended to highlight his own loveless, barren existence. Witnessing their mutual pleasure in each other, he craved physical contact and yet he could never resort to paying for the comfort of a woman, as some of the men he was with in Belgium and France had done.

His life was a mess.

Chapter Thirty-Three

'It seems to me, that all of my life I have journeyed through grief and that the journeying was merely preparation for the loss of Charlie. From time to time, I have glimpsed the splendour of a life that might have been; just sufficient to illuminate what it was by comparison.' Fanny looked up at Connor, sitting on the other side of the great kitchen fireplace. 'You know, when Charlie and I were young in Seaforth, we touched the edge of heaven together. We knew such exquisite joy.'

'I know...'

'No! You don't know. Nobody knows. There never was such happiness in the entire world. Sometimes, remembering, I think we threw it away, but this was not true; it was stolen from us piece by piece. It was as though the gods were jealous. There was Alexander and his bitterness, then my grandfather died, and my mother. They never saw our children. My father and brothers simply disappeared; they didn't care enough to try to find me to tell me of my mother's death.' She paused, as though choosing which of the myriad tragedies in her life to highlight next. 'William died even before he began to live. Joe died – Joe, who so loved life that he delighted in every tiny, new discovery. Then, as though these were just rehearsals for the final tragedy, I lost Charlie. But I am coming to terms with my fate now. Each morning, when I open my eyes, I spend a precious hour with him before I rise and we talk together. We each knew the other so well that this is quite feasible. I know what he would have answered in every circumstance. When he was alive, I shared him with the world but now I have him exclusively and we can go where and when we want. We can travel through time and space together. We can be young again in Seaforth and in Liverpool. Oh, Connor, you must think I am mad, but it is a survival technique ... the only way I can cope in a world without him.'

187

'You're still young, Fanny. You have to move on to the next phase of your life.'

'I can't move on to what you call the next phase, because this phase has not closed. Do you realise that I have no idea of how he died? From the time he left this house, just before you saw him embarking at the docks, I know almost nothing of what happened to him. He walked out of my life young and strong and healthy and full of love, and now he has ceased to exist. Sometimes I get to feel quite angry with him, that he left me with four children and another growing inside of me.'

'Ah, sure, Fanny, you wouldn't be without any one of them, so you wouldn't. They all have something of Charlie in them and, just think, most of us never get a smell of the happiness you and Charlie knew. Look at me, at my age, and still never found a woman that I wanted to settle down with, nor one that wanted to settle down with me, neither.'

'Has there never been a woman in your life, Connor?'

'Ah, yes, of course there have been several, but they never worked out. I've travelled about a lot. I suppose I never stayed long enough in any place to get to know a lady well enough to be married.'

'I suppose that today has made me more morose than usual. It's been hard to see everybody around me rejoicing that the war has ended and anticipating their menfolk returning, with me knowing that Charlie should have been coming home to me, but that he never will.' Her voice broke as she gave rein to the tears that were never far from the surface.

Connor moved from the far side of the fire to kneel before her and he took her hands in his. 'Have a good cry, Fanny. Get it out of your system. You'll feel better. Just let go.' His voice was warm and the gentle brogue seemed to increase the compassion in his words.

Fanny had come to rely on Connor, and to Sam, who was of course the only boy in the house in Walton Road, he had become a father figure. They would go out together to the park to kick a ball about, and the man would talk to the child about his father. Sam never mentioned Charlie at home, but he would open up to Connor as he did to no one else. The girls, too, adored Uncle Paddy and when, on occasion, he was absent from them for more than a few days, they would fret.

They were growing up fast. At twelve years old, Francie was tall, handsome and willowy, like a young colt, and Bertha, one year and

188

two inches less, had become breathtakingly beautiful and alarmingly precocious. When they walked together heads would swivel to follow them in awe, and Francie would squirm uncomfortably but Bertha would toss her head and turn to stare them out.

'Have you seen enough?' she would shout, and the people would look away quickly and hurry by.

There were infrequent occasions when Mr Peterson, contracted by some commercial operation to produce photographs for advertising purposes, invited them to sit for him for a small fee, and the girls were allowed to keep these windfalls, provided they were saved. Invariably, when there was a choice to be made between the two girls, Francie would be disappointed as Bertha prevailed, but at times the client needed, or preferred, a dark-haired child and Francie came into her own.

They were seventeen and sixteen years old respectively when Mr Peterson's assistant, who had first shown them into the studio fourteen years earlier, brought a note to the house. Fanny answered the bell and took the proffered note. She opened it where she was and read the contents.

Dear Mrs Cahill,
Enclosed you will find information about a proposed 'beauty contest' to find the loveliest young lady in Liverpool. As you will observe, the winner will go forward into the national finals to be held in London.
     If you were willing, I would like to take a photograph of each of the girls to enter into the contest.
     Perhaps you would call on me in the next day or two to discuss this further.
     Yours sincerely,
     Patrick J. W. Peterson.

Fanny folded the letter and put it in her apron pocket. 'Tell Mr Peterson that I will call on him tomorrow with my decision.'

She went into the kitchen and sat down. She took out the note and spread it out on the table. She was very uncertain about this. A beauty contest? She had never heard of this before. The whole idea sounded extremely unsavoury to her and, anyway, the girls were quite vain enough. Yet there was a part of her that took great pride in their beauty. She herself had suffered all her young life from a lack of self-worth caused by her harelip, and she did not want any of her children to lack confidence as she had. How she wished that Charlie were here to talk it over.

For a moment it was as though he were sitting opposite her at the scrubbed table. What would he have said?

'Fanny, my love, we have beautiful children. We're proud of them, aren't we? Let them take whatever opportunity the world offers. One thing is for sure, there won't be anyone to touch them for loveliness.'

Fanny smiled at the memory of him and was overcome by a sweet nostalgia. 'Oh, Charlie. Oh, Charlie. Oh my love.'

At eleven o'clock next morning, she stood outside the studio shop and studied her reflection in the plate-glass window as she had so long ago. Her clothes were shabbier and cheaper now than they had been then but her lace handkerchief was as white and pretty as ever over her mouth. She entered the shop. The russet-coloured carpet was gone, replaced by one of many shades of blue, and the pictures had changed. On the wall to her right, there was a photograph of two tiny children, one darkly lovely and the other exquisitely golden.

'So many years ago,' she muttered.

'Yes.' Mr Peterson's voice behind her startled her. 'It was, indeed, a long time ago. How many years, Mrs Cahill, ten … twelve … more? They are still very beautiful. You know, sometimes, beautiful children grow up to be plain and plain children, beautiful, but Francie and Bertha began lovely and have grown even more so as the years have passed. Do come in to the office. Come in, sit down, won't you?'

Fanny took the seat opposite the desk. It was all so fraught with memories.

'Now, have you had time to think this matter over?'

'Perhaps you'll tell me more about it.' She let her hand drop. Mr Peterson knew what she looked like, so there was no need for her small deception. 'What does it entail?'

'Well,' the old man took out a form and began to study it, 'initially, we would take photographs of the girls and send them to the regional judges. I will take the portraits without cost to you, but in return, I would expect to keep the copyright of them. If one of the girls wins and, believe me, I have no doubt that they will, the resultant publicity will be more than sufficient reward. As I was

190

saying, if one of them wins, her photograph will be sent to London and those who are selected for the final judging will travel down with a chaperone, at the organisers' expense of course, to be assessed in the flesh, as it were.'

'In the flesh?' echoed Fanny in alarm.

'No, no, no, no. That's just a figure of speech. It is a very respectable and prestigious event. The winner is to be painted by Mr Augustus John in addition to the financial benefit and the modelling opportunities.'

'I would be allowed to travel with her and remain with her all of the time she is there?'

'Without a doubt. There is nothing seamy about this, Mrs Cahill. Indeed, if there were, you would surely not expect that I should be recommending it to you.'

'Could we change our minds at any time between now and the … er … the London bit?'

'Of course, but I can't see why you would want to opt out if one of the girls has got so far.'

'I just want to be sure. There is certainly no harm at all in your taking photographs and sending them off. When would you like the girls to come for the sitting?'

'I'll advise you in a day or so, but I am not very happy about your wish to have the option of withdrawing the girls part way through the contest. Perhaps you will become more positive after the first adjudication.'

He opened the door for her and she rose and went out in front of him. She turned. 'I must seem very ungrateful to you. I don't mean to be. I just have to be so careful for Francie and Bertha. They attract all kinds.'

'Yes, of course, very wise. It must be hard bringing up the children on your own but you know that I have their best interests at heart.'

As she hurried home, the excitement began to rise in her. Of course her girls would win and the money would swell their savings from their work in the fish market. She thought it strange that one should receive money for being beautiful, as though it were not sufficient reward in itself.

The steam rose from the horses' flanks and nostrils as they strained in the icy November air, and the tramcars clanged and rattled along with their anonymous loads of humanity. It grew dark early, and Fanny relived that dread night in December when she

191

had hurried in the opposite direction with the near lifeless bundle that was William wrapped in her arms.

She reflected that this was her life now, one moment elated and the next brought low with remembrance.

The photographs were duly taken and delivered by Mr Peterson, personally, to the address given on the form. He was of the opinion that photography would make a contribution to the world of art no less important than the wielding of a brush on canvass and, as Mr John was to be one of the final judges, he happily anticipated the exposure of his work to such an august personage.

The girls, who could now be considered young ladies, were very excited at the prospect of winning the contest and visiting London for the first time, but were saddened at the realisation that only one of them could enjoy this experience. Neither of them considered the possibility that some other contestant might usurp them, though Francie secretly conceded that people were disposed towards Bertha's vivacious fairness rather than her own arcane brand of beauty.

As chance would have it, the judges in Liverpool were quite unable to decide between the two. The adjudicators concluded that they were so different in every degree that it was impossible to choose between them. So portraits of them both were forwarded to the illustrious panel in London who, without being apprised of their relationship, chose the two girls, together with one Alicia Tempest, as the finalists. In consequence of both of the girls being chosen, first-class tickets for two chaperones were sent in addition to those for the girls.

Fanny was undecided whom she should invite. She would have favoured Connor, and Francie and Bertha wanted him to go with them, but there was also Ellen to be considered. Finally, unable to decide between the two of them, she asked Mr Peterson.

Fanny and the two girls awoke on the appointed morning and made their way to Lime Street Station, their excitement and enthusiasm resulting in their arriving thirty-five minutes early. Fanny settled the girls in the waiting room, crossed the road to King George's Hall, and picking up her skirts, mounted the steps to stand before the naked nymph. Nostalgia filled her with a pleasurable melancholy. She walked around the plinth until she came opposite the Walker Art Gallery and, looking up, she relived the happiest moment of her life.

192

Dabbing at her eyes, she hurried back to the station and opened the door to the waiting room.

'Ma, what's wrong?' Francie was out of her seat and standing in front of her mother instantly. 'You've been crying. What happened? Are you all right?'

'I'm all right, Francie, dear. Bertha, come on, the train will be coming in at any moment. Gather up your things and come.'

She ushered them out onto the concourse, her eyes darting round, searching for Mr Peterson. She caught sight of him moving towards them from the entrance. Taking the tickets from Fanny, he led them through the barrier and onto the platform where the porter opened the door to a first-class carriage.

'Isn't this wonderful?' enthused Bertha. 'I've never been on a train before, let alone in a first-class compartment. I wish the girls at the fish market could see me now!' She lowered herself, with her instinctive grace, onto the seat next to the window and Francie sat down beside her. Mr Peterson waited until Fanny was seated before taking the seat beside her. They had the carriage to themselves.

A shrill whistle split the air and echoed around the vast glass-ceilinged structure and steam hissed and spurted upwards, spreading and then dissipating as it rose. The train lurched forward before settling into a regular motion, which quickened until it had reached speed.

'Bertha,' Mr Peterson addressed the younger girl, 'I wanted to have a word with you before the judging. You know that you are a beautiful young lady?'

'Yes,' Bertha replied without embarrassment.

'It is one thing to look beautiful in a photograph where you're still and in repose and quite another to exude an aura of beauty when you are before the panel. It is good that you know you are beautiful. Keep that constantly in the forefront of your mind all the time you are with the judges. The last thing I would want to do is to make you feel self-conscious. You are beautiful Bertha. You are very, very beautiful. But if I were forced to find a fault, I would have to say that you are, just faintly, round-shouldered. I want you to remember to sit up straight and pull your shoulders back. No, no, no! Don't strain them. That's right. Just pull them back gently. There, that's perfect. Lift up your chin and say in your mind, "Look, see how beautiful I am. See how straight, how relaxed, how very, very beautiful."'

With that peculiar talent that she possessed, Bertha mimicked the old man to perfection. Her shoulders went down, her back stretched, her long neck arched even further and her body relaxed without flagging.

Fanny squirmed uncomfortably. She seemed to spend most of her time trying to subdue Bertha's self-assurance. It seemed to her graceless to be quite so self-confident as her child was.

Now Mr Peterson turned his attention to Francie. 'Francie, my dear, you are elegant and slender and you have a natural grace, but you have a tendency to look down. I want you to lift your head and look straight into Mr John's eyes. Pretend he has a pimple on the end of his nose. Don't be afraid to smile at it. Focus on the judges. Don't look at your feet. Come, now, practice on me. Look in my eyes. See the pimple on my nose.'

Francie smiled, suffusing her face with light, and was instantly transformed from a chary little mouse into a delightful gazelle.

Fanny approved. Had it been so easy to change Francie's fragile self-confidence to this self-assurance – and she had not known it?

The countryside whizzed past the window between the stations and they looked out, unspeaking, each with their own introspections, onto a land bathed in that startlingly bright February sunshine that often penetrates the barrenness of winter.

Francie was thinking that she would be eighteen in a month. Surely she would have a lot more freedom. If only she could win this contest. To be painted by Augustus John! What would follow? She might meet some excellent gentleman who would want to marry her and take her away from the fish market. She might live in a big house with servants, just like her mother had told them of. She held her head high and gazed at the pimple on Mr Peterson's nose … and beamed.

Bertha, noticing how the smile enhanced Francie's face and how the raising of her head gave her a new, becoming confidence, felt threatened and began to concentrate on dropping her shoulders.

They reached London's Euston Station and alighted among the unruly crowd of travellers elbowing one another for a cab. In time, Mr Peterson prevailed, and holding back several fractious contenders, hustled Fanny and the girls into a black hire car.

The hotel was very grand. Their rooms were beautifully appointed and the girls delighted in the luxury, but Fanny had been here before, neither in these same rooms nor this same hotel, but in

194

others just like them. But that was a lifetime ago. This whole experience had carried her back to her youth, and the nostalgia brought a tightness to her chest.

The next morning was a bustle of industry as Bertha and Francie bathed and made ready. They used a little mercolised wax on their faces and heightened the colour on their cheeks and lips with a smear of rouge. Fanny brushed their hair until her arm ached, and finally, they slipped the beautiful new dresses, bought with previously earned fees, over their gleaming heads.

They left their hotel and stepped out onto the streets of London, excitement rising in them with every new sight and sound. The city was agog with people hurrying by. This was life as they had never seen or even imagined. This exceeded their dreams. This was a life they wanted to be part of.

The cab stopped outside an elegant building and they entered and were directed to the first floor. They mounted the staircase and went along a corridor until they stood before a door.

Mr Peterson, with an arm on the shoulder of each girl, turned them both towards him and without releasing his grasp on them, said, 'Now, I want you to remember what I have told you. Once you are through this door, you are on your own. You are the two most beautiful girls in the world. Now go and show them the very truth of this.'

Fanny and Mr Peterson waited in the outer room while the two girls went into the chamber. Mr Peterson remained calm and detached, but Fanny sat twisting her handkerchief around her finger, forgetting totally the reason for her carrying it. On the other side of the room, across to their left, sat a couple whom Fanny presumed to be Mr and Mrs Tempest, together with several other people whom she took to be sponsors of their daughter, Alicia. The woman wore a light cashmere coat with a fox fur collar and a cloche hat of the same material. She looked extremely elegant and expensive and Fanny recognised her own shabbiness by comparison. She was amazed when the woman, opening her purse, took out a cigarette and fitted it into a long holder of ivory. Her husband leaned across and lit it for her. She crossed her long, slender legs and threw a smile at Fanny who lifted her hand to cover her lip and gave a little nod of acknowledgement. She hoped that the assured Alicia was not engendering the same despairing self-consciousness in her girls.

The wait seemed interminable as the light that had shone brightly through the window began to dim and the shadows that it had thrown across the floor faded away. Fanny, exhaustion triumphing over anxiety, had difficulty in keeping her eyes open.

When at last the door opened, a tearful Alicia ran across the room to her mother and threw herself in her arms, sobbing loudly on her shoulder. Amidst much clucking, the other party gathered themselves and their belongings together, and were led away by an usher into an adjoining room. They swept past Fanny and Mr Peterson without glancing at them, evidently much perturbed by their child's obvious rejection. Fanny's heart constricted. Did this mean...? The wait continued and eventually, the door opened again and this time, Francie appeared through it, her head no longer held proudly. She gave Fanny a watery little smile and settled herself onto a chair beside her mother.

'I think Bertha's won, Ma. Isn't that wonderful?'

Fanny turned her eldest daughter to face her and drawing her head forward, kissed her on the forehead. At that moment, she felt prouder of Francie than if she had been chosen the most beautiful girl in the world, but now Bertha came into the room accompanied by an elderly man with white hair and beard, whose arm rested lightly on the girl's shoulder. His eyes alighted on Francie, sitting beside Fanny, and turning to Bertha, he asked, 'Who has come with you, Bertha?'

'This is my mother and this is our very good friend, Mr Peterson, who took my photograph. Having introduced the adults, she put her hand in Francie's and said, 'And Francie is my sister.'

The surprise on the old man's face was a picture. 'I had no idea,' he said. 'Well, well. Who would have thought there could be two such beauties in one family and each so different from the other?' He offered his hand to Fanny. 'I can see from whom their handsomeness comes.'

'Thank you, Sir.' Fanny spoke from behind her handkerchief.

His attention turned to Mr Peterson. 'And they are further advantaged, I think, by having the services of such a excellent exponent of the art of photography.'

'It's kind of you to say so, Mr John. It would be hard to take a bad likeness of these two.'

'Yes, I'm sure, but we must talk some more later, if you have time.'

Addressing Fanny again he said, 'I will need to talk to you about

196

the arrangements for Bertha, Mrs Cahill. Are you free for dinner tonight and you, too, Mr Peterson?'

Panic arose in Fanny's throat so that she could scarcely speak. She had nothing to wear. She couldn't leave the girls alone in London. He had made no mention of the cost of the extra night in the hotel. These thoughts swirled like a grey mist, through her mind.

'I'm sorry. I have another engagement in Liverpool in the morning. I really have to get back tonight.'

'Perhaps we shall have to order some tea to be brought in and deal with it now.' He flipped open his gold watch and glanced at its face. 'Oh dear, this is an unexpected difficulty. It leaves us very little time for discussion. Cannot your appointment in Liverpool be postponed? We could have you back at your hotel immediately after dinner and arrange for an early train in the morning.' Noticing the strain on her face he added, 'We will, of course, settle the hotel bill.'

Fanny, having had time to compose herself, replied, 'That is very kind of you and is, indeed, a consideration. However, I had not anticipated staying for the evening so I have brought nothing suitable to wear.'

'Will that matter if we dine in private? I can assure you, Madam, that I would take no offence if you were to turn up in the clothes you are wearing now. I do, in any case, hate dressing for dinner so that I shall be spared that minor vexation.'

Chapter Thirty-Four

The portrait that Augustus John painted of Bertha was exquisite. She was seated with one elbow supported by a table, her head tilted slightly to one side and her chin resting gently on an extended index finger. Though the pose was ethereal, there was no hint of contrivance as one might have expected, because Bertha was sensitive to the artist's purpose and possessed an uncanny talent for achieving the exact quality of expression he envisaged. The gold of her hair shimmered as though a zephyr were playing through it, and John had managed to capture this movement on canvas in a most remarkable way. Everybody agreed that it was a masterpiece.

Her photograph appeared in the *Tatler* and she was invited to go to Paris for a year, where she would sit for several distinguished artists. But the most attractive benefit was the money.

Initially, Fanny was adamant that under no circumstances would Bertha be allowed to take up the modelling assignments. She argued that the child was not even seventeen until the following month and much too young to be allowed to go away from home to live in town, let alone in Paris. Eventually, Mr Peterson prevailed upon her to keep the option open for twelve months, when Bertha would be eighteen and Fanny conceded this though she knew privately that she would not change her mind.

She spoke to Charlie of it during their morning 'meetings' and he told her, 'Let it be until the twelve months has passed, and then review it. It is a great honour and opportunity and, sure, Bertha will bring us no shame.'

'Charlie, you are impossible. She's much too young to be going off to Paris. You know how headstrong she is, and she will be amongst all those artists and other strange people and so far away from home.'

'All right, Little Goose, but it'll do no harm to wait for a year and see how you feel then.'

'You really are no great help to me. I thought you would have supported me on this one.'

Charlie just beamed that heart-wrenching smile that caused her to thrill.

'Who are you talking to?' Bertha burst through the door without knocking, interrupting her mother's rapture. 'I do believe you're talking to yourself. That is an indication of dementia, you know, Ma.'

Fanny smiled. 'Don't be so impudent, Madam. I was just thinking about this Paris thing.'

'Oh, Ma, you will let me go, won't you? Please. Ma, you can't stop me going. It's such a wonderful opportunity. Oh, please, Ma.'

'Bertha, be quiet for just one moment. I've been thinking and I have decided that we will not say "no" ...'

'Oh, thank you, Ma. I knew you'd let me go in the end.'

'Bertha. This is just why I am reluctant to allow it. You are so impetuous! You never listen to what you are being told. Now, listen and don't interrupt until I've finished. You are too young to travel to Paris now, so I am suggesting a compromise. We leave the decision for one year. We will decide on your eighteenth birthday. Do you agree?'

Bertha's face fell, and she looked as though she might cry.

'Do you agree, Bertha? That's the offer. Take it or leave it. We still have to contact the organisers to ascertain whether they are willing to postpone the trip. I can't see that you will be any less beautiful in twelve months' time, though sometimes I think that might be a good thing. If you have become more responsible and mature by then, you may go. In the meantime, you concentrate on your work.'

'Gutting fish? Oh, Mother, how can you want me to gut fish in preference to becoming a famous model?'

'I am worried about you becoming an infamous model, Bertha. If you don't like gutting fish, get another job, but not modelling in Paris! I don't know what your father would say.'

But she did know.

The organisers agreed readily to the postponement and the matter was closed.

One evening, some months later, when Bertha was making to go to her room, Fanny spoke to her.

'Don't go upstairs yet, my dear. Come and sit with me. I want to talk to you.'

199

The girl turned at the door and came to sit on the corner seat of the fireguard beside her mother.

'Your father and I have decided...' Fanny herself pulled up sharply as Bertha looked at her quizzically.

'I have decided to permit you to take up the offer of the work in Paris...'

'Oh, Ma.' The girl threw herself into her mother's arms.

'Bertha! There you go again. You really must learn to control your impetuous nature. It is very unbecoming and unladylike and will not serve you well when you are in France. I have given this much thought, and here is what we shall do. I shall write to Mr John and tell him that I think that you will be ready to travel to Paris next spring. We will then take some of the money that you were awarded and we shall shop for some suitable clothes and other requirements. But, I want to tell you Bertha, that you must not betray the trust I am putting in you. You must keep yourself modest and virtuous and regard the experience as work and not as an opportunity to behave in an unseemly manner. I shall expect to receive from you, every week, a letter telling me what you have been doing, and I shall also request a report from the chatelaine of the house where you will stay. If I even suspect any misdemeanour on your part, you will be recalled to Liverpool immediately and back to the fish market. Have you understood, have you understood completely, what I have said?'

'Oh yes, Ma. Of course I will work hard and be utterly demure and decent. I will be the most wholesome, the most moral, the most refined...'

'Bertha, you are being stupid again. Please stop it and realise the seriousness of what I am saying. I should tell you, Bertha, when you behave like this it reinforces my feeling that you are too immature to be allowed to go. It would have been so much better if Francie were going, too. She would have been a steadying influence on you and I should feel so much more settled in my mind. Anyway, there you are. It is decided. I will write tomorrow.'

Chapter Thirty-Five

Bertha had been gone for four days when the stranger came.

It happened on the first day of April. Fanny opened the door and her heart turned over.

'Richard,' she whispered, 'is it you?'

No sooner had the words left her lips than she realised her mistake, but she could scarce believe her eyes, for standing on the bottom step was a man so like her youngest brother that she still felt some uncertainty even after he spoke.

'No, no. My name is not Richard.'

'Of course not. Please forgive me and come in. I know who you are.'

'I don't think so. We've never met before. Obviously you have mistaken me for someone else.' His voice was deep and mellow and he displayed some embarrassment at the error. He was certain that he had the wrong house. This lady standing erect and framed in the doorway was educated and refined. She was not what he had expected. Charlie had been a fine man, but he was not from the same class as the woman who stood before him now. And she was beautiful except for the defect on her upper lip.

'Yes, I do know who you are. I don't know your name, but I know who you are. Please come in. Don't stand on the doorstep. Come in, I have something to show you.'

Hesitating and bewildered, Robert allowed himself to be shepherded into the parlour at the front of the house.

'Please sit down. I'll get Francie to make us some tea.' She moved to the open door and called, 'Francie, would you come here?'

Immediately, a tall, dark, enigmatically beautiful girl appeared in the doorway and Robert swallowed hard.

'Francie, this is a friend of your father's. They were in Belgium together and he has come to visit us. Would you bring some tea?'

With a little bob, the girl gave him a wan smile. 'How do you do?' and she left the room.

Fanny had moved to the sideboard and took from it a wooden box, which she set on the mahogany table.

'How do you know who I am?'

Without answering, Fanny opened the lid and took out a letter, spreading it upon the table and smoothing it out. She turned over a page and, finding the place she wanted, crossed to Robert and indicated it to him.

He read,

A strange thing happened to me today. I saw a young officer who was so like Richard that I was quite startled and approached to embrace him. I actually had my arms around him before I realised my mistake and it was a good thing that he was in shock or I could have found myself court-martialled. I was able to help him and, for Richard's sake, that gave me great comfort and pleasure.

Robert reread that portion of the letter that Fanny had indicated. Slowly he raised his head to look into her face.

'It was me. Charles was writing about me.'

'Yes, I know. You look so startlingly like my brother; not just in features or build but also in the way you stand, the way you move. It is quite uncanny. He used to push back his hair in the same way. One could swear that you were Richard as we last saw him. I can quite understand how Charlie mistook you for him for an instant, until he realised that Richard would have been much older then.'

'Would have been? Is he dead then, this brother of yours?'

A look of bewilderment crossed Fanny's face. 'Do you know, I really couldn't say. I haven't seen him for more than twenty years. It's much too complicated to explain now.' She brightened as she went on, 'I must tell you that I am so very, very glad to see you. Why has it taken you so long to come? I have longed to know what happened to Charlie before ... I have felt as though my life came to a standstill when he died. So many unanswered questions.' She settled herself opposite him and smoothed out her skirts. 'I know you must have known him well. He wrote of you several times.'

'I wish that were true. In fact, the reason that I am here is because

202

I so much want to know more of him. I thought that, meeting you, you would be able to tell me. I only know that he was the bravest man I've known.'

'What a lovely thing to say. Yes, Charlie was the dearest, sweetest man and I can imagine that he would have been quite brave and fearless in battle. But you haven't answered my question. Why have you come after all these years?'

There was a knock on the door and Francie entered, carrying a tray.

'Thank you, my dear. Just put it down. I want to talk to Mr … I'm sorry, I've just realised that I don't know your name.'

'Mawdsley. Robert Mawdsley.'

'I'll call you in a little while and you can ask Mr Mawdsley …'

'Major Mawdsley, actually,' Robert interrupted, his eyes never moving from Francie's beautiful face. She was like a gazelle.

'… Major Mawdsley, anything you want to know about your father.'

Francie withdrew while their eyes were still locked upon one another. He was so handsome, so tall. She could tell that he was taken with her and she thanked her God that Bertha had already left for France. Was he married? Did he live nearby? Would he come to see them again?

Fanny could not help but notice that her guest was finding it hard to concentrate on their conversation, his attention still upon Francie. Oh dear. Surely this was not going to prove tiresome. Francie was at an impressionable age and this man was old enough to be her father … well almost!

She began to pour the tea as she continued, 'Now, Major Mawdsley, you were about to explain why you have come to visit us after such a long time.'

'Charlie and I were in different regiments but our paths crossed several times. It was quite mysterious, the way he always seemed to be there when I was in need. I was wounded and sent back to England and after I returned to the front, it took me some time to find out his name and address. He died in my arms, and with his last breath he asked me to bring you a message. He told me that your name was Fanny and that you lived in Liverpool. He said something about a little goose.'

Her eyes lost focus as the tears rose, and for a moment she could not speak.

'What was the message?' Her voice was steady when she finally spoke.

Robert hesitated. 'He said 'Tell Fanny I love her.' I asked him where I would find you and he told me, Liverpool. Oh, yes, and he asked me to say that he was sorry. That's all.'

Fanny remained quiet for several minutes, struggling to retain her composure, until finally, 'It was so brave of you to stay with him as he died. I am so grateful that he had a friend beside him.'

He hung his head. 'It wasn't like that. Charles saved my life.' When she didn't respond, he went on, 'Do you understand what I'm saying? He stepped between me and the bullets. If it wasn't for me, he would have been here today.'

Fanny froze, her eyes burning into the man who stood before her. Her mouth opened and closed and, again, opened and closed, then she shut her eyes and staggered unseeingly from the room.

Francie heard her mother let out a half sob, half scream and hurried to see what had happened. She saw Fanny struggling to mount the stairs, one hand on the stair above, unable to hold herself erect. The girl looked to the parlour door and then took the stairs two at a time until she reached her distressed mother.

'Ma, what's the matter?'

'Francie, go and attend to our guest. I'll be down in a moment. Just go!'

Francie turned the handle of the door and went into the parlour.

'What have you been saying to my mother?' she flung at Robert. 'You have really upset her. What have you said?'

He moved forward to take her elbow but she shook him off.

'What have you said to her?'

'I was with your father when he died. I think she is overcome with emotion.' He shifted uneasily. 'Perhaps I'd better leave.'

'No, please don't go. That was rude of me. Ma gets easily upset at the moment. My sister has just left home and Ma's feeling very low. She'll be angry with me if you go. She'll know I've been rude to you.' She hung her head shyly. 'Please do sit down again. Ma will be down soon. She just needs a little time to compose herself.' With an effort she changed her demeanour. 'Have you come far? It is very kind of you to visit us. How well did you know Da?' Her mind searched for things to say until finally she fell silent, looking at her hands as they rested in her lap.

'I didn't know your father for long, but he was very good to me.

After he died I was sent home to England and spent several months in hospital in Southampton. I went back to the front when I was better, but my wound wouldn't heal and eventually I was given a desk job. I have left the Army now but I have never forgotten Charles so, as I was coming to Liverpool, I thought I would see if I could find your mother. Before your father died, he gave me a message for her.'

'I see.'

'It seems that I look a lot like your mother's … your uncle.'

'I never knew Ma's family, nor Da's either.'

They spoke of other things, and the conversation began to flow easily between them. Before long, it was as though they were friends of many years standing. Francie, excited by this mature and distinguished man from the first moment of their meeting, became more and more attracted to him as they spoke, and Robert thought her the most exquisite girl he had seen and found her quiet modesty endearing. Moment by moment they were building up a mutual liking and friendship and, beneath the formality of their meeting, there lay an unsettling sensation, which threatened to develop into an ardour.

Francie was quite flustered by Fanny's return.

'Ma,' she said, 'are you feeling better? Major Mawdsley has been telling me about Da.'

'Has he, indeed?' She moved to where Robert had risen from his chair. 'I'm so sorry, Major. It was very silly of me. I felt quite faint. I hope you will forgive me.'

He held the proffered hand, which he took to be her dismissal of him.

'That's quite all right. I'm sure it has been a shock for you. Perhaps I should have written before I came.' He hesitated for a moment longer and then went on, 'May I call on you again? It has been very awkward for both of us but I do feel that I want to know Charles's family better.'

'Will you be in town on Sunday?'

Without hesitating, Robert decided to delay his departure. 'Yes.'

'Would you like to take tea with us at about four o'clock?'

And so it was arranged, much to Francie's satisfaction.

Chapter Thirty-Six

A skinny teenager with an amazing mop of frizzy, ginger hair opened the door to Robert when he arrived at the appointed time on Sunday. She wore a grin that spread from one ear to the other.

'Come in. We're all waiting for you.'

They were, indeed, all waiting for him, for he found an unexpected number of people assembled when he entered the parlour. Sat next to Fanny was a giant of a man with a boy of about ten years old who had managed to squeeze himself into the narrowest gap between the man's thigh and the arm of the chair. A young man stood beside the piano, turning the pages of the music, and there at the piano, enigmatically beautiful, sat Francie. His mind had been unable to retain the extent of her loveliness so that he was startled by it again, as he had been a few days ago.

She stopped playing abruptly as he entered the room and stood, turning to receive him and moved to her mother's side as Fanny rose, extending both of her hands in a gesture of genuine welcome.

'Children, this is a dear friend of your father's. His name is Major Mawdsley and he was with your father when he died.'

The skinny teenager shouted, 'Hallo! I'm Winnie. They call me Skinny Winnie. This is Bunny, that's our Francie and Sam and this,' she crossed to where the man, looking even taller than when he was seated, rose to his feet and put his hand on her shoulder, 'is Uncle Paddy.'

'Thank you,Winnie, that will be enough. You'll have to excuse Winnie, Major Mawdsley. She is much too excitable for her own good.'

Francie stepped forward and offered her hand to Robert with the little bob that she had treated him to on his first visit.

'It's good to see you again,' he said, addressing Francie, direct. 'It's good to see you all.'

'Please sit down.' Fanny indicated a chair on the opposite side of the fire from Connor.

'Would you please excuse me?' Francie left the room.

'Winnie, go and help your sister with the tea, please.'

Winnie escaped from the stiff formality of the room and, once outside the door, collided with Francie who was propped up against the wall, waiting for her.

'Isn't he wonderful?' she addressed her younger sister.

'He's awright. Nuthin' speshull.'

'Oh Winnie, you are such a little idiot. He's beautiful. Did you ever see anyone so handsome and debonair?'

'Debun what?'

'Oh, never mind. Come and give me a hand.' Francie's nerves were tying themselves in knots from the back of her neck to the centre of her stomach.

They giggled as they hurried down the long corridor to the kitchen where they set about making the tea and completing the trays that had been made ready.

Back in the parlour, Robert was answering the questions that were being put to him by Connor and the two boys, while Fanny sat, her hands demurely in her lap, watching the proceedings with growing pleasure.

'Do you have a family, Major? Do you have children?' Now Fanny spoke.

'Yes, I have a son. We called him Charles after your husband.'

'Really. That is an honour.'

'How old is he?' Sam and Bunny spoke at the same time.

The boys liked this man, especially Sam who was usually very reserved and distant with strangers. He warmed towards him, and their conversation flowed easily. Connor was slower to relax and join in, but it was evident that, eventually, Robert had his approval. By the time the girls returned carrying the trays, the atmosphere had changed and everybody was laughing together, and Fanny considered that she had made another friend. After half an hour or so Fanny rose from her chair and crossed to Robert.

'Major …'

'Oh, please, "Robert".'

'All right, Robert. I still wonder why it has taken ten years for you to bring us news of my husband and what has prompted you to do so after such a long time. It would have been such consolation to us to

207

have known sooner how he died. Nevertheless, I know that I speak for us all when I say that it is wonderful to have met you now and to have talked about Charlie. I hope that you will come again when you are next in Liverpool.'

There it was again. He was being dismissed. This lady had a charming way of telling one when it was time to depart. Robert smiled and rose to his feet.

'I think it is time that I was going. Thank you for your hospitality. It has been wonderful meeting all of Charles's family and, yes, I would like to think that I could call on you again when I come to Liverpool.'

'I'll show you out.' Francie was on her feet and at the door before anybody could speak and Robert made a round of the room, shaking hands and exchanging pleasantries with everybody in turn, whilst Francie waited in the hall. As Robert came out, she opened the front door and standing on the top step, he turned, reached out and took her hand. He held it for several seconds and she made no move to withdraw it.

'Can I see you again … outside, by ourselves?'

'I don't know.' She was thrilling at the very suggestion of a clandestine meeting. 'I'm not sure. Ma would be very angry if she found out.'

'I have to go back tomorrow at the latest. I promise that no harm will come to you. I just want to speak to you. Where do you work? Can I see you for just ten minutes after work?'

'Meet me at the Corner House just after seven. I can't stay for long and you mustn't say anything to Ma.'

For the second time, she was glad that Bertha was away. She could never have met Robert if her sister had been at home. She would surely have told Ma.

That night, she hardly slept. All through the hours of darkness and even as the dawn rose, she was still full of fear and excitement. This was the most daring thing she had done in her life and to be doing it with Robert was like living a dream. Her happiness stopped her breath and caused her to gasp. She had never felt like this before. Never!

It was to be the beginning of a passionate love affair.

The day after that first, secret tryst, Robert's body returned home but his mind remained behind with Francie and he could focus on nothing but the thrill of being with her. Hungry for love, he became addicted to the exquisite creature who returned his passion with equal ardour. He travelled up to Liverpool each weekend and they met in the Adelphi Hotel where he had reserved a room.

He relived the memory of a previous weekend. He had travelled to Liverpool by train, tired of the regular return journey by car, and alighting at Lime Street Station, had dropped his valise in the hotel and continued to St John's Market. He had found the stall where Francie was working and stood at a distance watching her serving customers. Her graceful movements were at odds with her job. She handled fish as a duchess handles her jewels. She pushed back a strand of long dark hair and looked up. Catching sight of him, a smile spread across her face and she blushed. They could not acknowledge one another, lest someone who knew her family should see them, and whilst this was a frustration, it also added to the thrill. It was their secret. It bound them together against the world.

It had begun to drizzle as, at seven o'clock, she swung around the corner of the market entrance, where standing in the doorway of the chemist shop they had embraced.

'Phew! You smell of fish.'

'That's not so surprising,' she responded. 'Are you ashamed of me? Shall I get a job on a flower stall?'

'It would be a great deal more pleasant than the smell of cod,' he teased her.

As they began to walk arm in arm in the direction of Lime Street, the drizzle turned to a shower and the shower to a downpour so that they ran to shelter in an archway. Five minutes passed and the rain continued.

'Francie,' he covered her hand with his own, 'would you come back to the hotel with me? At least we would be dry, and it seems ridiculous to be walking around in the rain when we could be together in a room with a fire.'

He felt a shudder pass through her, but he did not know its cause. It could have been the coldness of the rain or it could have been the fear of his intentions. He waited, unspeaking, but she didn't reply. 'Francie?'

'I don't know, Bob. I don't know if we should.'

He thrilled at the unfamiliar form of address. 'Bob.' No one had ever called him that before. 'Bob.'

'It's all right, Fran, don't worry about it. Forget I asked.' He drew her close. She was almost as tall as he was but slender as a young elm.

'No, no.' She returned his hug. 'I want to. It will be lovely to be together indoors.'

'Are you certain? I don't want you to do anything you don't want to, Francie.'

'Yes.' It was no more than a whisper. 'Yes, I want to.'

He remembered, now, how he had stood, a hand on each of her shoulders, as the bellboy opened the door for them and he followed her inside. He had turned to tip the boy, and when he faced back into the room, she had moved to the fire. She stood, drenched with rain, her hair lengthened and straightened by the deluge, her clothes soaked and clinging to her body.

'Here, take off your coat.' He made to help her out of her coat but she took a step back and pulled it about her more tightly.

'Francie, I won't hurt you. Don't be afraid of me. I won't do anything you don't want me to.'

'That's the problem. I'm afraid I will want you to …' her voice trailed off and her hands dropped to her sides, loose and heavy. Her head fell upon her chest and the rain-soaked locks of her hair swung forward concealing her face.

Robert moved towards her and, with his arm around her shoulder, he pushed back the heavy curtain of hair.

'Oh Francie, Francie, Francie. My beautiful darling.' With an effort, he controlled his emotions and moved away. 'Look,' he said. 'I'll run you a bath and you can soak in it while your clothes dry in front of the fire. I don't know what your mother will think if you go home soaking wet. You can wrap yourself in my pyjama top or my one spare shirt until they're dry.'

He went to the bathroom, leaving her standing by the fire. When he came back, she was wrapped in the sheet off the bed. He turned his face away and felt her brush past him. When he looked again, she was gone, her clothes in a wet bundle on the floor. He drew in a deep breath and put his hands to his head. What was he doing? He knew that he was on dangerous ground. He didn't want to do anything that would hurt Francie, but he knew how much they were both struggling to keep control of a situation that was slipping away from them. He stooped to pick up her clothes. They were sodden, but there was nowhere to wring them out except the bathroom, and he must not go in there. He pulled the guard away from the fire and began to lay her shift and bloomers over it. He pulled the chair from the dressing table and laid her dress across its back. A cloud of fish-smelling steam arose from the wet garments. He unrolled her stockings and, closing his eyes, he held their wetness against his cheek. Her shoes squelched as he pressed the water from them. He drew out his handkerchief, wiped them inside and leant them against the guard.

Quite suddenly, he realised that his clothes, too, were saturated. But they would have to remain so. He could not risk upsetting Francie. He removed his jacket and wished he had had the foresight to bring a towel from the bathroom when he had run her bath. He began to shiver, despite the heat of the fire. Squatting on the floor before the flames, he warmed himself. He felt her hand on his shoulder and rising turned to see her there, wrapped in a towel. Her hair, a little while ago straightened by the rain, had now miraculously sprung back into tight, mahogany, gold-tipped curls, the white towelling enhancing the dark tumbling mass. Her scrubbed face was gleaming like satin and her cheeks were flushed from contact with the hot water. It was too much to bear. Nobody should be so beautiful. It was not fair to expect a man to behave honourably. He stepped closer and gathered her into his arms, and the towel dropped to the floor.

Even now, as he remembered, he could not be sure whether it was an accident or whether Francie had allowed it to happen. All he knew was that the sight of her, standing there was overwhelming. As he recalled the moment, his loins came to life and the tremor rose through his whole being until he was trembling all over.

Francie! He had drawn her against him so that he no longer had to look upon her. But control snapped. His mouth sought hers. She tasted sweet … she smelled sweet. He fought to re-establish control. His breathing slowed down, though he could still feel his heart thudding against the wall of his chest. He pushed her away, gently.

'Francie, we must stop this now.'

She moved into the space he had made between them, and pressed her body against his.

'No, Francie. It has to stop.' He broke away, and lifting his valise, he opened it, unpacked a shirt and shook it out. 'Here. Put this on.' His tone was sharp.

'I'm sorry.' She hung her head. 'You must think me a hussy. I feel so ashamed. I just couldn't help it. I love you so much. I'm so, so sorry. Please forgive me. I don't do things like this you know.' The

211

thought rushed into her mind. 'Oh, heavens, you don't think I've done this before, do you?' She began to cry.

Robert moved to comfort her, but came to a timely stop.

'Don't cry, Francie. I understand darling. I want to make love to you, but we should wait until we are married.'

She looked up through tear-filled eyes. 'Married? You would marry me? If you were free, you would marry me? Have I spoiled that now? You wouldn't marry a girl who has behaved like I have, surely?'

'Of course I would marry you. Will marry you. I'll get a divorce. We don't make love any more. It's a sham of a marriage.' It sounded false to his own ears. It was what men said. It was so trite. Again he fought the urge to embrace her. He shook himself vigorously.

'Look here. I'm going to have a bath, too. I'm soaking wet. When I come out, we'll talk some more and make plans for the future. Our future.'

She stood amazed, hardly believing her ears. He wanted to leave his wife and marry her. She was overcome with a sense of wonder. No thought of her mother's reaction. No thought of the pain it would cause others. He must love her. He must really love her. She sat on the edge of the bed, a vision in his starched white shirt. The bed was high, and her slender legs swung over the side and she glowed. Oh, how she glowed.

She was still like this when Robert, towel wrapped around his waist, stepped out of the bathroom. God in heaven, she was beautiful.

He moved across the room to where she sat and held her again, his eyes staring over her head at the wall behind her, his arms enfolding her, her cheek against his chest. His hands found the top button of his shirt and he released it and his index finger, in the hollow between her breasts, slid down to undo the buttons below until the shirt fell open. He pushed the fabric away from her left shoulder and his head came down to kiss the exposed flesh. Looking into her eyes, he slid the shirt from her other shoulder and lowered his gaze. As he watched, her soft, full nipples hardened and his lust was unbearable.

A shaft of sunlight falling across his face woke Robert. He turned his head to look at Francie. She lay facing him, the movement of the curtain in the breeze, making the shadows dance upon her cheeks.

As though cognisant of his gaze, she stirred and, with a flickering of her lashes, drew in a deep breath of contentment. She had a look of pure innocence on her face.

'And well she should have,' thought Robert, because what had taken place between them had been the purest joy imaginable. Far more moral and honest than what had, on very few occasions, passed as love between Cissy and himself. He adored her. They were meant for each other. He had no comprehension of the banality of the platitudes that ran through his mind. To him they were uniquely his own.

Unable to resist, he leant forward and kissed her eyelids. First the left … she shook her head a little as though relieving herself of a fly … then the right, causing both eyelids to flutter open in irritation, which turned to ecstasy, which turned to fear.

'Bob, what time is it. Oh, goodness, what will I tell Ma? Oh, Bob. She will be so worried. What have I done? I don't mean what happened between us, that was wonderful. I've no regrets about that but Ma will be so worried. Oh, Bob, what have I done?'

She threw back the bedding and Robert drank her beauty in anew. He reached out and caught her arm. 'Don't go, Francie. Wait a moment and listen. You have been out all night, another ten minutes won't make any difference.'

Francie relaxed a little and turned back to him.

'Let's think what we should do for the best. What are our options? Your mother will be very upset and, possibly angry …'

'Possibly?'

'Probably'

'Probably?'

'Certainly.'

'That's more like it.'

'We have several choices as I see it. Firstly, we can go back together and tell her that we are in love and want to be married.' Francie made to speak. 'Wait a moment till I've finished. Secondly, you can lie to her and tell her that you missed the last bus home and had to stay with Sally. Thirdly, don't go home at all. We can go somewhere together and wait until I can divorce Cissy and then marry. Then I can take you home and we can tell your mother.'

'No!' Francie interjected. 'No, Bob, I can't do that. You don't understand. I can't leave Ma without an explanation. She is such a lovely person and I love her so much. I hate to hurt her. We all do.

We couldn't have a better mother and it is so hard to cause her pain. No, I can't just leave without saying anything. Besides, there is my job.'

'You don't have to worry about your job. You'll never have to gut fish again. I am quite wealthy, and I'll be able to look after you well. Do you want us to go and tell her then?'

'No, I think I had better lie to her for the moment, though there will be ructions. I had better go home and say that I stayed at Sally's. Then I must go to work this afternoon and make sure Sally backs me up. What a mess.'

'I'm so sorry, darling.'

'No, Bob, don't feel sorry. I don't feel sorry. It was the most beautiful night of my life.' She raised herself on her elbow and looked down into his face. 'Did you mean what you said about wanting to marry me? Did you really mean it, Bob?'

'How can you ask me that, Francie? Do you really think that this means less to me than it does to you? I can't believe that you could love me. I will do anything in the world for you. There is nothing else in life but you. My Francie! My Love!'

Fanny was to look back in later years and wonder how she could have been so naïve as to believe the myriad excuses produced by her eldest daughter to explain her weekend absences. It was to be a long time before Robert returned to the house at Walton Road, and this saddened and puzzled her, yet still she did not connect the two things, even though she had seen the looks that passed between them. Well brought up young ladies just did not behave in this way and it did not occur to Fanny that any of her children would lie to her. It was unthinkable.

Chapter Thirty-Seven

The situation at home became unbearably tense. Cecilia was confused by Robert's sudden acceptance of the state of their relationship. He had become unmoved by her rejection of him and, indeed, he gave her no opportunity to repulse him. Bewildered by her unexplained loss of control over him, she felt an unaccustomed insecurity. Once or twice she had made approaches, gently laying her manicured hand on his arm, only to have it shaken off by her husband in an absent-minded gesture.

'What is wrong with you? You walk around like a zombie. It's as though I'm not here. You pay absolutely no attention to me. You go away weekend after weekend and leave me in this house all alone without telling me where you go, and when you are home you can scarcely be bothered to answer me. Really, Robert, I don't know what is happening but I don't deserve to be treated like this.'

She began to whimper, looking up at him between her fingers to gauge his reaction, but he made no sign of having heard her. Flying into a rage she rose from her chair and threw herself at him, hammering her fists on his chest. 'What is it? You have met someone else haven't you?' She waited for his denial. 'Haven't you?'

'Yes.' The word erupted from his mouth. There was complete stillness. It was abrupt, cruel and decisive! After a moment's silence in time, it reverberated around the room again, this time with greater authority, greater power and greater assurance. 'Yes, I'm afraid I have.' He threw it off like a heavy burden and a lightness entered into his soul. Suddenly, all things were possible. The deep, gnawing pain that had griped him ceaselessly since his first clandestine meeting with Francie, eased. He felt no shame, no sorrow or remorse, just a sense of liberty and euphoria. In a double wonder he had shaken off this harridan and embraced the possibility of replacing her with his beautiful Francie.

'Robert. You can't mean this.' She was astonished at his response to her rhetorical question. She had only thrown it at him as a rebuke for his coldness. She had never for a moment considered it as a possibility. 'You're angry with me. You are just making it up to punish me. Please, Robert, don't play games with me, there is no one else, is there? Come here and give me a kiss.'

'I have nothing to give you, Cissy. I gave you all I had to give, but you considered it worthless and now I want to be free of you. I want to be free of you, Cissy. I'm leaving you.'

The simpering fell away and anger began to rise in her. 'Don't fool yourself,' she spat. 'You are going nowhere. You are not going to cast me aside for some little tart. If you go, you will never see Charles again. I'll make sure of that. I wonder what your parents would think of their "darling boy" if he did something so disgraceful. You may be sure that I shall make certain they know how you've treated me – and your son. And don't imagine that I will give you a divorce. I will never divorce you and you can't divorce me. I am faultless in all this.' She flung out of the room.

Robert stood in the centre of the room, motionless. His emotions were being tossed and turned by changing events. One moment, as he caught sight of freedom and Francie, he had been elated, and the next he realised that escape was not so simple a matter, that not only Francie and he were involved, but many other people. For the first time, he felt a surge of gratitude that Charles was away at school and unaffected by what was taking place between his mother and father. He had fought a losing battle with Cecilia when she had first insisted that Charles should board. Then, recalling her threat that he would not see his son again if he chose to go to Francie, Robert felt a cold despair.

He lay in the spare room that night but sleep eluded him. He realised that he would never have found excuse for any other man to leave his wife and child to go to live with a young girl half his age. The world would consider it a contemptible thing to do, and despise the man who did it. His son would be ashamed of him. He would cause his parents such embarrassment and grief. He would not be able to hold up his head. The cost of happiness was high but he could not live without Francie. In any case, things had gone too far.

* * *

216

He was brought back to the present by a knock on the door.

He rose and crossed to open it. Cecilia was standing outside.

'Go to her.' She threw a suitcase on the floor between them. 'Go to her and don't come back.'

Chapter Thirty-Eight

Bertha arrived in Paris without understanding a single word of French. When she boarded the ferry to France she was alone for the first time in her young life. It should have been a liberating experience, but as she listened to unintelligible conversation and the small boat was tossed on the rough sea, she thought only of home. Bertha had no stomach for suffering and could only moan to herself, 'What on earth am I doing here?'

So when, at last, she stepped onto dry land she looked deathly pale and dishevelled and imagined that she must smell of vomit. Madame Patou, in whose Paris home she was to stay, met her off the boat. The French lady looked severe and humourless, and Bertha found her minute appraisal most disconcerting. The woman actually had the effrontery to walk around the bedraggled Bertha in a wide circle, her critical eyes scrutinising the girl from head to toe. Finally, she beckoned to a waiting driver standing beside a massive Rolls-Royce, turned and walked away without a word. Bertha stood uncertain of what she should do until Madame, turning to look over her shoulder, instructed the bewildered Bertha in brusque French. When Bertha did not respond, she repeated in English, 'Come, follow me. Non, non, non, non, non. Maurice will bring your baggage.'

The house was magnificent, and Bertha was overcome by its size and elegance. She was led up three flights of stairs to a small room under the roof. At first sight she thought it would be as dark and gloomy as the rest of the interior, but as she entered she was delighted to find that it was neat and pretty and chintzy, and suited her very well. She had never had a room to herself before. After the housemaid had left, she lifted the blind that covered the dormer window, and the room flooded with buttery sunshine. She knelt upon the window seat, opened the casement and looked out over the rooftops of Paris. She thrilled with excitement. The campanile of the nearby church began to sing the hour and the sound reverberated all around, increasing her elation. At the sound of the bells a flight of doves rose from the eaves, and circling around, came back to land again on the roof, where they strutted, flatfooted like fat, pregnant ladies. A ladder, which lay flat against the roof beside the window, led down to a fire escape that zigzagged its way to the ground far below. One of the birds stood on a rung and examined her, head cocked on one side inquisitively, his eyes reflecting the sunlight like two topaz gems nestling on pale grey velvet. Then the birds all settled down again, cooing softly. Unwrapping the remains of biscuits that she had not eaten on the boat, Bertha crumbled them between her fingers and sprinkled them below the window. Their appreciation was noisy and exuberant and infected her spirit with the same jubilation. Paris was intoxicating! The very air was different, heady and more pure. Surely she would burst. How she wished Francie were here to share her pleasure.

Dragging herself away from the window she opened her case and began to unpack her few belongings, shaking out her dresses and placing them on clothes hangers in the wardrobe. There was a tapping on the door and she shouted, 'Come in.' But no one entered. She called again but still the door remained shut. Crossing the room, she drew back the door. A young girl in black with a starched white apron and cap stood timidly outside. She began to speak in French, which was incomprehensible to Bertha, who drew the door wide open and beckoned the little maid in.

'Non, non Mam'selle, let me unpack for you.' She stopped and looked around the room. 'Bonté divine! Où est votre valise? Et votre garde-robe?'

Bertha pointed to the wardrobe and the maid's eyes opened wide in surprise at Bertha's sparse supply of clothes and to Bertha's discomfiture, she began to giggle.

*　*　*

'Auguste, mais que nous ont-ils envoyé? Cette petite Anglaise est une vraie savage. But why do they send to us this petite souris as a modèle?'

'Elle est très belle, Claudette.'

'Oui, she is beautiful all right, but she has no … comment dire … elle manque d'élégance. There are plenty of French models and they are better than the English.'

219

Bertha stood aside, a step or two behind her chaperone, having no conception of the tenor of their conversation.

Pym was leaning languidly over the balustrade on the floor above, looking down into the Académie foyer, when he saw her. He did not so much see her, as see a golden cascade swarming out from a shimmering crown. From this perspective she was just hair, but hair like he had never seen before outside of his imagination. Beside and in front of her stood a pair of shoulders and a feathered hat, and one of the tutors whose top view consisted of a shiny dome and a considerable paunch. The latter two were engaged in loud and urgent conversation, completely ignoring 'la cascade d'or'.

He felt in his pocket until his fingers encountered a piece of crayon. He drew it out and took careful aim at the centre of the golden circle, and his aim was swift and true.

Bertha felt something sharp sting the top of her head and turning slightly, out of the corner of her eye she saw a grinning face, topped by overly long curling hair. After a rapid appraisal of the risk, her gloved hand snaked up her back and she rippled her fingers. He was hanging perilously over the balcony when she turned her face up but she saw that the smile had faded to be replaced by a startled gaze and then he was gone from her sight. Her face coloured and she was thoroughly discomforted by his expression. Had she committed a terrible faux pas by acknowledging him? She looked around furtively, fervently hoping that no one else had witnessed her disgrace.

The more worldly girls in the market had always said it was wise at least to pretend to ignore boys. It made them more eager, they had said, and made the girls seem more chaste and, therefore, more desirable. But she deplored the etiquette that dictated that one's face and actions should contradict one's feelings. She had simply acknowledged a small mischievous pleasantry and now everybody would consider her gauche, a little fishwife. The tears stung behind her lids and she felt that her mother had been wise when she had countenanced her not to come to Paris. She belonged in Liverpool, in the fish market.

Madame Patou, having concluded her conversation, turned her head towards Bertha and said, 'Allez viens, petite Anglaise.' Indicating that Bertha should follow her, she led her across the foyer to the great staircase. As soon as they had rounded the column at its foot, the boy, who had been concealed by its girth, edged around, pressed hard against it. After Madame had passed, he stepped out in front of Bertha, who, although startled, recovered herself admirably, sidestepped him and lifted her head high, saying to herself as she did so, 'I am very beautiful.' When her back was towards him, she silently thanked Mr Peterson, and her face broke into a smile and she triumphed, 'Ha! He won't catch me like that again! I am not a common fish girl now. I am very beautiful.'

Pym watched her pass and his gaze followed her up the staircase. This girl was an uncommon beauty. He was in his final year at the Académie and so was long past feeling awe at the sight of a beautiful woman. But, truly, this was an awesome beauty, and she had seemed so delightful and ingenuous when she had acknowledged his fatuous action with that impish smile and furtive wave. But then, as he had lurked behind the pillar to catch a closer look at the perfection of her, she had adopted a churlish air of superiority that forbade any further dalliance. That look placed her beyond human aspiration. She was a goddess.

As the ladies reached the first floor, the stairs rounded to their left and Bertha, turning her head slightly over her left shoulder, saw that he was still staring at her, and her natural exuberance overcoming acquired discipline, she stuck out her tongue.

It was such a farcical sight. This goddess, this vision, this epitome of beauty and elegance, pushed out a small pink tongue between her white teeth and, withdrawing it, continued as though nothing had taken place. Pym threw back his head and laughed. She was glorious!

Each day he trawled the Académie for a sight of her. He looked in on every life-class. Surely she must be a model. He asked his fellow students on the sculpture course, but none of them knew of her. She had vanished as mysteriously as she had arrived. He had missed several anatomy studies as well as his sculpture classes. She became an obsession, sleeping and waking. She must sit for him. He must preserve that transient beauty in clay, in bronze permanence!

Today, having reached the last life class of the day, he surrendered the search and remained there, watching.

And then, when he had stopped trying, it happened. As he leant against the doorjamb of the studio, watching the model as she sat motionless, and wondering with a purely professional concern if Bertha's body could be as perfect as her face, he sensed her suddenly behind him, golden and cream and pink. She wore a soft, simple dress of ivory silk, which skimmed her body. The studio window was open against the oppressive heat and the slight breeze that entered there, rippled around the room in search of escape, until it found an outlet through the open door where they stood. It took hold of the flimsy fabric and pressed it gently against the contours of her body so that it undulated over her breasts and pelvis. They smiled at one another and his fingers curled around hers. She moved forward until she stood beside him and, with their fingers still entwined, she saw the nude woman sitting on a dais in the centre of the room. She felt the crimson rush. Never had she seen a naked body before, not even her sisters'. Ma had always taught them that they should never expose their bodies to another person, and she had heard, whilst eavesdropping, her mother imposing on Mr John, the instruction that Bertha must always be completely and modestly clothed when sitting for portraits. Yet here she was, standing hand in hand with a stranger to whom she had never spoken, let alone been introduced, and they were staring together at a totally naked and unembarrassed female. A tremor ran through her and, mistaking it for a chill from the breeze, he drew her closer.

'What a prim and prissy English girl I am,' she thought as she struggled to appear nonchalant. Not for the first time she felt gauche, like some uncultured peasant. She swiftly decided to accept and adapt to these novel circumstances.

It was to become Pym's abiding ambition to exhibit his bronze of Bertha in the salon.

A self assured young man called out 'C'est l'heure!' and the model slumped forward, her hair hanging down over her knees, and then she rose and stretched. She reached out and picked up her kimono, wrapping the sash around her waist as she padded, barefoot, to where water and a glass stood on a table. She poured herself a glass and began to sip it, looking around the room. Then she picked up a packet of cigarettes and shook one out onto her hand. As she did so, the sash fell undone again. Unconcerned, she lit the Gauloise and inhaled deeply.

Not all of the students put down their brushes and palettes immediately but they continued for different lengths of time, drifting one by one into small groups. A coterie of Dutchmen and one woman gathered in the corner nearest the window, and catching sight of Pym, waved to him to join them. He took Bertha by the elbow and guided her across the room until they stood in the middle of the Dutch group. Pym introduced her in French, and though she understood only a smattering of the language, she was able to discern what was being said. For some reason he had introduced her as 'Olivia' pronouncing the 'O' as an exaggerated diphthong.

The Dutchmen turned her this way and that, lifting her chin with a finger raising her hair onto the top of her head, all the time gabbling in an unintelligible guttural language. Bertha was becoming used to being prodded and poked like livestock, but she liked it no more now than she had when she arrived. For as long as she could remember, people had touched and stroked her, but since she arrived in France it had gained momentum to the point where she had to exercise great self-control to prevent her slapping appraising hands away. Just because she was 'quite pretty', people seemed to think that they shared ownership in her.

Pym sensed her discomfort and spoke quickly and low. The tallest and oldest Dutchman, Jan, said in excellent English, 'Forgive us, mademoiselle, it is the artist in us that craves to possess beauty that we might immortalise it, and it us. Let us all go now and take a glass of wine. The class is almost over, just one more session, we will not be missed.'

Bertha demurred. To both Pym and Jan she said, 'I can't come. I have to go back. I'm not supposed to go out without a chaperone. I only got out alone this afternoon because Madame had a headache and I had no sitting.'

'Nonsense, you will take a glass of wine with us and then we will return you to your "Madame". We want to know more about you, lovely Olivia.'

They were seven, seated around the table in the small café near the corner where Rue de Martyrs meets Rue Lepic in Montmartre. They spoke with great passion, arguing the virtues of Jean-Baptiste Pigalle and Rodin, but Bertha's French did not allow her to comprehend what they were saying. Her mind was in turmoil with a mixture of pleasure and fear. The atmosphere tingled with a joyous fever that filled her with elation, as though she and they were separated from the world outside, so that she started when Jan leaned forward and asked her, 'Whose classes do you sit for? I've never seen you in any of the studios.'

'I don't sit for students. I am here to sit for three portraits by the masters. I'm not a model … well, not really, though I have done a bit of modelling from time to time before I came to Paris. Mr Augustus John arranged my timetable. He's already painted my portrait and it was hung in the salon.'

'Ils gardent le meilleur pour eux, n'est-ce pas? We must go and see it.'

There was a wave of assent around the table and Pym leant towards her and whispered in her ear, 'He said that the masters keep the best for themselves,' and she flushed with pleasure.

'Would you sit for us privately if we could raise the money?'

'No, oh no. No!' Bertha was thrown into confusion by the turn the conversation had taken and her head was fuzzy from the wine. 'Forgive me. I have to go. I'm so sorry. Thank you for the wine.' Frenzied, she stood up to leave but the room moved with her and she stumbled and fell back onto the chair.

Pym, who had been leaning back on two legs of his chair, now stood up and moved around the table to Bertha. He took her firmly by the elbow and lifted her to her feet. 'I think I had better take Olivia home. I promised to look after her,' he lied.

The men rose and wished her 'bonsoir', and Pym steered her towards the cashier where he paid for the wine and they went out into the street to cheers and thanks in Dutch, French and English.

Outside, Bertha asked, 'Why do you call me Olivia?'

'Because that is who you are. I don't want to know what your mother called you. To me you are Olivia.'

Panic was rising in Bertha as they came out into the evening air, and she had only a nebulous idea of where they were. She didn't turn her head as Pym spoke to her, but looked straight ahead in stony silence. She'd never tasted alcohol before and she had the strangest, bemused feeling in her head. If this is what it was like to be drunk, she wondered why people desired it so much. But as they progressed along the road the feeling turned to a warm, carefree pleasure. It diffused through her body and she was unashamedly happy to be here in Paris, on a warm evening in early summer, with a handsome, considerate companion of indisputable charm.

Chapter Thirty-Nine

Fanny was distraught at Francie's behaviour and considered herself largely to blame. She had spent so much of her time worrying about Bertha in Paris that she had neglected her eldest daughter who had changed from an obedient and caring girl into a wilful and perverse creature that she could hardly recognise.

Fanny had not been able to talk any sense into her. Her attempt at discussion had resulted in Francie flouncing out of the door and not returning until nightfall. She was spending more and more time at Sally's house, and Fanny had vague misgivings about the amount of money that she had to spend.

'Ellen, where have I gone wrong? What did I do to deserve this?'

'Don't blame yourself, Fanny. Those two girls 'ave 'ad more temptations than we could dream about. Beauty can be a curse as well as a blessin' but, don't you worry, they'll be all right. They're both good girls an' they're just sowin' their wild oats. I'm sure you've nothin' to worry about with Bertha. She's got 'er 'ead screwed on right, an' Francie, well, she's just 'avin a good time while she's young.'

Francie was, in fact, spending her time in the new house Robert had bought in West Derby. She had given up her job and, during the day, she kept house for him, and in the evening they would curl up together and make love.

The only thing that marred her happiness was Fanny's constant nagging. She longed to tell her mother about her relationship with Robert, but the time was not yet right. She must do it step by step so that it did not come as a great shock, and when Cecilia gave Robert his divorce, she would be able to tell Fanny that they were in love and intended to be married. She constantly asked Robert if he had spoken to Cissy about divorcing him, but he procrastinated. However, she knew he loved her and wanted to settle down with her and have babies.

225

This happened rather sooner than either of them had hoped. Francie knew immediately that she had fallen pregnant, and she was frantic. When she told Robert he was enormously pleased, and seemed unable to understand why she should be so upset.

'We want babies don't we, my love? This is just perfect. We'll tell your ma and you can move in here.'

'But Bob, we're not married. You'll have to speak to Cecilia first and tell her that she must give you a divorce. I can't let anybody know that I am having a baby until we're married, then we can say it was premature. It'll be all right, but we must sort this out with Cecilia first and get married as soon as possible.'

But Robert knew his wife would never agree to divorce him, and that the knowledge that there was a baby on the way would make her even more adamant. As each day went by, Francie became more agitated. When she went home at night, she would climb straight up the stairs to the little room she had shared with Bertha, and wish that her little sister were there to confide in. She would open the door of the wardrobe and look at herself naked in its long mirror running her hands over her flat belly, looking for a sign.

One night she imagined that she was beginning to fill out, though she knew it was not possible at this stage. The next day she waited for Robert at the house and asked again, 'Have you spoken to Cecilia?'

Robert confessed that he hadn't, and a deluge of tears burst forth.

'I've got to go away,' she wept. 'I can't stay here, I'm beginning to show. Bob, I've got to get away somewhere until I've had the baby.'

'Don't be a little idiot, Francie, you can't be showing now. You're not even certain that you are pregnant. You could be doing all this worrying for no reason. You'll have to go and see a doctor.'

'No, I can't. How can I, Bob? I can't tell anyone. It would kill Ma if she found out. Please, darling, let me go away somewhere until I've had the baby and you'll be divorced by then and we can get married right away.'

Later that evening, after he had dropped Francie off at the end of Walton Road, he decided on what he must do and the next morning he telephoned Frank at his office.

'Frank, how are you?'

'We're both fine. Sophie is worried about you, though. We haven't heard from you for months.'

'No, I'm sorry about that, Frank. I have been rather busy. Life is a bit hectic at the moment. Listen, is there some way I can get in touch with Sophie quickly? I've got a favour to ask. Well, rather a big favour in fact.'

'Can I help you?'

'I think I'd rather run it past Sophie first, if you don't mind, old boy.'

'No, no, that's all right. Can she ring you in your office later on this afternoon? I'm going home for lunch so I can run her back to the office with me. We keep on saying we will get a house telephone, but I think it would only be used for telephoning you. Could she ring you about two-thirty?'

'Fine. You have my telephone number?'

'Yes. We'll call you later. Goodbye.'

At precisely two-thirty, Sophie telephoned.

'Hello, Robert darling, how are you? I do hate these telephone things. You really must keep in touch and come to see us. I haven't had a letter for months. What on earth has happened to you? We miss you so much. We'd got used to having you to stay regularly, and then you just vanish and we hear not a sound from you.'

'Just listen, Sophie, I've got something very important to ask you but before I do, please don't be judgmental, just try to understand. I really need you now.'

Sophie filled up with pleasure. Robert needed her. This was her whole ambition in life before she met Frank and transferred half her adoration to him.

'Of course, you know I'll do anything for you.'

'Well, you'll need to talk it over with Frank before you give me an answer.' He paused, unsure of how to proceed without shocking her.

'Yes, go on. I'm sure that Frank will feel exactly as I do. We would both do anything to help you. What's your problem, darling?'

'Since I left Cissy, I've been very lonely. You and Frank have been wonderfully good to me but I need someone of my own, Sophie. Do you understand that?'

'You've got another woman.' Her voice was flat.

'Yes. Well, a girl actually. I'll tell you all about her in a letter. She's the daughter of the man who saved my life. We want to get married, but Cissy has said she won't give me a divorce. Well anyway...' he trailed off.

'She's pregnant?'

'Yes.'

'How can we help?'

'This could have been a big mistake,' he thought.

'Never mind,' he said. 'Forget about it. I just wanted you to be the first to know how happy I am. She is a beautiful girl, Sophie, I'm sure you will love her when you see her. I'd like to bring her down to meet you. How do you feel about that?'

'Robert, if she makes you happy, she will be very welcome to stay here until after her confinement.'

'Oh Sophie, you are a wonder. How did you know that that is what I wanted to ask you?'

'As you are only too well aware, Frank and I have never been blessed with children. It will be wonderful for us to have a baby in the house. When are you bringing … what is she called, Robert?'

'Francie, her name is Francie.'

'When are you bringing Francie?'

'How would it be if we came on Saturday?'

'Fine, I'll make the bed up for her … for both of you. Oh, Robert darling, please forgive me. I'm finding this hard. I don't disapprove. I know how unhappy Cecilia made you … but it is just a little hard to handle. I'm sure she will be lovely if you love her. We'll see you on Saturday. About what time shall I expect you?'

'We'll start very early and be there for lunch. Is that all right?'

'Yes. Goodbye, dear.'

'Goodbye, Sophie. And thank you.'

'I've been offered a job in London and that is all there is to it!' Francie spat the words out at poor, bewildered Fanny.

'But why, Francie? It's such short notice and you've told me nothing about what kind of job it is.'

'Oh, it's OK for Bertha to go skipping off to Paris, but I can't be trusted to go to London. And she's younger than I am. Well, I'm going. OK?'

'Don't use that terrible American slang when you're speaking to me. You can go where you like. I don't care any more, though I wonder what your father would think if he were still alive.' Fanny left the room and went upstairs to talk to Charlie.

'I hate you,' spat Winnie. 'I hate you, Francie. Ma and me and the boys'll be better off when you're gone. You're nothing but trouble.' Winnie followed her mother upstairs in order to offer her comfort, and Francie dropped into a chair and sobbed softly. Then, she picked up the case which she had packed with her few belongings, and left, shutting the door quietly behind her.

There is an esoteric aura in the very early hours of the morning when only a few initiates are abroad. It is as though they share a secret that the sleeping world knows nothing of. Francie had this sense of belonging to this mystic society in the early dawn when they drove down to London. The morning was cool, detached from the dusty heat that was promised for later in the day, and the placid stillness evoked in her a serenity that she had not felt since she knew about the baby. She sat back on the leather seat of the black Jaguar. She loved this car! She longed for the day that she could roll up in it to the front door in Walton Road, a married woman with a beautiful child.

She hated the thought that she would only see Robert at the weekends, but as he had said, it was only for a few months and then it would all be worthwhile.

'You will ask Cecilia about the divorce, won't you Bob? She can't refuse now, not if you tell her we're having a baby, can she? Promise me you'll talk to her as soon as you possibly can.'

Robert drew her closer, his right hand remaining on the wheel, 'I promise, my love. As soon as I leave you in London I'll sort it out.'

'And you'll write to me won't you? You will let me know what she says?'

'Stop fretting, Francie. I've told you, I will sort it out.' He was faintly tetchy now.

They drove in silence for a long time, Francie happily anticipating her return home with her baby and settling again into their new house in West Derby, having her mother and Bertha to tea, pouring the tea into fine china cups like her mother had, tucked away in the kitchen cupboard.

Robert was thinking about how impossible this whole business was. He knew that Cissy would never give him a divorce, and dreaded telling her about the baby. She had threatened him with not seeing Charles again. He stiffened. They would see about that. If they divorced, he would get custody of his son and it would be Cissy who would be unable to see him. He would have to talk to Francie about Charles coming to live with them at an opportune time. What a mess he had made of things.

'Let's stop here for something to drink.' He pulled onto a

gravelled forecourt and came to a halt in front of a teashop. The moment had passed.

When they came out, the morning was established and there were people about. They continued their drive without much conversation, content to be together travelling along the country roads and through the market towns.

Eventually, London loomed ahead and Francie began to feel the excitement rise in her. She wondered whether Robert's sister would like her, and she felt like a country mouse despite her smart clothes and new, upswept hairstyle.

They pulled up in front of a delightful little house in Swiss Cottage and before the car had come to a halt, the door opened and a plain woman in a red and white spotted apron came out, holding a small dog in her arms. The dog, seeing Robert, wriggled and squirmed and the woman allowed him to jump to the ground. He ran yelping towards Robert and jumped up against his legs, his tail wagging with pleasure. Robert stooped to pick him up and ruffle the fur around his neck, and the woman crossed to him and embraced him.

'Robert, darling, it's wonderful to see you,' and bending down to look into the car she continued, 'and this must be the lovely Francie.'

'I'm sorry, Francie.' He opened the car door and helped her out. 'Yes, this is my...' he hesitated, unsure of how to proceed, and Francie realised that this was the first time he had introduced her to anybody.

'I'm Francie,' she held out her hand, 'Robert's fiancée.'

She was certainly very beautiful. Sophie appraised her from head to toe and noted nothing but perfection. The flecks of gold in her hair and eyes were quite unique. She made Sophie feel plain and dowdy, but if she made Robert happy, Sophie would make a real effort to like her.

Sophie's easy manner made Francie feel clumsy and awkward. They were very different. The only common ground they shared was their mutual love for Robert, but that was enough. The older woman took the outstretched hand and drew Francie into the house, her free arm around the girl's shoulder, urging her forward.

'I am so pleased that you are coming to stay with us for a while. Robert has told us all about you.' Over her shoulder she continued, 'You told us she was beautiful, Robert, but ... Sit down, Francie. No,

230

over here, it's more comfortable. Did you have a good drive down? It's such a long way, isn't it, but I must say, you both look very fresh.'

Robert followed them into the room, still holding the dog.

'Oh, do put him down Robert.' She took him from Robert and placed him outside the door. 'There you are, Jujube, now you be a good boy.' She closed the door, and smoothing down her apron, she sat on Francie's left and continued to question her. 'When is the little one due, Francie?'

'In the New Year.'

'What a lovely way to start the year. Do you hope for a boy or a girl? Have you thought about names? What are you going to call him … or her?'

Polite conversation continued, with Sophie trying hard to put the girl at ease, until she rose and said, 'I must go and see what's happening in the kitchen. We're having a late lunch if that's all right with you. Frank will be home any moment now. I do the cooking myself, but Violet helps me in the kitchen. I'll just go and see how she's getting on.'

She hurried out of the room and Robert crossed to the settee and sat down next to Francie, taking her hand in his.

'Are you all right?'

'Mm.'

'Do you like her?'

'Mm. Yes, yes I do.'

'I told you she was a dear, didn't I? She'll make you very much at home. I know I can trust Sophie to look after the both of you.' He patted her stomach and felt a sudden surprise at its roundness.

They pulled apart quickly as they heard a key turning in the front door and voices in the vestibule. The door opened and a burly man entered, his arm around Sophie who barely reached his shoulder. Her face was turned up and she looked tenderly into his. Frank disentangled himself from her embrace and greeted Robert.

'Good to see you, stranger. It has been too long. What have you been doing with yourself?'

'Francie, this is my husband, Frank.' Sophie continued to gaze up at him adoringly and Francie, seeing an ageing, balding, portly man, wondered what Sophie saw to idolise in him.

Frank leant forward and took her hand in both of his. 'Welcome to our home,' he said. 'We are both delighted that you are going to stay with us awhile. You must make yourself at home and treat our house as though it were your own.'

Sophie said, 'Robert, would you like to show Francie her room … your room. You know what I mean. Perhaps you'd like to freshen up, Francie. Lunch will be on the table in two or three minutes.'

Chapter Forty

Fortunately, but unexpectedly for Bertha, Madame showed no sign of disapproval at her late return. In fact she seemed more amiable than usual.

'Did you have a good day today, ma petite Anglaise? How does the latest portrait progress?'

Her headaches had increased in frequency when she discovered that she did not have to be with this tiresome English girl everywhere she went. It presented her with an excellent excuse to remain at home when Bertha went to the Académie.

'Perhaps it would be best if you did not mention my affliction to anybody else, Bertha. It would be unkind to worry people unnecessarily, ne c'est pas?'

'Oh, I agree, Madame, when your poor head is so troublesome, how can you be expected to traipse around after me in this hot weather?'

So the two had a secret arrangement that suited both admirably, since it left Madame to pursue her own interests and Bertha free to meet with Pym and his friends after her sittings. Sometimes she would observe the drawing, painting and sculpture classes, and most of the masters raised no objections. They were enchanted by Bertha. She loved the sculpture sessions because she could stand beside Pym as he shaped the clay into a wonderful likeness of the subject statue. He was frequently despondent and would knock down the clay and begin again and, on these days, he would be depressed and distant with her.

'Why are you like this, Pym? Look around you. Isn't yours the best? You are too hard on yourself. What is it you want?'

'I want to sculpt you, Olivia. I want you to sit for me and I will create the most wonderful work of art the world has ever seen. Sit for me, Olivia. Will you do it for me?'

'You know I can't. It's in the agreement that I must only sit for people who have been designated by the panel. You know that I would do anything for you, Pym, but I can't do this. It's not fair of you to ask me.'

Nevertheless, the moment of weakness came and Bertha succumbed. They were together alone in the café where they had gone on that first afternoon, drinking coffee, when Pym reached out and placed his hand over hers.

'Olivia, I'm going to ask you one more time. Please. You are the most beautiful girl in Paris, maybe even in the world ...'

'Maybe?' she teased him.

'Surely,' he said without smiling. 'But it is not only your beauty that makes the project so seductive. The fact that I love you brings an extra dimension to it.'

'Love me?' Rapture! 'Love me, Pym? Do you really love me?'

'Of course I love you.'

'I didn't know. You never said.'

'Surely, I don't have to say it with my lips for you to realise it, Olivia. After all, I know you love me but you've never said it.'

'Oh, I do, I do, Pym. I love you. I love you. There you are, I've said it.'

'And I love you. Will you model for me? I can't pay much, but when the statue is finished, it will command a high price and I will be able to make it up to you.'

'Of course I will. Oh yes. You don't have to pay me, Pym. I will love modelling for you.'

Elated, he leant over the table and kissed her on the mouth, and the excitement of that contact released a rush of adrenalin that made her delirious with pleasure and zealous for more. She, too, rose and they left the café, hand in hand. Their relationship had changed in pitch and intensity. They were in love.

Ironically, the more time they spent together, the less time they shared. Now, the proportions had changed. Ninety per cent of the available time was spent in the empty studio as artist and model, and only ten per cent remained to enjoy each other as boy and girl. They worked in an atmosphere of furtiveness, which made the work more difficult and laborious than it would otherwise have been, but Bertha adored Pym and learned to be happy in his company in any circumstances. Sometimes it seemed to her that he regarded her only as a subject, but when they rested from the work, he devoted such loving attention to her that she melted.

234

As for Pym, he enjoyed Bertha in equal parts. Sculpting her was absolute delight to the artist in him, and loving her was ecstasy to the man. He daydreamed that she would come to live with him in his room in Monmartre but he knew without asking that there was nothing of the bohemian in Bertha. She was excessively conventional, even a little prudish, but it was a trait which he found endearing in her. Yet he longed to make their relationship complete.

When he escorted her home, they would part on the corner of Rue de Marquise so that they should not be seen together.

'Let me walk you all the way. I want to see where you live.'

'What if someone sees us?'

'Does it really matter, Olivia? People are just going to have to get used to seeing us together. I think we are being too cautious. We've done nothing wrong, and I am proud to be seen with you. If they find out that we love each other, they'll just have to accept it. Come on, I'll walk you to your door.'

She was pleased and fearful at the same time but, defiantly, she linked her arm through his and guided him to the house.

'You live there?' His mouth fell open and he turned to look at her with eyes wide in exaggerated astonishment.

She laughed at his expression. 'No, idiot. I am just staying here until the portraits are finished.'

He looked up at the massive building again. 'Which is your room?'

'Round the back. Come, I'll show you.' They retraced their steps and turned left round the side of the grounds. As they reached the end of the stone wall, she pointed through the railings that topped it. 'There,' she said, 'that dormer window in the roof. That's my room. I love it. It's wonderful up there. The sun wakes me up each morning, that and the cooing of the doves, and I can see right over Paris. I wish I could take you up to see it.'

'I wish you could, too. Can you smuggle me in one day when there's nobody around? I would just love to see where you sleep. I could imagine you last thing at night before I close my eyes.'

'Pym! The thought of sneaking you in makes my blood run cold.' She moved closer until she was against his chest and raised her lips to be kissed. Then she shook him off, turned and ran back around the corner, leaving Pym staring at her window and the ladder that lay beside it … and the fire escape that ran up to it.

Occasionally Madame would accompany her, though Bertha knew it was merely for appearance's sake. She hated the days that she was chaperoned, because it set her aside from her friends and emphasised their freedom and her own bondage. When she thought about her time in Paris coming to an end, she would feel a massive lump weighing down her stomach, causing her such misery that she would feel physically sick.

Towards the end of autumn, when the leaves lay thick beneath their feet and the great plane trees, half-naked, let the grey sky show through their branches, they walked along the Quais towards the Pont St Michel. Her happiness turned to melancholy which, in turn, became deep despondency. So heavy was the sense of despair at the realisation that this idyll must end, that she shared her thoughts with Pym and he, too, became grave.

'It had not occurred to me that you would go back to England when your contract was up. Why do you have to go back at all, Olivia? Why can't you stay? You are happy here, aren't you?'

'How can I stay, Pym? I will have no money and nowhere to live.'

'I don't want you to go. We belong here. I can't see why you can't stay. You can share my room with me and you will be able to make money modelling. When your time is up, you will be able to sit for whoever you like and they will be queuing up to pay you whatever you ask. How can you leave me, Olivia? How can you leave me and your cooing doves and Paris?'

'I don't want to go home, my love, but what you're asking frightens me. I can't stay after my contract is up.'

It was the first time they had thought about the future. They had been living as though that summer would never end; as though they could spend the rest of their lives, sipping sweet, black coffee in the pavement cafes of St Germain or sitting under the trees in the Place St Sulpice, strolling hand in hand through the pleasant Jardin du Luxembourg, mooching through the musty books on the stalls along the quays. Relishing the wonder and glory and euphoria of Paris in an eternal spring!

Now, he guided her across the cobbles to a bench where they sat together, silent and sombre. A burnt umber leaf fluttered down, swaying from side to side until it lay upon its siblings on the hardening earth, a reminder that winter was just a breath away and their time together was almost over.

'When the next portrait is finished, I shall be going back.'

236

Hesitantly she asked, 'Will I see you again, Pym?' She waited for his answer, but it was as though he had not heard her. Mistaking his lack of response for apathy, she went on, 'No, I don't suppose I will. I'll return to Liverpool,' And the fish market, she thought, and you will forget all about me. A tear rolled down her cheek and she halted its course with the tip of her tongue.

'Don't be silly, Olivia.' His voice was brusque. 'There's no question of our being separated. If you really can't stay here in Paris, then I will go to Liverpool with you, but we need to think about it. I'd much rather we stayed here. We've been so happy, haven't we? And I don't want to finish my studies just now. I want to live with you, Olivia. I want us to be married. Will you marry me, Olivia?'

'Pym, my darling Pym, you want to marry me? You really want us to be married?' Amazement, elation and sheer incredulous joy filled her whole body as she flung her arms round his neck.

'Of course I want to marry you. How else will I get to finish your statue?'

She punched him playfully, and then, controlling her excitement, she became serious. 'I'm only eighteen and we will have to wait until I'm twenty-one.'

'Not if your parents agree. We'll go to Liverpool together and I will utterly charm them so that they can't say no.'

'My father is dead, but I know my mother will like you and you will adore her. She is wonderful; she is the love that is always there.'

'I am sorry about your father, but I, too, will be the love that is always there, Olivia.'

They sat motionless, wrapped in an embrace, Bertha deliriously happy, but Pym weighing in his mind the deprivation of leaving his wonderful Paris against the loss of his fabulous muse, Olivia.

A lone dragonfly settled on the lovely curve of her neck where it flowed into her right shoulder and, tired from its summer exertion rested, hovering now and then. Pym took out his pencil and rummaged in his pockets for some scrap of paper to immortalise the tiny creature, but could find none.

'Don't move,' he instructed Bertha, and as she froze into complete stillness, he slid his hand beneath the neckline of her dress and eased it to expose a patch of ivory skin. He rapidly sketched the hovering insect on her shoulder, just below the clavicle, before it rose in the air with one last, weary effort and receding into the distance, vanished from their sight.

'I want to see it, Pym. How can I see it? I haven't got a mirror.'

He guided her to the nearest salon and Bertha, turning her back to the plate glass window and looking over her shoulder saw a beautiful, fluttering image poised on the curve where her neck and back met. He had so captured the feathery quivering of its wings that she held her breath as though not to unsettle it.

'Have you got a handkerchief, Olivia?'

Bertha took one from her pocket but as he made to take it, she snatched it back. .

'What do you want it for?'

'To rub it off. Do you want Madame to know what a brazen hussy you are, exposing your body to a decadent artist?'

'No, don't wipe it away, Pym. I want to keep it as long as possible. I wish I could keep it always.'

'Do you really, Olivia?' He raised one eyebrow in question. 'You can, you know. Come with me. Let's keep it there forever. It will be my seal of ownership.'

Taking her hand, they retraced their steps into the Latin Quarter and, turning right, away from the Seine, twisted and wound down a maze of narrow medieval streets and alleys until, breathless, Pym stopped in front of a small shop. There was no one around but it was open. The bell clanged as they entered and a slight woman with clouds of black floss floating in a vast circle around her face, appeared through a curtain.

'Oui. Que vous fallait-il?'

Pym spoke to her in rapid French and she nodded her assent, hair rising, floating and falling in all directions. She pushed it back and, gathering it together, anchored it with a long, colourful scarf.

'Oui,' she said again, giving her attention to Bertha and turning her around. 'Voulez-vous vous asseoir ici?' She indicated the dragonfly. 'C'est charmant.'

She sat a terrified Bertha on a high stool and began to prepare her equipment.

'Pym, I'm scared. What's she going to do? Is she going to tattoo me?'

'Don't worry, my little Olivia, she will just trace faintly over the lines that I have drawn. If you are apprehensive, shall I go first?'

Bertha nodded wordlessly and Pym spoke in French, too fast for her to comprehend and, putting his hand beneath her elbow, he helped her from the stool and settled himself in her place. The tattoo artist stood Bertha beside Pym and began to copy the pattern from Bertha's left shoulder onto Pym's right. Bertha watched in fascination as the ink penetrated the skin and reproduced an exact copy of her dragonfly. When it was finished, the lady held up a mirror for Pym's approval, and satisfied of its accuracy, he said to Bertha, 'Are you ready? Are you sure you want to do this?'

She nodded twice but made no sound, and she lifted herself up onto the stool that Pym had just vacated. She felt her skin being dabbed gently with an ice-cold swab, and flinched at the first prick. It felt as though a sewing machine were piercing her skin with a hot needle but after the first few stings, it was nothing more than a tingle.

When it was finished and they stood side by side, inspecting their tattoos over their shoulders, the pleasure that they felt far exceeded the pain they had suffered. The twin dragonflies were small, faint and discreet … and very, very lovely.

On the next three days, Madame, for reasons unknown to Bertha, insisted on accompanying her to her sittings. It may have been because Bertha's departure was growing imminent and she felt that she should be seen with the girl during her last few weeks, or she may simply have been having feelings of guilt at having neglected her obligation. Wherever they went, Bertha dutifully followed two steps behind her, her eyes darting backwards and forwards in search of Pym. She was anxious that he should know the reason for her non-appearance, but could find no way of getting a message to him. It was essential that he should see her with Madame and know that she was unable to escape the steely eye of her chaperone. On the afternoon of the third day, she saw him and a look of love and frustration passed between them and then he was gone.

That night, as Bertha lay on her bed, thinking about Pym and wondering how they were to meet if Madame insisted on her renewed vigilance, there was a tapping on the window. At first she dismissed it as the wind, but when it persisted, she rose and crossed the room. She pushed open the casement and there, crouching beside the window, on the roof ladder, was Pym, his grin creasing his face. He held the ladder with one hand. Looking down at the ground three floors below, Bertha was reminded of Joe and fell back against the inside of the eave.

'Pym,' she whispered. 'Oh God in Heaven, Pym. You could have killed yourself.'

He wriggled through the dormer like a caterpillar and it swung shut behind him. Bertha, her hands under his arms, dragged him in and they fell in a heap together onto the floor. Her terror was mixed with joyous excitement and they rolled over and over clasping one another, kissing hair, faces, necks. Finally, exhausted by their passion, they lay together on the floor, neither speaking but their eyes locked. They were both amazed at the calm that fell upon them. It was as though they were wrapped as one in peace and gentle bliss. It is, thought Bertha, like a religious experience. They had entered a different realm. They were one in spirit. They lay, still looking into each other's eyes. Pym took the end of the ribbon that closed the neck of her nightgown and pulled it gently. The neckline parted. Then, his eyes still holding hers, his fingers found the next ribbon and he drew this towards him and the bodice fell open. He gazed at her, his mouth dry, his breath abated. Full of fear lest he should break the spell, he ran one finger down between her breasts and parted the fabric, and it was just as he had always known it would be. She was as perfect as in his waking dream. Rising onto his knees, his arms slid beneath her and he lifted her onto the bed and, still holding her shoulders raised, he slipped the nightgown over her head. Then he undressed and lay down beside her.

Dawn must have been breaking, because the room was filled with a pale pink glow. Pym rose softly, so as not to disturb her, and pulled on his trousers and shirt. He crossed to the window and looked out. It had been raining and now the rooftops were frosted and glistening in the fresh, dawn light. He would have to hurry. Crossing back to where Bertha lay, he bent over and kissed her lightly. He tied his shoes together by the laces and slung them around his neck. Standing on the chair he placed one hand on either side of the aperture, and levered himself up on his arms. Turning, he sat on the ledge and pulled his legs up after him. His left foot made contact with the roof ladder and he transferred his weight from the window to the third rung, but as he moved his hand to take hold of the upright, a dove rose and, fluttering over his head, startled him and his foot slipped on the wet steel. He slithered uncontrollably down the roof and over the parapet, grasped at the top of the fire escape, missed, and hit the cobbles, thirty feet below.

240

Bertha was awakened by his scream and was filled with mortal dread. She sped to the skylight, climbed upon the chair and looked over the sill. The angle of the roof hid the ground immediately below from her view but instinctively she knew what had happened.

'No!' The word reverberated across the Paris rooftops. 'No-o-o-o!' Like a wounded animal, all anguish and suffering in that one word, 'No!' She slipped from the chair and lay crumpled, like a discarded puppet on the floor.

Fanny reread the letter with mounting horror.

Madame,
It is with regret that I must ask you to meet your daughter, Bertha, at Lime Street Station on the morning train from Euston. The train leaves Euston at 11.30 am. I regret I have been unable to ascertain the exact time of arrival in Liverpool.

I am sorry for the short notice but your daughter has brought disgrace on my house and I can no longer tolerate her outrageous behaviour. I must confess here, that I had reservations as soon as I met the girl and that, in spite of my constant vigilance and care at all times, she has managed to exceed my very worst fears.

She has been receiving young men into her bedchamber during the night, the only time, which for modesty's sake, she has been left unchaperoned, and one of her paramours fell from the roof when leaving her room and was killed.

The scandal that has ensued has caused great trouble to my household and myself. I suggest, Madame, that you lock up this wayward girl when she returns to you that she may cause no more trouble to those who have, out of the goodness of their hearts, offered her hospitality and sought to guide her.
Yours sincerely,

It was signed Claudette Patou.

Fanny sank slowly into her chair, using her right hand to steady herself, and holding the letter loosely in her left. She lifted the notepaper again and stared at it vacantly. 'This cannot be happening to me.' She was alone in the house and she looked around the room as though searching for someone to comfort her.

'Charlie,' she sighed. 'Why did you have to go? I can't do this on

241

my own. It's not fair.' Now the tears were flowing. 'You didn't have to go, neither did you have to come between that man and the bullet. You owed more to me, to us, the children and me, than you did to some stranger. I can't do it any more, Charlie, I can't do it any more.'

'Hush, now, Little Goose. You are strong. You have to do it. There is no one else. I trust you, Fanny; I've always trusted you. You will look after our little ones. It doesn't matter what they have done, they're our children. Do you remember how we dreamt of them when we were very young? Do you remember when we were all together in the beginning? Do you remember all that love and laughter, Fanny? You mustn't give up on them now, and you mustn't believe the words of a stranger until you have spoken to our daughter. You give her the benefit of the doubt until she can defend herself. I don't believe there is a bad streak in either Francie or Bertha. Wait, Little Goose, wait until Bertha comes home and, whether it's right or wrong, she is still going to need your love. I haven't left you alone, Little Goose; I'm here with you always. In your head, in your heart.'

Drying her eyes, she murmured, 'Thank you, Charlie. You're always such a comfort.'

The girl that Fanny met at Lime Street Station was not the Bertha that she had said goodbye to nine months earlier. This girl was beautiful, maybe even more beautiful in her pathos, but she had a haunted look in her eyes and an air of tragedy and misery surrounded her.

'My good God!' She stumbled forward in her haste to take her child in her arms and shelter her as Bertha's knees gave way. 'Bertha, whatever has happened to you? Oh, Bertha, my dear, my love! Come here to me. Come let me take you home. Don't worry Bertha, no one's going to hurt you now.' She knelt on the platform and rocked her daughter backwards and forwards, oblivious to the curious stares of other passengers.

The dam gates, which Bertha had kept sealed, burst open. Crouching on the floor, her mother holding her tightly, great sobs exploded from her frail body as all the anguish of the past days emptied out of her in a torrent.

Chapter Forty-One

Francie received Bertha's letter when she and Sophie returned from shopping in the mews. The two had become firm friends, with a genuine appreciation of one another's virtues. After the first flush of marriage and home-making, Sophie had come to feel lonely during the day while Frank was at the office, and now Francie had become like the daughter she had never had. They laughed together as they unburdened themselves of their acquisitions but at the sight of the familiar handwriting Francie froze. How could Bertha know where she was? She had given no one this address except Sally and she had sworn her to secrecy. Besides, Bertha was in France and the postmark on the envelope was Liverpool.

'Well open it, silly, and then you'll know!' Sophie laughed as she handed her the paper knife from the bureau.

Francie slit open the envelope and took out a single sheet of paper.

> My darling Francie,
> Yes I'm home – in disgrace – and I so very much need you. Oh, Francie, I really need you. Forgive Sally for giving me this address. I tortured her until she gave in. Ma only knows that you are working in London. It sounds so exciting. But, Fran, Ma is so miserable that she doesn't know where you are so if you come home you will make both of us happy. I must see you. I can't tell you anything in a letter but I do need you. Please Fran.
> Love always, your sister Bertha.

Panic set in and the alarm transferred itself to Sophie as Francie ran her fingers through her hair.

'Whatever is the matter, Francie?'

'Oh, goodness, Sophie. It's from my sister. She knows where I am.

If Ma finds out about my pregnancy … I don't know, I don't know. Oh Sophie, what am I going to do?'

'Calm down, Francie,' she laid her arm around the distraught girl's shoulders, 'calm down, it'll be all right. Robert will be here tonight. He'll know what to do. You're quite safe here. No one can harm you. Shush, shush now.' She drew Francie towards her and gently patted her back to soothe her.

'Oh yes. Thank goodness Bob will be here soon. He can go and see Bertha for me and find out what's wrong. Oh, I hope she doesn't tell Ma where I'm staying.' She was composing herself now as she spread out the letter and read it again.

'Something's wrong, Sophie, I know it is. I should really go to Bertha but just look at me! I can't hide my condition any longer.'

'Francie, sit down and I'll make you a cup of tea. Don't get yourself upset. Leave it to Robert. Maybe he'll bring Bertha down to see you here and your mother need not know but you know she's going to find out some time. As long as you and Robert love each other, it doesn't matter. You'll be married as soon as he can get rid of that dreadful Cecilia. I really wish he had met you first.' She hugged the girl again before ringing for Violet. Tea was needed at a time like this.

The hours seemed interminable before Robert's Jaguar pulled up in front of the house. Francie had spent most of the previous hour at the window, and now she saw the car and ran to open the door. She flung herself into his arms and the tears, that she had been fighting back all afternoon and evening, now cascaded from her eyes. The words that accompanied them were incoherent and Robert, with great difficulty, guided her into the house and tried to placate her.

'Francie. Stop now. Francie, sh, I can't tell what you're saying. Calm down and tell me what's wrong.' He took his handkerchief from his breast pocket and wiped her eyes.

'Now, quietly, tell me what's so terrible that you're falling apart.'

After he had taken off his coat, she showed him the letter and reluctantly admitted that she had given Sally, Frank and Sophie's address in case of emergency.

'It doesn't matter,' he said. 'It's not important, Francie. Of course you must get in touch with Bertha and find out why she needs you, but your mother doesn't have to know where you are. When I get back, I'll go to the house to see your mother and I'll make an

244

opportunity to talk to Bertha. When we know what has happened, we can decide what to do. It may be best to bring Bertha down here, if that's all right with Frank and Sophie.'

'Of course it's all right. It'll be nice for you to see your sister anyway, Francie. You see? I told you it would be all right when Robert got here. Come now, both of you sit down and we will plan how we should handle this.'

'Have you spoken to Cecilia yet? Has she agreed to a divorce? If only she will agree, none of this will matter. We can be married right away and then I can go home.'

'It's not as easy as all that, darling. These things take time. I think one has to wait two years before a divorce is made absolute, so Cissy agreeing isn't going to help at the moment. Things have to be arranged. We will have to find someone willing to be sited as co-respondent and all that side will have to be set up.'

'That sounds very sleazy, Robert. Is there no other way of managing it?' Sophie was reluctant to see her brother branded an adulterer, though she supposed that was exactly what he was, and yet she could not but feel happy that he was going to shake off the hated Cecilia and marry this dear little girl. She wished that the precious relationship between these two people whom she loved would not be seen by the world as a sordid affair.

'I think you are trying to avoid the issue.' Francie was becoming tearful again. 'I asked you whether you had approached Cecilia; whether you had talked to her about it at all. I don't believe you've …'

'Francie! I've had a long drive. I'm very tired and I am not in the mood for wrangling. Cissy will never agree to a divorce and, even if she did …' Francie made to interrupt, but his voice grew louder, 'even if she did, she would never let me see my son and I'm not prepared to give up Charles. Just leave me to manage this in my own time, in my own way. When the time is right, I'll talk to Cecilia.'

But Francie had already left the room.

Sophie had remained silent throughout this altercation and now she moved to Robert and placed her hand upon his arm.

'She's very young and she has never met Cecilia. She doesn't have any idea how self-centred and nasty she can be. Give her time.' They sat down together side by side on the sofa, Sophie turning to face her brother. 'What is to stop you saying that you are married? Who would know the difference? Nobody is going to demand to see your marriage certificate.'

'Her mother knows that I'm married and have a child. She will also know that it is not possible to obtain a divorce in such a short time. Anyway, she would hate Francie marrying a divorced man. Sophie, we are weaving such a web of deceit that I wonder sometime how it's all going to end. I adore Francie, but since she became pregnant she has developed into a harridan. I feel as though I am falling out of the proverbial frying pan into the fire. As soon as I arrive here, does she say, "Hello Robert, I'm so glad you are here. Did you have an awful journey?" No, the first question she asks is, "Have you spoken to Cecilia yet?" I tell you, Sophie, I'm beginning to dread coming down.'

'Oh, come, that's not fair. The poor girl loves you and she's pregnant. She's away from her family and friends and all she wants is to be with you. I'll be sorry when she is gone. She's such good fun and she has a sweet nature. Be patient with her Robert, this is a very hard time for her.'

It sounded like an echo of a past conversation … with his mother-in-law. He'd heard it all before, but he patted the hand that lay on his arm.

'You're right of course. It's just been a long drive and it is wearing me out driving down each weekend. I'll go up to her and apologise.'

He reached up and pulled the bell. Like a naughty schoolboy, he felt like running away and hiding before anybody came to the door, but he was a man with more than his fair share of responsibilities and it was no consolation that his troubles were all of his own making. He was about to ring again when Sam opened the door and his face broke into a grin so reminiscent of Charlie's that Robert was stunned for a moment. The boy was beginning to look more like his father with each passing month. Memories flashed through Robert's mind. 'Charlie.'

'Come in, Major.' Sam came down a step to welcome Robert into the house. 'It's wonderful to see you. Come in,' he said again, 'I'll tell Ma you're here.' He opened the parlour door for Robert and continued towards the kitchen at the end of the corridor. Robert went into the parlour and looked around. It was as though he had never left. Everything was exactly the same, as though no one had used the room since he was there. The piano stood open against the wall on his left, a sheet of music lain on it. The marble bust of a child reading a book sat on its top. There was the chair where the big

246

Irishman had sat with Winnie and Bernard on either side of him. If he could go back to that moment, would he change anything? What he was doing was hurting so many people and yet he couldn't help himself.

Fanny came bustling in, wiping her hand on her striped apron. 'Major, how very nice of you to call. It seems such a long time since we saw you.' She looked flustered. 'But, then, such a lot has happened since you were here. Never mind that, though.' Turning to Sam who stood behind her, she continued, 'Sam, would you slip upstairs and ask Bertha if she would make some tea for the Major?'

'Please don't bother with tea. I don't want to be any trouble. I just happened to be in the area and thought it would be nice to see you all again.'

'Well, Bunnie is at school, he is the clever one in the family, and Winnie is at work, and I'm afraid you've missed Francie. She's away for a few days.' She looked vacant for several seconds before, with a slight shudder, she continued. 'You haven't met Bertha, have you? You must meet Bertha. We've told her about you and I know she would like to see you. She knows you were a friend of her father. Sam, ask Bertha to bring some tea anyway.' She turned back to Robert. 'So many questions have occurred to me since you were last here. There is so much I want to know. Now, please sit down and we can have a good talk.'

While they were talking, there was a knock on the door and Bertha entered. She stood framed in the doorway for several seconds, looking at Robert. He sat very still, holding his breath. This girl was like an angel; thick, golden hair framed the most exquisite features. Francie was beautiful, dark and enigmatic but Bertha was golden and serene. Her poignantly beautiful face suddenly broke into a smile, and it was as though a switch had been thrown and the whole room lit up. She offered her hand as she stepped towards him; the smile disappeared as rapidly as it had come and the haunted expression returned. She was more delicate than Francie, more fragile, and the hurt in her startlingly blue eyes evoked in Robert a feeling of deep compassion. He wanted to draw her into his arms and comfort and console her, though he did not know for what.

What was he thinking about?

He let her hand drop, but not before Fanny, with a deep sigh, recognised the overwhelming power of her daughter's pulchritude.

Bertha said not one word during the whole interlude. She sat

247

demurely on the piano stool, her back to the keyboard, and held one of Fanny's treasured old teacups in her lap. She neither spoke nor drank, but remained unmoving. Robert tried hard not to look at her, but his eyes, like polar magnets, were drawn to her constantly. He would drag them away, only to be overcome by their determination to dwell on Bertha's face. Bertha was aware of his fascination, but it was no different than that to which she was well accustomed, and the man himself was of no interest to her whatsoever. She was vaguely annoyed at her imposed attendance upon him. In short, she wished that he would go.

So the time dragged on for Bertha, and on more than one occasion she had to be recalled from a trance-like state to answer a question. Her mind was on Francie. She could not understand why Francie had not answered her letter, and it disturbed her greatly. She desperately needed to talk to somebody about Pym, and there was no one else in the world in whom she could confide.

As the time went on, Robert began to worry that he was not going to have an opportunity to speak to her alone.

'Are you still working in St John's Market, Bertha? I remember that your sister Francie told me that you both worked there before you went to Paris.'

'No, I haven't started back yet. I'd rather try to get work some-where else, perhaps nearer home. It would not be the same working there without Francie.'

This was news to Fanny. 'But she'll be home in a few days,' she lied. She did not want to share their problems with a virtual stranger. 'Still, my dear, if you could find employment closer that would be very good.'

The time went quickly until Winnie came bursting into the room still wearing her outdoor clothes. 'Whose is that big car outside?' she shouted. 'It's marvellous. Whose is it?' Then seeing Robert she asked, 'Is it yours?'

'Yes,' began Robert.

'Winnie!' exclaimed Fanny. 'Mind your manners. Now say, "How do you do?" to Major Mawdsley, take off your coat and sit down.'

'Ma! Have you seen it? Come and look at it.'

Fanny sighed but she went to the window and pulled back the curtain.

'It is certainly a handsome automobile, Major. Yes, very hand-some.' She let the curtain fall back into place.

'Can we go for a ride in it?'

'Winnie!'

Robert just smiled. 'I don't see why not, Winnie. Perhaps Bertha would like to come with us for a spin.'

'Is it all right, Ma?'

'Well,' Fanny hesitated, 'If the Major really doesn't mind, as long as Bertha goes with you.'

Bertha gave her mother a long-suffering look, and her sister, a withering one.

'Please, Bertha,' coaxed Winnie.

With a sigh, Bertha rose and went to fetch her coat. When she came down the stairs, Robert and Winnie were standing outside the door waiting for her.

'Come on, slowcoach, hurry up.' Winnie was bursting with excitement.

'Don't be long, now, and be careful. Do as you're told, Winnie and don't be a nuisance.'

Robert held the front passenger door open for Bertha.

'I want to sit in the front,' Winnie groused, but Robert, ignoring her, took Bertha's elbow and eased her into the front seat, then he opened the rear door and pushed Winnie playfully into the back.

'There you go, young lady, and if you don't stop grumbling, we'll leave you behind.'

He drove along Scotland Road, inscribing an arc until they had circumnavigated Walton Road and were back at the house, while Winnie, praying that someone she knew would see her, jumped up and down in the window, pointing out the familiar landmarks. When they came to a stop, she flung open the door and ran up the steps, laughing hysterically. Bertha made to open the car door but Robert leant over and took her hand off the handle.

'Don't go just yet, Bertha. I have a message from Francie.'

Bertha looked startled. She turned two huge, cornflower-blue eyes to stare at him before pulling her hand away and drew herself up into the corner as though he were threatening her. Robert withdrew his hand.

'I'm sorry. I didn't mean to alarm you. It is just that Francie doesn't want your mother to know where she is just yet.'

'Why? Why doesn't she want Ma to know? How do you know? What has it got to do with you?' Then her demeanour changed and she asked, 'Where is she? I don't understand. Tell me.'

'We can't talk now. Your mother will wonder why we're sitting out here. Where can I meet you?'

'Where's Francie?' It was as though he had not spoken.

'Bertha, Bertha, listen! I can't tell you here. Meet me somewhere later. Where can we meet? I'll tell you everything.'

'Is she all right?' Bertha continued not to hear.

'Yes. She's all right. Where can we meet?'

'I'll slip out later and meet you around the corner. There's a small sweet shop. I'll meet you if you wait there. I'll be as quick as I can.'

'Right, but don't tell your mother. Do you understand?'

She nodded absently. Robert got out of the car, walked around, opened the door and helped her out. She stepped out of the car and went up the steps and into the house. Robert followed.

'I'll be leaving now, Mrs Cahill, but I'll come and see you again, if I may.'

Fanny was perplexed at his abrupt departure, but she came to the door and watched him as he drove away. She could not determine what made her feel uncomfortable, but something was not quite right. Whatever happened during that drive had altered Bertha's mien. She was more erect and more composed.

'Very strange,' her mother thought.

But now her mind was on other things. 'Winnie,' she called, and Winnie, still exhilarated from the ride, came hurrying to see what she needed. 'Would you slip down to the shop for me?'

'I'll go,' interjected Bertha. 'I could do with some fresh air.' She had not yet taken off her coat and was opening the door before she had finished talking. 'What is it you want, Ma?'

Winnie, delighted to be relieved of this chore, disappeared into the dark of the long hall.

'We have no bread. Could you slip to the bakery and buy a loaf?' She took her purse and opened it but the girl was gone.

As she turned the corner, Bertha saw the car parked outside the sweet shop, and Robert, seeing her approach in his rear-view mirror, made haste to hold the door open for her.

'I haven't got long. What is all the mystery? How do you know Francie, and where is she? Why won't she come home?'

'Whoa! One thing at a time. First of all, Francie is in London, as you know. I presume Sally told you where she was staying.'

She nodded.

'Francie is all right. She is having a baby, but she is all right.'

Bertha's hand flew to her mouth, and Robert took it and drew it away. He continued to hold it.

'Don't worry, Bertha. She particularly asked me to tell you not to worry. She is very happy and she'll come home as soon as her child is born.'

'Who is the father?'

'That doesn't matter at the moment. The man loves her and he will take care of her and the baby when it comes, but in the meantime, I've made arrangements for her to stay with someone I know in London.'

'When is the baby due?'

'January.'

'When can I see her?'

'I can take you to her any time you are ready.'

'What would I tell Ma?' She was becoming very agitated, and Robert feared that she was going to break down.

'Bertha, I wish I could stop you worrying. Francie is very happy. Here, she gave me this letter for you. No, don't open it just yet. We need to make arrangements. We need somewhere we can meet. I'll act as a go-between for you until you can find an excuse to go to London.'

'Where do you live? Do you live around here?'

'No. I have a house in West Derby but I can meet you at the café outside of St John's Market if you'll go back to work there. I can bring you letters each time I go to London on business.'

Bertha was acutely aware of curious stares of passers-by. Luxurious motorcars were a rarity in Walton, and she dared not think what would happen if she were to be seen by someone who knew her.

'Oh, why has she done this? This is impossible.' With a visible effort she gathered herself together. 'I'll meet you on Monday afternoon. I'll tell Ma that I am going to see if I can get my old job back. Five o'clock. Now I've got to go. I'll see you then.'

Robert watched her form recede until she was a small speck and then she vanished around the corner and he drove away.

She took off her coat in the hall and walked down the corridor to the kitchen. As she entered, her mother looked up.

'The bread, Bertha? Where's the bread?'

Her hand flew to her mouth. 'I forgot. I'll go now.'

As she turned and left, Fanny slowly shook her head. What was happening? There was something very strange going on.

251

Chapter Forty-Two

Francie opened the letter in haste. It was the first one for two weeks, where previously he had written each day, sometimes twice a day, ever since she had been in London. And he had come down to be with her every weekend, but last weekend, without warning, he had missed. She tore the envelope apart and took out a single sheet of paper. She turned it over in her hands and peered again into the ruins of the envelope looking for more, but the missive she held in her hand was all that there was.

> My dear Francie,
> I am truly sorry that I am unable to come down again this Saturday but work is pressing upon me and I have been neglecting it whilst I have been visiting you at the weekends. Also, I must go down to see Charles and to talk to Cecilia about a divorce.
> I know this will be a great disappointment to you but these things happen. It is hard to express things in a letter but I will see you soon and explain everything then.
> Forgive me, my dear Francie, if I hurt you. I'll definitely see you next weekend.
> Yours, Robert.

Francie stared at the letter and then read it through again. She looked down at her other hand, which rested on her swollen belly, and she moved it slowly over the curve. He had made no mention of the baby. The letter was so impersonal, so lacking in any kind thought, that it chilled her to the marrow. Once again she raised the sheet of paper and read it, but this time, when she came to the line where he had written 'to talk to Cecilia about a divorce', she brightened. Of course, that was much more important than his coming down to London. At last he was doing something positive about ending his marriage to Cecilia. She should be rejoicing instead of sulking. It must be her condition that was causing her to behave like a silly child. Poor Robert was doing everything he could to ensure that they could be together with their baby and all she could do was complain. Still, the letter could have been more loving.

She folded it and placed it back in the envelope, pulling the torn edges together in an effort to restore it to its original state.

Sophie came into the room. 'What does Robert have to say for himself?'

'He's not coming again this weekend, Sophie.'

'That's too bad of him.' She sounded distressed. 'He really ought to be here now that the baby is almost ready to come. Men are so thoughtless. Does he say why?'

'He's going to see Cecilia about the divorce.'

Sophie's eyes lit up and a smile broke across her plain yet pleasant face.

'Darling Francie. That's wonderful. At last, he is trying to move on. I do hope he is firm with her. She can be so difficult; you have no idea. I'm sure he'll be here the next weekend with good news.'

But he did not arrive the next weekend, with or without good news, nor did Francie receive any letters from him. She felt utterly dejected.

'She must have said "no", otherwise he would have been here to tell me straight away. He knows that I am waiting anxiously to know what happened so why didn't he, at least, write to me? It must be bad news, Sophie, or he'd be here. The baby could come any time now.'

'No, Francie, you still have a month to go. Don't worry about things that have not happened.'

'What if it comes early and Bob isn't here? I do want him with me when our child is born. Oh Robert, Robert, Robert.' She lowered her head into her hands.

Christmas came and went, low-key and gloomy, because Robert didn't come. By now Fanny was sure that he was having second thoughts and that he no longer wanted to marry her. She cried constantly, and felt that she just wanted to die. She received only two letters in this time, both couched in cool terms, neither referring to his confrontation with Cecilia. In response to her many letters, asking for his wife's reaction he merely wrote, 'I will tell you when I see you.' She was inconsolable, so that Frank, at Sophie's behest, telephoned him on many occasions, but was told each time, that he was 'not available'.

Francie was almost suicidal, and it was while in this state of mind that she gave birth to a boy. He was a beautiful baby with dark curling hair. Sophie adored him from the moment he was born, and Francie was happy to allow her to take over the main care of the child, but she herself would hold the little boy to her breast and weep.

Sophie was intensely disapproving of her brother and could not understand how he could treat Francie so abominably. It was now almost two months since he had visited her and he had sent only a smattering of short, curt letters.

What on earth, she wondered, had the poor, forlorn girl done to deserve such treatment? She had been the epitome of goodness and gentleness. Not complaining about his neglect of her and yet so obviously broken up by her grief.

When Robert did eventually turn up, she would give him a piece of her mind. She couldn't reconcile his actions with the Robert that she knew, the man she had hero-worshipped since they were children together.

'Have you decided what you are going to call him?' She tried to occupy Francie's mind with positive thoughts.

'Francie looked up from feeding her baby and replied, 'Samuel. I think I want to call him Samuel for my older brother. But of course it depends on what Bob wants.' She forced a watery smile. Sophie said nothing but raised one eyebrow.

'He will come, Sophie. He's just so busy trying to get everything ready. You'll see, he will come.' But she bit her lower lip and turned her eyes back down to the child, and Sophie felt a deep and tender sympathy for her friend.

They were into February when the letter finally arrived. The pavements were sparkling white with snow, and so bright was the sun that shone upon them that it drained all colour from the surrounding buildings so that the world was like a monochrome painting. It was bitterly cold, and Francie drew her dressing gown tightly around her as, hearing the postman, she hurried to the front hall as she had done each day for the past two months. This morning there were two letters, and she recognised Robert's handwriting on the second. Her heart stopped beating for a short moment and she held the letter against her breast as she hurried back upstairs to her room. Sam was awake and murmuring in his cot.

'It's from your daddy. He's coming down to see you, I know.'

She opened the envelope as she spoke, took out the letter and, with her eyes closed in silent prayer, held it before unfolding it and reading.

Dear Francie,

I don't know how to begin this letter, but I'll try. First of all, I am longing to see my son and can't wait until you bring him home to me. I am enclosing a money order to cover the cost of your rail fare and any other expenses you may have and if you send me a telegram to let me know when you are arriving, I will meet you at the station.

Bertha has told your mother that she has been in touch with you and that you will be coming home.

Francie, Cecilia has agreed to the divorce. I may not see Charles but he is growing up and will make up his own mind when he does, and I have had to agree a substantial settlement but it will be worth it in the long run and it will not stop me continuing to provide for you, of course. I have something to tell you but it will have to wait until you get to Liverpool, as it is not something I can discuss in a letter.

I await your telegram and the chance to meet my new son for the first time.

Yours Robert

'Sophie, Frank, Sophie! It's Bob. I have a letter from Bob. He wants me to go home. He wants me to bring Sam home.' She picked up the baby and ran onto the landing where Frank and Sophie were coming out of their room, tying the cords of their dressing gowns around them.

Holding the baby close with one arm, she raised her free hand and waved the letter. 'I told you he'd write. I told you. He's sent me a money order to get some things for the baby and myself and for my rail ticket. I've got to send him a telegram. I've got to start packing. He wants me to go to him. Cecilia's agreed to the divorce.'

Sophie took the letter and read it and icy fingers ran down from the top of her spine to her coccyx and caused her to shudder visibly. Frank put his arm around her shoulder and drew her close. 'Are you cold, my love? I'll go and ask Violet to light the fire early.' He left the two women standing together on the landing, Francie with a great feeling of happiness, Sophie with a deep sense of foreboding.

'I wonder why he has decided to tell Ma about us. I suppose now that Cecilia has agreed to the divorce, he feels it doesn't matter. Oh, Sophie, dear Sophie, I'm so happy,' and taking Sophie's silent brooding as regret that she was to leave, she went on, 'Oh Sophie, I shall miss you so much but we'll come down and see you often, the three of us. It'll be wonderful. We'll take Sam to the zoo and go shopping together. Bob might bring us down and leave us here for a few days, though to tell you the truth, I never want to be separated from him again. I'm going to start packing and then I have to get my rail ticket and send a telegram. There's so much to do!' She kissed Sophie on the cheek and handed Sam to her. 'Will you take the baby for me? Just for a short while. I'll be down as soon as I've packed.' She turned and hurried into her room leaving Sophie and Sam, motionless, on the landing.

The day passed in a flurry of excitement for Francie. There was the dash to the station to find out about train times and buy her ticket, and then, on to send the telegram. After this, she went shopping. She bought herself a pretty nightdress and some talcum powder. When she had finished she had sufficient left over for a small bottle of Evening in Paris perfume, an extravagance she knew, but it was a rare and special occasion; she was going home to Robert and taking his son for him to meet. Happiness caused her nerves to vibrate almost to the point of being sick. She could barely stand it.

The next morning they all rose early.

'Francie, my dear,' Sophie ventured, 'are you sure you don't want me to come with you? I can throw a few things into a case and be ready in seconds. I'll be able to buy my ticket at the station.'

'No. Honestly, Sophie, I don't need anyone. I'm all right now. Robert will look after us when we arrive and I only have to sit on the train. It would be pointless for you to leave Frank and come with me.'

A glance bounced between Sophie and Frank. 'This is a disaster' and 'There's nothing more we can do.'

Dismayed and troubled, they waved Francie and her child out of the station.

Francie wrapped her coat around her more tightly and secured the shawl snugly about Samuel. It was cold in the carriage, but she

256

supposed that it would become warmer as they progressed. She leant her head against the frosty window and dozed as town and countryside sped past. From time to time her eyes opened and closed, like the shutter on a camera. Frame after frame of small houses and people then fields, until she slept, agreeably comfortable and contented. Her last thought before her eyes closed in sleep was of Robert. 'I'm coming home, Bob.'

Sam, stirring in her arms, woke her up. She was alone in the carriage so, turning towards the window she unbuttoned her blouse and fed him. They sped through Crewe without stopping, the train screaming steam as it travelled through the station. 'It would not be long now.' She looked down at the child and happiness surged through her again.

'Your daddy's waiting for you, my darling. Even now, he is striding impatiently up and down the platform at Lime Street and he won't be disappointed because you are beautiful. He is going to love you and we're going to be so happy at last. We'll take you to see your grandmother and Aunty Bertha and Winnie. Bunny will be there, too, and your namesake, Uncle Samuel. Oh, my little Sam, this is what I have always wanted, longed for. I am so happy and you'll be happy too.'

She eased him across to her other arm and lay her head against the back of the seat. She remained like this until she was aware of movement in the adjacent carriages and the train began to slow down.

The carriage door swung open and banged against the side of the train. The noise was unnerving after the calm, rhythmic click of the wheels. As the guard handed down her case and she adjusted Sam against her left shoulder, she looked down the platform and her heart leapt as she saw Robert, waiting. Bertha was with him. Her feelings were mixed. She longed to see Bertha, but she had wanted these first few moments with Robert alone so that they did not have to be conscious of watching eyes as they embraced and kissed and kissed again. Still, here were the two people she loved most in the entire world, except Ma, of course, and she would see her soon.

The waiting couple advanced towards her and Bertha stood back a little as they came together. Strangely, Robert didn't embrace and kiss Francie as in her vision, but reached out and took Sam, hugging him closely and then holding him away to examine him. Then he hugged him again and, finally, turned and handed him to Bertha.

He turned towards Francie again and kissed her lightly on the forehead before picking up her suitcase and taking her arm to steer her towards the concourse.

The Jaguar was waiting outside and Robert held open the front passenger door for Bertha, holding the baby while she seated herself. She held out her arms for Sam and Robert placed the child in them. Francie was astonished and perplexed, but before she could protest, he opened the rear door for her and, closing it, went around to the front of the car and slid in behind the wheel.

He was stouter than Francie remembered, and looked much older. Bertha looked older, too, there were dark rings around her eyes which were somehow not unbecoming. She seemed so mature to Francie, so changed that Francie felt uncomfortable with her. And there was something in the way in which she had commandeered Sam, and in the way that she and Robert had taken over. An uncomfortable feeling was overtaking Francie. Something was not quite right. She had not seen her sister for almost a year, and yet she seemed to be avoiding eye contact. She kept her eyes fastened on the baby, occasionally glancing up at Robert as though for support, but looking at Francie not at all.

Francie felt a coldness wrapping itself around her heart. 'Is something wrong?' Nobody replied so she went on, 'What is it? Cecilia hasn't gone back on her word, has she?'

Robert sighed. 'Can this wait until we get home, Francie. And then we can explain everything. Just be patient.'

'Just tell me,' Francie almost screamed. 'Tell me she hasn't gone back on her word to give you a divorce.'

'She has not gone back on her word to give me a divorce.'

'Thank God for that.' She sank back into the corner.

Bertha's head had disappeared below the top of the bench seat, and the baby with her. Francie felt a tear roll down her cheek. This is not at all what she had envisaged. This was not the homecoming she had expected. Something was wrong, but what? She was going home, she was with Robert, her baby was well and beautiful and even her dear sister Bertha was here. Ma! It was Ma!

'Is something wrong with Ma?'

'For goodness' sake, Francie, your mother's fine. She's looking forward to seeing you. We've told her you're coming home tomorrow. We wanted you to have a good night's rest first.'

They travelled in silence until they reached Queen's Drive, and

Bertha spoke for the first time since they had met. 'I'm sorry Francie, I'm sorry.'

'What have you got to be sorry for? It's not your fault. What have you to be sorry about, Bertha?'

Robert interrupted loudly, 'Wait until we get home. Just wait, you two.' So both of the girls just waited.

When they drew up in front of the house in West Derby, the unloading procedure was the same as before, in reverse. Robert went around the back of the car and helped Francie first. Then he held Sam as Bertha alighted. Francie made to take the child from his father but he edged him away from her and handed him back to Bertha. He closed the big gates behind the car and opened the front door of the house and Bertha entered and took Sam straight up the staircase.

Tenderly, Robert drew Francie into the hall and placed his arm aound her shoulder to guide her into the living room. Once inside the room, he turned her round.

'Now, I don't want you to get upset, Francie. You know how much I loved you. I'd have done anything for you. Sit down. I need to talk to you.'

Fear was rising in ever increasing stages. She put her hands over her ears. She wanted to be back in Swiss Cottage. She didn't want to know, whatever it was. Robert removed her hands from either side of her head.

'Listen, Francie. You have to listen because this won't go away. Sit down. Bertha and I went to see Cissy and we explained to her that I wanted a divorce because of the baby. I told her that we wanted to get married and she has agreed.'

'You told her that we want to get married? You told her about our baby?'

'Not about your baby, about Bertha's. Francie, Bertha and I are having a baby and we want to get married.'

The world stopped, and a cold dread engulfed Francie. For a minute she froze, only her eyes gliding from Robert to the floor, from the floor to the ceiling, from the ceiling back to Robert, and then to the window. Her body never moved, but her eyes kept on swivelling. Finally, they rolled up to the ceiling again and her legs gave way as the room swum around her. She was in the epicentre of a vortex, which swirled closer and closer until everything went black and oblivion reigned.

She was woken from a disturbed sleep by a movement beyond the door and she found herself, not in the bedroom they had shared before she went to London, but in the small guestroom at the back of the house.

It was not a nightmare, then. It was true. She wished that she had not woken up. She was still numb with horror, but she knew the pain would be unbearable when it came. Bertha and Robert! These had been the only two people she could turn to in the fraught circumstances but now they were the enemy. They were the perpetrators of this perfidious betrayal. Still feeling like an observer looking in on the scene, she lifted her legs over the side of the bed and moved unsteadily to the window. She looked out over the large garden towards the woods that boarded Lord Derby's Estate. It was a beautiful garden. While she had been waiting for Sam's birth, she had imagined him playing on the long lawns, perhaps with brothers and sisters. Now, there was nothing left of the dream. There were just herself and Sam and what would she do? How could she go home to Ma with a fatherless child?

She heard the door creak open and turned to find Bertha with Sam in her arms.

'Francie.' Her tone was wheedling, and Francie hated her even more for that. 'Eugene is hungry. He needs feeding. I've got some milk powder for him but I thought you might want to feed him yourself.'

Eugene? Francie made no reply but stood staring, abject hatred in her glare.

'Don't look at me like that, Francie, I couldn't help it. You don't think that I wanted this to happen, do you? I didn't know that Robert was the father of your child, too. Francie, answer me. Don't just stand there looking at me as though you detested me.'

'Detested you? Detested you? I loathe you. You are repugnant to me. I could squash you like a slug, like the slug you are, and feel no compunction. I feel nothing but revulsion for you, Bertha. All our lives you have betrayed and abused me. You have delighted to disparage and demean me. It has been all your joy; and now, this; your crowning act of treachery. You are evil. Now give me my baby and get out!' She snatched the child from her sister's arms with such tenacity that he began to cry. Crossing over to the bed, she lay down, holding the tiny, frightened body against her own and sobbed softly.

Bertha felt dread at the savagery of her hatred and fled.

260

Only moments later, Robert knocked on her door and entered. Francie turned over on the bed and looked at him through a film of tears. She was finding it hard to believe what was happening. She looked at him imploringly.

'Tell me it's not true, Bob. Tell me it's all a mistake.' She turned away again. 'I want to die!'

Robert moved around the bed until he was facing her, then he lifted the child out of her arms and after a moment, laid him in the waiting cot and came back to the bedside. He lay down beside her and put his arms around her.

'Francie, oh God, Francie. What have I done to you? I never wanted to hurt you. You were everything to me, but when I met Bertha I was helpless to resist. It would have been wrong for me not to tell you, to have married you and spent our whole life together with her sitting in your chair and lying in your bed. She would have been in my head always, Francie. Every time I looked at you I would have seen Bertha. Every time I lay with you I would have imagined I was with her. I am obsessed with her, Francie. I can't help it. I can't help myself.'

'Is this supposed to console me?' she screamed. 'What about me and Sam?'

'Sam?' For a moment he did not understand. 'Sam who? Oh you mean the baby. I thought you meant your brother. No, we're going to call him Eugene. Bertha wants to call him Eugene.'

'What does it have to do with Bertha? He is our son, not Bertha's.'

'Bertha and I will look after him and bring him up as our child. You can't go home with a baby, Francie, it would kill your mother.'

Her face was puce. 'Are you suggesting that she should have my child as well as my husband? She has taken everything I have ever wanted in life. She sat like a vulture watching, and when she saw that I wanted something badly, she pounced and tore it away from me. No, not like a vulture. A vulture would have the decency to wait until its prey was dead. She enjoys the kill. She is not getting Sam. She is not getting my baby.'

Her voice was strident and angry now, and it brought Bertha running up the stairs, slowing only to push open the door. Inside she found her sister, now standing and pounding the chest of her lover with both fists. Francie tried to cross to the cot but Robert caught hold of her wrists and held her in a vicelike grip.

'Get the baby, Bertha. Take him downstairs. We'll come down

261

when she has gained control over herself.' And to Francie, 'This is doing no good at all, Francie. You're upsetting Bertha. Just calm down and we'll talk about it. Your mother is expecting you tomorrow and you can't go home with the baby. Leave him here with us until things get sorted out. It would be cruel to give her another shock. She is not at all well since Bertha's expulsion from Paris. Bertha and she have fallen out and Bertha has already left home. She is living here with me so no one needs to know about Eugene for the time being. You can see him as often as you like.'

'Thank you very much. How magnanimous of you. Aren't I the lucky one? I can see my own child whenever I want to. Well, no thank you! Sam is my child and he stays with me. We'll be going back to London on the morning train.' She stopped suddenly as something occurred to her. 'Sophie wanted to come with me. Did she know about this? Is that why she wanted to come because she knew what was waiting for me when I got here? Is she in cahoots with you over this?'

Robert didn't answer. He didn't lie, but left the impression that Sophie had been a party to the deception. If Francie's spirit could have sunk further, it would have done so. Sophie, too! Now she perceived that she was entirely alone, and desperate beyond her imagination. The realisation sapped her energy so that she collapsed onto the bed and sat, soulless and oblivious to all else except her deep desolation.

She wanted her mother.

Chapter Forty-Three

'My girls will be only nineteen and twenty this month and yet it is as though they were both lost to me. Francie spends most of the time in her bedroom and I've heard nothing from Bertha since she left with that man. Her father gave his life for him and he repaid him by seducing his daughter.'

Connor said nothing but gazed sullenly into the flames as Fanny went on.

'He's old enough to be her father.'

'Hardly that, Fanny.'

'Well,' she sounded petulant. 'How could he abuse my hospitality like that? I welcomed him into our home. I can't think what Charlie would have said. Francie won't hear their names mentioned. Whenever I want to speak to her about them, to look to her for comfort and support, she rises from her seat and leaves the room without a word. Was I so wrong to allow Bertha to go to Paris and not stop Francie from going to London, Connor?'

'Times are changing, Fanny. Nowadays some girls leave home before they're married, and yours are very high-spirited and gifted. They have so many more opportunities than plain, simple girls. They'll turn out all right and, anyway, you'd have heard if Bertha were in trouble. You can be sure of one thing and that is that news travels fast if trouble propels it.'

Fanny lowered her voice furtively. 'But he has a wife already, Connor and a child, too. The shame of it.'

He leant towards her and reached across the front of the fire to take her hand. 'I seem to remember two other lovers who defied convention and family and society to be together. It's very hard for someone who is outside the relationship to understand what drives people to do things, Fanny. It must have been as hard for the Master and Mistress to accept you and Charlie being in love as it is for you to come to terms with Bertha and the Major.'

'This is different. It is against the laws of God.'

She was interrupted by Bernard's entry into the kitchen. He was not yet eleven years old but, against all odds, he had been awarded a scholarship and was regarded with respect verging on awe by Sam and Winnie. Fanny warmed at the sight of him. At least she had done something right here. Her youngest son was strong and handsome and clever. He had a bright and loving personality and an enviable ability to rise above his circumstances. When everything seemed to be conspiring against them, Bernard remained buoyant. He was a great blessing to her.

Connor greeted him. 'How is the great scholar and how is he liking his new school?'

'It's good, Uncle Paddy. They don't treat you like a baby and the work is really challenging, exciting. I love it.'

'Go and get changed, Bunny, and when you come down I'll have tea ready. Make sure you smarten yourself up, now. Sam is bringing Lilly-Anne home for tea and I don't want her to think we're uncouth.' Turning to Connor, 'You will stay for tea won't you? It'll be a chance for you to meet Sam's fiancée. Please say you'll stay. I could do with some mature company. I'm so tired of the young people's problems.'

Connor liked Lilly-Anne as soon as he saw her. She was unremarkable and rather shy, but there was a gentleness that defined her whole nature, and her adoration of Sam was heartening to see. Sam had an aura of pride about him. The girl gave him confidence, self-assurance and an appreciation of his own self-worth. Here was a good match, that would grow stronger with the passing years.

Connor wanted to ask if they had set a wedding date, but hesitated lest they should think that he was interfering or exceeding his authority. He made a mental note to ask Fanny later.

The meal passed very pleasantly until Fanny rose and Lilly-Anne hastily followed her to help her clear the table and wash the tea things. Alone with Sam, Connor's curiosity got the better of him and he asked, 'When are you thinking of getting wed, Sam?'

'As soon as we can afford it. I've been making a few enquiries, Paddy, but I had no idea that getting married cost so much. I don't understand why there needs to be a fuss. After all it's me and Lilly-Anne that are getting married not her mum and dad and uncles and cousins.'

'Won't her father be paying for the wedding? It is usually the bride's Da who foots the bill for all the celebrations.'

'To tell the truth, they're not all that well off. I couldn't leave him to stand the whole cost, and in any case, we're going to need money for somewhere to live. I wish it were all over and Lilly-Anne and I were in our own house.'

'Why do you need your own house?' The door had opened and Fanny had overheard Sam's last remark. 'Surely this house is big enough for us all. Now that Bertha's moved out and Francie lives a solitary existence in her own room, there's plenty of space. You and Lilly-Anne could have the top floor to yourselves. What do you think, Lilly-Anne?'

Lilly-Anne, following behind her future mother-in-law, looked towards Sam. 'I'll do whatever Sam wants.'

'I just want to be married to you.' He crossed the room and put his arm around her shoulders. 'I don't care where we live as long as we're together.'

Everybody turned as the door opened and Francie came in. Connor was shocked by her appearance. Her hair was wild around her ashen face, which looked transparent as though a light was shining from within, and her dark eyes were ringed, as if with kohl. Her shoulders were slumped forward and she faced the floor.

'Francie!' Connor started forward, 'Are you ill? You look...' he trailed off, not knowing how to finish the thought.

'Hallo, Uncle Paddy. Lilly-Anne, how are you?' Then, without waiting for reply she went on, 'Ma, is there enough water for a bath?'

'Yes, my darling. Are you sure you don't want anything to eat?' But the door had already closed.

'Fanny, what on earth has happened to her? She looks...' but again he could not find the words to express himself.

'She's been like this since she came home from London. She's not eating and not caring for herself. She won't go to work and I can't get her to go out of the door. I'm becoming really afraid for her, Connor, I truly am. It's as though she has lost her mind.'

The truth was that Francie did not want to go out of the house. She did not want to see her sister or her paramour, but she desperately wanted to see her child and she was pining for him with an unrelenting ache. Mentally, she was on the verge of insanity, and physically she was starving herself. She had to express the milk, without Fanny knowing, when the pain became too intense and the

265

more she expressed the more her body made. She longed to suckle Sam at her breast as she had done in London, and such was the intensity of her maternal feelings that she felt she would even face Robert and Bertha just to hold him again.

The day came when her need was beyond bearing, and without saying anything to anyone she put on her hat and coat and stepped outside into the brightness of the spring sunshine.

She had no memory of how she had come to West Derby. It was as though she were an automaton, set to follow a designated path, but she alighted from the tramcar and turned without conscious thought towards the house that she had shared with Robert for those few precious months.

As she came in sight of the house, she stopped and was suddenly aware of her surroundings. This is the way it ought to have been when she arrived home from London. The sun should have shone like this, the lily of the valley should have been springing up, their stems heavy with delicate white bells nestling on the shiny, dark green leaves. The grass should have been laid out, young and smooth, like emerald velvet, displaying the gold of celandine and kingcup, and the last of the daffodils tremulous in the slight breeze. The sky should have been clear azure with white fluffy clouds scudding across its vastness and Robert should have been overflowing with the same passionate love that he had for her before she had left. For this was how she had imagined her homecoming would be.

It was still cool despite the sun, and she drew her fur collar up around her neck and held it there. After a few moments, she turned and began to walk away until, halting, she thought, 'Why should I be afraid? Why on earth should I feel embarrassed? It's not me who has committed this calumny. They're the ones that should dread facing me. Sam is my child, mine!' She turned again towards the house and with firm resolve, walked up the drive and knocked heavily on the door. She stood a moment, wistfully gazing at the deep purple clematis that she and Robert had planted, and remembering. The door opened and Bertha stood before her, as delicate and beautiful as ever, but with her hair shorn into a fashionable bob.

'Bertha,' she gasped, 'What have you done to your beautiful hair? Why did you let anyone cut it?'

Tears sprang into Bertha's eyes and she wiped the edge of her hand beneath her nose.

'Oh, my poor Bertha, don't cry.' Her arms went around her little sister and they stood clasping one another as Bertha wept into her shoulder.

'I'm so sorry, Francie. I just want to die. I can never forgive myself for what I have done to you.'

'Let's go inside and sort this thing out. I didn't realise, Bertha, that you were so unhappy. Is Robert treating you badly, too?' She eased Bertha back through the door and closed it with her foot. 'Let's go into the living room and clear up this dreadful mess, once and for all.'

Bertha continued to weep as Francie had never seen before, and she felt compassion for the little sister whom she loved enough to rise above the acrimony that their circumstances had engendered. She held her in her arms and rocked her gently. 'It doesn't matter any more. We'll get through this together.'

'Eugene is upstairs having a nap,' Bertha mumbled through her fists. 'Shall I go and get him for you?'

Francie had come to West Derby for no other reason than to hold her child in her arms, but she replied, 'No, leave him for a moment. We don't want him to see both his mother and his aunt in this condition. Come, dry your eyes and talk to me. Why did you cut your glorious hair?'

'Oh, Francie. It has caused so much pain to everyone I love. I have been so vain, always thinking that my looks would get me anything I wanted. I loved my hair but it was like a spider's web, like a trap entwining everybody who saw it. It was as though it defined my whole way of life and it destroyed the people I loved. Don't you see that I had to cut it off to be normal? I long to be ordinary. This so-called beauty has been a curse.' The tears poured from her eyes.

'Oh, Bertha ...'

'No, let me go on, don't stop me now, there's something I need to tell you. It's about Robert and me.' She paused, drawing her eyebrows together so that that perfect brow was cleft between her eyes. 'It was all my fault, Fran. I am to blame for this sorry mess. Robert had no interest in me. I seduced him but I swear I didn't know that he was your lover. Robert told me that you were pregnant and that he had sent you down to stay with friends of his in London, but I didn't know that he was Eugene's father. I didn't even love him, Fran. I don't even like him. I just needed somebody, anybody.' She began to cry again. 'What have I done? I destroy everyone who comes close to me.'

Francie drew her close again and looked over her head, the room swimming through her tears. It was more tragic than she had realised. She was aching for Robert with unrequited passion, and her little sister was living with a man she didn't love.

'Was Bob furious about your hair? Where is he now? Is he working in Liverpool? Will he be back this evening?'

'Yes, he was really angry. He should be home by seven. Can you stay to see him? We all need to talk together, Fran.' She stood up and moved to the mirror, and lifted her arms to straighten her hair.

'What's that on your shoulder?'

'It's a dragonfly.' As Francie began to speak again, she said, 'Don't ask me now. I'll tell you sometime.'

She adjusted her blouse to conceal the tattoo and leaned over, opened her bag and took out her compact, wiping the skin around her eyes and nose with a puff. 'I'll go and get Eugene.'

'Can I come up with you, Bertha? I'd like to see him asleep again. I used to watch him for hours as he slept. It was so calming. I'd like to see his room, too, to know where he sleeps. Then I can imagine him when I am in Walton Road.'

She followed Bertha up the stairs and into a bright, sunshine filled room. As she moved towards the cot her heart filled up with a melancholy joy. In a shaded corner lay her precious baby, dark curls just beginning to show sprouts of gold at their tips. His long lashes lay on his cheeks, each one turning from black to gold.

'Isn't he beautiful?'

She was startled by Bertha's voice coming from behind her. For a moment in time, there had just been Sam and herself. She had forgotten the rest of the world, lost in her adoration of the child. 'Yes,' she murmured, 'incredibly.'

'He is so like you, Fran. Everybody who sees him will know that he is your son.'

'That could be a problem but he is like his grandmother, too. Ma will love him … and I'll never be able to tell her that he's mine.'

It was Bertha's turn to give comfort now, and the two sisters stood together, arms entwined around each other's neck. Fran broke away first. 'May I pick him up? May I wake him?'

'He's your baby, Fran.'

She lifted her son with great tenderness and he stirred in her arms. Instinctively he searched for her breast, and she unbuttoned her blouse and guided his mouth to the nipple. She felt a great surge of joy and a deep sigh escaped her lips as she sank into the wicker chair and shared, once again, a glorious moment with her beloved child. After the baby was satiated, a great tiredness came upon her, released by her contentment and, with Sam lying in her arms, they slept together.

Bertha let her sleep. She sat watching the two together for several minutes before she made her way downstairs and began to prepare the evening meal. She felt happier than she had done since she had left France. The baby moved inside of her and she leant against the sink savouring the moment. Joy and misery met in her in equal proportions as she gazed at the knife in her hands.

The day was a turning point in this threefold relationship. Francie went back to Walton Road much more contented, so much so that the family remarked to one another that her melancholy seemed to have lifted and she appeared to be building her life again after whatever misfortune had happened in London.

Robert had insisted that the arrangements must remain the same for Fanny's sake, but suggested that Francie should become Eugene's godmother, which gave her a legitimate role in the upbringing of the child. She visited West Derby whenever she had the opportunity and established a close and loving relationship with her son.

Still no one told Fanny that she was a grandmother, and still she did not know where Bertha was living.

In August, when the country was sweltering in tropical sunshine, Bertha went into labour and was delivered of a beautiful baby girl. She was a placid child and golden, like her mother, and Bertha treasured her possessively.

Robert adored the child, the daughter he had longed for after his two sons.

'What are you going to call her?' Francie asked when she saw the baby for the first time.

'I think we should call her Eleanor. It was my mother's name …'

'Olivia!' Bertha interrupted. 'We're calling her Olivia.'

As Robert made to demur, she repeated, 'Olivia. It's not open to discussion. She will be called Olivia.'

'It's a nice name.' Francie calmed the situation when she saw that Bertha was uncompromising in her manner. 'I love the way you put the stress on the "O". It sounds like a Shakespearean character.' She tested the name with her tongue, 'Olivia, yes that is really nice. Don't you think so Robert?'

'I would have liked to be consulted,' he sulked, but he reluctantly agreed that it was, indeed, a pretty name.

Something had been bothering Francie for four months, and she decided that this was the moment that she should broach it. Robert and Bertha now had their own child and perhaps they would be prepared to relinquish some of their control over her son.

'Can I ask you something? It has been on my mind since I first came back here in April. I would really love to take Eugene to Ma's. I know she would be ecstatic and I do so much want to show her my son.'

Robert exploded! 'Francie, you must stop calling him "your" son. You must break this habit now before he begins to understand what you are saying. He is not "your" son. He is my son, and he will be brought up as my son, mine and Bertha's.'

His ferocity frightened Francie, so that she murmured apologetically, 'I didn't mean to upset you. Of course I won't tell Ma that he is mine; I'll tell her that he is yours and Bertha's but it's just that I think it's time she met her grandson. It can't do any harm, Robert, and we will want to show her Olivia, won't we?'

'Oh, great, Fran turns up with our son, Eugene, this week and next week we miraculously present her with a granddaughter. It's to be hoped her arithmetic isn't too good.'

'Well, let me take Eugene as soon as possible and then we must wait awhile before we tell her about Olivia. The sooner she knows about Eugene, the sooner you can tell her about Olivia.'

There was considerable reluctance on Robert's part but the sisters were formidable when they were of one mind and their wishes prevailed. The following weekend Fran collected the boy and took him back to Walton. Robert drove her in the car and Bertha and Olivia accompanied them, but after dropping Francie on Everton Brow the others drove into Liverpool and waited in the Kardomah until an hour had passed.

Francie heard the bell clanging from inside the house and breathed in deeply while she waited until Winnie opened the door. She was as wild and unruly as ever despite her fifteen years.

'Fran! What a lovely baby. Whose is it? Is it a boy or a girl? Can I hold it? Coo, it's lovely. It's a boy isn't it? Ma, Fran's got a little baby.' She shouted this last into the long hall and Fanny loomed out of the darkness, wiping her hands on her striped apron.

'Francie, whose baby is it?' She stepped forward into the light and

270

pulled down the edge of the light shawl with her finger to see the baby's mouth and she smiled as she went on, 'He's a lovely little chap. Whose is he?'

They ushered Francie into the house.

'He's Bertha's, Mum.'

'Bertha's! How can he be Bertha's? She never said anything.' She did some quick arithmetic. 'The father must be a Frenchman …'

'No, Eugene was two months premature, and see how he's grown. See what a big boy he is. Robert Mawdsley is his father. Honestly, Ma. Robert's the father. I know that for certain. Aren't you pleased to have a grandson?'

'I could have wished for his mother to have been married, and I could wish for a different father,' she turned to the child who now lay in her arms, 'but that's not your fault is it, my little sweet? Winnie, put the kettle on and make your sister a cup of tea.'

She turned her attention back to Francie. 'Where is Bertha? Why doesn't she come home? Is she living with him, Francie?'

'She's fine, Ma. They are living together and they are both very happy.' She knew that she was lying, that Bertha was far from happy and that they were all living a lie. She knew that in spite of everything, she herself was still deeply in love with Robert. Her heart still turned over when she was near him, and she still mourned for the love they had shared. It would have been so different if she hadn't gone to London, but had stayed here to face the music. It would be she, and not Bertha, who would have been sharing their home with Robert and bringing up this beautiful child together. She turned away so that Fanny would not see her distress, but Fanny was much too involved with her first grandchild to notice.

After a time, Fanny asked, 'Where is she, Fran? Why doesn't she come home? Is it because she thinks I would be very angry about the baby? You know, don't you, that although I might appear annoyed, I would never turn her away. You are both my children and there are times when I really ache to have all of you together. Where is she, Fran?'

'I can't tell you at the moment, Ma. Bertha made me promise. She loves you, Ma, and she'll come home in her own time. We all have ghosts to lay, and we need space while we do it. She feels she has let you down, we both have, but she'll come to see you when she's ready.'

Winnie came in, pushing the door open with her hip as she carried in the tray with tea things on it. 'Here we are. My turn with Bertha's baby. Gosh, I'm an aunty. Give me the baby, Ma.'

'Sit down first, Winnie, and be careful with him.' Fanny placed the baby in Winnie's arms and went back to her chair. They had been talking for some time before Fanny said, 'Tell her I want to see her, Francie. Tell her I want her to come home … but I don't want to see him. Tell her not to bring him!'

'Does Bertha know that Sam and Lilly-Anne are getting married, and I'm going to be a bridesmaid?' Winnie broke in. 'Will Bertha come do you think?'

'I don't know, Winnie, but I'll ask her when I take the baby back. Oh, look at the time. I have to go right away. I promised to have him back for his evening feed. Bertha made me promise; she wouldn't let me bring him until I promised. I don't want to be late so that she won't let him come again.'

'Try to persuade her to come with you … please! Please, Francie.'

'I'll try.' She took the baby from Winnie and kissed her mother on the cheek.

'Goodbye, Ma. I'll be back in a couple of hours.'

'He's a lovely baby, my grandson. Eugene. That's a good name. Tell Bertha I think he's lovely.'

Francie took her son home to Walton Road regularly from then on.

Though Bertha never raised any objection because she was totally wrapped up with Olivia, whom she carried everywhere, Robert was very uneasy with the arrangement and concerned that, after one of her visits, she would not bring him back. He had already lost one son to his mother and he was not about to allow it to happen again.

Francie collected Eugene and took him to visit the family every second weekend and Fanny looked forward to these visits with her grandson. On occasion, when she had broached the subject of Bertha coming with them, Francie had become impatient, shaking herself and making ready to go, so that Fanny bit her lip whenever she thought about seeing her second daughter.

'How is Bertha, Fran?' she asked nervously.

'I have some good news, Ma.' She shrugged off her coat and draped it over the chair. 'Bertha's pregnant again. She's delighted. They loved Eugene so much that as soon as he was born she and Robert decided to have another. She must have fallen pregnant right away. I can't tell you how pleased she is.'

A deep, sorrowful sigh escaped Fanny's lips. What had she done to make Bertha shun her like this? She was to be a grandmother twice over, and yet there was this chasm between them.

Later, when she was relating their conversation to Ellen, the realisation ʰat she had done the same thing with her own mother struck her, and she now knew what pain that must have caused Irene.

'Oh, Ellen. How cruel the younger generation can be. I had no perception of what my mother must have gone through when Charlie and I just left. She never saw us again, nor bounced her grandchildren on her knee. No wonder she died soon after, her heart must have been broken.'

'Bertha'll come when the new baby is born, love. Why don't you write 'er a letter an' ask Francie to take it? Just tell 'er how you feel. Tell 'er how sorry you are.'

'But I didn't do anything, Ellen. Honestly, she just left without a word. I wouldn't know if she were dead or alive if it wasn't for Francie. If we had had a quarrel I could understand but you couldn't call it a quarrel. Yes, we disagreed over her behaviour, but I never blamed her for what happened in Paris. I never doubted her story and I supported her as best I could. I brought her home and loved her … and yet she left with that man. I don't have anything to apologise for, Ellen.'

'That doesn't matter, girl. What does it matter oo's wrong an' oo's right? You're 'urtin' an' she's probably 'urtin', too. Write to 'er. Tell 'er your door is open to 'er an' 'er children.'

'I can't. I just can't. I might have been able to if I had done it right away but it's been six months. I've left it too late.'

'Why not invite 'er to the weddin' an' put a letter in with the invitation?'

'Yes. Oh, that's a good idea, Ellen. There's nothing wrong with me inviting her to her brother's wedding…' she broke off. 'Will I have to invite him? I don't want to see him.'

'They come as a pair now, Fanny. You don't 'ave a choice. Or rather, you do 'ave a choice. You can never see your daughter an' 'er children again, or you can accept 'er choice of 'usband.'

'He's not her husband!'

'No, but 'e will be. You mark my words, she'll be 'ere as soon as the new baby comes, anyway.'

But Bertha did not come. Fanny counted the weeks off until the new baby should be born and continued to count long after what she calculated must be the latest date of her confinement.

It was a day of great rejoicing when Sam married Lily-Anne, but the occasion was spoilt for Fanny by the continued absence of her daughter. The weeks of waiting turned to months, and the months to years, and Fanny grew weary of waiting. Francie told her that the child had been born, and that it was a beautiful baby girl whom they had called Olivia.

Before the year was out, Lilly-Anne had produced a daughter. She had none of the Hall beauty, but she was a comely child and much loved by her parents. It did not stop Fanny longing to see Bertha's baby girl.

Chapter Forty-Four

Cecilia never did divorce Robert, neither did she allow him access to Charles, but she was unable to prevent him visiting the school to see his eldest son, which he did at least once a term. The year the boy became eighteen and gained a modicum of freedom, Robert was able to bring him home to meet Eugene and Olivia for the first time. It was a bizarre moment when they confronted one another. Charles had known of his half-brother and sister but he had expected, in some strange way, to recognise them and had not anticipated the awkwardness that he felt. By their third meeting, he decided that he loved them.

Although Eugene was some ten years younger than Charles, the older boy gave his brother lots of attention and took an interest in everything he did. They would spend hours making models together and rambling in the woods behind the house. The six-year-old Olivia idolised her new big brother and tried to scale the fence to join the boys in their adventures, but even with a tower made of old boxes, she was unable to reach the top. When he began his engineering degree at university, Charles would visit them for part of each holiday, much to his mother's chagrin.

Still Fanny had not seen her granddaughter. It seemed to her to be wretchedly unkind. There had been no quarrel between Bertha and herself. There well might have been if she had known before her daughter left that she was leaving to live with Robert Mawdsley. Bertha had simply walked out of her life and made no contact with her since. Had it not been for Francie, she would not know if she were dead or alive. She would not know that she had two grandchildren, one of whom she had never seen.

So Francie had a foot in two different worlds. At Robert's insistence, she now lived in an apartment converted from outhouses in the grounds of their home in West Derby. His main reason for insisting on this was that he feared that if she remained in Walton

Road she might weaken and tell Fanny the truth, and then Eugene would be taken away from him. So afraid was he of losing his son that he constantly harangued her, insisting that it would break Fanny's heart if she learned the full extent of her daughters' shame. Also, he found great solace in being able to talk to Francie. Bertha seemed to have so little time for him. Her whole life was taken up with Olivia to the exclusion of everybody else, and the times when she would wander off in her mind to another place were becoming more and more frequent.

'Some days she speaks neither to Eugene nor me, and yet she smothers Olivia with her maternal concern. On many occasions she locks herself in her room and speaks to no one. She seems to care only for Olivia. Several times I have gone into her room and found her lying on her bed crying and clasping the poor child so tightly against her that the she could scarcely breathe. When I enter, Bertha releases her and she scampers away with obvious relief, as fast as she can.'

'Does she look after Eugene properly, Bob?' Francie asked anxiously.

'Oh, yes, she is never unkind to either of us. Just preoccupied. It's as though she lives in a world of her own. I know I shouldn't be saying this to you, Fran, but I sometimes think we all made a terrible mistake; that if I had never met Bertha at that time, or if you had stayed in Liverpool, you and I would have been married and been very happy.'

'Don't, Bob,' she could hear the choking in her voice and hated herself for her weakness. This man had abandoned her at her most vulnerable time. He had been utterly heartless in his treatment of her, and still she longed to be with him … was even content to be a lodger, just to be near him. This was not going to get out of hand. 'Don't. Just don't.' Her voice was harsh and abrasive. 'You've already messed up at least six lives. Just don't do it again.'

'I'm not flirting with you, Francie. I just want you to know that I still have deep feelings for you. That I regret what we did – what I did.'

Francie tried hard to dismiss this conversation from her mind, but couldn't prevent herself from relishing the moments they spent together.

She remained in the apartment, from where she watched her son grow tall and strong and uncommonly handsome. The loving bond that had developed between her and Eugene grew stronger as Bertha retreated further and further into her solitude. She heard him call her Auntie Francie and felt her heart drop like lead each time. When she went to Walton Road, she was constantly harangued about the whereabouts of her younger sister and squeezed dry for every last detail of Olivia. She continued to take Eugene to visit his grandmother, but Bertha would not allow her to take Olivia. That is, until the day of the child's ninth birthday, when Francie finally prevailed with her sister and Robert to permit her niece to accompany them.

She had been standing beside Bertha watching the children enjoying the party.

'Do you remember, Bertha, the day we were ten and eleven and we had a joint birthday party? It was during the war, a couple of years after Da died. Aunt Ellen's children came, and Uncle Paddy told us about Ma and Da meeting in Seaforth. It was the first time we had heard anything about our grandmother and grandfather and about Ma's grandfather. Even at that age it seemed strange that we had no family, either on Da's side or Ma's. I remember feeling a deep sense of deprivation and resentment that we had never met either of our parents' families. No grandmothers or grandfathers, no aunties or uncles, no cousins, nobody. It was as though we had no roots. It was an empty, lonely feeling. We had to adopt an uncle, Paddy, and Ellen became our surrogate aunt. Isn't that awful?'

'Yes, I suppose it is, though I've never thought of it before.'

'Ma and Pa left Seaforth before we were born, so that their parents never saw their grandchildren.'

'How sad.' Bertha lay her head upon Francie's shoulder. After a few seconds, she looked up. 'You're thinking about Ma not seeing Olivia, aren't you? Oh, Fran, what shocking blackmail,' she laughed.

But Francie did not join in her laughter. 'You owe me, Bertha. I've never mentioned it in all these years, and I wouldn't bring it up now but I ache for Ma every time I go there, and Winnie has told me that she cries when I am gone. You must let me take Olivia to see her.'

Bertha nodded slowly. 'I'll talk to Robert. I'd like Ma to see Olivia, but perhaps I should go with her. It will seem very strange to the child if she meets her grandmother for the first time without me. I really do want to see Ma, Fran. Sometimes it's a real physical pain. But Robert and I are not married, and not only that, but I've been so afraid that she would see the children and realise that we have lied about their ages.'

'Why should she? Nobody else ever queries it and, anyway, what does it matter after all these years. I won't tell her that Eugene is mine, if that's what you're worried about. I promise you, Bertha. Let's go together. She would be overjoyed. Oh, Bertha, let's do it. Don't let Bob stop us.'

It was Sunday and the bells were ringing, summoning the faithful to church. Francie stood on the doorstep again, but this time her sister, her son and her niece were with her. She was trembling with elation as she anticipated her mother's delight.

It seemed an age before the door was opened and Fanny stood there. For several seconds she just stood in the doorway and stared from one to the other.

'Ma?' Bertha broke the silence.

'Bertha!' Tears began to flow down Fanny's face as she reached out to draw her daughter into her embrace. She held her for a long time before wiping her eyes on her apron, and then she turned to Olivia. 'And this must be Olivia,' she choked.

Olivia bit her bottom lip and looked up from the embrace at her mother in bewilderment that this strange lady should be hugging her like this.

'Say "Hallo" to your grandmother, Olivia.'

'Shouldn't we go inside first?' Francie interjected. 'We're making a spectacle of ourselves on the doorstep.' But she, too, was choked up with emotion.

Shouts reverberated throughout the house as the occupants relayed the news to one another. Bertha was home!

Fanny never visited the house in West Derby, despite many invitations and she and Robert never met except for the odd, unavoidable family occasion, when she acted as though he were not there. It could not be said that Robert didn't make great efforts to mend the rift. He would regularly send her gifts. Sometimes the products of one of his flourishing businesses, and sometimes simply lovely articles which he had thought would give her pleasure, but always she would lay them to one side with a sniff, until eventually Bertha would offer them, ostensibly from herself or the children.

Sam and Lilly-Anne, once in a while, would take Virginia to join the other children in play. The occasions were rare because Lilly-Anne always felt inadequate when faced with the comparison of her own circumstances to Bertha's. Francie, too, was discontented at these family gatherings because she felt excluded from this mystic maternal sisterhood, and more than ever at these times, she wanted to shout to the world that Eugene was her son.

In May Bunny turned twenty-one and Bertha and Robert invited the whole family, including Charles, to celebrate his birthday. It was one of those wonderful spring days when nature gives the world a foretaste of high summer and it was warm enough to spread out the feast in the garden.

After they had eaten, the adults wandered back into the house while Francie, Winnie and Lilly-Anne cleared up the remains, but the children stayed in the garden. After a time, five neighbouring children joined them in their play.

Eugene gathered his sister and cousin and their friends together at the back of the potting shed. 'Let's go into the woods and play hide and seek.'

'The girls can't climb over the fence,' one young boy pointed out.

'Follow me.' Eugene led them to the corner of the garden and behind the rhododendron bushes. When they were out of sight, he pulled back the brushwood and revealed a small hole, just big enough to crawl through.

'I'll go first and then the rest of you follow.' In seconds they had vanished from the garden into the trees.

When the clearing up was finished, Lilly-Anne and Winnie went back into the house and Francie looked around the garden for the children. She went all through the grounds but she couldn't find them and was beginning to panic when she heard laughter and shouting from beyond the fence and, finding a place where the ground was slightly elevated, she stood on her toes and looked over the top. Not twenty yards away she could see her son.

Eugene … her young god … wonderfully big and strong for his years. He stood astride a branch of a candle-flowered horse chestnut, the threaded gold in his dark curls reflecting the late afternoon sun. His chiselled good looks and the proud angle of his head suggested a certain arrogance, but alongside that supreme confidence he wore an easy charm, which compensated, it was so endearing. She stood awhile, watching their game. He was a born leader and had an ability to make the other children feel immensely important without compromising his own pre-eminence. Her heart contracted. She promised herself that, one day, she would tell the world that this was her son. The vision was to stay in her mind for long years.

'Isn't he handsome?' She was startled by Charles's voice behind her. 'In fact, he is probably the most attractive child I have ever seen, he and Olivia, that is. Yet they're both very different, Eugene so dark and Olivia so fair. The same as you and Bertha, I suppose.'

Francie wondered, fearfully, if she should read something into this last remark, but she thrilled at the young man's approval of her son. 'Yes, he is, isn't he? They're both beautiful children.'

They stood together awhile, Francie enjoying the wonder of her beloved son and Charles captivated by the loveliness of his ten-year-old half-sister.

The Halcyon days were coming to a close and another war in Europe threatened. On the eve of the Munich Conference, the *Daily Express* had carried the headline 'There will be no European War', but the unease remained with the issuing of gas masks and the distribution of air-raid shelters.

'How could they even think of going to war again, Connor, after what happened in nineteen-fourteen? What did it achieve except years of mourning for so many young lives?' She turned the shell over in her hands as she spoke.

'There've always been wars, Fanny, so there have, and there probably always will be.'

'Do you think that Sam and Bernard will be called up?'

'It'll be a different kind of war this time. It will be bombs and planes. I don't believe they will send men into battle with guns again.'

'Well, even if they do, you'll be too old and that's a blessing.' She looked at her friend intently. He had, indeed, aged. His hair was a thatch of white silk rising over a wrinkled, leathery skin. She remembered the young Connor. Now, she saw him shrunken and bent, it was hard to believe he had ever been tall and handsome, in a rough kind of way. He must be on the shadowy, mysterious, other side of eighty, she thought, and he looked tired, as though he had had enough of living. She sighed for the past.

'It seems to have brought it all back, remembering my dear

Charlie going away. I have never stopped resenting his going. I even resented you for a while because you had spent precious time with him after he had left me. We could have had such a happy life. We'd overcome such problems, come through periods of unmitigated tragedy, and were settling into a period of peace and contentment, when he left. The girls would not have behaved the way they did if Charlie had been alive. Oh, this is no use is it, Connor? He's dead.' She began to sob softly. 'He was my purest joy.'

Connor moved across the room to where she sat, and put his arms around her. She made no move to prevent this token of his fondness and affection. She felt no threat. Status was irrelevant. Passion had long since been exhausted. Here were two old and dear friends exchanging consolation in their advancing years. It was a chaste, benevolent tenderness and warmth, and Fanny valued it above all.

Sometimes it seemed to Fanny that her children had merged together again into one cohesive and loving family and she had remained an outcast but Connor was from her time, her generation. He understood.

Her fears came to pass on a sunlit Sunday morning in September when the headline changed to 'Britain declares War', and the ubiquitous brown cardboard box containing a gas mask became what was to prove an unnecessary accoutrement for each man, woman and child. Soon, everywhere, the air was pervaded with an eerie smell of musty sandbags. The very atmosphere had changed.

When the call-up papers came, Sam and Bernard went together to the recruiting office. Much to his regret and shame, Sam was rejected, not only because of his age but also because of an ongoing illness. Lilly-Anne never dreamt that the stomach ulcers that marred their life would make her so happy. She felt as though a death sentence had been lifted, but her euphoria was to be short-lived, as the school that Virginia attended was earmarked for evacuation and her beloved daughter was despatched to the country.

Lives were turned upside down, but Bernard was elated by his acceptance into the 1st Airborne Division.

'What is it about men?' Fanny was to ask Charlie during one of their early morning conversations. 'Why do they go so willingly into their own destruction? You all pretend that you are defending honour but you revel in it.'

281

'It is true, Little Goose, but no one and nothing can ever prepare a man for the terrors of battle. Killing and being killed is a vague concept. By the time men learn the truth of it through experience, it is too late to turn back. If I had realised that I wouldn't see or touch or hold you again, I would have deserted. I thought I was indestructible. But I'm here now, aren't I. I never left you, Fanny. I won't go until you come with me.'

Robert, too old for active service, was called up to serve in administration. Bertha took everything in her stride, showing neither sorrow nor pleasure at his departure, but Francie was deeply saddened.

After he had left, Bertha, at thirty-two, found herself to be pregnant. She had not been a reluctant lover for she had, long ago, learned to imagine that the arms that held her were Pym's, but she had not wanted another child at any age, let alone now.

It was Francie who, at Bertha's behest, wrote to Robert to tell him that he was to be a father. It was a painful occupation for her, and Robert was not at all pleased that Bertha had chosen to tell him through a third party. He recognised that neither of them felt overwhelming ardour any longer, but Heaven knew he tried to keep their love alive. It lay heavily on him that he had hurt Francie so deeply and so unnecessarily. The only justification for such a massive betrayal was overpowering passion. If that had been unreal, then there was no excuse.

And now he was to be a father again.

When Charles arrived at the front door of the house in West Derby, smartly kitted out in his new Royal Engineer officer's uniform, Olivia became hysterical.

'You can't go. I won't let them take you.' She held on to his sleeve, pulling him into the house in sheer desperation. 'Tell him he can't go, Mummy. Aunty Francie, tell him he can't go.'

She fell onto her knees in abject misery, sobbing pitifully and wrapping her arms around his legs, her head resting against his thigh. Charles squatted down beside her.

'I'll be back soon. It won't be for long and I'll write to you.' He enclosed her in his arms and held her until the sobbing subsided and they rose to their feet, still clinging to one another.

Charles had stayed for an hour when, having said his goodbyes to everyone, he kissed Olivia on the forehead, held her at arm's length and then, delivering her into her mother's arms, strode away without looking back.

The last of their men was gone.

Chapter Forty-Five

September was balmy. The sort of atmosphere that is as warm as summer, but quiet and still. Ironically, it was as though a deep peace had fallen over the country. The leaves that covered the earth around their feet reminded Fanny of Seaforth, and Bertha of Paris, and both were filled with that sweet melancholy which is part misery, part joy.

In August, the War Office had need of experienced senior officers who were able to speak French and German, to interrogate prisoners of war, and Robert was dispatched to France.

He had three days' leave before he had to go, and on the fourth day, Bertha drove him to the station with Francie, who stood forlornly on the platform while her sister embraced the man that she, Francie, loved, and waved him off dry-eyed. Several times Robert had tried to engage his wife in conversation.

'I'll miss you, my dear, and I'll write every opportunity I have.' If his words lacked passion, they were caring and concerned in a brotherly way.

'Mm.' She had a faraway look in her eyes as though she responded from some automatic reflex.

'You'll write to me won't you? Tell me how our baby is doing and look after yourself.'

'Mm.'

To Francie he said, 'Look after her for me, Francie. Make sure she doesn't try to do too much.'

It was all that Francie could do to keep herself from breaking down as the train grew ever smaller in the distance, but Bertha was already moving towards the turnstile.

They drove home in silence but when they reached the house, Francie asked, 'Don't you feel concerned that Bob is travelling into danger, Bertha?'

'Yes, of course I do. He's a dear man and I shall miss him, but it has to be. No use worrying over it.'

'What were you thinking at the station? You seemed preoccupied. Poor Bob tried so hard to ...'

'Francie, it is obvious that you have still not got over Robert, and I am sorry, truly I am, but don't expect me to spend my life trying to explain that I don't feel the same. I love Robert, of course I do, how could I not? He has been very good to me. You ask me what I was thinking? I was thinking how lucky he was to be going to France, probably to Paris. Do you have any idea how much I would give to be going to Paris? It is the only place on earth I want to be, war or no war. I shall never be happy away from it. It is my soul's home. I ache for it!'

Reaching out to comfort her, Francie began. 'What is it, Bertha? What draws you back?'

'Nothing. Nothing. Forget it. Robert has promised to take me there when the war is over, though I'd rather go by myself.'

She hung her head. 'It's no use, I can't truly love him.'

Francie winced as though she had been struck.

'I'm sorry, Francie. I wish I could put the clock back. If I had known that you and Robert were lovers, I would never have taken him from you. It wasn't Robert's fault, you know. I threw myself at him. I was pregnant and I thought that he was doing what he considered to be the honourable thing when he offered to marry me. And here I am, pregnant again. It must be painful for you, Fran.'

'Don't, Bertha, don't let's talk about it. Neither of us is married to him. No one forces him to stay with you. He has made his choice.'

Bertha was delivered of a boy seven months, almost to the day, after Robert left.

'What will you call him?' Francie asked.

'His name is Paris.'

It was a strange name.

'He was the lover of Helen of Troy, wasn't he?'

As Francie held the child in her arms, she remembered with utter clarity the moment that she had first held her own son, and thanked God that Eugene had been deferred from military service. She had been very wise to advise and guide him into a career in engineering and, specifically, armaments.

Chapter Forty-Six

One after the other the Stirling's four engines were switched on. After each roar, eleven echoes reverberated along the runways, confirming that they had passed the point of no return. Like a swarm of voracious hornets through the haze of a sunny September morning, the planes rose into the sky above Fairford, each carrying a load of sixteen paratroopers. Travelling in the deep gloom of the Short Stirling's belly, Bernard was at first but dimly aware of his surroundings. Only the smells emanating from the plane's structure impinged on his mind. A tight knot in his chest and stomach muted his customary ebullience.

It took two and a half hours to reach their destination in Holland, time which was spent unspeaking, each man engrossed in his own thoughts. The sporadic badinage that had accompanied their embarkation had drifted into silence as soon as the engines had begun to roar and they had risen into the air.

Approaching Arnhem, the atmosphere of stark terror in the plane was as solid and constricting as the metal that encased them as they sat in two rows facing each other, unseeingly. Flying at six hundred feet, the pilot could see the dropping zone. Bernard silently checked his equipment as he awaited the green light which would signal their rapid exit.

His hands were raw with cold as he gripped the side of the seat. There was an icy dread inside his chest and a screaming in his head. The wags of the unit were atypically introverted, as petrified as their more sombre brothers. They were bound together in an unholy fear.

The order was given and they rose as one, all chauvinism prostrated, all heroism subdued, all fearlessness replaced with paralysing panic. There was no choice, no last-minute change of mind. There was only one way – down. The raw air bit at Bernard's face as he tumbled out and plummeted towards the earth. He felt the familiar jerking movement, as though he were returning to the plane, before he began to glide like an eagle. He released his kit bag and, looking down to check on its descent, he could see the landing zone bordered by pine forests. His mind went blank and the fear was replaced by the feeling of liberation that always accompanied his gliding through the air beneath a 'chute. In less than twenty seconds the ground came up to meet him and he landed hard.

An agonising jolt shot through his arm and side, and he lay there for several seconds before painfully taking off his harness and making his way to the rendezvous point. They set up the beacons and smoke markers, working hard and fast. When all was made ready, they lit up their cigarettes while they waited for the gliders and Dakotas to arrive.

In the distance they could hear the occasional rapid fire of a Spandau machine gun, like the sound of ripping canvas, and the slower chatter of a Bren gun. Some of the men in the platoon had encountered German resistance, but they were minor skirmishes. Had it not been for these distant clashes of arms, it would have been difficult to believe that they were in occupied Europe, so peaceful seemed the flat countryside around them.

The pain of the impact was receding. 'Perhaps this won't be too bad,' thought Bernard as he inhaled the smoke with pleasure.

The man in front of Bernard was the first to hear the rumbling of the tanks. He stopped so suddenly on the narrow track that Bernard, close behind, stumbled into him.

'Sh! Listen, can you hear them? They're ahead of us.'

They all stood motionless as they listened.

'No. It's coming from our rear. They're behind us.'

Suddenly it was as though the whole forest was closing in around them. They could neither advance nor retreat, as mortar shells began to explode on every side. Some ran off to their left and were gunned down by small-arms fire. Bloody fragments of others flew into the air as high explosives landed amongst them. Bernard and Nobby with three others rolled down into a dip, where they cowered, pressing close to the moist earth, their hands covering their heads as splinters of shells rained down over them. Cries of agony added to the terror and the massacre seemed to go on for hours.

Bernard whispered to the sergeant who lay nearest to him, but

287

there was no response. He turned him over and looked at his face, but wide, startled eyes gazed back at him above bloody tissue that had been a nose and mouth. He retched, and overcoming his revulsion, covered the hideous lesion with its owner's helmet. The shelling stopped but the small-arms fire continued.

A burst of machine gun fire struck the edge of the ditch six yards to his left and he ducked back and rolled towards Nobby and the others.

'We've got to knock out that gun. As long as it's there we're trapped. Cover me.'

Cocking his Sten gun and checking its magazine, he crawled out of the ditch and inched his way forward, hugging the ground and seeking the tenuous cover of the long grass. He crept cautiously, his progress halted each time bullets flew too closely over his head, until he sighted the position of the German machine gunner and proceeded on his stomach towards the tree from which the firing came. He felt the stinging of the scratches on the side of his face as he pressed it down against the harshness of the forest floor. His fear was replaced by fury at the fate of his comrades, focussing his mind on the task he had undertaken. Thirty yards, twenty yards. He stopped for a moment as bullets flew above his head. They had not seen him. Ten yards. He never heard the pistol shot that rang out behind him as he rose to take aim at the assassin in the tree. He didn't have time to realise that he had come between Nobby's shot and their mutual target. He didn't feel the bullet striking him. His blood-stained helmet rolled across the ground beside him.

The slight tremors which had fleetingly overtaken his limbs, ceased. His body was cradled in the grass and a gentle breeze wafted the strands of flaxen hair. But for the wound at the base of his skull, he looked as if he were sleeping. An irridescent dragonfly settled briefly on the butt of his gun before rising into the air, untainted by death or war, and the scudding clouds above the canopy offered no tears of compassion to mourn his passing.

Fanny was alone when the telegram came. Her hands were covered in flour as she hurried down the corridor to the vestibule and pulled open the door. The red bicycle was propped up on the edge of the pavement and the boy had moved down off the steps and to one side, so that Fanny knew before she saw him, before she took the envelope from his hand, before she died inside yet again.

*   *   *

Eight months later, the church bells rang out, the floodlights went on, there was dancing, there were parties in the streets to celebrate the end of the war. Spring was in the air, but it was still winter in Fanny's heart, and this time there was no Connor to assuage her pain. The old man, made deaf by the encroaching years, had slept through the whining of the siren. Unaware of the stick of bombs that rained down from the sky, he had died instantly as the tenement in which he lived collapsed around him.

Chapter Forty-Seven

On May 8th, all of the newspapers carried the same headline: 'Germany Surrenders'.

Olivia and Eugene were visiting Fanny. Bertha had sent them with a precious gift of two bags of coal and a bottle of Urillac. Fanny was truly grateful. The winter was over but nobody had thought to mention it to her aching legs and back. Her rheumatism had not improved with the weather and Bertha considered that her mother's need was greater than theirs and they could afford this benevolence now that the warmer weather was here.

The journey had been difficult. People were thronging the streets as the bus moved imperceptibly through the crowds, so that it was late afternoon before they arrived at Walton Road.

Auntie Winnie answered the door, and the young people burst into the room, overjoyed.

Olivia flung her arms around her grandmother's neck. 'Isn't it wonderful? Charles will be coming home.'

'And Father,' Eugene reminded her. 'Not just your precious Charles. He isn't the only one who went to fight.'

'He's the only one I care about.'

'Olivia, what a dreadful thing to say.' But Fanny smiled indulgently. She loved Olivia dearly. If she were to be honest, she would have to say that Olivia was her favourite though she never admitted it, even to herself. She was so beautiful that Fanny found that, when she was unobserved, she would devour the child with her eyes. She was all Cahill, so like Charlie, there was none of the arcane beauty of the Halls and she looked not at all like her father.

'But it is wonderful. If only your Uncle Bernard were coming home, too. It would have been his birthday in three days' time.'

It was July before Charles finally came home. Olivia, who had sat at the window every free moment, was the first to greet him. He arrived just before lunch. She saw him before he reached the gate of the house and she tore through the hall yelling, 'He's here! He's here!'

She flung open the front door and tore down the path into his arms. They clung together crying with happiness. No longer the child that had said goodbye, for one month short of her nineteenth birthday, she was almost as tall as her twenty-nine-year-old brother. Francie followed close behind her, holding Paris in her arms, her eyes narrowing as she observed the emotion with which the two young people greeted one another, while Bertha studied the group from the living room window.

As for Charles, he was astounded by Olivia's maturity. For years he had been writing to a little girl, and now he found her to be an exquisitely beautiful young lady.

'Charles, oh Charles. I've missed you so much. I'm so happy that you're back. Why has it taken you so long to come?'

'I went home first, to see my mother. She's been quite ill. I stayed with her for a while but, hey, I'm here now and just as happy to see you … all of you,' he added hastily.

He was ushered into the house where Bertha greeted him with a hug, and murmured how good it was to see him.

'Father's not home yet, then?'

'No, he's had to remain behind. Intelligence has to interrogate German prisoners – or something?' Bertha replied in her usual absent manner. 'He's in Paris Headquarters but he has leave coming up in two weeks.'

After he'd freshened up and lunch was over, Charles produced the presents he'd brought for them. Coty perfume for Bertha and Francie, and Maison Lyons chocolates for Olivia. 'I would have brought perfume for you, too, if I had known that you would be such a grown-up young lady. You are amazing!'

Olivia glowed with pleasure. 'I'm really delighted with the chocolates. Do you know how long it is since we had luxuries like this? How on earth did you manage to find them? Of course, I shall never open them. I shall keep them as a memento of today, of your coming home to me.' She kissed him again, and Francie glanced sideways to gauge her sister's reaction, but Bertha made a 'What?' expression in return.

Talking together after the three young siblings had gone out, Francie said, 'Bertha, how can I say this? Can't you see? They are more loving than they have a right to be.'

Understanding rose slowly in Bertha. 'Don't be silly. How could you think such a thing? They're just pleased to see each other after so long. You know Olivia has always hero-worshipped Charles.'

'I'm not so sure. Their affection seems to be a little excessive to me. To tell you the truth, it has always seemed somewhat extreme, even when they were children. I'm quite worried about them, Bertha. They're both so dear; I would hate them to get hurt. They've been brought up apart. The normal restrictions haven't been in place.'

'Francie, even if they were not half-brother and sister, he's ten years older than her.' Francie's eyebrows shot up, questioningly, and Bertha blushed. 'It was different with us. You're worrying about nothing. Don't say anything to Robert; the suggestion would upset him. It'll pass, and they'll be quarrelling like all brothers and sisters, after they have got over the euphoria of their reunion.'

'I have to go home, little sister. I can't leave my mother as she is. She needs me. I'll come back as soon as her health improves.'

'Charles, if you weren't working for your father, you wouldn't be able to flit backwards and forwards from her to me.' Olivia began to wheedle, but in a charming way. 'Please, Charles, don't leave me. I can't stand it when you're away from me.'

Charles clasped her hands and removed them from around his neck.

'Don't try to make me choose between my mother and my sister, Olivia.'

'Stop calling me your sister. I'm your half-sister, and I need you so much more than she does. Anyway, why can't I come with you?'

'Stop being childish!' The words came sharp and harsh, and Olivia stepped back as though lashed by a whip. She stared at him for several seconds through eyes awash with tears, and then turned on her heel and fled from the room.

He never said goodbye to her. After speaking to Bertha and Francie, he left the house without turning back.

Eugene found Olivia on the swing in the small orchard. Her eyes and nose were red and she held a bunched-up handkerchief in her tight fist.

'Ollie, you've got to get over this, you know. You're going to drive Charles away from us all if you insist on this possessive obsession. You're nineteen, for goodness sake. Act like it.'

292

'I can't help it, Gene. Life without Charles around is kind of ...' she let out a breath through pursed lips as she tried and failed to find expression. 'I'd feel just the same way if you went. I love you both, honestly I do, but you've been with me always and Charles just comes and goes. And I hate that woman!'

'That woman?'

'Yes. His mother. If it wasn't for her, Mummy and Daddy would be married and Charles would be living with us all the time. I heard Auntie Francie call her a spiteful wretch, when she and Mum were talking about her. I don't believe she's sick at all. She's just playing upon his good nature. Do you know, Gene, he wouldn't even tell me when he's coming back?'

'Come inside, Ollie. It's getting dark.'

Charles arrived at his mother's bedside after midnight, and sat beside her until 11 am the next day, when she died.

When she heard of Cecilia's death, Olivia felt no contrition about her mean thoughts and words. Robert's wife was not mourned by anyone except Charles. Robert, Bertha and Francie, all of whom had at some time longed for the freedom that her death bequeathed them, no longer felt the same urgency. Whilst they held no love for her, they would not have wished her dead.

Several months passed before Charles visited them again. He arrived unannounced late one evening and Olivia was not at home.

'Eugene, would you come and have a drink with me?'

'There's plenty to drink here, Charles. I think we have most things, let me see, brandy, whisky, gin. Can I get you something?'

'If you don't mind, I'd rather go out. We could slip into town and have some supper at the Adelphi.'

'Right.'

Charles drove in silence.

When they reached the hotel, they ordered a light supper and a bottle of wine. Still Charles had not indicated what was on his mind.

'Is something bothering you, Charles?' Charles stared pensively into his drink without replying. 'It's Olivia, isn't it? Oh Charles, don't take any notice of her. She'll get over it. It's just a juvenile crush; she is so immature. If it weren't you it'd be the gym teacher. I know she must be getting on your nerves, but just try to ignore her.'

'It's not that easy.' The words hung in the air. After a moment, Charles went on, 'It isn't just one-sided.'

Eugene fell back in his chair as he absorbed the statement. 'What are you saying? Charles, you're crazy. I don't want to hear this. Why are you telling me? Just let's drop the subject. You're off your head. It's impossible. I thought it was bad enough when it was just Ollie, but Dad will knock your head off if he thinks you like Ollie … like that!'

'I can't help my feelings, Eugene. I've tried so hard to change things. I've stayed away for months, but I can't get her out of my head. Eugene, we're not … doing anything. Olivia doesn't know how I feel. I've never spoken to her about it.'

'I should hope not. My God! It's obscene.'

'I thought you would understand. You're our brother. I couldn't speak to anyone else about it. I've kept it bottled up inside me, but it's killing me. It's like a pain in my gut and I don't know what to do.'

Eugene recognised that his brother's heartache was very real and that he was suffering. At twenty he was old enough and experienced enough to know the agony of love, but still he couldn't stop the feeling of revulsion. He wished that Charles hadn't told him and, since he couldn't help, he saw no reason that he should have been involved like this.

Chapter Forty-Eight

Robert took Bertha to Paris as he had promised, but nobody had told Charles that they were going.

Eugene was away when his brother came, and Olivia was at home alone.

'Charles, how wonderful to see you. Come in. Oh, it is marvellous that you're here.'

Charles removed his overcoat and they went into the sitting room together.

'Would you like a drink?'

'No thanks, Olivia, but I'd love something to eat. I'm starving. Where is everyone?' he continued, looking around the room. 'Are you here alone?' An uneasy feeling arose in him and left a trail of fluttering footprints across the back of his neck.

'Yes, Mum and Dad have gone to Paris and Eugene is away for the Company. I'm not quite alone, Francie is in her apartment.' She moved across to where he sat and leant over to kiss his cheek, but he turned his head away.

'No, Olivia, let's go out somewhere. I really am hungry. Can we go somewhere to eat?'

She was stung, but managed to control her feelings and say, 'I could boil you an egg.'

'How could I resist such culinary delights? No, I think I'll pass on that one. Get your coat and I'll treat you to an excellent supper at a quiet little out-of-the-way place I know. By a "quiet little out-of-the-way-place", I mean it's cheap.'

'I don't care how cheap it is as long as I'm with you. I've missed you so much. She lowered her voice and asked plaintively, 'Do you think it's fair that you punish me like this for caring about you?'

'Olivia, don't make this difficult. I'd never have come if I had known you were on your own. We can't be alone together, Olivia. You ask me if I think it's fair. Do you think it's fair to put me in this position? I'm a man, Olivia and I love you so deeply, and not in the way that a brother should love his sister. Do you know what the world would call me if it knew?'

'You love me?'

'Of course I love you. You are beautiful and intelligent and utterly lovable. Do you know what they would call me? I tried to tell Gene, and he was horrified – you would have thought I was a leper. Oh Olivia, I don't know what to do. How could this have happened? Surely I couldn't feel like this if it were so wrong, and yet I know it is.'

'No, no. It's only convention, Charles. You know that Cleopatra was married to her brother. There are many historic precedents for siblings loving one another. None of this matters; nothing matters now that I know you love me, too. You have no idea how lonely and miserable I've been, adoring you the way I do and thinking that I was nothing more to you than a nuisance. It doesn't matter now that I know that you feel the same way. I can put up with anything!'

'Stop it, Olivia. You're just making it harder. Get your coat.' He moved towards the door and held it open for her to pass. She said nothing, but swept through the door and shrugged into her coat, refusing his assistance.

They both remained silent in the car, Olivia not knowing whether she was ecstatically happy or totally dejected, Charles feeling deepest despair.

He parked the car and sat back against the leather seat.

'What are we going to do, Olivia?'

'We're going to have something to eat, and enjoy our stolen moments of happiness. I am not going to be separated from you, Charles. Whatever our relationship has to be, I am prepared to accept and adjust to it, so long as I am allowed to be with you.'

They sat opposite each other in a booth, and Charles took her hands in his across the table. As the waiter approached them, they let go guiltily. Their eyes locked, and suddenly they laughed together as they realised how ridiculous it was to be concerned with what he thought.

'You see, it's always going to be like this. Worrying about what people think or say, even though they know nothing about us. The guilt is deep in us, the guilt of just knowing that we care for one another. How much worse would it be if we were to give in to our feelings?'

'Do you really love me, Charles? Did you really mean it when you said it? Do you feel the same aching, longing that I do?'

He lifted his head and looked at her, nodding slowly.

'Then we live together. We live together as brother and sister. We accept the crumbs that we are offered by fate. We make a vow that we will be celibate and satisfied with this love. We will not go to the extremity of passion.'

It was a very different Paris than the nineteen-year-old Bertha had left over twenty years before.

'Could it have been so long ago, Pym, that spring, that summer, that autumn? That autumn!'

It seemed to Bertha like a previous existence. Short, incredibly sweet and in the end, cruel beyond comprehension. Sorrow welled up inside of her, leaving her enervated.

She looked across the Rue de Marquise to where the house had stood. Time and the war had even robbed her of any remembrance, for there was nothing there, not even the stones; the site had been cleared. It was as though it had never happened.

'Oh Pym, if only it hadn't rained in the night. If only you had not awoken with the dawn. If only … if only.'

She glanced at her watch. She must get back to the hotel before Robert returned. She had feigned a headache and told him that he must not waste the evening but go out himself. She would sleep it off, and in the morning they should go together and explore.

'You can show me where you worked when you were stationed here, and I'll share all my beautiful places with you.'

'Are you sure you'll be all right? I don't like leaving you, darling, not when you are feeling ill.'

'Yes, yes. Go.'

'All right, but I'll be back in a couple of hours. You get some sleep.'

She glanced at her watch again. The couple of hours was nearly up. She turned and retraced her steps.

The concierge told her that Monsieur had collected the key.

'How long ago?' she asked.

'Before I came on duty, Madame. I do not know.'

She took the lift up to the third floor and knocked on the door of their room. It was flung open and Robert was standing there, distraught. 'Where have you been, Bertha? I've been out of my mind with worry. I thought you had taken really ill, but the concierge had changed and didn't know where you were. Where have you been?'

'Oh, darling, you shouldn't have worried. I couldn't sleep and I thought a short stroll might blow away my headache. I'm sorry if you've been upset but it did me good. I feel so much better now. Let's ring for room service and have a drink before we go to bed.'

Robert drew her to himself and held her for a long time, while, unseen by him, the tears glided down her cheeks.

The next morning Bertha arose early and was showered and dressed before Robert was awake. She stood in a shaft of golden sunlight that streamed in through a gap in the curtains. She looked forlorn and very, very beautiful. She realised that he was no longer asleep.

'You're awake, then? I've been thinking, let's miss breakfast and take a croissant and coffee in Montmartre. I can show you the Café Petite Maison Rouge where we used to go. Oh Robert, I was so happy then!'

'And aren't you happy now, my love? I don't know what it is, but I always get the feeling that that part of your life is separate and secret. I wish I had known you then.'

'We met not long after. I didn't change so much in a year.'

Oh, but I did, she thought. Oh, how I changed.

The Maison Rouge still stood, unchanged. The place where Pym had first told her that he loved her. The melancholy was unbearable. Why was she sharing this with Robert? She should have come alone, then she could have wept openly, she could have thrown herself on the cobbles and sobbed, she could have sat at their table and relived that glorious moment, she could have laid her ghosts. But, Robert *was* here, and there was a need to exercise self-control.

'Let's go inside.' Her laugh was affected, and left Robert with an uneasy feeling, but he followed her into the café and to where the table had stood. She halted and looked around, but she saw no one she recognised. What had she expected, ghosts of the Dutch students, laughing and drinking, raucous and abandoned? But the café was quiet at this time of the morning and they drank their coffee in silence. It seemed that she was as anxious to be gone as she had been to come, for now she was rising and moving to the door. Robert paid the bill and followed her. She led him through the Bohemian quarter, past the Hotel Beausejour and up the steep rise

298

of Rue Lepic until, reaching the top of the winding narrow streets of Montemartre, they stood side by side looking over all of Paris in the morning light.

'So this is what captivated your soul? It's very beautiful.'

'I was never here in the morning. This is where we came after classes finished at the Académie, and sometimes after dark when Montmartre came to life. It was so wonderful in the twenties, it hurts even to remember.' She gave a deep sigh and moved to walk back down the hill.

'What are we doing this afternoon?' Robert asked. 'Would you like to see my old Headquarters?'

'Let's walk along the river first. There used to be a little shop on the left bank. I'd like to see if it's still there.'

'Right. And we'll have some lunch over there.'

'And can we have a look at some of the art galleries to see if there are pictures by any of the students or masters I used to know.'

The tattoo shop was no longer there, at least Bertha could not find her way back to it, but they spent a pleasant morning exploring the streets that lay behind the bank.

Suddenly Bertha was anxious to be gone and, in the event, they lunched at The Dome. As they ate, Robert asked, 'Would you like to go to the Champs-Elysées and we'll buy you a dress?'

'I don't need a dress.'

'Women don't buy dresses because they need them. I thought you'd jump at the opportunity to sample the latest Paris fashions.'

'Am I so frivolous, Robert?'

'No, of course not. Something else then? A souvenir of our time together here.'

'I'd rather look around the art galleries, if you don't mind.'

It was while they were looking that Robert came to a sudden halt outside an impressive salon.

'Bertha! Bertha, come and see this.' She came beside him as he pointed at the window. 'It looks like you. It must be you ... just as you were when I first met you. Bertha, it's you, isn't it?'

Then she saw the statuette, and she leant her forehead heavily against the window, feeling shocked and faint. Behind her, as though at some great distance, she heard Robert repeating, 'It is you, isn't it? You never told me that you had been sculpted. You never mentioned it and yet it's so exquisite. Who sculpted it, Bertha? Why didn't you tell me?'

'It's not me. It's just someone who looks like I used to. See, it's taller than I am and she has long, curling hair.'

'But you had long, curly hair when you were in Paris. Surely it is you. You must remember having sat for it.'

'Robert, it isn't me! How many times must I say it? It isn't me!'

Panic rose in her, and she didn't know why. She couldn't comprehend why she was lying and all her nerves were jangling. It must have been the shock of seeing the statuette so long after Pym had worked it. She swayed, and Robert caught her by the elbow and supported her through the glass doors and to a chair in the salon.

The vendeuse brought a little brandy in a glass and she sipped it slowly.

'I'm all right, darling. Just let me rest here a moment.'

'I think we may have tried to do too much in one day. Do you want to go back to the hotel?'

'No, no. I'm all right now. I just felt a bit faint.' She looked up into his face and went on, 'Robert, you said you wanted to buy something for me to remind me of this time in Paris. Could I have the statuette?'

Robert took a deep, noisy breath through his nose. 'Well, we could ask how much it is, but it looks very expensive. Of course, if we can afford it you shall have it.'

The cost caused him some concern, but Bertha's pleading was impassioned. She had never been a covetous woman, but it seemed that she wanted this more than anything in the world. He paid for the statue and the proprietor offered to have it delivered to their hotel, but Bertha would not allow it out of her sight for a moment. She watched intently while it was being packed, and insisted on carrying it herself.

'What's its provenance? Who is the artist?' asked Robert. 'Do you have any more of his work?

'Non, Monsieur. I understand that he was a most talented student who died in tragic circumstances, but because he was so young, there is very little of his work and, certainement, nothing of the quality and perfection of this.'

'When did he die?'

'Robert, come on, I'm feeling unwell again. Please take me back to the hotel.'

Back in West Derby they carefully removed the packing and took out the statuette.

'Bertha, it's you,' gasped Francie. 'It is a wonderful likeness. Who did it?'

'Bertha says it's not her, Fran, but I can't believe that it could not be. The resemblance is uncanny. Watch out, she'll get enraged if you insist that it is her.'

He took the figure from where he had stood it, and turned it over in his hands. His eyes narrowed as he squinted. 'How can you say it isn't you, Bertha? There is a tattoo on her left shoulder.' The two women craned forward and a gasp escaped Bertha. There, faint as a wisp of smoke, was the outline of a dragonfly.

'Of course it's you, Bertha.' Francie looked at her sister in bemusement, and Robert, too, was perplexed. 'You must have sat for it. Nobody could do this from memory.'

'I don't know. I don't. Sometimes the sculpture class would … I don't know!' She was agitated and gasping for breath.

'It's not important, darling.' Robert's arms were around her. 'It's not important,' he repeated. 'It is a very beautiful model, and all the more poignant that it is actually you and you never knew it was being done. We'll stand it here. Move the flowers, Fran. There, it shall have pride of place.'

'No, it's mine. I want it in my bedroom.'

'But no one will see it there, darling.'

'I don't care. I will see it. Did you buy it for me or for everybody else? I want it in my room.'

Chapter Forty-Nine

The two brothers rose as Olivia approached the restaurant table through a wave of turning heads.

'She is so lovely,' Charles thought. 'How can I be blamed for loving her?'

It was not merely that she was beautiful; she carried her head proudly on her long, slender neck. She was tall and willowy, and there was something about the way she moved, the way she carried herself. She glided rather than walked, as though she were on ice.

Lowering herself gracefully into the vacant chair, she placed her hands on the table in front of her. She looked pensive, as though she were expecting a two-pronged attack.

'Well, I'm here, though what good it will do I really can't imagine, and if you two conspire to bully me, I shall leave.'

'Nobody's going to bully you, Ollie,' replied Eugene. She was being exasperating already. We just want to talk about … about this situation.'

'There's nothing to talk about. I want Charles and I can't have him. I understand that, but there's nothing to stop us living together. We don't have to be married, and we have to accept that we can never be like other people. I will not be separated from him, not now that I know he feels the same way. Lots of brothers and sisters, who don't marry, live together quite happily and all I want is to be with him, to be able to look after him, to touch him and hold him. We don't have to share a bed. We don't have to commit incest.'

'There is no reason to be crude, Ollie.'

'What on earth is crude about that, Neanderthal man?'

'And there's no need to be rude either. I didn't want to be here. I only came because Charles asked me.'

'He should never have told you.' She turned to Charles, 'You should never have told him.'

'It's hard, Olivia, I needed to talk to someone about my feelings.'

302

'I didn't speak to anyone. You could have spoken to me. Charles, we don't need anybody's approval. We're both adults and able to make our own decisions. Sometimes I have felt suicidal, but I haven't confided in anyone but you.' A frown appeared between her eyebrows, and she laid her hand across her mouth. 'I feel betrayed.'

'I can't see any point in discussing this, Charles, she's just unreasonable.'

'Sit down. We'll order dinner and when we've eaten we'll decide what's to be done.'

'I've already decided.'

'Olivia!'

There was silence during the meal, broken only by the occasional banal remark that required no discussion, and Charles told the waiter that they would take coffee in the lounge.

As they settled in their chairs, Eugene began, 'As I see it, you have two options. Either Charles goes away and doesn't come back, which to my way of thinking is the best solution, or you go away together and live as brother and sister.'

'That would be an unbearable strain, Gene. I don't think that's an option. I think you're right and I have to go away. It means that I won't see any of you, and I will not even be able to explain my conduct.'

'Where would you go?'

'I thought I'd spend some time with Aunt Sophie and Uncle Frank. It depends on where I can get a job, but I'm an engineer, it shouldn't be too hard. I can't go on working in the family firm if I am not to keep in touch.'

Olivia listened to the two men through this conversation until, finally, she said, 'And I am not to be consulted about this at all?' She turned to Charles. 'You said you loved me, you didn't want to live without me, and five minutes with my brother and you are prepared to abandon me. Charles, if this is the total of what our love means to you, perhaps you'd better go now.'

'Olivia …'

'Be quiet. You two have had your turn. Now it's mine. I suppose it's the difference between men and women. For men, love means just one thing, but women can love unconditionally, accepting limitations. Just look at Auntie Francie. Now you make up your mind, Charles. Do you want to be with me or spend the rest of your life away from me? The choice is yours. When you've decided what it's to be, let me know.'

Pushing back her chair, she rose and walked regally out of the lounge.

Charles followed her, leaving Eugene at the table, and caught her by the arm. Turning her to face him, he said, 'Olivia, darling, it's not Gene's fault. I asked him to come; he didn't want to.'

'Why did you ask him to come?'

'Because he is your brother. He is your closest relative. I thought he would understand.'

'Don't be so naïve, Charles. He is no closer than you are. We all share the same father, but have different mothers. He is my half-brother, too. Surely you must have guessed that.'

Arrested, he gazed at her aghast.

'Charles, how can you not have worked out that the time between our birthdays is too long for us to be twins and too short for us to be brother and sister? Gene and I have always known this. You must have suspected. When our wonderful father made Auntie Francie pregnant, he sent her down to stay with Aunt Sophie, and while she was away, he shacked up with Bertha and they had me. We come from marvellous stock, Charles. Is it any wonder that we are hopelessly confused?'

He was aware of several dozen pairs of curious eyes upon them. He let his hand fall from her elbow and she was gone.

Bertha sat in the corner next to the window, staring into her glass as she swirled the rich red liquid around in it. She removed the stub of the cigarette from her holder and replaced it with another. Eugene leant forward to light it. She always insisted that she didn't chain-smoke because she never lit one from another but stubbed out the spent cigarette before lighting the next.

Charles sat next to Olivia with his head in his hands, and Francie sat on her other side. Robert was standing in front of them all, like an irate headmaster.

'You are not going anywhere,' he addressed Olivia, and turning to Charles he went on, 'and as for you, I wash my hands of you. Pack your things and get as far away from here as you can and don't come back. I never want to see you again.'

'Just take it easy, Robert,' said Francie. It isn't something that they can help. I know it's a difficult situation, but even if you stop them now, Olivia will be twenty-one soon and then they will be able to go where they like. We must try to work this out so that Charles and

Olivia understand the impossibility of what they are intending. The more you harangue them, the less inclined they will be to reason.'

'It's really none of your business, Francie, Olivia is my daughter, mine and Bertha's, not yours. I don't know why you are here. It's nothing to do with you.'

Francie was stung. 'I still care about them both. If I had been listened to in the first place, this would never have arisen. It would never have got to this point.'

She looked directly at Bertha, who was listening intently to the argument without making any comment.

Charles raised his head from his hands. 'Olivia and I have got to work this out ourselves. We didn't expect a blessing, but we did expect more understanding, especially from the three of you. After all, you're not outstanding examples of normal relationships. Olivia and I have decided that we are going away together. We are not going to do anything that would be contrary to the accepted norm. For us to live together as brother and sister, in celibacy, is the lesser of two evils. I will not be without her as long as she wants to be with me. If she should meet someone else later on, I shall release her with my blessing. I have fought this obssession with Olivia since I was the age she is now. Even as a child I knew I loved her. I am going to take her away on her next birthday, with or without your blessing.'

'We'll see about that. We'll see what the law has to say about it,' Robert blustered.

'Oh, let them marry.'

All heads turned to look at Bertha.

'What did you say?'

'I said let them marry. Give them your blessing and let them marry. For goodness sake let someone in this family find happiness in love. Let Olivia marry him.'

Robert shook his head in bewilderment. 'What are you saying, Bertha. She can't marry him. He's my son.'

'But she is not your daughter.'

He moved his head head slowly from side to side, as he strove to understand her meaning.

'She is not your daughter, Robert. They are not brother and sister. They are not even half-brother and sister. You are not her father. Olivia's father is dead.'

'The dragonfly.' Suddenly, Robert knew, and wondered how he had not known before.

Still staring at her, the others saw the tragedy etched on her face.

'We have spent our adult life tearing one another apart. It has to come to a stop. We have to stop abusing each other for our own ends. I am sorry you had to find out, Robert. I had thought to take my secret to the grave. Charles, will you take Olivia and Eugene out while I try to explain to your father and Francie.

'No. I won't leave. We have a right to know this. Who is my father? I have a right to know,' Olivia repeated.

'She's right. They should stay. No more secrets. We all have an interest in your explanation.'

Bertha shrugged in resignation.

'All right. You want to know.' She rose, moved to the window, and took the cigarette end from her holder, stubbing it out in the ashtray and replacing it with a new one. She permitted Eugene to light its replacement and she inhaled deeply, eyes closed, head raised.

'When I was in Paris, I met and fell in love with a young Dutch student whose name was Pym. Pym died, and I was blamed for his death. Before he died, we made love – just once – and Olivia is the result.' She looked across at where her daughter sat motionless and then she crossed the room as Olivia rose to her feet. She rested the back of her hand against the girl's cheek. 'Your father was a wonderful, talented young man. He made that statuette which your father – which Robert – bought for me in Paris.'

'You knew?' Olivia addressed Robert.

Bertha answered for him. 'No. He never knew. I never told him until now. I met him as soon as I arrived home in disgrace, and I set out to seduce him. I thought that if he could arrange for Francie to have her baby in London, surely he would help me if he thought the baby was his. I didn't know that Robert was the father of Fran's baby, too.' She turned to address her sister. 'Honestly, I didn't Fran. I would never have done that to you if I had known.'

Francie lowered her head and covered it with her hands to hide the despair written on her face and Eugene, stunned at what he had just heard, moved across to comfort her.

'Well, you all know the rest of the story. Olivia isn't your daughter, Robert. I'm so, so sorry for all the misery I have caused you. I know that you and Francie still love each other, and that if I hadn't deceived you, you would both have lived happily together for all these years.'

306

It was as though the consequence of this revelation had suddenly struck home with Olivia. She rose abruptly, 'So there is nothing to stop Charles and me getting married?' She turned to Charles, and he stood up and caught her to himself, as she half sobbed with relief into his shoulder.

'No. And there's nothing to stop Francie and Robert getting married either. There has only ever been me between all of you and happiness.'

'This is all too much,' Robert said quietly. 'I feel as though I am going mad. You can do what you want. Just leave me but don't imagine you are taking Paris. He stays with me.'

She left the room, mounted the stairs to her room, and opening the drawers, she began to pack a small suitcase. Taking up the statuette, she stared at it for a long time, then held it to her breast lovingly. After a moment she wrapped it in a silk nightdress, one that she had worn many years ago in Paris, and laid it gently in the case.

Chapter Fifty

So her daughter had returned again to that cursed city. Fanny rued the day that she had weakened her resolve and permitted Bertha to take up the prize.

'In fact,' she thought, 'if I could turn back the clock, I would never have allowed Mr Peterson to submit their photographs.' That had been the turning point. Until that time they had been two ordinary children, remarkable for their beauty, it was true, but unspoilt and normal. After Augustus John and his colleagues had chosen them, they had changed and grown wild and wilful. Now she had gone to Paris again, and no one thought fit to tell Fanny what was going on. Why had she left 'that man' and abandoned her children? Francie would be here soon and this would be Fanny's first opportunity to ask the questions about Bertha's sudden departure. She hoped her eldest daughter would be able to throw some light on the subject.

Right on cue, the front doorbell clanged and she heard Lilly-Anne moving along the corridor, and muffled voices outside of the kitchen door. Since she had been unable to take the stairs, she had spent her days in Charlie's snug where it seemed to her that she could feel his presence.

'That man' had bought a bath chair in order that she should be a bit mobile and, though it had proved to be a blessing, he need not think that it altered anything between them.

Lilly-Anne entered, Francie following close behind.

'Here's Fran, Ma. I'm sure you'll be very glad to see her. I'll get us some tea and then leave you two alone. Can I get anything else for you?' She busied herself, moving the cushions behind her mother-in-law's back.

She was a dear girl, Fanny thought, but her anxiousness to please could be infuriating. Now she left the room and Francie came forward, bending over to hug her mother.

308

'How have you been, Ma?'

'I'm all right, my dear. Just getting older and more tired, but I've nothing to complain about. How are the rest of them?'

'Everybody's fine now that they're all getting used to Bertha having gone. I went across to France to see her last week.'

'Is she well, Fran? Can you tell me what happened? Come and sit down and tell me all about her.'

'She's living in Paris in a small apartment in Montmartre and seems happy in her peculiarly melancholy way.'

'Yes, strange that permanent air of sorrow. She was never the same after she returned in nineteen twenty-five. What does she do there?'

'She does a little painting herself, and sells the odd picture from time to time. I was surprised, Ma, she's quite good and although she's getting old, she is still beautiful and models when she needs money. She smokes some disgusting cigarettes incessantly, and drinks copious amounts of red wine. Her apartment has a small verandah and she stands on it, staring out over Paris, and in some strange, esoteric way is content, even happy.'

'Is she all right for money? I have some put by ...'

'Robert has provided quite well for her and she says her needs are minimal. As long as she has enough for her cigarettes and wine she doesn't care about money.'

The two women fell silent, each with her own memories and thoughts. Lilly-Anne came in with two cups of tea, slopping over into the saucers, and when she had gone and the door closed behind her, Fanny remarked, 'She's a dear girl, Fran, and makes Sam very happy, but sometimes she drives me mad. She never uses a tray, doesn't know what a napkin is for, and is continuously and irritatingly happy.'

She poured the slops from her saucer into the cup and sipped the hot beverage. 'I shouldn't complain. I couldn't manage without her. Now what were you telling me about Bertha? What caused her to leave the children, especially Paris? He is so young.'

'Paris lives in West Derby with Robert and me, Ma. He is a lovely child. I think of him as my own especially now that Eugene has gone to live in Canada.' The tears welled up in her eyes. 'I miss him so much already.'

'Yes, I always knew he was your favourite, even when I thought he was Bertha's son. You know, Francie, sometimes I despair of understanding. First Bertha brings up your child as her own, and then you bring up Bertha's children. It's an alien world. I suppose I'm just too old to adjust.'

'It is quite convoluted, Ma. It's best not to ask.'

'Then may I ask if you intend to marry that man? Is he going to make an honest woman of either of my daughters?'

'That's not fair, Ma. His wife would not divorce him.'

'But she's dead now, isn't she?'

'Yes, but it doesn't seem important any more.'

Fanny turned away and sighed. It all seemed so meaningless.

'Have you seen Winnie lately?' Francie changed the subject.

'Yes, she and Reg come every week with their monstrously ugly children. Winnie, so plain and graceless, and yet she lives in a bubble of bliss with her dull, uncouth husband.' Francie recalled her feelings when she first met Sophie and Frank, and Fanny went on, 'They are like a couple of delirious garden gnomes and have no interest in anything except each other. She behaves like an infatuated fourteen-year-old when he is about. Neither of them is tempted to stray, because no one else could tolerate them for long. Who would have thought it?'

'You know, Ma, you are getting very cynical in your old age.'

'I know. I'm getting quite horrid. It's being cooped up in here all day. I long to get out. I'd love to go back to where I lived as a child and see the old house and my grandfather's house, too. You know he turned it into a home for single mothers before he died. Doesn't that just go to show what a wonderful man he was? I loved him so much. Almost as much as I loved your father.'

'I know. Would you really like to go back? Robert and I would take you.'

'No! No! I don't want Robert to take me anywhere.'

'Ma, you ...'

'No!'

'He's the only one in the family who's got a car.'

'No!'

The house lay derelict. The elaborate wrought-iron gates and railings had been removed. As Robert opened the door and helped her into her bathchair Fanny turned her head away from him so that he should not see her tears. Robert didn't notice. She had treated him with less courtesy or consideration than she had paid

310

Rupert when he had driven her, long years ago. To be beholden to this man who had been responsible for her husband's death and had ruined her children's lives was an anathema to her. She had only succumbed to Francie's entreaties because of her deep longing to visit her old home one time before she died. And now she was sorry she had. Robert was behind her, pushing the chair, and she was glad that she didn't have to look at him.

She let her eyes, swimming with unshed tears, roam over her old home. The house was just an empty shell, but the roses, which had run wild, swarmed over the ruins in a storm of pink and white blossom. The stumps of the net posts on the tennis courts were covered with bindweed so that they looked like termite hills, and here and there, patches of orange hardcore peeped through the overgrown surface.

She raised her hand and pointed to the ghost of the drive where the stables had been, and Robert obligingly propelled her in the direction she indicated. They came to the area where the kitchen garden had been and passed between ancient lavendar bushes until they came to the site of the lych-gate.

Fanny sat unmoving, staring at the place. Robert and Francie exchanged frowning glances. What was the old woman seeing? It was just a wilderness of hawthorn with an old stone almost hidden by weeds.

'I want to sit on the coffin rest. Just for a moment. Please?'

Robert cut a swathe through the branches with a stick but when he tried to help her out of the bathchair, she shrugged him off and indicated to Francie to give her her arm. Francie hesitated for a moment, stung by her mother's rebuff of her lover, but Robert smiled, took her hand and put it under her mother's elbow.

Sadness and joy mingled to produce the strangest melancholy in Fanny. 'See, Charlie,' she thought, 'I am waiting for you here where I waited for you so many years ago.' She sat there weeping silently, not knowing whether it was pleasure or pain that caused her tears.

'Ma, I had no idea that you had lived in such an imposing house. I would imagine it was quite, quite beautiful in its heyday. Grandfather must have been very rich.'

'Yes, it was, and my father was the wealthiest man in Seaforth. I was so happy then, Fran. Sometimes I didn't even realise how happy I was; I constantly complained about my lot. All I ever wanted was to be with your father.' She grew pensive. 'We could have stayed here.

We didn't have to leave like that. Alexander went to France, in any event. It could all have been so different.'

She looked up as an elderly man approached from the direction of the former house where Charlie and she had lain in the shadows of the ruins when they were young. As he drew closer he wished them 'Good morning', and stopped to talk.

The mansion, he told them, used to belong to gentry who owned the local brickworks. A couple had bought it shortly after the lady of the house died, but they had moved away when the war started.

'Aye, it used to be a magnificent house but the gates, all the railings and everything made of metal was requisitioned to make ammunition during the war. For a short time it was used as a billet for army officers but after it was destroyed by land mines in nineteen-forty, it became nothing but an empty shell. I remember it from when I was a young man. One of the finest houses in the county, it was.'

As he made to leave, Robert shook hands with him and, thanking him, explained that his 'mother-in-law' had lived there as a child.

The man peered closely at Fanny and exclaimed, 'You was Miss Fanny, wasn't you? I remember you. You used to ride out in the landau. Didn't recognise you, because I never saw your face. Well, well, fancy that. Miss Fanny.'

They left him still marvelling at the strangeness of the meeting, but it had cheered Fanny to see someone from so long ago, even though she had no idea who he was, and getting back in the car they headed towards Crosby. Fanny did not recognise much. Either the road had changed to keep pace with the rest of the world, or her memory was fading, but as they passed the five lamps she gave a sob of remembered joy. She closed her eyes as they covered the rest of the journey, and began to doze, caught between the present and the past of forty years ago.

Francie shook her gently and she realised that the car had stopped. As her eyes focussed, she saw that they were at the end of the long drive that led to the great house that had been her grandfather's. Robert began to edge the car forward slowly so that Fanny might take in the view.

The authorities had added hideous extensions and there were prefabricated buildings scattered carelessly around the grounds like an abandoned miniature village, which some wilful child had neglected to return to the toy box.

'Strange, unprepossessing phenomenon, prefabricated buildings,' muttered Fanny. 'The lake has been filled in; I suppose to stop the children falling in and drowning. Still …'

'Pardon?' Francie leaned forward to catch the words.

'Nothing. It doesn't matter. Nothing matters any more. I wish I hadn't come back. I can't stand the loss of such elegance and grandeur, even for the benefits that caused its demise. Poor Grandfather, I'm glad he never saw the true cost of his benevolence. You know, Fran, altogether I wish that I had left the past untarnished and remembered it just as it was when your father was alive. Not that I am not grateful to you and Robert for today, you've both been kinder than I deserve.' Her voice had softened and sounded like a young girl's and she reached her hand over the leather of the front seat and laid it upon Robert's shoulder. 'If you don't mind, I don't want to get out of the car. It's too cruel. I'd like to go home now.'

Robert covered the hand on his shoulder with his own and gave it a squeeze. 'All right, Ma. We'll go back now.'

Arriving at Walton Road, Robert and Francie helped an exhausted Fanny out of the car. She could scarcely stand, and Robert lifted her and carried her up the steps and into the house.

'Would you mind just taking me to Charlie's room?' she asked.

Robert looked at Francie who indicated the door at the end of the corridor. He continued past the parlour and stopped outside the small sitting room beside the kitchen. Francie leant across him and opened the door, and he put Fanny down on the settle.

'Just leave me here for a moment. Just leave me alone. I'll call you when I need help.' As they turned to go, she said, 'Robert.' He turned to her. 'Thank you so much for today.' He smiled and left the room, closing the door quietly behind him.

After an hour passed with no summons, Francie asked, 'Should I see if she's all right?' and having received agreement from Robert she went to the next room and turned the handle. Fanny was fast asleep on the settle, her arms resting on the supports and her head fallen back. A soft whisper of a snore escaped her lips.

'Ma. Ma, would you like me to help you to bed?'

Fanny stirred, her eyes blinking as she sought to focus and recall where she was. She had been dreaming, she realised. She had been young again, hurrying down the path on a beautiful summer day, the blazing sun teasing the perfume from the lavender bushes …

and Charlie had been waiting, his cap pushed back on his head and his thumbs resting in the armholes of his waistcoat. And that smile!

'Oh, Fran, I was having such a lovely dream.' She looked at her eldest daughter through timeworn, watery eyes. 'I'm so tired. Yes, I'll go upstairs and lie down. Perhaps I can recapture my dream.'

It took a great effort to help her to her feet and, unable to stand, she allowed Robert to lift her frail body and carry it up the stairs.

She lay in the same room, on the same bed that she had shared with Charlie; on the same bed in which she had borne her children; on the same bed in which Bernard had been born the night she heard that Charlie was dead, that night when Ellen and Connor had kept her alive.

They were all gone now, Charlie, Ellen, Connor and Bernard. Little Joe and William, too. She sank deeper into oblivion, as though she would join all her dear ones.

Chapter Fifty-One

Grandma. Grandma, are you awake?'

Fanny ascended through a swirling mist, up, up until she emerged onto the plane of consciousness. Until she thought she made out the face of her wayward daughter.

'Bertha?'

'No it's me, Olivia.' She leant over and kissed the old lady on the forehead. 'I've brought someone to meet you. Are you well enough?'

Her eyes closed and then her lids fluttered open again, searching for recognition. She peered through the fog and her breath caught in her throat.

'Richard?'

'No,' Olivia said again, 'this is Charles. We want to tell you our news. Can I get you anything?'

She was awake now and saw her mistake. Olivia sat on the side of the bed, a tall young man standing beside her. It was Charles. It was Robert's son. She had met him once or twice before. He looked like his father; he resembled dear Richard. He was Robert's son but, of course, Eugene was his son, too. It was all too confusing.

'Could you move my pillows so that I can sit up further, Olivia?' She let go of the shell that she had held and placed her hands on either side, as Olivia lifted her and adjusted the pillow to support her. 'So, what is this news?'

Olivia turned to look at Charles before she began, 'Perhaps we should fill you in about some other things first. To begin with, Grandma, this may come as a shock to you, but Charles and I have discussed it and we feel that it's something you ought to know. I hope we're not making a mistake. We have weighed it against your frailty and we both feel that, if it were us, we'd want to be told. Besides, if we're to tell you our good news, we have to tell you this first.'

'Olivia, my love, what is it you have to tell me?' She had no patience with procrastination and sounded a little fractious, even to her own ears, so she reached out wearily and took the girl's hand.

'Grandma. Oh dear! Grandma, Bertha is not Eugene's mother.'

Fanny allowed herself a gentle smile ... such a waste of long restraint. 'Of course not. Francie is.'

'You knew?'

'Of course I knew. I've known for years. Do you all take me for a fool? He is the image of his mother. There is no mistaking it. When you were both quite small, before the world had taught you how to lie, you told me when it was your birthdays and how old you were. When I realised the discrepancy, I asked Francie about it, and of course she told me. But Bertha doesn't know I know. Is that what all this secrecy and heart-searching is about?'

'Well, that's not exactly all. You had better get ready for another shock.'

'My dear child, I'm much too old and experienced for anything to shock me. What else is there that I don't know?'

'Robert is not my father.'

This time, Fanny sucked in her breath and held it. 'I see. Now that is something new. Then who is?'

'Mother met a boy when she was in Paris, and they fell in love. They were going to be married, but he died. She came home and discovered that she was pregnant, then she met Robert and they became lovers. She let father – Robert – think that I was his.'

'Paris!' Fanny thought. 'So that was the trauma that destroyed my child. Poor Bertha, she has had to live with this awful pain all these years. Why couldn't she tell me? And poor, poor Francie. What sort of mother have I been that my children had to go through such experiences alone? And I had no idea.'

'But, you see, it's really good news for Charles and me. We're in love ... have been for years, but we thought that we were brother and sister. Now that we know that we are not blood relatives at all, we can be married. Everybody still disapproves, but at least it is legal and, just think, I don't even have to change my name. There is no hindrance to our marriage now.'

Fanny listened but it was rather a lot to take in at one time. There was a sense of shock, and a necessity for some serious adjustment and she was oh, so tired.

At last Charles spoke, 'You can see it makes things difficult for

316

everyone. How do they explain to people who know us that it's all right for Olivia and me to marry? It means that we are going to have to move away. Well away! That way we'll save them all embarrassment, and we, Olivia and I, need not worry what people are thinking.'

'We've come for your blessing, Grandma. No one else, except for mother, has felt inclined to give theirs. Will you bless us, Grandma?'

'Olivia, darling, would you go downstairs and bring me the box that's on the sideboard?' Olivia rose and left the room. 'Charles, you and Olivia come from a bizarre family, to say the least, but it seems to me, from the vantage-point of old age, that life without love is worth nothing. If you are to take Olivia away, you must cleave to her through all troubles, because she will have no one to fall back on. I left my home and family after I married her grandfather, and I know what it is to surrender everything for love. There will be a lot of pain along the way and it will seem meaningless sometimes, a chasing after the wind, but if you cherish it, love lasts through eternity. Give me your pledge, now, that you will treasure her and work your way through the times of trouble, and I will give you my blessing.'

He took her thin, knarled hand in his and bowed his head. After a moment, he looked straight into her eyes and said, 'It seems that I have the best of the bargain. My pledge, which you could have had without condition, in return for your blessing, which is of inestimable value to Olivia.'

Olivia pushed open the door with her foot and stood for several seconds looking at the scene before her.

'Come in, darling.' Fanny withdrew her hand and stretched it out to Olivia who came forward and placed the box on the counterpane. 'Thank you, my dear. Now would you do something else for me? She took a small Bible from the box and handed it to Olivia. 'Open it at Song of Solomon and read the part that is marked.'

Olivia turned the pages and began to read:

'Set me as a seal upon thine heart, as a seal upon thine arm:
For love is strong as death; jealousy is cruel as the grave;
The coals thereof are coals of fire, which hath a most vehement
   flame.
Many waters cannot quench love, neither can floods drown it:
If a man would give all the substance of his house for love,
it would be utterly contemned.'

The tears were flooding from Olivia's eyes as she struggled for control to finish the verse. They each meditated on the words without speaking. Fanny took from the box a black velvet pouch and, opening it, took out the ring that her grandfather had entrusted to her so many years before.

Handing it to Charles, she said, 'Five generations. This was my grandmother's engagement ring. Through all our poorest, hardest times I have kept it. I want you to give it to my granddaughter as a token of your love and fidelity.'

He made no move, but stared at the lustrous gem. The light from above their heads danced on every shimmering facet.

'Take it.'

Charles took the ring in his right hand, and Olivia's fingertips in his left. He slid the ring upon her finger and turned her hand over and kissed her palm.

The old lady sighed with contentment and closed her eyes. She was back in the brickworks yard, outside her father's office. Her hands shifted on the counterpane and she felt the kisses on her upturned palms.

'Although I do nothing more than lie here, yet I am tired, Charlie. I close my eyes and the whole of my past drifts before me. I have clung to your promise that you will not go until I am with you and, now, I think that I am ready to come.'

'What a sweet felicity that the pale horse should bring its rider so gentle to my end.'